WWW.BEWAREOFMONSTERS.COM

PRAISE FOR JEREMY ROBINSON

"[*Hunger* is] a wicked step-child of King and Del Toro. Lock your windows and bolt your doors. [Robinson, writing as] Jeremiah Knight, imagines the post-apocalypse like no one else."

—The Novel Blog

"Robinson writes compelling thrillers, made all the more entertaining by the way he incorporates aspects of pop culture into the action."

—Booklist

"*Project 731* is a must. Jeremy Robinson just keeps getting better with every new adventure and monster he creates."

—Suspense Magazine

"Robinson is known for his great thrillers, and [with *XOM-B*] he has written a novel that will be in contention for various science fiction awards at the end of the year. Robinson continues to amaze with his active imagination."

—Booklist

"Robinson puts his distinctive mark on Michael Crichton territory with [*Island 731*], a terrifying present-day riff on *The Island of Dr. Moreau.* Action and scientific explanation are appropriately proportioned, making this one of the best *Jurassic Park* successors."

—Publisher's Weekly - Starred Review

"[*SecondWorld* is] a brisk thriller with neatly timed action sequences, snappy dialogue and the ultimate sympathetic figure in a badly burned little girl with a fighting spirit... The Nazis are determined to have the last gruesome laugh in this efficient doomsday thriller."

—Kirkus Reviews

"*Threshold* elevates Robinson to the highest tier of over-the-top action authors and it delivers beyond the expectations even of his fans. The next Chess Team adventure cannot come fast enough."

—Booklist - Starred Review

"Jeremy Robinson is the next James Rollins."

—Chris Kuzneski, NY Times bestselling author of *The Einstein Pursuit*

"[*Pulse* is] rocket-boosted action, brilliant speculation, and the recreation of a horror out of the mythologic past, all seamlessly blending into a rollercoaster ride of suspense and adventure."

—James Rollins, NY Times bestselling author of *The 6th Extinction*

PRAISE FOR KANE GILMOUR

"*Resurrect* is high adventure in the grand tradition, with a brash hero, relentless villains, beautiful women, and breathtaking locales from the Himalaya to Hong Kong. It is as addictive as hot buttered popcorn—you'll keep coming back for more."

—Stephen M. Irwin, award-winning author of *The Dead Path*

"I know I'm not the first to say it, but it bears repeating. Kane Gilmour has tapped into the same creative vein that energized Clive Cussler's earlier Dirk Pitt novels. It's all there, from the pitch perfect character chemistry to over-the-top action. If you've been craving some old school Cussler, you really need to read *Resurrect*."

—Sean Ellis, international bestselling author of *Magic Mirror*

"*Resurrect* is a thriller teeming with action-adventure goodness: an intriguing historical mystery, a tough and resourceful hero, a dangerous villain, and a globe-hopping adventure filled with chases, escapes, and action to spare."

—David Wood, *USA Today* bestselling author of *Atlantis*

"I understand that *Resurrect* is a first novel and to say it was impressive would be an understatement. A very entertaining action thriller. Well paced and hard to put down."

—F. Bard, ThrillReads and Reviews

"*The Crypt of Dracula* is how a vampire novel should be written. It's suspenseful, frightening, dark, and realistic. It harkens back to the day when 'monster' movies played at Saturday matinees and at midnight showings. Somewhere, Bram Stoker is smiling. He's beaming from ear to ear because someone finally got it right, and that someone is Kane Gilmour."

—Mark Adduci, Suspense Magazine

"[Kane Gilmour has] mastered the considerable challenge of fantasy world-building"

—Publisher's Weekly (for *The Mammoth Book of Kaiju*)

"The team of writers [on *Refuge*] have done the impossible; they have woven a tapestry of word and emotion into a quilt of brilliance. The only thing better than the story is the end."

—Suspense Magazine

ALSO BY JEREMY ROBINSON

The Didymus Contingency
Raising The Past
Beneath
Antarktos Rising
Kronos
Pulse
Instinct
Threshold
Fracture
Torment
The Sentinel
The Last Hunter
Insomnia
SecondWorld
Project Nemesis
Ragnarok
Island 731
The Raven
Nazi Hunter: Atlantis
Prime
Omega
Project Maigo
Refuge
Guardian
Human After All
Savage
Flood Rising
Project 731
Cannibal
Endgame
MirrorWorld
Herculean
Project Hyperion
Patriot
Apocalypse Machine
Empire
Unity
Project Legion
The Distance
The Last Valkyrie
Centurion
Infinite
Helios
Viking Tomorrow
Forbidden Island
The Divide
The Others
Space Force
Alter
Flux
Tether
Tribe
NPC
Exo-Hunter
Infinite²
The Dark
Mind Bullet
The Order
Khaos
Singularity
Hunger – The Complete Trilogy
Nemesis
Point Nemo
Good Boys – The Lost Tribe
Good Boys – Unleashed
Kingdom

ALSO BY KANE GILMOUR

Action-Adventure
Resurrect

Action-Adventure Comics
(Co-authored with Jeremy Robinson)
Island 731

Nostalgic Horror
The Crypt of Dracula
"No Hallows' Eve"

Military Sci-Fi Adventure
(Co-authored with Jeremy Robinson)
Callsign: Deep Blue
Ragnarok
Omega
Endgame
Kingdom

Post-Apocalyptic Science Fiction
(Co-authored with Jeremy Robinson)
Refuge 5 – Bonfires Burning Bright
Viking Tomorrow

New Pulp Science Fiction
Warbirds of Mars: Stories of the Fight!
(Edited Anthology)
Warbirds of Mars (webcomic)

KINGDOM

A Jack Sigler Thriller

JEREMY ROBINSON
AND KANE GILMOUR

Visit Jeremy Robinson on the World Wide Web at:
www.bewareofmonsters.com

Visit Kane Gilmour on the World Wide Web at:
Kanegilmour.com

Jeremy would like to dedicate this book to
Kane Gilmour, Sean Ellis, Kent Holloway, David Wood,
Ethan Cross and David McAfee for their amazing contributions
to the Chess Team universe. If your favorite characters don't
make it to the end of this book, blame Kane!

Kane would like to dedicate this book to
Mike Pastore, for years of enthusiasm, friendship, and
long phone calls where we acted as personal therapists for each other.
Your support was invaluable, my friend.

THE STORY SO FAR...

Years ago, a US Army Delta operator named Jack Sigler, callsign: King, discovered documents that led him to insurgents planning to use a devastating sonic weapon to destroy the world. The American President, operating in a deniable capacity as callsign: Deep Blue, arranged for King's highly efficient group—Chess Team—to stay active for times when threats were so great that conventional forces could not handle them.

Sometime later, King's brother-in-law, George Pierce, accidentally stumbled upon a rogue geneticist named Richard Ridley, who uncovered the legendary Lernaean Hydra's head and used its genetic code to create regenerating soldiers. Chess Team fought the geneticist and a revived Hydra with help from a man named Alexander Diotrephes, who might have been the Hercules of myth. Along the way, Erik Somers, callsign: Bishop, was infected with the Regen serum, gaining immense strength, but was slowly losing his grip on his humanity.

The following year a rampant strain of Brugada virus was unleashed on the world, and Chess Team was put into action in Vietnam, protecting Dr. Sara Fogg, who was searching for a cure. The team fought Vietnamese Army *Death Volunteers* as well as Neanderthal-human hybrid creatures. During the mission, Bishop discovered a strange crystal that temporarily cured him of his affliction, and Alexander left a young girl named Fiona for King to find and keep safe, who eventually became his adopted daughter.

Six months later, after being granted legal custody of Fiona, King attended his mother's funeral only to discover she was still alive, and that both his parents had been Russian sleeper agents who defected to the West. The team deployed around the world to protect the last speakers of dying languages, including the Neanderthal hybrid creatures who were slaughtered by Richard Ridley's animated golem monsters, as he sought to use the Mother Tongue to control the world. This protolanguage bestowed its speaker with the ability to animate the inanimate. The team members broke into separate missions, Bishop was cured of his Regen condition, and ultimately Ridley was defeated by King, with help from Fiona who learned enough of the Mother Tongue to bring him down. At the end of the catastrophic battle, Stan Tremblay, callsign: Rook left the team without notice, after a squad of soldiers under his command had been ruthlessly killed.

With Rook AWOL, and Queen assigned to hunt for him, King made his way to Ethiopia for a meeting with Dr. Sara Fogg, with whom he'd become involved. He soon encountered Dr. Felice Carter, a woman whose mind was quantum entangled with those of the entire human race. They battled a near omniscient artificial intelligence computer network called Brainstorm, which sought to reap the secrets of a fabled Elephant Graveyard.

Hunting for Rook, Zelda Baker, callsign: Queen, followed his trail through Russia and diverted to Chernobyl. Urban explorers had been attacked by something resembling a werewolf, and Queen soon found a deathtrap-laden abandoned amusement park run by a splinter faction of Richard Ridley's crumbling empire.

After rescuing a young Russian woman, Rook made his way to Norway, where he stumbled on a decades old Nazi creature terrorizing the countryside. And the threat of something more...

King once again went up against the Brainstorm AI, as he and George Pierce investigated bigfoot-like creatures in the Arizona desert. The creatures were being attracted by antimatter technology, which King and Pierce destroyed, while evading a professional hitman.

Bishop thwarted a terror group that got its hands on a bioweapon from Ridley's old company, Manifold Genetics. He also found that his biological father was involved with the terrorists.

Shin Dae-jung, callsign: Knight, was vacationing when he was sent to a Chinese ghost city, where he met up with Anna Beck, the former Manifold agent who had assisted Chess Team in their first fight with Ridley. Together, they took down a rogue scientist attempting to create a Hydra-like creature. Beck went to work for Chess Team after leaving China.

Back at the Chess Team's new base in New Hampshire—captured from Ridley's forces and retrofitted—former President of the United States, Tom Duncan, callsign: Deep Blue, found himself and his support crew, including Beck, trapped inside the base. Assaulted by genetic monstrosities and a former mercenary team of Ridley's, Duncan and Beck repelled the invasion.

Graham Brown, the man behind the Brainstorm AI, evaded a trap set by King, while Sara Fogg and Fiona were temporarily abducted by Alexander, who needed Fiona's Mother Tongue abilities to save the world. King tracked down Brown and a hacker with a death wish, who unwittingly unleashed a sentient black hole. King, Alexander, and Fiona were able to quell the threat, but Alexander slipped away with a piece of rubble containing the black hole.

Huge energy globes appeared around the world, wreaking destruction, and acting as portals for fast, wolf-like creatures from another dimension. Members of Chess Team battled the threat globally, before coming together to battle the source in Norway, where Rook was in the thick of it, and the woman he had rescued, Asya Machtcenko, was revealed to be a Russian sister King never knew he had. Bishop and Knight were trapped in the alternate dimension for an unknown time, but they were rescued, and the Chess Team defeated the man behind the threat, although his technology was stolen by Alexander, who claimed to be holding King's parents hostage.

King and Asya set off to find their parents, while clones of Ridley begged Chess Team for help against Alexander. They all converged in North Africa at an abandoned Manifold facility where the elder Siglers were unharmed, but King and Alexander came to blows and were engulfed in an explosion. The remains of the team fought a protracted battle against the resurrected Ridley and his clones, thinking King was dead. The truth was far stranger, as King and Alexander were whisked into the past. Alexander shared an immortality serum with King and enlisted his help in rescuing his wife and returning to his own dimension. King was left to live out the centuries, traveling from the ancient sands of Babylon, through the Roman Empire at its zenith, to the birth of the American Revolution, until he rejoined Chess Team in the Tunisian battle, ending the threat of Richard Ridley for good.

The next year the team was embroiled in a governmental struggle for control over the Congo and the birthplace of humanity. Knight was injured, losing an eye. Bishop and Felice Carter made a connection and Chess Team thwarted a terrorist named Monique Favreau, whose parent organization would continue to plague the team for some time. In a final battle, Bishop appeared to die at the bottom of a lake, preventing a bomb's detonation.

George Pierce, now in control of the ancient society Alexander had led, gathered allies including Fiona Lane, Felice Carter, mythology professor Augustina Gallo, a hacker named Cintia Dourado, and a man going by the name Lazarus—who just might have been the long-lost Erik Somers. The new group used their skills and resources to stop an organization from seizing the power of the Well of Monsters, unbeknownst to Chess Team.

Still recovering from the tragic loss of Erik Somers, King led Chess Team on a snatch-and-grab to capture a drug cartel leader. But the mission escalated out of control, involving an enemy from their past and infectious, ravenous monsters. The team's support organization was disbanded, and Deep Blue surrendered to the government, so the rest of the team could avoid being officially reined in under US military control.

Deep Blue was whisked away to a Black Site in Arctic Canada, after quietly being tried for treason against the United States.

An altered Chess Team—with Asya Machtcenko fulfilling Bishop's role, Lewis Aleman functioning as Deep Blue, and Knight now armed with a cybernetic eye and Anna Beck as callsign: Pawn by his side—took down a Bright Tomorrow terror cell in Mongolia. In the middle of a Siberian anti-cyclone storm the team tackled genetic weaponry and giant Mongolian Death Worms.

Disavowed and on the run, Chess Team hunted for Tom Duncan who was abducted from his Canadian prison. But King saw a broadcast with a woman he thought long dead—Julie Sigler, his and Asya's sister. The team got drawn into a Russian scheme to topple the US government, and King faced off against his own family members and stopped the Russian President from achieving immortality.

As Earthquakes ravaged the planet, George Pierce and his Cerberus Group uncovered an apocalyptic death cult determined to use the sun to destroy all life on Earth, which led to a hunt for an object out of antiquity—the Ark of the Covenant. No longer calling himself 'Lazarus,' Erik Somers has yet to reveal himself to Chess Team.

And the hunt for Tom Duncan continues...

KINGDOM

"In the kingdom of the blind, the one-eyed man is king."

—Erasmus

"Man must evolve for all human conflict a method which rejects revenge, aggression, and retaliation."

—Martin Luther King, Jr.

"Now this is not the end. It is not even the beginning of the end. But it is, perhaps, the end of the beginning."

—Winston Churchill

PROLOGUE

The Desert

Today

A single set of feet pounded the dry soil, filling the air with the sound of a tyrant on the march. The determined woman's long strides suggested a mission. She had a destination in mind, and nothing would stop her from reaching it.

She paused to catch her breath and cluck at humanity's folly. On the edge of the arid plains, she had seen the place where a truck driver—not paying attention or perhaps attempting to avoid a toll—had allowed his vehicle to careen off the road, plowing over the 2000-year-old geoglyphs etched into the ground. The vehicle left deep scars and, due to the dry, windless climate, the gouges across the ancient symbols would remain for the next two thousand years or more.

As the woman strode on, she fumed at the stupidity, and mused over the fact that it wasn't even the first time. Greenpeace activists had also damaged the site in 2014. Unlike those 'save the planet' types, she respected the ancient designs, and followed a specific course, already tread upon by another, a few years previously. That trail followed a set of footprints planted on the plains in antiquity, leading to a specific boulder.

Her destination.

Buried under the rock were the remains of the most dangerous man the planet had ever known. He would have been a worthy adversary for her once, but now his ravaged corpse would serve another purpose. But first, she would need to see about restoring him.

The huge woman reached the boulder, and ignored the carved glyphs in its side, including the most recent—a stylized letter K. She threw her immense strength into the side of the stone and, at first, it refused to budge. But then she heard a grinding as the massive stone scraped over the dry grit of what passed for soil below it. In a few more minutes, she had unearthed the entrance to the Stone Whisperer's tomb, but it had been filled with dry soil.

Only then did she sit, rest, and take a sip of water from one of her many canteens. The water would need to be rationed. She did not know how long it would take her to excavate out the passage under the boiling sun. After just a handful of minutes, she stood once more, and began to dig.

Eventually, she activated a brilliant LED flashlight and crawled through the low tunnel's entrance. Her huge frame barely squeezed through the tight passage.

Deep under the stone, the air was just as hot and dry as it was outside, but the flashlight sliced through the dense shadows, and she quickly found her prize. She had expected a stale stench of decay, but the complete lack of humidity on the plains had stolen even that. The burlap sack was covered in fine gray dust.

Her fingers—incredibly delicate, despite her size—worked the frayed, rope drawstring that sealed the sack. The Stone Whisperer's head rolled out, the desiccated flesh looking for all the world as if it had been petrified. She could see where the nerves, ligaments, and blood vessels had been cauterized at the neck, and the man's face had been shattered inward. One eye socket was hollow and dark, and the jaw was absent, leaving what was left of the man's nose hovering over a void.

Using precise motions, the woman dripped water from a canteen onto the remains, careful not to waste a single drop on the hungry desert floor. Once the severed head's outer surface was moistened, she withdrew a syringe from her pack. She injected the sharp needle directly into the sole remaining, lidless eyeball. She depressed the plunger, then removed the syringe, which made an audible sucking noise. She did not consider the man's pain, because at this point, he was completely inert. He might as well have been dead. Just as he had been for the last few years.

She knew, between the serum and the moisture she would apply over the coming hours or days, the Stone Whisperer would move again. His face would be restored first. Then, with agonizing pain and slowness, the head would beget a torso. Once the man's mouth and lungs were partially grown, the process would accelerate. The Stone Whisperer would use the language of the ancients, a language before there were human languages—the language of God. He would manipulate flesh and bone as easily as he could manipulate soil and stone. In days, she knew, he could be whole again. A man of staggering intellect, dogged determination to match her own, and a chilling lack of morality. Under other circumstances, he might have been the perfect match for her. A soulmate. Someone who would *understand.* But fate had other plans. Now, she needed him for an entirely different purpose.

The Stone Whisperer would help her to achieve a specific goal.

She had come far from her origins, but as she had navigated the world, she learned that, to ultimately succeed, she would need to rely on the skills and strengths of others, while guarding against betrayal.

The severed head was once again as dry as tinder, and she had yet to see any signs of tissue growth. She opened another canteen and poured the water in small droplets into her open palm, then spread the moisture on the rough texture of the parched skin. The impoverished surface soaked in the liquid, once again feeling dry and scratchy to the touch. She grunted and poured a thin stream of water into the dehydrated eye socket, ready to cease the flow if the water began to drip out of the skull.

It never did.

She dumped the entire canteen into the corpse's head, and not a drop dribbled out. Five minutes later, the skin that remained took on a glistening sheen. Then, finally, the edges of the damaged skin turned pink, and began to stretch.

The woman opened another canteen.

Three hours later, the missing eye had formed, and the eyelid had grown back. Most of the upper lip had protruded, although the skull still lacked a mandible. As soon as the eyelids had grown, they closed, the newly created muscles squeezing them tightly shut. The woman knew the muscular clench was from the abject pain of regeneration, not the light her feeble flashlight cast in the cave.

Another hour passed, and the woman kept feeding the growing head more water. A flap of neck skin and a jutting pink tendril of spinal cord now dangled from the back of the head, and the first nubs of growing jawbone were sprouting from the fleshy mass. Eyelashes had grown on the newly formed lids, although the head remained bald, and the eyebrows had yet to begin growing.

Without preamble, the eyelids snapped upward, revealing brilliant blue irises. The eyes seemed to scream in pain, anguish, and confusion, but overall, they boiled with hatred and a single sizzling question.

Why?

The woman raised the head in her hand, moved the flashlight's beam toward her own face, and unleashed her gravelly voice.

"Welcome back to the world, Richard Ridley."

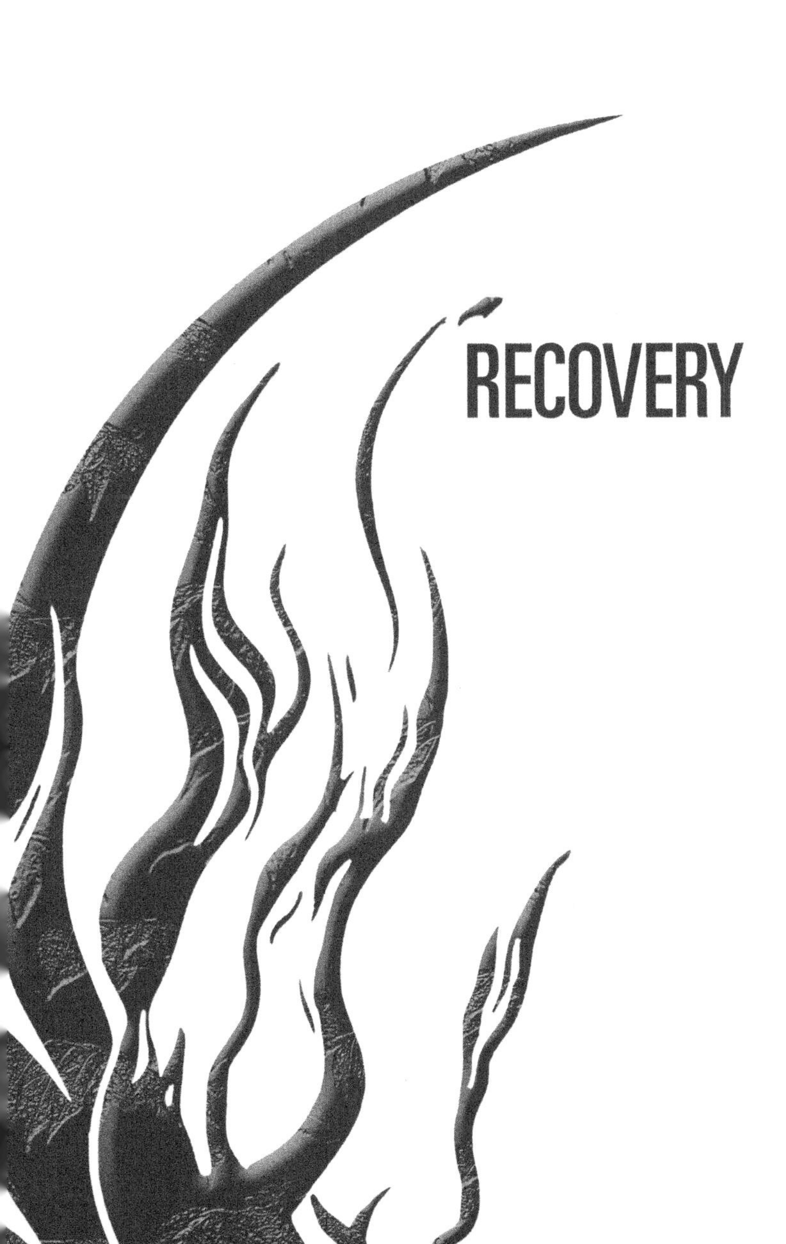

RECOVERY

ONE

Grand Terre, Kerguelen Islands, Southern Indian Ocean

Six dark shapes split the crackling clouds, razor sharp knives plunging through electrified cotton. Even though the storm raged and thrashed, the elongated egg-like slivers continued their downward trajectory. Lightning flashed across the sky, throwing hues of green and blue through the tormented, billowing mass. In seconds, the shapes slit the last of the clouds and darted lower, toward the rain lashed, howling madness below.

The fast-moving shapes continued, as if alive and determined, despite the weather that battered the island under the storm.

Located in the Southern Indian Ocean, between the Roaring Forties and the Furious Fifties, the island and its neighbors were frequently slammed with winds over 90 mph, and their geographic isolation from other land masses lent the islands another name in 1776, when Captain James Cook rediscovered them on Christmas Day. The gloomy, sterile landscape has lived up to its name.

Desolation Islands.

The vicious, black daggers, moving down toward the island at a terminal velocity of 180 mph, were another matter entirely.

The skinny, elongated eggs were just that—pods to contain living bodies. The Vehicle for Orbital Deployment and Kinetic Attack (VODKA) was unsurprisingly designed by the Russians, once they had gotten their hands on the US Prototype for a High Altitude, Low Opening (HALO) Pod of a similar design. The American pod was built with heat-resistant ceramic, titanium, and 'reinforced carbon–carbon,' which gave its nose the same black snout as the space shuttle. But the VODKA pod was coated in a slick, next generation polymer that reduced friction on the way down, and reflected all radar and laser attempts to detect it.

The older HALO pods contained impact foam and a harness that barely allowed the passenger to breathe. The VODKA was filled with a nanite gel that would absorb all impact and redirect it outward.

The pod performed double duty. It protected the passenger from the extremes of atmospheric temperatures. But, unlike the older pods, which would deploy parachutes at a designated altitude, jolting the passenger's speed down to a reasonable pace, and then ejecting them—to freefall farther and then pull their own parachute—this pod's secondary purpose was shock and awe.

It did not slow down, and it did not eject the passenger.

The six pods screamed past an immense rock formation and slammed into the loose rocky soil at the side of a shallow river. The resulting sextupled impacts were like six bombs going off, spraying rock and dirt for hundreds of yards, and leaving the eggs embedded in the ground, steaming in the lashing rain. They were surrounded by a crater of sand and rock turned glass, a thousand feet in diameter. Had anything in the vicinity of their landing zone been alive before, it would be annihilated now.

But the ferocity of the storm had seen to the last of any living creature, long before the pods shattered the ground. Anything with a heartbeat had fled the area, and nothing was present to hear the gentle cooling tick of the six canisters.

Despite the furor of their arrival, the passengers inside the pods were unharmed. The nanite gel had both insulated them from the heat of entry and protected them from the craterous impacts. As designed, the gel had redirected the massive forces outward, adding to the devastating effect around the pods. But to the passengers inside, the shock was less than that of hitting a large pothole in a battered Honda Civic. Military engineering at its finest: protect the personnel and devastate anything in a half mile radius of the landing.

The VODKA pods' steaming outer shells detonated outward, turning the huge eggs into gigantic fragmentation grenades, further shredding the landscape in the vicinity. As the reverberating booms dopplered away, the next layer—an outer core of the nanite gel—slid away to reveal an inner shell, which cracked and hissed. These fragments fell to the rocky ground, as the pounding rain diverted the nearby river toward them.

The water swirled around the strange protrusions, sweeping away the larger fragments and the melting goop of industrial gel. When the gel's structural integrity finally gave way, six objects from the now disintegrated inner pods collapsed to the water.

One of the objects was a large plastic case.

The other five were among the deadliest soldiers known to man.

The smallest of the soldiers—who were all dressed from head to toe in black environmental battle suits with full helmets—rolled with the fall, coming to his feet. He scanned the immediate terrain, then located the plastic canister. He began moving toward it before the other four had recovered.

As the four others gained their feet, the first man cracked open the case, reached in, and began passing out weapons and small tactical backpacks. The crate contained four Steyr AUG rifles with grenade launchers, and one Remington Mk 21 Precision Sniper Rifle. Combined with the handguns and knives each team member already carried on their battlesuits, it was all the ordnance this team would need.

The objective would be in close quarters, and the team was expecting little resistance on the way to the target. Without a word, they moved east, heading toward the mile distant town of Port-aux-Français. There was little variation to the low-lying ground between the impact site and the loose scattering of shelters, Quonset huts, and shipping containers that comprised the town. Plus their arrival was devastating. So, instead of opting for subterfuge, the team focused on speed. They covered the ground at a near run, sweeping their weapons left and right as they ran.

One of the members slowed and turned in a 360 degree arc, guarding the team from a rear attack and making up for the limited visibility of the full head helmets. Halfway to the only human settlement on the island, the smallest team member left the others, carrying only the Remington. In minutes, he was lost to them in the howling rain.

Finally, the remaining four members of the strike team skirted two reclining sea lions in the scrub grass and made their way up to the first building on the edge of the settlement.

Expecting fire, the team took cover against the structure's wall, back-to-back at the corner. But no attack came. Still, they held their position, waiting for confirmation that they could safely move.

The sniper said nothing over their comms. They had previously used some of the most sophisticated communications gear on Earth, but on this particular mission, they used a system common in the world's regular military forces—and their messages could still be intercepted. Instead of speaking, the sniper made a double-click noise with his tongue. It wasn't much but, in the completely silent helmets of the four-man team, it meant everything.

You're covered. Proceed.

The lead man knelt on the ground, waiting. Looking over the small encampment. As he'd expected, nothing moved. Not even a lazy sea lion rolling about. Just pounding rain and the flapping of a tattered flag on a pole. The French Southern and Antarctic Lands' official flag was a blue field with a tiny French *tricolour* where the Union on an American flag would be, and a grouping of white stars and stylized letters. But the tattered remains of the cloth suggested months of neglect.

The broadest team member, who had been facing the rear of the building, turned and surveyed the scene. Then he spoke aloud.

"We've got two problems, boss."

The leader stood up and turned to face the broad man. "What are you thinking, Rook?"

"That this place stinks of 'empty' more than my sweaty Aunt Petunia's love life. But the second problem is even worse."

TWO

"What's the second problem?"

The broad, muscled man opened his helmet visor, so his sincerity could be seen. Piercing blue eyes topped a worn, craggy face and a long dirty blond goatee. "The second is, I gotta bust a grumpy the size of an anaconda."

A slim, lithe figure—one of two women on the team—stepped between the men, flung her own faceplate upward, and glared at the man who had spoken. She, too, was a blonde, with her own Arctic blue eyes. On her forehead, she had a scar in the shape of a star with a grinning skull in the center of it. A brand, seared into her skull by a now-dead asshole.

"Damnit, Rook," she said. "You better be joking."

Stan Tremblay, callsign: Rook, gave the woman his largest, toothiest grin. "About this place having nothing more exciting than cobwebs? Sadly, no."

The woman, Zelda Baker, callsign: Queen, continued to glare.

"Okay," he said, "but that descent from the C5 was a little wobbly, and the landing shook a few things loose..."

Queen sighed and turned away from Rook as she spoke, "Like your last remaining marbles." Then she spoke to the team leader. "But he's right, King. This place looks deserted. What's the play?"

King, slightly shorter than Rook, and far slimmer, although still packing plenty of muscle, flipped up his own visor. His brown hair showed wisps of silver at the temples and had grown a little shaggy, certainly out of regulation, but Delta operators were rarely held to the same standards as other branches of the military—at least where appearance was concerned. And in this case, the team was not the typical Delta unit. King wasn't even sure whether they were technically in the Army or not anymore.

But it didn't make a difference.

"He's here somewhere. Or he was. We need to turn this place upside down and inside out. If there's even a fraction of a hint about his current whereabouts, I want it found."

King turned to scan the empty research station in the distance. Then he turned back to the empty flatlands behind them. "Knight? Any sign of movement?"

"Zip." Shin Dae-jung, callsign: Knight, was the team's sniper, and the small Korean-American man was both deadly and deadly serious about his work. If he said nothing was moving, then nothing was—anywhere.

"Go ahead and come in then," King said. "We could use your eyes."

When King turned back around, the other female member of the team—King's own sister, Asya Machtcenko, callsign: Bishop—was already picking a door lock a few feet away. Rook and Queen moved in opposite directions to cover both corners of the building as Bishop worked.

King smiled, and turned again, to see if he could spot the stealthy sniper's approach. As usual, he saw nothing, until Knight wanted him to, when he jogged from King's left toward the building, from a small outcropping of rock. Of course, he was far closer than King had thought, and he came in at an angle King never would have suspected. Knight was always unpredictable.

King slid up behind Bishop, raising his weapon, ready for whatever might be inside the building. But if he was expecting a fight, he didn't get it. The building was a warehouse that smacked of disuse, with poorly sealed windows, and a small hole in the corner of the roof that was letting in a spray of rain. Broken wooden pallets littered the floor, and rows of empty metal shelving filled the rest of the space, covered in discarded plastic wrapping and sliced away, thick, plastic straps. Whatever had been stored in the space was long gone or used up. Probably perishables.

Next, the team checked out several of the other fifty or so abandoned structures at the station. Some scientific equipment had been left behind in the other structures. But they all held the same air of abandonment and neglect.

Hours passed as the team moved like clockwork from structure to structure. Huts, buildings, and even shipping containers had been used for all manner of purposes at the empty research station. There were scientific laboratories, tech buildings for meteorology and communications, living quarters, and even a tiny movie theater. Some of the shipping containers had been used for storage, and one had held old, battered cots and sleeping bags. But there were no signs of life.

"This is bananas," Rook complained. "We know there were people here just two days ago. Where the hell is everyone?"

They stood at the water's edge, near a line of twelve enormous propane tanks. They had searched every significant structure. All that remained were a few shipping containers and a couple of shacks on the edge of the station's layout. The rain had ceased, but the winds coming off the sea still battered their bodies, and in some cases blew tiny pebbles on the ground, skittering across clumps of grass and hardpacked earth. Already, the ground was drying from the blasts of cold air.

King knew Rook was right. They had all seen the video footage.

Five years earlier, the team's founder and friend, former US President Tom Duncan, had been arrested and quickly whisked away to a US government black site in the Canadian Arctic. Chess Team had immediately attempted a rescue there, but Duncan had already been further abducted by an unknown enemy and moved to a new location. For the next few years, King and his people tracked down every wisp of a lead, often going on little more than hints and rumors. They usually arrived at each possible detention location just a step too late.

Two days ago, everything had changed.

King's best friend, George Pierce, ran an obscure society dedicated to preserving ancient secrets and archeological treasures. His people had seen a video of Tom Duncan being herded off a boat, handcuffed and blindfolded, and onto a pier here at Port-aux-Français—where several scientific staff were waiting to board the same boat. But not nearly enough people to empty the station.

Where the hell did the scientists go? King wondered.

Chess Team planned their assault, prepped for their mission, and were in the air in under forty hours. Their friend and liaison, Lewis Aleman, callsign: Deep Blue, had been tracking the airspace over the islands and all boat traffic in the southern oceans. No one else had come or gone since. The weather was notoriously lousy. Flying a plane in or out was impossible.

King also quickly discounted that the hostiles had moved Duncan to a different part of the island. While the imposing craggy landmass was littered with former whaling stations, geomagnetic camps, seismographic stations, and even an old sheep farm, all the structures had fallen into disrepair, and none had been manned in ages, according to Deep Blue. Plus, travel overland was treacherous at best, due to cliffs, mountains, and glaciers. The story was the same on the other outlying islands. Port-aux-Français was the only current settlement, and it was usually on a skeleton crew this time of year.

"Hey," Bishop said. "I've got a question."

King smiled at the woman's careful pronunciation. She had only recently lost any sign of her accent. He'd not known of his sister's existence until just a few years prior, as she had been raised in secret, in Russia. But since joining Chess Team, Asya strove to fit in with every aspect. She had filled the role of the former Bishop, a man named Erik Somers, who had been killed on a mission in Africa. But if there was one thing King could say for his sister, she was diligent. She had proven herself an excellent hand-to-hand combatant, mastered numerous weapons—even those the others on the team thought would have been too much for her, like heavy machine guns. She had even mastered the language and the culture. To anyone who didn't know her, Asya could pass for a woman who had been raised somewhere in the US. Her accent was now American, but regionally indistinct.

"What's on your mind, Bishop?" King asked. They might have broken radio silence, but he would stick with callsigns until the mission was over.

Asya pointed far out to the western edge of the camp, a half mile away, where a lone, rusted, red shipping container was the only man-made structure to ruin the line of the natural horizon. "Because of the weather, all the structures of the camp are tightly clustered together. Everything is repurposed and reused. Even some of the shipping containers looked like they were used as dorms. So, what's that one doing, all on its lonesome, way the hell out there?"

THREE

The small hairs on the back of Queen's neck stood up. Something was very wrong here. As soon as Bishop had spoken, all heads had snapped toward the distant shipping container, which stood alone on a small rise.

Without another word, the team advanced toward the edge of the camp and the one structure far from it. Queen felt as if a trap would be sprung at any second. Yet nothing happened. Rain spattered in fits and starts across the island, but nothing moved. The land was barren of even animal life now, and there was still no sign of any of the humans that should have been there.

As the team approached the shipping container, she and Rook fanned out to the far side, while Knight slipped to the back of the rusted structure and pulled himself silently on top of the red roof of the container. He pointed his weapon downward at the roof, ready to put holes in it and anyone hiding inside.

King and his sister had stayed by the container's doors, which were bolted shut, but not locked.

After circling the structure, Queen and Rook joined the others at the door. She shook her head at King, indicating they had seen nothing. He scowled and turned his attention to the bolt on the door. He slipped his pack off and procured a small canister wrapped in gray duct tape. Then he leaned in and sprayed liquid from the canister on the bolt, covering it. The spray started to foam and turn white.

Queen wondered what it was and, when King turned to her, he saw her confusion. He handed her the canister, and she could see from the parts of it that were not covered by the duct tape, that it was a slim can of WD-40.

Smart, she thought.

It wasn't a part of their standard kit, but King had thought to bring some. Now the bolt on the rusted door would slide with much less friction and be nearly silent.

Queen stood back and raised her weapon at the door. King sprayed the door hinges, then he and Rook also stood back, forming an arc, covering Bishop as she slowly wiggled the bolt loose. King raised his hand, silently lowering his fingers in a countdown. From above the container, Knight kept a watch on King's hand, his eyes darted around the landscape as well, but his weapon stayed pointed at the roof of the shipping container. If there was trouble inside it, the others would blast it from the front, while Knight punctured it from above.

Before King's final finger dropped, Queen turned her attention to the door. Then Bishop pulled hard on the door and stepped out of the line of fire with it.

For a split second, Queen was about to fire at the lone object she saw inside before she realized what it was. Centered near the front of the mostly empty shipping container was a single wooden pallet stacked four foot high with sacks of wooden pellets to be used in heating stoves. The sacks were still tightly bound to the pallet in plastic. It was possible that an assailant was crouched behind the stack, and completely concealed, but Queen doubted it.

The others apparently did, too. They lowered their weapons. Seeing King relax, Knight turned his attention to scanning the horizon, but he stayed on the container's roof.

"All that tension, I thought we were finally gonna see some action," Rook said, as he entered the mostly empty container, along the side of the pallet. "But nooo. Instead, we're like a virgin on his wedding night, waiting for his bride to finish a nap."

Queen rolled her eyes.

"What? It's fuckin' frustrating." He sighed. "Now that we've checked literally everything—"

Rook's mouth stopped moving at the same time that his hand went up.

Queen's weapon snapped upward.

Rook just waved his fingers, indicating the others should follow him into the container and see whatever he had spotted on the far side of the plastic wrapped stack. Queen entered on one side of the pallet and Bishop followed Rook in on the other.

Rook turned on his rifle-mounted flashlight. He pointed it at a metal hatch set into the floor of the shipping container. The hatch was round and had a wheel on top of it, like those on submarines.

King tapped Queen's shoulder, and then stepped around her and squatted down next to the hatch. Where the bolt outside was rusted and had looked disused, the wheel on the floor hatch was heavily coated in a thick grease. King didn't bother with the WD-40. He just put his hand on the wheel, and it spun easily under his touch.

Again, the team took up stances around the hatch, and King opened it to reveal a vertical shaft with a ladder. The shaft descended for fifteen feet before meeting a horizontal subterranean corridor. White LED lights were recessed into the walls. Without another word, King slid down the ladder. Queen was next. She knew the other two would follow, and Knight would still be outside, providing them cover.

The corridor ran fifty feet to a single brown metal door. Like the shipping container above, it was sealed with just a sliding metal bolt, but no lock in front of its hasp. Asya moved forward to inspect the door for traps and held out her hand to her brother. This time, the duct-taped lubricant can was going to be used—just to be on the safe side.

Rook covered the group's rear, keeping a constant eye on the ladder and the open hatch back to the container. King inspected the corners of the corridor, above the door, looking for a video camera or anything else.

Queen knew something here wasn't right. *A single door? Down a single corridor? Hidden under an abandoned shipping container?*

Then she heard King's tongue make an almost imperceptible sound over the comms. Three clicks. Then two. She understood he was signaling to Knight that they were about to breach the door.

Queen moved left against the wall and crouched down, her weapon pointed at the door. Again, Bishop flung the door open.

The hinges were well oiled, and the door swung wide without a sound.

Beyond the door was a single room. A prison cell. It had a tiny stainless-steel toilet bolted to one wall and, near it, a small, matching wash basin. There was a cot along one wall, and blankets were heaped high on it. A bolted metal grate on the ceiling provided air flow.

The room also held a single occupant.

He was on the floor, doing pushups, his back to the doorway. He was dressed in pale blue medical scrubs, and his feet and muscled arms were bare. His head was covered in brown hair at the back and on the sides, but the top showed skin in a male pattern of baldness that practically resembled a monk's tonsure. The man's beard was long and scraggly, displaying each unshaved day of the five years he had been incarcerated.

"Tom?" King asked.

The man whirled around on the floor into a crouch, but upon recognizing King, Tom Duncan reached out his hand and began to scream. "King, No! Wait! It's a trap!"

But it was too late. King had stepped through the doorway.

FOUR

As soon as King's leg swept through the doorframe, it broke the beam of an invisible electric eye, and a blaring klaxon sounded. The tunnel and the room were snapped into darkness, and then the recessed LED lights snapped back on with strobing red. Tom Duncan, a former President of the United States, and a former US Army Ranger, was already running toward King.

Sonovabitch, King thought. *I should have checked the doorframe.* He could see the electric eye nestled into the metal frame now.

"Can you run?" King asked, turning as Duncan reached him.

"We're going to need to," Duncan said, passing King.

The others were already making their way up the ladder.

"What's coming?" King asked.

"Not sure," Duncan said, as he reached the ladder. "But they bragged that it would be bad."

"Knight?" King said into the comms. "Status?"

"Alarms going off. Fucking loud. But no movement."

King could hear the wince in Knight's voice. Even though he knew Knight was encapsulated in the relative quiet of a padded helmet, King could still hear the klaxon behind Knight's voice, slightly off from the sound of it down in the tunnel.

"We have the package but need a minute to wrap it," King said.

"Understood," Knight replied.

At the top of the ladder, Bishop opened her pack and handed Duncan an armored bodysuit. He quickly tore off his medical scrubs and struggled into the suit. King noticed his friend and former boss had lost almost twenty pounds since the last time they had met, but the rest of the man's body was taut and wiry. Strong, despite having been a prisoner for years.

Bishop next produced boots, gloves, and a helmet like those each team member wore. Once Duncan was suited, they all snapped their faceplates closed, and King decided it was time to contact support. "Switching to Channel 2," he told the others through comms, and they all switched their gear. The team had been using a lower powered channel to make signals to each other on the ground. The clicks and tongue noises would not have been easily identified—if anyone had been listening. But now that an alarm was blaring across the island, support would be better than silence.

"Deep Blue, we have the package. Gig is up. We need transport." King was speaking to Lewis Aleman, who had been Tom Duncan's right-hand man and had then taken over the role of tactical and technical support for the team when Duncan had turned himself in to the US authorities five years earlier. Aleman had also taken over the callsign of Deep Blue.

"King, the LZ was compromised. Proceed to Pick-Up Point Aurora," came the terse reply. "Afraid we can't get any closer. Let us know if you'll be coming in hot."

"Will do," King said, and then he turned to Duncan. "I know you can sprint, but can you handle long distance?"

"I'll make it," Duncan said. "But wherever we're heading, we better get there fast."

"King, what's the plan?" Knight asked, unseen.

Queen, Rook, and Bishop watched the doors to the shipping container, but the group had yet to move out of it.

"Back into the camp. Find some wheels. There's a road to the satellite station. I'd rather ride than run. Everyone set?" King waited just a second. "Go."

The team, along with Duncan, ran toward the nearest sheltering building in the camp. Knight was already ahead of the group and peeled off to the left. "There was a pickup at the northwest corner of camp. I'll come to you, King."

"Route 66," King replied, referring to the major road of the camp, which ran through it, along the shore and beyond, to a defunct satellite tracking station a mile and a half out of the main camp.

Once the group reached the first structure, they moved quickly from building to building, constantly seeking cover, and looking out for any movement.

"Where to?" Duncan asked.

"Aurora is on the other side of the peninsula from the camp."

"Where are we?"

"Oh, sorry. Desolation Islands."

"Ah, Port-aux-Français." Duncan said. "The only thing on the other side of the peninsula is the Norwegian Bay."

Rook turned to him. "How the hell do you do that? You're not even anywhere near a computer."

"I know things," Duncan said. He almost needed to shout to be heard over the klaxons.

"Man, that noise is brutal. Like a kiss from my Auntie," Rook shivered. "Ugh. That mustache."

"Move," King said, and the banter stopped. The group leap-frogged from building to building, weapons up and looking for an attack coming at them from anywhere but the sea. They scanned the mountains in the distance, and the squalid buildings of the camp, but the only motion was a plume of dust rising above the buildings on Route Rouen—which was little more than a dirt track through the camp.

"Proceeding," Knight said over comms.

The group moved toward the sole hotel in town, where visiting scientists had stayed when the camp was populated. That reminded King of a question he had.

He turned to Duncan. "Where the hell is everyone? Two days ago, when they brought you here by ship, there were people everywhere. Scientists. Staff. We got a still picture taken by someone waiting to board the ship you came in on. What happened?"

Duncan shrugged. "No clue. I was put in the cell, and food came later in the day. No food came yesterday. No one came today—until you did. I thought it was just a tactic to soften me up."

By this point, Duncan was shouting to be heard over the klaxon. The alarm burst from several loudspeakers mounted on telephone poles around the camp. One of the faded white poles stood above where they waited for Knight. King could see the gray speakers at the top of it, each pointing in a different direction.

"Damnit," Rook shouted. "I oughtta just put a round in the friggin' thing. No one is coming to answer that alarm."

"Wait," King said. He noticed the alarm wasn't just loud.

It was getting louder.

He was about to suggest that Rook act on his impulse to shoot the thing, but then his hunch about the sound was confirmed. The klaxon's volume jumped—probably doubled—and each of the team members bent over in pain, trying to clutch their ears through their helmets. King couldn't imagine how loud the sound would be *without* the protection of the helmet, but he expected it would be enough to rupture an ear drum. He could feel the pulsing noise in his chest.

Rook stood up straight and took aim at the loudspeaker with his Steyr AUG—and then he vanished, as a fast-moving wall of green and brown plowed into him from behind like a bus.

FIVE

Rook's body flew through the air.

The impact rattled him, but the weave of the wetsuit-like body armor he wore absorbed the brunt of it. He was stunned. Disoriented thanks to being made into a pool ball.

Assess the damage, he thought. Then the realization that should have come first finally hit.

Oh shit, I'm still in the air. I'm gonna hi–

His body slammed into the concrete wall of the hotel, and dropped four feet to the ground, crunching against the asphalt of a paved road. Three hard hits inside thirty seconds.

Rook tried to speak, but the only noise he could make was a high-pitched whistling.

Shit, he thought. *Broken rib? Punctured lung?*

Before he could move to check his body for breakage, she was there in his view.

"Rook," Queen shouted, flipping up her visor, despite the noise. "Sweet fuckery, are you okay?" She slipped an arm under him as he sat up.

"Yeah," he said, relieved that his voice had returned. "I'm–What the fuck hit me?" Rook saw that Bishop, Duncan, and King were all standing still, weapons aimed across the street. They formed a wall between Rook and whatever had flipped him aside like a rag doll. His breath back, and the strange lung whistle sound gone now, he staggered to his feet, with Queen under his arm the whole way.

At his full height, Rook was taller than anyone else on the team, but he still needed to go up on his toes to see over King's helmet. When he did, what he saw took his breath away again.

The thing looked like a giant crocodile or a Komodo dragon. Except it was huge. The size of an old station wagon. Green and brown thumb-nail-sized colors coated the thing like camouflage. The muscles in its legs rippled and pushed against the skin like they were trying to tear their way out of the beast. Its tail was thick and long—equally muscular. A forked tongue like a snake's flitted from the creature's mouth, and its entire front end was drenched in a thick, viscous drool that was alternately clear and pea-soup green. Four and a half feet tall, Rook estimated. And twenty feet long.

As unexpected as the nightmare lizard was, its behavior was stranger. It had rammed itself into the telephone pole with the gray loudspeakers. Now it was viciously chewing and clawing at the noise's source, even though the falling pole had snapped the wires connecting it to whatever hidden device had started the noise.

This pole was down, but the noise from the alarms had not ceased. It continued to blare from several other nearby poles. The gigantic animal was frantic to end the noise, though. It seemed to comprehend that its first victim had ceased functioning. It raised its elongated head, turned, stuck out its long tongue as if tasting the air, then barreled toward another pole thirty feet away.

"What the actual hell is that?" Bishop was the first to find her voice.

"Megalania Prisca," Duncan said.

"A what?" King asked.

"Extinct giant monitor lizard."

"Doesn't look extinct to me," Queen said, looking around. Behind them, she saw another immense lizard racing parallel to the shore, its mighty clawed feet scrabbling at the stones and rocks, sending up sprays of grit behind it as the creature wiggled.

"Didn't *feel* extinct," Rook said, as Knight arrived in a tan Ford 150 pickup truck. The truck slewed as he crushed the brakes and skidded to a stop. Rook walked to the passenger door, opened it, and heaved himself in. "Sup?"

"What did I miss?" Knight asked, as the others clambered into the bed of the truck. Bishop and King took up a defensive position at the tailgate. Queen took the forward view with Duncan behind her. She slapped the roof of the truck's cab.

"Just friggin' Godzilla giving my nuts a moose-clap."

Knight stamped on the accelerator pedal. "So, just another day, then?"

As they drove along the road, Rook saw three more of the enormous lizards—all attacking the poles with the klaxons on them. Some were even larger than the one that had bushwhacked him.

"You said 'extinct,' Tom," King said, over their comms. "How extinct?"

"Fifty million years, at least," Duncan said. "I watched a documentary about them. Mostly just guesses based on the fossil record. They would have been about twenty feet long, like these things. But these could just be really large Komodo dragons, too. Hard to tell for sure, but they're in the wrong part of the world, if they are."

"Think this was the trap left for us?" Queen asked.

"I'd rather not wait around to find out," Duncan replied, and Rook thought the man sounded tired. Deeply tired. Rightly so, after being held prisoner for years. Rook was about to ask whether Duncan would be able to haul ass on foot if their road ran out, as he knew it did on the far side of the satellite tracking station, a few miles past the camp. But then something happened. He was preparing to shout over the noise of the alarms and the revving engine, when he noticed something jarring.

The alarms all just stopped.

On their own, and at the same time, in the middle of the klaxon's plaintive whine, it died. Abruptly. No dwindling, diminishing fade. As if it had been cut off. Rook twisted around in the cab's tight confines to peer through the rear window's tiny sliding door.

In the distance, the large lizards were coalescing around the last building of the camp—one of the first the team had investigated, and the last one before the solitary road on which they now travelled.

The super-sized creatures, like a herd of dinosaurs, looked conflicted for a moment, mulling around, crawling over each other.

Then they all turned as one, toward the road, and the team's pickup truck, which was doing fifty miles per hour and threatening to tear itself apart on the pot-holed, uneven, asphalt surface. The engine moaned as if the pistons would explode through the hood. If Knight didn't cool it soon, the truck would throw a rod.

The next thing to happen convinced Rook that he *would* see that engine meltdown. There was no way Knight was going to slow down. Not until the truck broke or flipped when they ran out of road.

As if the starter's pistol of a race had gone off, the entire group of Megalanias broke into a frantic sprint, straight toward the truck's retreating rear end.

SIX

The tough, leathery-looking skin of the creatures seemed to boil and bubble as they scrabbled over each other in their haste to follow Knight's commandeered pickup truck. He glanced at the squirming bodies, each the width of city buses, in the sideview mirror. Then he jammed his foot down on the accelerator pedal.

But the old truck had nothing more to give. He could feel the engine straining now. It would die soon, and they'd need to hump it three-miles to the shore of Baie Norvegienne—the Norwegian Bay—where transport *should* be waiting for them. It didn't look good.

"How fast are these things?" Knight asked.

"Fast," Rook said. "Way too fast. The first one we saw plowed into me like a train and kept on going, before we even had a chance to see it."

In the back, Bishop started shooting at the distant, but still approaching, lizards. Single shots from the Remington rang out, and Knight wondered if she would hit any of the creatures—and if she did, whether a single .338 round would make any difference. Worse, there appeared to be about thirty of the creatures before they started climbing all over each other in the fury to chase the team. Since then, a few more had raced in from the shore to join the herd. Knight had no idea how many of them followed the truck now.

The pickup's right front wheel found a deep pothole in the barely paved road. Rook bounced so hard that his head smashed into the corner of the cab's roof, where the liner was starting to fall down.

"Sonnuva ball-less monkey-fuck! Keep it on the road, wouldja?" Rook cried out.

Knight chuckled and said "Sorry," then kept his eyes on the road instead of the encroaching threat behind them. From the truck bed, Bishop kept firing single shots. But Queen and King had yet to open fire with their rifles. He'd be able to know when the lizards were overtaking them, once those two joined in with rapid-fire bursts.

Knight swerved the truck left to avoid another pothole. This one had grown so large it covered the majority of the road. As the truck jolted, Knight heard another shot, and then he heard Bishop swearing in Russian. He smiled, knowing what that was like. You were sure that *this* time, the shot would not miss. But then external forces acted, and you were right where you started, needing to line up another shot.

"Quarter mile to the tracking station," Knight said through comms. "Let's hope there's another vehicle there. Not sure this one will make it far off-roading."

"We're already off-roading," Rook complained, as Knight swerved to avoid another huge pothole, which forced them into a third.

"Scanning already," Queen replied.

Knight glanced in the rearview mirror. She was facing forward, over the roof of the cab. She would be using a monocular, checking the upcoming station for any other vehicles they could appropriate. It was going to be close.

The buildings ahead all looked whitewashed—or washed out by the elements. There were some spherical radar dome structures on the left of the road, and a few small buildings to the right, with one large radome. The radomes looked like giant golf balls, but they were actually shields made from fiberglass, and they were designed to protect delicate machinery from hail and high winds. Knight had examined the satellite imagery of the entire site before they had departed for the mission. He knew that, beyond the structures he could now see, the road jagged to the left, and then swept around to a tight cluster of twenty satellite dishes that resembled the famous Very Large Array in New Mexico. Beyond those, the road was dirt, and it ran another two hundred feet. Then they would be off-road.

And they would still need to travel another mile and a half.

"Found one," Queen said. "I can see the rear end of a Jeep behind the building at the far right. By Epcot Center there."

Of course, Knight thought.

It was in the wrong direction from where they needed to go. He hoped the Jeep would work, because stopping to transfer to the other vehicle would potentially kill them all.

"Hey," Rook said, slapping the back of his hand against Knight's arm, and switching off his comms.

Knight glanced over at him. The man had a huge grin on his face. Knight switched off, too. "What are you thinking?"

"Sweep right before we get to the buildings," Rook said. "Pull in tight against the side of the last one, and I'll dive out. Then you keep going toward the array."

Knight looked dubious.

"Keep going as long as you can. If I can get the Jeep rolling and it's better than this shit heap, I'll come to you, and we'll transfer by the array. If not, I can take shelter from those things in the big building." When Knight's raised eyebrow didn't lower, Rook continued. "I'll have a better chance with concrete than out in the open."

"Queen's gonna be pissed," Knight said.

"Not her call," Rook replied. Then he switched comms back on, and said, "King, I'm gonna get the Jeep. You guys stay with Knight. If I can get the Jeep rolling, I'll join you. We'll transfer at the array."

"What?" Queen started.

King cut her off. "Agreed. Do it. If you get cut off, we'll circle back after leading the herd astray."

The instant King said 'Agreed,' Knight swerved the truck off the road and onto the mostly flat, hardpacked ground. He had to steer around a few large rocks, but it was a smoother ride than the road had been. The bigger problem was that the truck tires were sending up a huge plume of dust behind them. He was shocked how quickly the ground had dried out after the rain but now the dust was obscuring their view of the pursuing lizard pack. They would only know if the giant creatures had closed the distance if they burst out of the dust right behind the truck. By then it would be too late.

"Hold on," Knight said over comms, then he dragged the wheel, turning the truck at a sharp right angle to their previous path. There was a thick two foot high pipe that ran above ground and parallel to the back of the building they approached. Also, the new course would keep the dust plume at an angle to their desired course—and the Crazy Ivan aspect of the turn would reveal if the Megalanias had closed the gap. But there was no immediate sign of the giant lizards.

"Get ready," Knight cautioned over the straining engine. "I'm just going to slow, but not come to a full stop. I'm not sure this thing would make it past first gear again."

"Fuck it, man. Don't even slow down. The suit and helmet will protect me."

Knight just nodded, and he yanked the steering wheel hard in another right angle turn, taking the pickup onto a curving driveway that was equidistant from the rear of the faded red Jeep Wrangler and the next nearby structure—a standalone radome. He held his fist up, and Rook bumped it. Then the big man flung the passenger door open, and he leapt out, headfirst.

Knight stamped on the accelerator pedal again, wanting to throw up a huge dust plume, and draw the pack away from Rook. He cranked the wheel hard, bringing the pickup back onto the road that ran around the front of the building and swept wide toward the distant array. But then he heard the noise he had been fearing: Queen, King, and Bishop—who had switched weapons—all opened fire with their Steyer AUG rifles. Worse, they weren't using controlled three round bursts. They were firing on full auto.

Knight didn't even bother looking in the rearview mirror. He knew the first giant lizards were right on them. And right on Rook.

SEVEN

The impact knocked the air out of Rook's lungs, even though he was expecting it. After his earlier collision with one of the Megalanias, his body still wasn't operating at full capacity, and he regretted telling Knight to not even slow down.

He landed on his right shoulder, and rolled, but meeting the ground at forty miles an hour—even with the cutting-edge body armor—still made his head ring and his chest vibrate like he was next to a Marshall amp at a Motörhead concert. He pulled his legs in tight and tried to make an egg shape with his body, rolling and flipping, until his momentum was spent. He landed on his back and wanted nothing more than to just stay still in the dirt and gravel until the hurting stopped.

He forced himself up anyway, in a sloppy sit-up maneuver, that immediately told him that, this time, he *had* cracked a rib. A sharp pain stabbed into his right upper chest, stealing the breath he was just about to take. He rolled to his knees, and struggled to his feet, trying to get his bearings.

As he stood, he could hear the straining engine of the pickup fading, automatic weapons fire, and a skittering, scrabbling noise coming from behind him. Rook realized he was facing the wrong way. Ahead of him was the immense fiberglass radome, which looked more yellow than white, up close. It was stained with streaks of rust, and a few greenish patches of mold on the concrete walls below the semi-sphere. The problem was he was way too close to it.

Rook turned fast and, despite the rising cloud of dust from the pickup's passing, he could see that, with his roll across the ground, he was now far closer to the radome than to the Jeep. There was a hundred and fifty feet of open ground between the building with the Jeep and the radome at his back. And he was forty feet from the radome. Some of the Megalania pack had already made the corner and were pursuing the team's truck. But the stragglers were still coming, and one of them—a huge brown lizard with a massive scar stretching across its face and over one eye—caught sight of Rook and altered its course. Two more of the lizards, greener and smaller, pursued the big brown one.

Ah, shitnuggets, Rook thought.

He turned and headed for the radome instead of the Jeep. The spherical structure sat on a twenty foot high concrete base, looking like a giant scoop of ice cream on top of a wafer cone. Rook didn't see a door into the interior. He did, however, see the one item he was counting on. Rook had visited a similar structure at New Boston Space Force Station in New Hampshire. He knew that radomes were usually fabric or fiberglass. He understood they were constructed to keep snow and rain off equipment, and he had witnessed first-hand the incredibly low-tech procedure for removing piled up snow from the tops of the giant golf ball like coverings.

Rook poured on the speed, his arms pumping at his sides, and he stretched out his running stride as much as he could. His rib throbbed with each step. Just as he heard a loud scrabbling noise behind him—claws on the pebble strewn ground, his imagination shouted at him—he leapt up, grabbed the rope hanging down from the top of the radome, and swung forward, pulling his legs up into a crouch like position. He frantically pulled himself up the rope, arm over arm, as he swept over the ground.

Eat your friggin' heart out, Tarzan.

Just then, the beast that had been on his tail blasted past, just feet underneath him, unable to stop its locomotive speed. He was grateful the creature hadn't lifted its head upward as it went, or he'd have been a snack.

Rook hauled himself up, as the backswing began. Below him, the giant brown lizard skittered to a stop and turned, darting left and right, looking for its prey. Rook silently swung back over the creature, and the two smaller green ones. From above, he could see that they were twenty feet long each, but were smaller than the brown leader.

He didn't think the massive dinosaur like beasts could climb the walls of the radome's concrete base, like little geckos, or that they could go up the rope like he had, but he still slowly pulled the end of the rope up out of reach—just in case.

Years earlier in New Hampshire, he'd been impressed with the fact that radomes had just a simple rope hanging from them. An airman would grab the end of the rope and walk a circuit around the radome, pulling the rope with him. The rope would effectively dislodge all the piled snow on the roof, and it would tumble harmlessly to the ground behind the walker. Low tech. Like the Russians using a pencil for their cosmonauts, while NASA had supposedly spent millions developing a pen that would write in space—or so the apocryphal story went.

Rook had expected the rope to be present on this radome, and he'd spotted it hanging off the fiberglass roof before he'd told Knight he was jumping out of the truck. But he hadn't planned on needing to use it to escape the frantic giant lizard creatures. He'd expected to be in the Jeep by now. He had escaped the lizards temporarily, but now he wasn't sure what his next move would be.

Then one of the green lizards ran away from the wall, skittered in a circle, and raised its head.

It saw Rook and let out a warbling growl. It was nothing like any other creature Rook had heard, but the grinding, almost mechanical rumble was exactly what he expected these things would sound like.

The immense brown lizard and the other smaller green one stopped and turned to look at the wall. The scarred brown beast craned its head up, while the green Megalania ran to the base of the concrete wall and started scratching its way up, with foot long, curved claws making shallow divots in the wall.

"Oh, well that's just fucktastic," Rook said aloud. Then he hauled himself higher up the rope, as fast as he could go.

He didn't slow until he reached the end of the concrete support wall, and he began to ascend the lower portion of the dome. He glanced down and saw that the two green lizards weren't gaining on him. One was still on the ground, and the other was only four feet up the concrete wall.

The large brown one was farther back, its head craned up, and its forked tongue slowly slipping out of its mouth, tasting the air.

Rook pulled himself up higher, the broken rib throbbing in pain now. When he crested the hemisphere of the radome, he pulled on the rope until he could stand upright with its assistance, at a little more than a 45 degree angle. He could still peer down over the edge at the green lizards, who were attempting to scale the wall, but falling back down after just a few feet.

The large brown creature just stared at Rook, making no attempt to get at him. Rook's own progress was halted now, too. He needed to get down off the radome and over to the Jeep, but he saw no way to get it done safely. He just hoped the Megalanias would give up and join the others in their pack.

Pulling on the rope, Rook walked higher up the dome until the view of the creatures was obscured by the angle of the sphere. He tugged harder and kept walking until his body was perfectly upright and he could balance on the dome's top without the support of the rope.

"Now what?" he asked himself, glancing back at the neighboring building with the Jeep.

Then the fiberglass floor beneath his feet groaned. His eyes darted downward, and the dome crumbled beneath his weight.

EIGHT

***This is not** going well,* King thought.

The mission was simple. Get in, grab Duncan, and get out. But their transportation was supposed to be closer, there should have been a few guards to eliminate, and there definitely should *not* have been prehistoric creatures on a rampage. Now, here they were again, getting split up. King was just about to give Knight the order to start a wide slow arc back toward Rook's location when they all heard a pained grunt over their comms.

Queen was the first to reply. "Rook? Status report. We need that Jeep."

A groan was the only response.

"Rook? Are you alright?"

Then finally, a response. "No. I'm not alright. I'm sitting in a nest of bones, with freaking Godzilla barreling toward me."

"Please tell me that's a euphemism for how much you miss me," Queen replied.

"Hah," Rook's barked laughter was loud over the comms, but then the rest of what he was about to say was drowned out by an automatic burst from his Steyr.

A second later, a slavering set of armored jaws lunged out of the dust cloud behind the tailgate, and King had to focus on their own predicament before he could think any more about Rook. He let loose a blast with his Steyr AUG, then switched to the pistol grip on the under barrel grenade launcher.

The shell spat straight down the nearest creature's throat and, out of the corner of his eye, King saw that his sister, lying prone in the back of the pickup bed next to him, had also just fired a grenade down a different creature's throat.

Suddenly, both giant lizards at the head of the pack chasing them detonated—the shockwave knocked the back end of the pickup off the ground and launched geysers of multidirectional gore that splashed onto the following horde.

For a fraction of a second, King worried the battered vehicle would flip over from the force of the blast, but then the wheels slammed down, jolting him up and off the tailgate. His body crashed back down, stealing his breath. He scrambled to his hands and knees as a gust of wind tore at the dust cloud behind the truck. He could see the bulk of the Megalania pack had paused to dine on the detonated remains of their fastest.

The breather was exactly what Chess Team needed.

"Knight, take us around in a wide arc and head back for Rook. We're not leaving anyone behind this time."

King turned around to see Duncan crouched behind the cab of the truck, one hand on the bottom of the slider window and one braced against the top, to prevent him from being thrown. Queen was on the passenger side, with a single loop of nylon ratcheting strap through the truck's frame looped around her leg for the same reason. She had her faceplate up and, as she glanced quickly at King, he could see the gratitude for his decision.

She would never say anything, but he knew she was worried about Rook. The decision seemed sound at the time, but plans had to be fluid in the heat of battle. Now King regretted letting Rook dive out, but if they had to make a stand back at the huge radar dome, so be it. He just didn't know how long of a stand it would be. They didn't have a lot of grenades, and the Megas didn't want to collapse under a spray of 9mm rounds. Unless you hit them in the eye and got their brains, but with the whole pack squirming and thrashing like eels—and from the back of a jostling pickup on non-existent roads, that was tricky.

"Blue?" King said over comms.

The response dopplered through his earpiece, with both Lewis Aleman—from his remote location—and Tom Duncan from King's side, replying with a "Yeah?"

Then there was silence over comms for a second.

King decided to clear it up quickly. "Sorry, sir. There's a new Deep Blue. Your codename is now...Eagle."

King saw Duncan just nod. Then he continued with his original question. "Blue, any chance of air support?"

"Already checked. They're too far out," came the response from Lewis Aleman, the new Deep Blue. "We can get you cover once you reach the bay."

"Copy," King replied.

The temporary distraction the feeding frenzy provided elapsed. King could see the pack through the fog-like haze kicked up by the pickup's wheels, as the vehicle jounced hard on the uneven ground. Knight's wide arc had nearly brought them back to the big radome, which had a new ragged hole in the top of the sphere. A bent piece of metal frame stuck up and out of the hole at an angle.

Asya opened fire again at the approaching swarm, catching one creature in the eye. It dropped, and the others scurried over it in their haste to get the truck.

"Rook," Knight's voice called. "Where are you? We're approaching the Jeep, but I don't see your location..."

"Wait one," came Rook's labored reply.

The pack was inching closer, but the ground had leveled out closer to the buildings. King took a chance and stood in the back of the pickup, aiming the grenade launcher at the pack's leaders, looking to repeat his earlier stunt. Asya let loose a shot first but, before the grenade met its target, there was a huge boom from in front of the truck.

King whipped his head around in time to see a massive brown Megalania bursting through the concrete wall of the big radome's base. Cinder blocks scattered away from the ruined wall, as the rampaging creature powered toward the truck. Riding on top of the brown monstrosity, was Rook, hanging on to his single handhold: a KA-BAR knife with a seven-inch blade buried deep into the top of the Mega's skull.

"Oh, I see you now," Knight said with a practiced calm, as he swerved the truck for the stationary red Jeep Wrangler, and away from the incoming behemoth.

The brown creature passed the pickup and headed straight toward the remaining pack, as yet another creature detonated from a launched grenade. The twin disruptions—the explosion and the arrival of a huge Mega heading the other direction—caused momentary chaos. Then the rest of the pack chased after the big brown Mega wearing food on its back.

Asya climbed to her knees and held on to the truck's tailgate, as King crouched and held the sidewall, while Knight skidded the pickup to a halt. Right next to the inert Jeep.

"Are we chasing Rook or getting the Jeep?" Knight asked.

King was about to say they should go after Rook, whose steed was now far ahead of the pack, but the creature was leading them all in the correct direction—toward their waiting pickup.

Before he could respond, the battered Ford answered for him, blowing a jet of smoke up from under the hood before it caught fire.

NINE

Queen jumped out of the pickup's bed and ran toward the Jeep's driver's side door. The others quickly followed. Knight caught up first.

"I'll drive. We'll need your eyes up top," she told him.

He proceeded toward the back of the vehicle and climbed the roof of the weathered soft top, lying down over the roll bars. Asya climbed up next to him.

Queen slipped into the unlocked door on the driver's side, just as Duncan climbed in through the flapping unzipped back window, and King slid into the passenger's seat. He slammed the door shut, then kicked the fabric hard, shredding the cracked material and launching it right off the door frame.

Queen bent under the hood to hotwire the vehicle, but King put his hand on her arm. "Did you check the sun visor?"

Queen sat up, grabbed the visor, and—nothing.

"Pretty sure that's just in movies, boss," she said, and then glanced down at the console cup holder where a single key sat. "You've got to be shitting me." She picked up the key, from which dangled a rubber ducky keychain.

Queen stabbed the key in the ignition, said a quick prayer in her mind, and turned it. The engine roared to life, as she had stamped down on the pedal a little too hard, expecting to need to goose the engine to life. But there was no need. The fabric top might have faded from too many storms, but the engine sounded good.

"Everyone ready?" Queen asked, one foot hovering over the accelerator, the other on the clutch pedal, and her hand on the stick shift, ready to launch them after the chasing pack of ancient lizard creatures.

Suddenly, a fist punched through the roof above King's shoulder, to her right.

Then another just behind her head.

"Need something to hold onto up here," Asya said over comms. "We're good. Go."

Now with one of Asya's hands through the roof and holding the roll bar above King, and one of Knight's hands grabbing the steel above her head, Queen let the vehicle go, and haltingly found her way through second gear and into third.

"That was a little rough," King said.

"Been a while since I drove standard," Queen said smiling, then she was racing into fourth.

While Queen stamped on the accelerator pedal, she saw King pull out his knife and then pause. "Asya, Knight, pull forward over the front seats. Eagle and I are gonna cut the roof away, so you can stand in back. Plus, we're gonna need room for the bronco buster once we catch up to him."

"Good idea," Duncan said. "Hand me that."

King passed the KA-BAR knife backward.

"All clear," came Knight's voice.

Queen kept her eyes on the dust cloud ahead of her as Duncan sliced away the back half of the fabric roof. Asya's legs dropped down into the back seat, next to Duncan. Then she slid all the way down until she was sitting next to him.

Queen turned her eyes to the cloud again. She addressed Rook over the comms, "How you doing, ma puce?"

"Oh, fine," Rook's voice sounded relaxed. "It's breezy up here, and there's no way to get down without being eaten alive. I can't believe this fuck is still running with a knife jammed into his noggin."

"Hang tight, we're proceeding," Queen replied.

"Problem is I can't steer this brown bastard, and he's breaking right—away from the rally point."

"Rook," Duncan said. "This is...Eagle. Do you have another blade on you?"

"Uh, no. But maybe I have something else. Why, Chief?"

"You could try stabbing into the creature's right eye. Might veer left for you."

"Will do," Rook said. There was a beat, and then Rook's voice came back. "Okay. That's disgusting, but it worked, Eagle. He's turning left."

"What did you use?" Queen asked.

"My friggin' thumb."

"That hand is never touching me again," Queen said.

"Only need one hand, baby," Rook responded.

Asya cackled with laughter from the back.

Then King spoke. "All the funny aside, I'm still not sure how we're getting Rook aboard and outrunning the masses. We have a long way to go, and the ground will be worse the closer we get to the water. Anyone have ideas? Deep Blue, any guidance?"

Aleman's voice came over the comms. "Keep your present course, and skirt the left side of a large pond, then hug the right bank of the river. Sand and a few rocks. Should be pretty smooth with the Jeep. That'll take you right to us."

"Blue is in the field?" Duncan asked.

"Almost," King answered, not elaborating.

Queen sped up, taking the Jeep to sixty. They were on a dirt track, and the path was uneven, but far better than the cross country they'd been doing. She was almost parallel with the rear of the Megalania pack now, and she sped up even more. It was a risky move. If they hit a massive pothole, the Jeep might flip, ending the chase. But if she didn't pick up speed, they'd lose Rook, or the lead Mega might veer again. So, she edged the Jeep up toward seventy and started passing the laggard lizards at the rear of the chase.

Her other concern was that, once she really got going, the pack might notice the Jeep and break away from pursuing Rook and his steed.

Asya fired a grenade at a fatter lizard near the middle of the pack. It rolled under its backside and detonated. The creature shot up into the air in a ball of fire, its tail flying one way, and the rest of the creature flipping the other. All the monsters behind the newly dead carcass stopped to eat. Three of the smaller lizards that had been ahead of the explosion turned back.

With one shot, Asya had cut their enemies in half. At least temporarily.

"Nicely done," Queen said.

She sped up around a slight curve, gaining on the pack's remaining members. Rook rode the big brown Mega at the head of the chase, but it was the way he was doing it that took her breath away.

Rook clung, one-handed, to his knife, which was still firmly embedded in the big creature's skull, the cross guard of the knife wedged tight against the reptile's skin. But the rest of his body was swinging on the creature's right side, like a trick rider on a horse. He was lifting his leg up and kicking the side of the lizard's mouth every time it tried to turn its head to the right.

Then she realized he was attempting to steer the beast.

And it was working.

But then it wasn't.

Because the big brown Megalania was slowing down—either because it was dying from the knife wound or because it was exhausted.

Or maybe because it was tired of getting kicked in the face.

As it slowed, the creature finally turned to the right, away from the speeding Jeep. The rest of the pack—twenty remaining lizard monsters—poured on the speed and closed the distance.

TEN

Tom Duncan felt great. He was fit, alive, and free at last. More to the point, he was finally back with his friends. His *family*. Even though they all faced constant peril from the moment King tripped the alarm, and they might all be devoured by slavering prehistoric reptiles at any moment, Duncan was sure he'd never felt better in his life.

Through the years of his imprisonment, no one had ever tortured him, for which he was grateful. He had been interrogated multiple times, by multiple groups—the accents were always slightly off—but none of them had been harsher than giving him a shove when was being moved from one location to another. His skin was a pasty white from not having seen the sun in years, but after a month or so of being held, his mysterious captors had even provided him with Vitamin D tablets along with his regular meals. He wasn't sure why he'd been held for so long, but he was clearly considered a high value prisoner. No one roughed him up. No one blatantly hurt him. He'd even had regular medical checkups the last few years, always with a different masked doctor.

Initially, his captors wanted information on America's space program, and he'd given only answers that were already public knowledge. The questions were always different, and the people asking never showed their faces. He was usually interrogated over an intercom system, although, once one of his doctors started asking him questions about the International Space Station.

As the years went on, Duncan used the solitude for two purposes. The first was to keep his body in the peak of perfection he'd had as a younger man in the Army. As such, he followed a punishing regimen of alternating exercises, focusing one day on back muscles and biceps, the next on legs and abs, and the next on chest and triceps. At first, he used the bars in the doors or the windows, and the floor and the bed of his cell. Over time, he was given dumbbells in his cell, and then given an adjacent room with a full universal weights system—at least until he'd been moved to, and abandoned in, the cell here.

The second thing he did with his time was sharpen his memory, using mind games, brain teasers, and the enhancement of an incredibly elaborate 'mind palace.' A mental image of the structure of his mind—memories, thoughts, ideas, and plans. The imagined building grew larger and larger over the years. He'd first heard of the 'loci method' of mnemonic device for recalling large amounts of data when he was a Ranger. He'd put the technique into practice while studying economics, and later utilized it to great effect in meet-and-greet functions as a US Senator. Later, as President, he was able to retain and recall large sets of data, statistics, and even complex diagrams and maps. His staff joked that he had a photographic memory, but it was really a system of remembering *where* in his memory he'd placed a given thought. As he had moved on with Chess Team and the Endgame organization that supported them, he'd come to rely more on the ever-present computers, but he still always practiced his personal mental system. 'Maintained the grounds' of his palace, as he liked to think of it.

After his imprisonment and his initial relocation to a black site in the northern wastes of Arctic Canada, Duncan started retreating *into* his mind palace. No longer merely checking the exterior grounds of the structure, he spent hours and days remodeling the interiors, and making the building more and more labyrinthine. As a former President of the United States and as the former leader of Chess Team, Duncan knew many things he could never let fall into the wrong hands. Things his interrogators would not even know to ask him about. His plan was to bury those things deep into an ever more complex maze of memory pathways. They were so convoluted that even *he* might have trouble recalling the information when desired.

When he had fully redesigned the space to improve his current mental security needs, he began using the palace for fun, recalling past adventures, innocuous conversations, and happier times. He had no idea if, or when, his imprisonment would ever end, but in the meanwhile, he would live a full, internal life. His mind was still free.

Each day of his imprisonment, he fully expected his unusual privileges to be taken away from him as a form of demoralization, and then the torture would begin. But that day never came. Instead, he was one day loaded on a plane, and then a ship. After days at sea, he was placed in the cell where Chess Team found him.

Even up to the hour before King had burst into his cell, Duncan was spending at least some time each day working on that gigantic palace in his brain. There were hidden spaces, nooks, tunnels, deep shafts, and booby traps. Large rooms and tiny crevices. At the middle of it all, a deadly and impenetrable fortress, deep in the recesses of the maze like structure. There he kept one specific piece of information he knew he needed to bury deep in his subconscious.

Because he eventually figured out what the interrogators were looking for, even though they had never clearly stated the desired information.

He understood exactly what they wanted.

He just didn't know why.

However, he knew if they could get that information, it would not lead to anything good. The research and the data—and more to the point, the ramifications from it—could alter the face of the globe in any number of doomsday scenarios. But, cut off from the world for years, Duncan had no way of knowing if his captors had accessed the information they had sought. He had no way to know whether any of those terrible scenarios had been put into action. Once he was back fully in the world, he would be able to look at the global situations, the increasing tensions, the hotspots of the globe, and possibly he could piece it all together.

But first they had to survive.

Up on their right, Rook's rampaging Megalania slowed to a complete stop, a cloud of dust erupting around them. Queen cranked the wheel hard, driving the Jeep right into the side of the beast. The Jeep jolted to a hard stop from the impact, and it sent Rook rolling up the hood of the vehicle, where King reached out an arm and grabbed on to Rook's leg.

"I've got him. Go! Go!" King shouted.

Asya and Knight focused their fire behind the Jeep, at the oncoming rush of reptilian bodies.

Everything seemed to recede into molasses like slow motion for Duncan. He felt helpless, because the group had given him a bodysuit, but no weapons. All he could do was attempt to process all that was going on. King hauled Rook to the side of the Jeep as Rook reached up toward the roll bars. Queen reversed the vehicle a yard, and then slammed on the brakes again, shifting back into first, and steering away from the cloud and the impacted brown lizard. Duncan wondered if the creature was dead. He turned in his seat in time to see a smaller, faster Megalania right behind the vehicle—just before its head erupted in gouts of blood from a fully automatic spray of bullets at the end of Asya's weapon. Four more creatures at the head of the remaining pack descended on their fallen comrade, fully ignoring the Jeep as it sped away.

Her weapon emptied, Asya slid back down into the rear bench seat beside Duncan. Her hand slid onto his thigh, and she looked directly at him. "Are you okay, sir?"

"Wondering what our exfil strategy is here," Duncan said.

"I'll just be alright if nothing else smashes into me today," Rook grumbled.

"The plan," Queen said, mashing through the gears, "is to get to the water."

"Where our ride will be waiting," King added.

Duncan could see the shimmering glare of water up ahead, as Queen stamped the accelerator to the floor. He turned back for another glance behind them. The pack of the Megas—more than a dozen—was still on their tail. And gaining.

Duncan turned to the bay. The river they had been following dumped into a wide expanse of dark water ahead. There was a tiny island in the bay. But no boats. No ships. No military greeting.

The sky opened up with a torrential downpour again, the wall of water so strong that Duncan could no longer see the bay up ahead. Queen wasn't slowing down, and Duncan knew the Jeep wasn't secretly some Transformer that could convert into a boat.

This is going to hurt, he thought.

Queen jerked the wheel to the right, and the Jeep raced toward a rise in the rocky ground that formed a natural ramp, right at the water's edge.

"Everyone hold on!" Queen shouted, and they were airborne.

Duncan had just enough time to voice the concern raging though his thoughts: "Has anyone considered whether these lizards can swim?"

Then the front end of the battered Jeep dipped down. Knight flew over the vehicle to the left. Rook and King bailed to the right. Water rushed up at the cracked windshield.

ELEVEN

King's last view from the air, as he neared the surface of the water, alarmed him. There were thousands of brown shapes in the bay near where they would hit the surface. Could be millions of them. He thought they were sharks at first. Then he remembered there were no sharks this far south. But that didn't rule out other predators.

Then he was hitting the water, feet first, with dozens of the six-foot-long brown creatures elegantly skirting out of the way. King held his breath and pulled his arms in tight. He sliced deep into the water, grateful it was high tide, then he swept his arms forward, gliding farther from where the Jeep would impact. He tapped a finger to the underside of his helmet, and exhaled, as his helmet's pressure seals engaged. The helmet had a very small reserve canister of oxygen built into it. Not enough to go SCUBA diving for an hour, but certainly enough to breathe underwater for a short swim. The device was rated at five minutes, but he would only rely on three.

With his faceplate now clear of bubbles from the impact, he could see the retreating shapes more clearly. They were Antarctic fur seals. The sleek mammals were between four and six feet in length, and they were all varying shades of brown. They were also all swimming away from the impact as fast as they could.

Sorry, King thought.

Then he turned his thoughts back to Duncan's last words before the crash. He was right, of course. The Megalanias were probably fast and powerful swimmers, like huge water monitors.

Rook was in front of him. Swimming away. Deeper into the bay. In the distance ahead of him, King could see Knight swimming in the lead. Above them, near the surface, Asya was with Duncan. King knew she would get his helmet's pressure system working, and then they would be on their way.

That left–

"King, your six!" Queen's voice was shouting over his comms, as he quickly turned his head. He was just in time to see a huge green Mega launch its open mouth his way. Then an arm slammed a seven-inch knife into the creature's eye. It stopped in place, shook its head back and forth, wrenching the blade away from the hand, and then the big lizard peeled away to the left. King turned to see Queen already swimming after Rook.

He turned one final circuit to look back for any more pursuing Megas. The water by the shore was a roiling, frothing mess, with Megas feasting on the copious brown seals. The panicked seals were retreating in every direction. The bloodstorm in the water would soon attract more predators, like leopard seals.

King turned again and stroked hard through the water after the others.

"Blue, do you read?" he asked. "We're in the water and coming in hot. Lots of reptiles will be in pursuit."

Lewis Aleman's voice came back immediately over the comms, loud and crisp. "Putting out the welcome mat. Expect support in two minutes or less."

Asya and Duncan descended to join King's position, and they all swam hard, chasing after Rook and Queen. Knight was already so far ahead, King couldn't see him.

Then a pod of seals raced past King, brushing by Duncan's leg, and causing the man to twist.

"King, incoming," Duncan said with utter calm.

King turned and drew his own knife—the only weapon he had with which he could fight off any of the much faster Megas. He didn't have much hope he could do any damage with the KA-BAR blade, unless he could score a direct hit in the eye, like Queen had done. More likely, he would sink the blade to the hilt in one of the creatures, and it would keep going, like the brown lizard Rook had ridden.

When he saw the threat, three large green creatures, all hope of fending them off with the knife vanished. But then the water was suddenly another battle zone. The pod of seals had returned, and they rammed into the lead Mega. King guessed there were ten in the pod, and they all attacked the first lizard in such a fury that the other two immediately turned away, in search of easier prey. The males in the pod were much larger than the females, and far more brutal, ramming and biting at the Mega, until it began twisting and flipping like an alligator in a death roll.

King retreated, grateful for the interruption, but wary that the males in the pod might turn their rage on him after fending off the reptile. He and Chess Team had also burst into seal territory, and the males might be whipped up into such a frenzy that they would view any trespassers as the enemy.

Plus, there was the possibility that the harried Mega might still come out on top in the battle. And any of the remaining Megas could easily skirt the fight and still come for King and the others.

He turned once again, and he stroked hard to catch the others. He realized in the melee, he'd lost track of time, and he knew their tiny supply of air would run out soon. There was no time to get sidetracked.

"Swim hard," he said over comms, but it was mostly directed at himself. "And everyone chime in."

"Help's on the way," Knight replied.

"Just need the welcome wagon," Rook agreed.

"Good," was all Queen said.

"We're catching up," Asya said.

Because she had spoken for him, Duncan relied on economy and stayed silent, as King knew he would. He was about to ask about the support that Aleman had sent for them when he was rammed hard from his left.

King's view swirled in a crazy kaleidoscope of bright and dark water as his body tumbled around in a fog of bubbles.

He raised his knife hand only to see he'd lost the blade in the collision.

King's head was ringing from the strike, and he wasn't sure which way was up. He tried to stick his arms out to create more drag, slowing his underwater tumble, but something slammed hard into the back of his legs, flipping him again.

He swept his arm side to side, then kicked hard, to get free from the cloud of bubbles. He almost immediately realized he was descending, and switched directions, aiming for the surface. If he was going to run out of air during this battle, he'd rather be near the shallower water.

This time when the Mega swept in at him, he saw the creature coming. It was a green one, and smaller than many of the others King had seen, but it still ran a dozen feet in length. It was easily large enough to swallow him. Just might take the reptile a few bites to do it.

The lizard sped in on King's left and, as it approached, he pulled his booted legs up and kicked as hard as he could. The drag in the water blunted the impact of the kick, but it was just enough to serve two purposes. It nudged the Mega away from its original trajectory, and it launched King up and to the right, farther away from the beast.

King shot upward like he'd been launched from a cannon, but when he turned his head to look in the direction his legs had propelled him, he saw only the open jaw of another waiting reptile. The darting tongue was out, and the mouth was wide, as the creature attempted to swallow him whole.

The last thing King saw was his head going into the creature's gaping maw.

TWELVE

Utter blackness.

But the expected crunch of the creature's jaw down on King's upper shoulders never came. Instead, the giant lizard's movement slowed. Then went still. King shoved against the beast's sides, and his head popped out of the lizard's mouth.

Five shiny metal rods, each two feet long and thinner than a finger, protruded from the side of the Mega's head, near the top of its skull.

Spears, from underwater pneumatic spearguns, had punctured the creature's thick hide. One of the barbed spears had sunk several inches deeper than the others. A killing blow.

The immense beast floated inert as King looked for his rescuers.

Five divers dressed all in black, with powerful flippers, full-face SCUBA masks, and armed with long spearguns, kicked toward King's position. US Navy SEALs, sent by Aleman.

"Good to see you boys," King said, but the men swam right past without acknowledging him, taking aim at even more approaching Megalanias. King recognized that they had a job to do, and also that their communications equipment might be set to a different frequency, so he swam on to catch up to the others. Until he was equipped with a speargun, there was little good he could do in the underwater battle. Air was the other issue. It would soon run out.

Ahead, Queen, Asya, and Duncan were in a small group, with Rook treading water off to the side. Knight was nowhere to be seen, but King knew the man would be watching for approaching lizards from whatever vantage point he'd found.

A glance back confirmed that a furious battle between Navy and nature had begun. Megalanias darted back and forth, getting skewered by the SEALs and their pneumatic guns. As soon as a Mega died, several more were on it, eating its corpse. The last of the Antarctic fur seals had long since fled the scene of carnage. After firing a few more spears, ensuring the buffet would continue for a while, the sailors turned and headed back toward King.

He looked to his team, wondering where their ride was hiding. The SEALs would have used an underwater sled to get them in this close to Chess Team's position. King figured the SEALs would have to share oxygen from their tanks with the Chess Team soon. That or they would all need to head to the surface. He wasn't sure what the plan was–only that Aleman had arranged pick up with the Navy.

As King closed in on the rest of the team, yet another massive shape blurred past him, but this one was all dark, and moving far faster than anything he'd seen in the bay so far. Patches of white marked the creature as an Orca–the Killer Whale. The creature raced into the bloody swirling waters, where the Megas were feasting on themselves.

King knew very little about Orcas, but he knew they travelled in pods. If there was one here, another three would be nearby. Either way, with Megas and now Orcas in the water, along with lots of blood, it was getting extremely dangerous for humans to remain submerged.

"Blue, we need that pickup pronto. The neighborhood is getting crowded." King saw that the SEALs had all returned and were forming a loose cluster with Duncan, Asya, and Queen. He swam to the grouping, not knowing what their next move would be, but knowing it would need to happen fast. Knight had materialized close to the group, and Rook was swimming toward the cluster of humans. Whatever Aleman was planning, King trusted that it was well thought out. They either had secured a ship, or they were planning some kind of airlift despite the legendarily awful weather.

"We're coming to you," was Aleman's only reply.

One of the SEALs looked at King and held out two index fingers, side by side, like railroad tracks. King understood the SCUBA signal to mean 'stay together'. Then the man waved his flat hand horizontally, and King understood it meant 'level off' or to maintain his current depth. King responded with an 'okay' hand signal. Then he held a fist up against his chest, indicating to the SEAL that he was low on air—and that all the others would be as well. The man just responded with an 'okay' hand signal, communicating that he understood their predicament.

Rook was still in far deeper water than the rest and making his way back toward the others with powerful strokes. But King could see the man was shaking his head to himself as he did, and King knew Rook well enough to read his irritation in his body language—even underwater. The water beyond Rook was dark blue and murky, but as King again checked a full three hundred and sixty degrees around him, he noticed that visibility in the water was far less than before. *Storm clouds above,* he thought. *Blocking out the sun.*

It worried him that he could no longer keep track of the Orca or see any of the Megalanias, but the SEALs appeared relaxed, as if they knew the tough part of the day was already over. Now King's irritation began to grow. His team was about to run out of air. The SEALs could afford to wait on whatever was going to happen next, but King's people could not.

He was about to attempt signaling again when the dark in the deeper part of the bay grew suddenly darker. Something big was moving toward them, and it was coming in quickly. Something much bigger even than the Orca that had breezed by King earlier.

When the dots all connected in King's mind, he understood what was going to happen.

"Oh shit, Rook!"

But that was all he could get out of his mouth before the advancing submarine grazed Rook as he was still swimming back to the group. The vehicle was slowing, but it was immense. Thirty-four feet across and almost four hundred feet long, the fast attack submarine's nose hit Rook at a shallow angle and his body was spun along the side of the vessel, flipping and flopping until he stopped moving. The SEALs and the rest of King's team, including Duncan, were all closer to Rook than King was, and all of them swam for his position as fast as they could.

King was in motion, too, but as he moved his arms and kicked for all he was worth, he noticed that his friend was not moving anymore.

THIRTEEN

Knight was there first. He was usually first. He'd gotten used to it.

Rook's body was floating in the water, but he wasn't moving. The sub had slowed to almost a stop. So slow that Knight couldn't tell whether the vehicle had completely ceased power and was drifting or if it was still moving but on very low propulsion. He hadn't spent that much time around submarines—even the one Chess Team used to have in the appropriated base in New Hampshire. He'd been aboard them a few times but, from inside, it was impossible to see what slow movement on the outside looked like.

"Rook," Knight called through the comms. "You okay, buddy?"

The floating body did not move or respond.

Knight reached out his hand and touched Rook's arm, and the man came to in a flurry of movements. Knight backed off, calling out again through the comms.

Rook calmed and saw Knight. Then he made hand movements indicating that his comms were out, but that he was okay.

The others arrived, but the SEALs urged everyone to follow them, and they made their way up the side of the massive submarine. He was so close to the side of the immense vehicle that Knight couldn't tell how big it really was. It just looked like a wall of black. But as they approached the topside, a hatch on the surface slid open, and its interior was white, easy to see in the gloom. The SEALs urged everyone down into the hatchway.

Knight checked the Suunto wristwatch on his arm and saw why. Chess Team and Duncan were about to run out of air. Knight did a quick headcount and saw that the first SEAL had gotten Duncan and Asya down the hatch already. He was shooing Queen in, and Rook was swimming to join her. King was last, and Knight swam in with him. The remaining SEALs followed then, and already the hatch was closing.

One of the Navy men was already tapping on Duncan's face shield and holding up a hose with a regulator on it. The hose was attached to the SEAL's own air supply. It was a buddy regulator, and it would probably be necessary for all of them to use one. The airlock chamber, or 'lockout trunk,' into which they had swum, was small and cramped, with no chairs or anything else. It barely had room for the eleven people and the metal ladder now wedged into the space. Just white walls and a glowing red LED light on one wall. There was another hatch set into the wall below the light. Once the outer hatch closed and the compartment had been drained, and its pressure regulated with that of the interior of the sub, the door would open.

But he had no idea how long the process would take, and all six of them would run out of air in under a minute. Knight hoped the other SEALs also had buddy regulators on their personal tanks. But that was still five regulators for six additional mouths. It was going to be close, and people were going to have to hold their breath for a while until the next opportunity to take one.

Knight watched as Duncan held his breath and released the pressure seal on his helmet. The helmet immediately filled with water, and he opened the faceplate, accepting the offered regulator. Next to him, Queen started signaling that she was completely out of air, by making a chopping motion across her neck, and another SEAL provided her with a regulator.

Knight knew he would be out of air any second, so he tried taking shallow breaths and conserving as much of what remained as possible.

The outer hatch moved slowly. Knight watched it, willing it to seal faster. The second the last sliver of white disappeared from sight, he heard a loud clunk vibrate through the water. Then the water in the chamber began to drain with air appearing at the top, which was about a foot over his head.

When he looked back, King and all the others were breathing from buddy regulators, supplied to them by the five SEALs. King was looking at Knight.

He signaled using his hands, asking whether Knight was okay.

Knight took a tentative breath, and he found that he still had air. He nodded and showed a hand signal of 'Okay.'

The water level lowered rapidly, forced out of the chamber by the air being pumped into it. As soon as the level fell below the tallest SEAL's face, he pulled off his facemask and began to breathe the air. Knight realized they wouldn't have to wait for the room to clear entirely, and he pulled his own helmet off. Slowly the rest of the team pulled their helmets off as the SEALs all began removing their equipment.

The air was fine, and Knight was secretly pleased that he hadn't run out of air at all. He must have been seconds shy of it, but the Korean American man had smaller lungs—or he just didn't breathe as rapidly as the others. Any number of reasons could be involved in why he hadn't run out of air before them.

"Thank you, gentlemen," King said to the nearest SEAL.

The man's face was covered by a coarse, dark, five o-clock shadow. He just nodded and said "No problem. That's the job."

Knight detected no undercurrent of hostility from the Navy man, or from any of the others. They just all seemed not to care one way or the other about what had just happened, as if it really *was* just another day on the job for them.

The chamber emptied, and as soon as the last water drop hit the drains in the floor, the green light on the wall flicked on, and a loud hiss sounded.

Then a *thunk,* and the door opened. Knight noticed that, unlike a typical hatch on a submarine, this door did not have a spinning wheel handle on this side of it. The airlock could only be opened from the interior of the sub.

Standing on the other side of the door, wearing his dress blues, was Admiral Ward. He was a slim African American man in his fifties with fully gray hair. Knight had seen the man before, but his hair was only starting to gray when Knight had first met him—and this was the first time the Admiral was wearing his dress uniform in front of Chess Team. Among the veritable ocean of ribbons on the man's chest, Knight spotted the Kuwait Liberation Medal, both Arctic and Antarctic service ribbons, as well as the much more rarely awarded Silver Star and Navy Cross. There was also a Purple Heart, meaning the man had been wounded in battle. The only thing missing was a Medal of Honor.

But Knight knew how very rare those were.

He had one.

Each member of Chess Team had received one, for services beyond the call of duty during the Brugada virus incident.

Before Ward could speak, it was Duncan who stepped forward and snapped a salute. "Permission to come aboard, Admiral?"

Ward crisply returned the salute, and then his face softened. "It would be my honor to have you, Mr. President."

Duncan reached out and shook the man's hand and smiled. "Jon, I've told you before, you can call me Tom."

Finally, a true smile reached Ward's eyes. The first time Knight had ever seen the man genuinely happy. "Yes, Sir, Mr. President. You have."

Duncan shook his head. "You're never going to do that, though, are you?"

"Welcome aboard the *New Hampshire.*"

FOURTEEN

USS New Hampshire (SSN-778)

Ward led them out of the chamber, and showed them to the berthing area, where there were spare uniforms for everyone, including Duncan.

"You can all get cleaned up in here, and then come forward when you're ready. Oh, and Sigler?"

King turned to look at the Admiral.

"How about letting me know now, where I am supposed to take you folks?"

Chess Team's relationship with Admiral Ward had been testy at best. The last time King had met the man, face to face, he had reluctantly agreed to allow Chess Team the freedom to search independently for Tom Duncan—but only after Chess Team had done their best to retrieve Ward's missing men in Russia. Prior to that mission, Ward had seemed hell bent on drafting the team members back into the military under his direct command through JSOC. Now it appeared he really had allowed them to run completely free. King had expected the Admiral would take them all back to the United States—and Duncan possibly back to US imprisonment. That Lewis Aleman had even convinced the Admiral to lend a submarine and a special forces team to the rescue operation was impressive. But King doubted the man's willingness to keep them unleashed, now that Duncan had been located.

"We have friends in Cape Town," King suggested. "And a facility where you can dock undetected."

The Admiral just nodded and left the members of the team to get showered and change their clothes.

King used the time to assess himself for injuries, but he was fine, beyond a bruise or two. He wondered about Rook, who had been uncharacteristically quiet after getting bashed by a prehistoric lizard, rammed through a wall, hit by a Jeep, and finally slammed into by a fast attack submarine. The man appeared to be in a foul mood, and King suspected he had a deeper injury. Anything that took Rook out of a fight usually made the burly man sour. He always wanted to be where the action was.

Although Rook was romantically involved with Queen, you would barely know it from their professional behavior in the field. But now, as they changed clothes, King observed her looking at Rook with deep concern in her eyes. He wondered about the state of the relationship, but he would never ask. As long as it didn't affect their performance in the field, that was their business.

Knight appeared serene as usual. Since the last upgrades to his cybernetic eye, he had ceased having crushing headaches and was mostly back to his normal self. But deeper, King detected that the man missed his partner, Anna Beck, who frequently joined Chess Team in the field as callsign: Pawn. Beck was in Thailand but would eventually meet them with George Pierce's Cerberus Group people in South Africa. The Group was waiting to hear whether the assault on the Kerguelen Islands was successful, or if another team of George's people would need to form Plan B. King liked Beck, and he thought she was good for Knight—especially after Erik Somers, the former Bishop, had been killed in Africa, some years earlier. Knight had been close to Somers, and he had taken the man's death very hard.

The new Bishop, Asya Machtcenko, was King's biological sister. He'd only learned about her existence a few years back, but they had become quite close in that time. King expected she might soon be closer to someone else. She had barely left Duncan's side since they had freed the former president from his cell, and King knew she had been attracted to the man before his abduction.

Duncan looked fit for a man who had been imprisoned for years. He was obviously older, and he appeared tired from their ordeal. Still, the light of fierce intelligence shone behind Duncan's eyes. King wondered what the former Deep Blue would have planned. Would he voluntarily turn himself back over into the hands of the US government, even though his original arrest was mostly at the vengeful hands of Senator Marrs, who was now dead? Would Duncan opt to remain a rogue element, sending Chess Team out on missions of his own choosing? King knew the team members would follow the man's guidance—as long as those rogue missions did not go against the interests of the United States. But King had come to know Duncan well in those last years before the man's abduction. He knew Duncan would never go against the will of the US government, and he worried that his friend might seek to once again surrender, to keep Chess Team free.

For his part, King had never really considered what his next move would be once Duncan was freed. The last few years, Chess Team had followed up lead after lead, searching for their former commander, and nothing else had been in the planning.

For the first time in a long time, King had no idea what was next. He could keep fighting battles for years to come. He was physically fit enough, but he knew he wouldn't be able to stay in the action forever. Plus, he had a family now. His wife, Sara, was researching the polio vaccine testing and development that had been done in the Congo in 1950. There had been allegations over the last few decades that they might have directly or indirectly led to the first outbreaks of HIV in that same region. Scientists had been outraged at the controversial claim that the two diseases were linked, and at the suggestion that Hilary Koprowski's work in the Congo was somehow responsible for HIV and AIDS. Sara, of course, became fascinated by the story once she'd heard it, and she decided to investigate for herself, edging slightly out of virology and into scientific journalism. Although the scientific community had discredited the hypothesis, there were enough loose ends to suggest a cover up and a conspiracy—at least to Sara's way of thinking. It had been two months since King had seen Sara. But that was the life they led. Intense periods together separated by sometimes months apart between her job and his.

King's daughter, Fiona, was off with George Pierce, learning about the world through the archeologist's adventures and through their acting as stewards of the Herculean Society. The organization was originally placed in King's care but, as the demands of Chess Team continually took priority, he had asked Pierce to take control of the Society, and Pierce had even used the organization's resources to take over a business entity called Cerberus Group. King had yet to meet any of George's agents face to face, although he assumed the organization was well in hand these last few years.

Before King could ruminate more, Tom Duncan cleared his throat and said to the assembled group, "Let's get a move on. The Admiral deserves some information, and I've got quite a bit to tell you all. And I expect you have some things to tell me as well, but those will need to wait. If what I suspect has actually happened, the world might be about to face some serious consequences."

"How serious could we be talking about here?" Rook asked, having donned a set of USMC fatigues with no stripes or name tags, just like the others. "I mean we just dealt with prehistoric lizard monsters for breakfast. How bad could it be?"

Duncan's face was grim as he started from the berthing area toward command and control. "Three words: Orbital Death Ray."

Rook's face sagged. "Okay, this sub is cool and all, but we're gonna need a much bigger boat."

FIFTEEN

Admiral Ward brought the group forward to a small conference room. It was a cramped space, but just enough for the seven people to sit around a large table. Computer monitors lined the walls, but this talk would be without visual supports—or any communication with Lewis Aleman, who would be waiting for them in Africa. The sub was running dark, under deep cover, and potentially in hostile waters.

Admiral Ward looked at Duncan for a long time before speaking. "It's your show now, Mr. President. At least until I get conflicting orders from the present Commander in Chief."

Duncan smiled at the man, appearing grateful for his assistance. "Let's hope it doesn't come to that, Jon. But it might."

"The Consortium thing?" Ward asked.

"You knew about that?" King interjected.

"I know about a lot of things, Sigler," Ward said and, despite the fact that he and King had not always gotten along, the comment lacked any malice. It was just a matter of fact. As commander of the Joint Special Operations Command (JSOC), King didn't doubt the man knew an awful lot more than most.

"What have *you* uncovered, King?" Duncan asked.

King turned to face Duncan. "That there was an organization responsible for the attacks in Africa a few years ago, and the attacks on Endgame, and some troubles we had in Russia after your abduction. The Russian President was involved, and certain factions in the US government might also have been involved." King didn't come right out and say it, but he made clear the implication of those who'd had a hand in Duncan's rendition.

King left out that his and Asya's own sister, Julie Sigler, had been a part of the Consortium. The woman was dead now, and it seemed unimportant for him to bring her into the discussion.

Duncan sighed. "Yes, Senator Marrs was likely unaware of that organization, but his political vendettas got him right into the middle of it all. Admiral Ward and a few others—Mike Keasling, before his death in New York, was one of them—and I have all been working on getting to the bottom of this conspiracy for quite a few years."

"I'm sorry to say that I wasn't fully on board with President Duncan's theory at first," Ward said, "but after that mess in Russia, I started looking deeper. I'm pretty certain President Chambers is involved in this."

Duncan sighed deeper. "As you know, Jon, I was hoping that would not be the case. Matthew Chambers was a good man once. If he is involved in this conspiracy, I'll have to believe he stumbled into it or was coerced, rather than having made the decision willingly. At least, I'll believe that until it's proven otherwise."

Duncan looked around the room at the Chess Team members. King did, too.

No one appeared unwilling to tackle a global conspiracy in which the President of the United States was involved.

King spoke for the others.

"We're all in."

Duncan just nodded, like he expected no different. "That's good, but we might have a different problem to tackle first. Or the two might be the same issue."

"Let me guess," Rook said, with just a tinge of weariness in his normally jovial voice. "Mars is invading, too?"

"Let's hope not. If they get involved, we'll be in trouble," Duncan said with a scowl.

"Wait one—" Rook leaned forward. "Are you saying there really are Martians?"

Queen slapped his arm. "No, moron. He's telling you to shut up and let him finish without interrupting."

Duncan smiled, but just a little.

King saw that Knight's face was impassive, but Asya was smirking.

"As I was saying," Duncan said, "I'm not sure who was behind my abduction. And I'm pretty sure I was passed from one group to two entirely different entities. Any one of them could have been connected with the Consortium. Or all of them. Or none of them. But someone out there, somewhere, is interested in a space based weapon."

Ward leaned in against the table. "What kind of a weapon, Mr. President?"

"Well, that's the problem. It could be any number of things. My interrogators always asked me questions about space missions. But eventually I came to realize they were all a smokescreen for the one they really wanted intel on: LCROSS."

"I kind of remember that one," King said. "Wasn't it a Lunar mission of some sort? A communications satellite or something?"

"Close," Duncan said. "The Lunar Crater Observation and Sensing Satellite, or LCROSS, had a stated mission of looking for Lunar water at the Moon's poles. It was also launched with a separate orbiter designed to map Lunar surfaces."

"You said 'stated,' sir," Knight said.

"Exactly. You were paying close attention, as always, Shin."

"So, what was it, really?" King asked.

"Our first serious attempt at an orbital strike weapon that could target any nation on Earth. It was a program I inherited when I got into office, and as soon as I learned about it, we had a lot of discussions in the Situation Room about the morality of such strikes. We discussed different orbital assault concepts from kinetic weapons to biological attacks. The science wasn't the hard part. DARPA long ago figured out how to infect a specific country with a virus from space or how we could drop a telephone pole made of tungsten from orbit and achieve the same results as a nuclear strike—free from radiation. So, the delivery is easy, and satellites could drop any number of things on a human populace. The challenge was in how to achieve plausible deniability."

Ward understood immediately. "No matter what we dropped on Russia or China or a rogue terrorist state, they would know it was us."

"That's just it," Duncan said. "And the spooks and creepy NSA types had thought long and hard about this issue since the first manned space program, and probably even before. And..." Duncan looked around the room at each person, his eyes lingering on King's just slightly longer than the others. "What I'm telling you all now is a deeply held secret in the US government, and I'm only telling you because I stopped being questioned about the LCROSS issues after a time, which led me to believe that even without me revealing anything sensitive, my captors eventually got their hands on everything they needed anyway. The tech. The delivery systems. The operational procedures. And the deniability solution."

"I'm afraid to ask, but what was the solution?" Rook asked.

"I know," King said. "It's simple. And horrible."

Duncan just nodded his assent for King to fill in the others.

"If you want to drop orbital strikes on someone, say Russia, the perfect way to avoid anyone thinking it was the US—"

"Oh God," Ward said, realizing what King was about to say, and pinching the bridge of his nose.

"—is to attack your own people with the weapon first. So, if it's a Kinetic Strike with a tungsten rod, for example, you first drop one on Kansas City, before you hit Moscow. Then you can be outraged first and start pointing the finger at other nations, before the second strike ever happens. No one would ever suspect the US of attacking its own cities. Some people have put forth the conspiracy theory that we attacked the World Trade Center in New York, and caused the deaths of three thousand people, but no one would ever think we'd nuke an entire city of two million from space."

"You got nearly everything right, Jack," Duncan said. "Except the spooks wanted to kill Cincinnati. I had a fit when I learned about the whole thing, and I killed the program. I thought there would come a time for space-based attacks, but we weren't there ten years ago. Someone, somewhere, has this knowledge and the tech. If it's the Consortium, they could attack anywhere. If it's a single nation-state, they'll most likely attack themselves first, before attacking anyone else—most likely the United States. It could be a biological agent. It could be physical. Acoustic. Any number of things. So... What has been going on in the world, in my absence?"

SIXTEEN

Rook's ribs ached. His body hurt.

And his mood was worse.

The discussion with Ward and Duncan had gone nowhere. The consensus was that the Consortium conspiracy was a problem, but they had precious little on which to proceed. The LCROSS connection was also tenuous. They had brought Duncan up to speed on the things going on in the world since his capture and imprisonment, but no one could point to a clear usage of the sort of technology—or warped moral compass for plausible deniability—that Duncan had described. The world had suffered natural disasters, outbreaks, and cultural uprisings, but nothing connected to a space based weapon. And there hadn't been any major attack on a country that led to a retaliatory strike. The premise horrified Rook, but for all he wracked his brain about world politics and upheavals over the last few years, nothing stood out as a clear pattern.

The team was still aboard the submarine—it would take them a few days to reach Cape Town—but Rook was glad for the down time. It gave him time to rest and heal. Chess Team didn't have a path forward yet, and Duncan didn't have an overarching plan regarding hunting down those connected with the Consortium. But Rook knew that sooner or later—probably sooner—the team would be called upon to go into battle again. He needed to be ready, mind and body, but he felt the farthest he'd been from that state, since going AWOL through Northern Russia and Norway several years back.

Something nagged at him. At his soul. He couldn't put his mental finger on it, but it always seemed to be there, in the shadows of his mind. Of course, getting rammed into by a giant lizard, a Jeep, and a submarine all in one day hadn't helped.

The image of his body flopping through the air—and underwater—after all those impacts made him grunt and grudgingly laugh, but it sounded more like a sigh when it hissed from his lips.

"What?" Queen asked, speaking softly.

They were each lying on a bunk in the crew quarters of the sub. Asya was sleeping on the bed above Queen's. The others were all awake, but somewhere else on the vessel. Queen and Rook were on bottom bunks, opposite each other. It was the closest they could get aboard the sub, while still displaying some measure of decorum, in deference to the Navy men who might not see their partners for months.

"Just thinking about that frickin' island, and the lizards...and stuff."

"Stuff? Can you vague that up for me a little?"

"Just wondering where we go from here, Zel. Duncan is still probably a wanted man by the US government, even though Ward is helping us. We have no real clues about this Consortium group either, except maybe for King's grandfather. I don't know about you, but I don't really want to head back to Russia to find out."

"From what King said, though," Queen said, "the man was less involved in the whole Consortium thing than Julie was, and she's gone now."

Rook remembered their time in the Ural Mountains, and the fact that King's—and Asya's—sister, a woman named Julie, had been brainwashed and had been working with the President of Russia, who it turned out had been the legendary Rasputin. Although killing the man would have caused an international upheaval, King had reduced the man's power. And shortly after Chess Team's involvement, Rasputin had retired and gone into hiding. Or so the Russian media said. Who could really be sure? Julie Sigler had died in the battle. No, their last big adventure in Russia held no further clues or information on how to root out the conspiracy.

"You know what's bothering me?" Queen asked, her voice dropping even lower.

"That you can't order a cappuccino on this tub?" Rook said, a little of his normal wisecracking persona resurfacing through his gloom.

"No. Although cappuccino. Yum. It's the giant lizards back on Desolation."

"You mean who is doing genetic tinkering on that scale?"

"We've had some problems with genetically engineered creatures in the past..." Queen said.

Rook just grunted.

"If I didn't know better, I'd think–"

"Ridley," Rook finished. "Yeah. Occurred to me, too."

The team had faced down a genetics lab in South America run by a megalomaniac, Richard Ridley, who went on to plague the team again and again for years, in the States, in Asia and Europe, and in North Africa. Chess Team felt like they were cleaning up the remains of that man's devious affairs for years–until his demise in Tunisia.

"He's dead. King made sure," Rook said. "But it could be someone who has access to that bastard's technology."

"Or someone else entirely, who developed similar–or worse–technology."

"Thanks, Zel. You're really cheering me up."

Queen sat up and reached across the bunk, taking Rook's hand in hers, pulling it to her mouth, and kissing his knuckles. "You really are in a foul mood, *ma puce*. What's really going on?"

Rook sat up and looked into the eyes of the woman he loved and admired. "We've been fighting this fight for a long time now. I'm getting older. We're all getting older. I don't really know how to do much other than fight and farm—and I didn't love the farming. But I can see a day in the future when we get a place somewhere. Settle down. Just breathe clean air and listen to the wind in the trees, and not have to worry that Bolivian death monkeys are going to fly out of them and try to eviscerate us every day, you know?"

"Settle down. You mean start a family? Children?"

Queen looked apprehensive, but she didn't reject the idea out of hand. Rook was well aware of her past. She'd been a victim of abuse and had lost a child. He knew that 'family' wasn't really something she aspired to, and that Chess Team had taken the place of those familial connections for her. But he also knew that she'd overcome all those traumas, and a dozen phobias to boot, and she'd become one of the finest soldiers alive. In his mind, if she wanted a family, she would find a way to overcome any residual feelings of fear or trauma from her early life. This woman would find a way to overcome anything if it stood in the way of what she wanted.

"I don't know. Maybe? Right now, I think a little house and a piece of land, somewhere quiet, might do the trick for me. How about you?"

Queen smiled in a way Rook had only ever seen her smile for him. She leaned across the walkway from her bunk, and kissed his forehead, then she sat back down, still smiling.

"It sounds pretty nice. Let's just say I'll think about it. A lot."

SEVENTEEN

Bloubergstrand, Cape Town, South Africa

The underwater tunnel began deep under Robben Island. Little more than a scrubby slab of land four miles off the coast, the island was most well-known for its former prison, and one of its most famous political prisoners from the 1960s to the 1980s—Nelson Mandela. The island was slightly lesser known as a maritime hazard, with over twenty shipwrecks around the tiny spit of rock.

An archeological team investigated the wrecks in the 1990s but, unknown to the public, the operation had secretly been under the purview of an organization called the Herculean Society. The Society was, at the time, led by a man named Alexander Diotrephes—the 'Hercules' of legend. The man was long gone from the world now, but his legacy lived on. The Society still cared for ancient sites and secrets around the world. The underwater tunnel below Robben Island, which traveled miles eastward to the shore, and to a Society safehouse on the outskirts of a suburb of Cape Town, was one of them.

The *New Hampshire* was not the largest submarine in the world, but it was still a very narrow fit. Admiral Ward's crew was nervous as they approached the tunnel and all but held their breath as they traversed four miles inside a deep passage, skirting volcanic rock and reef walls. There was an audible sigh of relief when the tunnel opened out into a huge subterranean docking station, a mile under the surface, beneath a steel factory.

When the vessel was docked, King led his team, Duncan, and Ward up and out of the sub and onto the concrete dock. He was disappointed to see that there was no one to greet them in the facility. It was huge and could probably hold five or six vessels the size of the *New Hampshire*. There was even room for the sub to make a full 180 degree turn before departing. The dock was utilitarian, with concrete decks and hanging metal catwalks above, illuminated by energy-saving LED lights. But the entire place had the feeling of abandonment that usually comes from disuse.

King didn't see a door leading out of the docks up to the main Herculean Society facility. Although Diotrephes had placed the Society in King's care, King had never been to this location before, despite having used many of the global facilities run by the secretive organization.

"Not quite the welcome I was expecting," Rook said.

"Not really a welcome at all." Duncan turned to King. "How are things between you and George?"

King had explained on the sub to Duncan about how he had asked his friend George Pierce to take over the running of the Herculean Society, and how George had set up his own team and handled some major world issues on his own. The Herculean Society assumed control of a former corporation called the Cerberus Group. Pierce and his team now used the Group as a cover organization. King's adopted daughter, Fiona, had even joined Pierce's group. King had seen Fiona a few times in the last few years, but she was often busy with Pierce's projects, and King had been kept busy with the hunt for Duncan. It was only now that he realized that, despite periodic phone calls, it had been a few years since King had met Pierce face to face. He had assumed Pierce was doing a great job with the Society and with the preservation of all its secrets. But maybe it was time King took a firmer hand in the organization.

Too many things slipping through the cracks, he thought.

"He should be here," King said. "Lew should be here, too."

King scanned the walls around the huge dock, both on the concrete platforms and at the end of the suspended metal catwalks. Everything led to perfectly smooth walls. There were no doors anywhere. He started to wonder if it was some ancient puzzle Diotrephes had put in place. But then he realized the metal catwalks were all modern. There were stairs leading from the docks up to the catwalks. One had a huge hoist on a steel I-beam that ran parallel to it, presumably for loading or unloading freight. But there was no obvious entry. No video camera his eye could spot on a wall. No motion detectors. No doorbells.

"Maybe the entrance is submerged?" Queen guessed.

"No," King said, lowering his weapon. He started walking toward the wall, and then ran his hand along it. "The entrances were removed. This wall is smooth. *Too* smooth."

Duncan stepped forward to touch the wall. "You think this was—"

A deep rumble filled the cavernous space. The team's weapons all snapped up.

All except for King's.

At the end of a metal catwalk above them, where the grating met a completely flat wall, dust shook from the wall's surface. Then, as King watched, the dark outline of a doorway formed in the rock, as if the stone had turned to malleable sand.

King quickly made for the metal stairs leading up to that catwalk. The others followed him, their weapons drawn and ready for anything. Knight split off from the group and made for the wall on the lower level, aiming up at the door, and whatever might come out of it.

The door was filled with shadows from deep inside the newly formed tunnel.

King moved across the narrow walkway, approaching the pitch-black opening, his eyes straining to peer into the darkness. He still had not raised his weapon. "Fiona?"

Years ago, his adopted daughter had learned that she had the ability to manipulate inorganic material with an ancient and forgotten language that only she knew. He knew she had been working on perfecting her abilities.

What concerned him was that his daughter hadn't emerged from the tunnel, all smiles and open arms, ready for an embrace. Instead, all was quiet. Not exactly a warm welcome.

His hand dropped to the handle of his rifle, which was slung around his shoulder. He raised the barrel toward the darkness, thought he spotted a shifting in the black before him, and then he heard a slight scuffle.

Then he heard a deep hiss.

Definitely not Fiona.

A quick thought occurred to King and, rather than snapping the rifle up into position the rest of the way, he lowered the barrel, and took a single defiant step forward.

He breathed in as deeply as his lungs would permit, and then he let the breath out in his own protracted hiss.

Faster than he could see, something lunged out of the darkness at him.

EIGHTEEN

Rather than dodging to the side, King stood his ground, leaned forward, and hissed louder. The thing that lunged out of the tunnel at him was so fast, Knight's electronic eye had trouble tracking it. Knight almost pulled the trigger on the creature. But something stopped him at the last microsecond.

Knight had known King for a long time now. He'd known all the players in Chess Team long enough to learn their tics and mannerisms, their postures, and their moods. King wasn't showing any fear and, as if with a sixth sense, Knight had picked up on it—just as the creature leapt out of the dark. That sense was the only thing stopping his trigger finger.

The Forgotten were once human.

Long ago.

King explained them to Knight years earlier, after a mission in Tunisia. The man the team had known as Alexander created the wraith-like creatures in his quest for immortality. They were failed experiments, but the man had cared for them—and eventually passed that duty of care on to King.

Shrouded in a tattered gray cloak, this creature had hideous, wrinkled charcoal skin. It was missing its facial features—no nose or mouth. The eyes were sunken hollows. The creature had a single vertical slit where its nose should have been. It had a jaw that hung obscenely low. Its taut skin clung to the muscles and skeletal structure, the texture rippled and crossed with lines and bulges, like deep burn tissue.

Knight knew that these fierce creatures, once the source of the vampires of myth and legend, were supposed to be subservient to King now. But it looked like maybe King's long absence in the field would result in the creature's betrayal.

Maybe they only serve George Pierce now, Knight thought.

The wraith-like creature stopped an inch from King's face, hissing loudly and making stuttering jolts forward, as if it wanted to fight but was being held back by something.

King did not back down and, if anything, Knight thought the lack of recognition in the yellow eyes was making King angrier. He advanced on the creature, and the wraith retreated into the tunnel's shadows.

Knight used the brief reprieve to scan the dock area for more of the creatures. He recalled seeing a veritable tidal wave of the things swarm the enemy in Tunisia. But those years ago, the Forgotten wraiths fought for Chess Team, and not against them. Their population had been severely diminished, perhaps just ten of them left alive. But the creatures were nearly immortal. They could crawl on walls and ceilings, and they were lightning fast. If there were nine more of them secreted around the dock, the team would be in deep trouble.

Knight made three retreat contingencies in his head, and he added a fourth just for good measure.

King held his ground at the mouth of the tunnel. He stopped hissing and listened. Knight could no longer hear the Forgotten creature.

Admiral Ward broke the silence. "Someone tell me what in the hell that thing was. And then tell me why we did not perforate the sonuvabitch."

Duncan spoke softly. "The creatures were once loyal to King."

King turned his back to the tunnel entrance, still exuding no fear. "That was a while ago. And even if they were still under my command, they bear constant watching. They could suck the life out of you in minutes, and they're not known for self-control. But they *will* shrink back from light." He activated a strong LED flashlight on the barrel of his weapon and swept it across the tunnel entrance.

A deep hiss emanated from the gloom, but it sounded much farther away now.

"So, keep an eye out for them. Stick together. Keep the lights on. They'll let us pass." King entered the tunnel, and Rook followed him. Queen waited for the others to go in after them, and then she motioned for Knight to join her on the catwalk, while she covered him.

The tunnel was long and straight. Just large enough for a human to pass through without bending. Off to the sides, separated by random distances, were side tunnels that were sometimes little more than fissures and sometimes larger alcoves. As Knight passed the latter, he could swear he heard more hissing. But when he angled his high-powered LED lamp into the dark recesses, all he saw was smooth stone.

Still, the hairs on the back of his neck stood up as he moved. He felt sure something was following them, even though he couldn't see it in any of the spectrums detected by his cybernetic eye.

The group was quiet until the tunnel's end, where a large freight elevator awaited them. With no other choice, they boarded the lift, and pushed the only button on the vehicle. A digital display lit up, informing them they were headed for the 'Ground' level.

The movement was so slight, Knight could barely perceive that they were ascending. But he knew they were a few miles underground at the dock, so the ride would take a while. The elevator was built to carry heavy loads and not for speed, so the group waited, tense, for a full two minutes.

Knight was astonished that Rook didn't fill the silence with wise-cracks, but he noticed the man was scowling, and standing a little closer to Queen than was tactically wise.

Finally, the lift ground to a halt with a slight jolt. The doors began to part. Everyone leveled their weapons. All except Knight. His eye allowed him to see through the elevator doors, and into the large space on the other side.

It was some kind of immense command room. There were computer stations along the wall, and a huge table filled the center of the space. Knight recognized George Pierce from his outline, and one other person, waiting right on the other side of the door.

"Stand down," Knight said, just before the doors opened completely. "It's Fiona."

He wasn't sure the warning would come in time.

NINETEEN

Queen almost shot Fiona.

Her nerves were so jangled after the last few days of heightened emotion, that she nearly shot her own goddaughter. She admitted to herself that, despite being a professional, the extraction of Duncan and the desperate battle with the overgrown lizards, followed by thinking a submarine killed Rook, then the strange reception in the base with the Forgotten creature, and now the elevator ride to who knew what, all of it was contributing a fair amount of stress. But her subconscious knew it was something else.

"Dad!" Fiona yelled, and she rushed in, hugging King before he'd even stepped off the elevator.

Once again, Queen was reminded that the little girl she'd known was no longer a child. Now in her twenties, Fiona was three inches taller than Queen—a difference she couldn't help noticing when hugging the girl. "Look at you," Queen clapped the girl's shoulders. "Absolute badass."

Fiona just smiled and continued her rounds of embraces with Rook and then the others, while Queen scanned the rest of the room.

George Pierce, King's long-time best friend and Chess Team ally, was standing just beyond Fiona, sheepishly awaiting his turn to share some hugs and handshakes. Queen noted, not for the first time, the man's uncanny resemblance to King, and the fact that they both had the same strange, orange-flecked brown eyes. If Queen didn't know differently, she might have suspected they were brothers, even though George was significantly older. Beyond him, deeper into the immense room, was a conference table with file folders and old printed maps strewn across it. On the other side of the huge room, a wall was covered with electronics and monitors. A woman sat at an office chair there, turned so she could watch them, but acting as if she was keeping her attention on the screens. The woman wore a loud, lime-green pair of pants and a garish floral blouse. Her hair was a mess of dreadlocks dyed a fluorescent pink, and she had more hardware in her face than Queen had ammunition in her belt.

Of more concern to Queen, the woman was a stranger to her.

Across the space to the right, another woman entered the large command center. Well dressed, with long, flowing black hair, and stunning good looks, Queen recognized the woman immediately. She hadn't spent much time with Augustina Gallo, the professor of mythology from the University of Athens, but the woman was all Southern charm, so she left an impression.

"George," Duncan was saying. "So wonderful to see you again."

"Thank you, Mr. President," George said, a bit embarrassed.

"Please, George, it's 'Tom' to you," Duncan told him.

"Yes, Mr. President," George said, and his grin suggested that no matter how close the two men might ever become, George would always use the other man's full honorific.

Queen watched what was going on in front of her, but she still kept her eye on the strange woman by the computers. She also noticed Knight slowly moving to the left along the back wall—in the opposite direction of her. She knew him well enough to know that he too, was keeping one eye on the woman they did not know. Queen doubted George Pierce would have anyone on his team he didn't trust and hadn't fully vetted. But just because he knew and trusted her, didn't automatically mean Chess Team should trust her. Queen could tell that Knight felt the same. King, Asya, Duncan, Rook, and Ward all seemed to be at ease now, though.

But was that because they implicitly trusted anyone on Pierce's team or because they knew Queen and Knight wouldn't and were staying alert?

Queen admitted that maybe it was just her, and Knight was just spreading out, giving the others space for their reunion. Or, maybe still self-conscious about the scarring on the left side of his face, he naturally gravitated toward that side of the room.

All she knew for certain was that she felt jittery.

And she knew why.

It wasn't the hostile reception downstairs with the Forgotten.

It wasn't the past few days or the strange woman with the bright pink hair.

It was Rook's plans for his future. For *their* future.

They had talked more about it, and she had told him she needed time to think about it, but she knew what her answer would be. Rook wanted to retire from Chess Team. He wanted her to retire with him. He wanted to buy a farmhouse somewhere and settle down.

He hadn't specifically told her so, but she knew that he wanted to have children. Years before joining the military—almost a lifetime ago—Queen had already been a mother. After a childhood filled with abuse that left her nearly paralyzed with fears and phobias, she had found a partner who abused her just like her father had. The man had given her a child—and his abuse had also taken it from her. After learning to live alone, conquering her fears, Queen had vowed to never be vulnerable again—and to never have another child.

But now, she had found a partner who treated her with respect and awe, tenderness and affection. Rook never made her feel vulnerable. He made her stronger. He complemented her in so many ways.

Still, Queen had noticed that her increasing feelings for the man had led to concern and worry for his safety, which was not a good thing on missions. She should be on task and watching out for her own safety and everyone else's—not focused on only one member of the team.

She knew he was overly concerned with her safety on missions as well. Retiring was the sensible option for both of them. She had been prepared to say yes to the retirement, the house, and a quieter life with him. They both had enough injuries from previous missions that growing old in the field was out of the question. They would either need to pull back from field operations or learn to raise chickens. *Well,* she thought, *maybe* I'll *need to learn. Stan already knows, I'm sure.*

She had been so ready to tell him yes. The idea of a life filled with lazy mornings, big breakfasts, and quietly wandering around a small couple of acres somewhere had formed itself fully in her imagination. She found herself thinking about it before she fell asleep at night. The fantasy life took on a hint of perfection in her mind's eye. While she knew Rook wanted children, she also knew he would be okay without ever having them. Content, with just the two of them.

But that damn pregnancy test ruined it all.

Back before they had left for the mission to rescue Duncan, she had seen those devious blue lines staring at her from that little white plastic device.

She hadn't told him yet. She knew he would be thrilled, but first she had to make sure that *she* was thrilled. And despite her vow to herself lifetimes ago, despite her past, and all the craziness of the life Chess Team had thrown her, despite everything: She was beginning to imagine a different life. One where she and Stan were not the only ones ambling around their hay field in northern New Hampshire. There was also a Newfoundland dog now in her dream. And running alongside the dog...a small boy. Around seven years old. With shaggy shoulder length hair that made him look a little like a tiny version of King. The boy would run and play with the dog, and Queen and Rook would slowly walk the perimeter of their land. Smiling and laughing.

It wasn't what she had been thinking of in her quiet moments for the last few years, but over the last few weeks it was slowly coming to take the place of any other fantasy. Maybe it could work. She was a different person now. She could do anything she set her mind to. Being a successful parent couldn't be harder than suffering torture at the hands of a crazed Vietnamese general. But being happy as a parent?

She just didn't know. And until she did know, she couldn't talk to Rook about it. She knew that was childish and ridiculous, but it was the way it had to be. At least until she could see that little boy and that dog in her mind's eye easier than the sunsets and the growing old in the childless versions of the dream.

"That was quite a reception with the wraiths," King said to Pierce, when Queen's attention turned back to the greetings.

"Sorry," George said. "I thought they would recognize you immediately. There's just the two of them now, and they've become very protective of me."

"Two?" King asked, genuinely startled. "There were so many of them..."

"They've been dying, over the last two years. As far as we can tell, the serum used to keep them unnaturally alive all these years is finally wearing off. But we should really wait until the rest of my team gets here. Dr. Carter can explain it better than I can."

"Carter. Not Felice Carter?" King asked in naked disbelief, his agitation beginning to show.

"Yeah," George said, holding up his hands to calm King, "She has her...condition...completely in check. Nothing to worry about. She's an invaluable addition to the group. But there's something else I need to tell you—"

"What the actual fuck?" the woman with the pink hair shouted from her seat by the computers, and she was typing furiously at a keyboard.

"Cintia?" George asked, calling the woman's name.

"That's not possible," the woman shouted. "There's a missile—"

Queen's heightened sense of alert went through the roof.

"Where?" King shouted, running toward the woman.

Cintia turned to the group, her face white, panic in her eyes, "Incomi—"

But she never finished her screamed warning.

The room exploded in a cloud of dust and grit, as thunder filled the air, and the stone ceiling came crashing down on them all.

TWENTY

The first thing King knew was he needed to cough, yet his lungs wouldn't respond. He first needed to take a deep breath in, but his lungs refused that, too. His head felt fuzzy, and a noise rang in his ears that vibrated all through his body. And he couldn't move.

He opened his eyes, but the darkness from behind his eyelids was matched by the darkness outside of them. But then everything blurred to the left, and the all-encompassing shade of black shifted to a muted gray, and finally to an opaque white, as if he was now inside a cloud.

Then his lungs remembered how to work, and he drew in a gigantic whooping breath—and immediately began coughing so hard that snot flew from his nose and tears rolled down his cheeks. His upper body curled forward. He ended up in a sitting position. Now he was up, each breath a strained whoop inward, followed by wracking spasms.

Then he noticed strong hands, guiding him up onto his feet. He went with them, because remaining seated felt worse.

As the coughs died down, his eyes went up, searching through the hazy dust cloud all around him for the face that went with the hands.

But it was the wrong face.

Had to be.

The man in front of him was huge. He was easily five inches taller than King, and over 250 pounds of rippling muscles in a black and dusty T-shirt. The man was vaguely Middle Eastern, but despite the thick beard he wore, and a bandana tied tightly over his mouth, King recognized him instantly.

"Bishop?" King staggered back a step, his head spinning, more from the confusion of his dead friend standing before him, than the explosion. He reached out a hand, placing it on the big man's shoulder, ensuring he wasn't hallucinating. The muscular arm was very real.

Bishop was alive.

"Hey, Jack," the man said in his soft voice. "We've got to go. No time for a reunion now."

With that, Erik Somers, the man who formerly held the callsign: Bishop, and whom King believed dead for the last few years, quickly led King by the arm across a tight cave of rocks and rubble.

King's mind whirled, but then it all came back to him.

The Herculean Society base. George Pierce. The screaming woman, Cintia.

And a missile headed right for them.

"Where's Fiona?" King asked, as another bout of coughing shook him.

Somers gestured to the woman near the door, looking upward and straining, her arms held aloft like she was summoning a storm. King realized his daughter was doing just the opposite. She was keeping the roof from falling in on their heads through sheer force of will.

"She's over there. Knight's securing our exit. We need to dig out the others," Somers said.

King and Somers started pulling up rocks and sweeping piles of debris away using their hands. Rook and Queen were doing the same on their side of the cavern, Queen limping, and Rook with a rag tied around a bleeding gash on his forehead.

They found Duncan first, under a desk that had sheltered him from the worst of it.

On his side of the cavern that used to be a room, King unearthed Augustina Gallo's foot and quickly called to his former teammate. They had her uncovered in minutes, but the woman was dead. King wanted to rage, and he wanted to grieve for her, but Erik Somers just moved on and kept hauling rock.

"How many more on your team?" King grunted, knowing that George Pierce and the woman with the pink hair were still unaccounted for. But he was having a hard time remembering who else had been in the room—or who else George had told him about.

"Felice Carter. Cintia Dourado. George." Somers said, pulling back an enormous slab of ceiling and rebar.

"Shit. If something happens to Felice..." King started.

But Somers cut him off with a growled reply.

King whipped his head around to see the other group had pulled Ward out from the collapse. The man was in shock. He looked around dazed, and Duncan quickly escorted him toward a doorway.

Halfway between the other search team and King, he saw a pile of rock shift on the floor, and he started to move toward the pile. Before he reached it, the rocks erupted upward with a flurry of movement and a shout of "Shluha vokzal'naja!"

His sister, Asya, burst from a new cloud of dust and rocks, her arms flinging wildly about her, as if she were still digging her way up and out of the rubble.

He knew from the strength of her unearthing herself, and from her voice that she would be mostly fine, but he quickly saw that one of her flailing arms was swinging a little more freely than it should.

"You're okay," King called to her, and she immediately calmed. "Looks like a broken arm."

The woman, covered in dust, looked down at the limp forearm, and spat on the ground. Then she looked up at King, still all business. "Are we being attacked?"

"Unknown. Knight is covering the retreat. Medical appears to be that way," he said, pointing toward the door where Duncan had led Ward just seconds earlier. He could see that Asya was about to protest. She wanted to pitch in with the rescue efforts, but he knew her injury could only be made worse with her stubbornness. "Go."

He turned back to Erik Somers, the former Bishop. The big man was still furiously moving stone. King joined him. His mind started to close down, with nothing but breathing and exertion filling his thoughts. Somewhere in the back of his lizard brain he understood that the survivors would need to leave their current location as soon as possible. Someone had attacked them with a missile—either Chess Team or George's Cerberus Group was the target. But each time he tried to think things through, his mind went blank again and he just lifted another rock.

Out of the corner of his eye, King saw Rook and Queen delicately making their way across the space to the far wall—the place he knew the pink haired woman had been at her bank of computers when she screamed out her warning. The warning that had probably saved most of their lives. From the height of the pile of debris and twisted rebar on that side, he didn't expect the woman would have made it.

"Jack," Somers said softly.

King turned around and saw that the large chunk of stone the man had just lifted revealed George Pierce's face—and his caved in skull.

"Godamnit," King sighed, dropping to one knee, tears in his eyes. They'd been friends for so long King didn't remember life without him. He was the kind of person King could go years without seeing and yet reunite with as though only minutes had passed. Even worse, while George's first experience with the strange world of Chess Team hadn't involved King until George called him for help, King leaving George in charge of the Herculean Society had guaranteed his friend would always be in danger. And now he was dead. Buried beneath rubble. In a cave no one knew existed.

And he wasn't alone. Others were dead. People who had fought to save the world on his behalf, while he spent his time trying to locate Duncan.

King clenched his fists, wracking his mind for some unnatural solution. George had been brought back from the brink before. As had Erik. And King himself, hundreds of times, during the few thousand years he'd spent living in the past.

But he couldn't think of anything.

Couldn't think at all.

Somers gently placed his hand on King's shoulder. He didn't say he was sorry. It wasn't necessary. King could feel the empathy from his old friend and former teammate.

"Dad?" Fiona shouted, still struggling to hold up the ceiling. "Dad, what happened? Who is it?"

When King looked up and Fiona saw his eyes, she knew.

She shrank a little bit, devastated by the loss of the man who'd become her uncle and then mentor and team leader. Then she led King by example, setting her jaw and doubling her effort, whispering a chant that held the power to repel the tons of stone over their heads. Because whoever had sent that missile was still out there, waiting for the Siglers to find them, and they would not disappoint.

"I can give you...maybe another two minutes," Fiona grunted. Sweat was pouring down her face, cleaving streaks through the thick layer of dust. Her upper body was trembling, and her teeth were gritted together from the strain.

"We've got the pink haired one," Rook shouted. "I'm sorry, she's gone. And she's buried deep. Not sure we're going to be able to get her out."

King turned back to Somers. "Erik," King said, and using the man's first name felt weird, since he had usually referred to him as Bishop or Bish—even in their downtime. "We have to go."

"Not until I find Felice," the man said, and the rage in his voice was apparent. And then it was quickly eliminated by surging hope.

"Erik," Tom Duncan's voice called. He knelt over the body of a woman, and the look on his face said enough. The Cerberus Group's ranks had been cut in half.

TWENTY-ONE

USS New Hampshire,
Somewhere in the Indian Ocean

Tom Duncan felt stupid and cursed himself again, the tenth time in the last half hour. They were all aboard the submarine again, and Admiral Ward's medics had tended to all the minor injuries, Asya's broken arm, and the woman in the coma–Felice Carter.

There was no knowing if she would ever come out of it, and it was clear to all that Erik Somers was involved with her, because he wouldn't leave the inert woman's side. Somers's resurrection was enough of a shocker, and Duncan was mad at himself for not performing a stronger search in Africa when the former Bishop had gone missing.

He was also upset at the deaths of George Pierce, Augustina Gallo, and the Dourado woman. They had only been able to retrieve Gallo's body before Fiona's extraordinary ability to hold up the roof of the collapsed building was at an end. The young woman was now in a deep sleep, recuperating.

But none of that was what Duncan was kicking himself in the metaphorical ass for the most.

At some point during the years he was imprisoned, his captors must have drugged him without him noticing and placed a small tracking chip in the back of his neck. If he'd been sedated until after the small incision had healed, he'd have just woken up one morning and assumed it was the next day.

As soon as everyone was safe aboard the sub, he'd discussed with King and Ward how someone might have been able to target the team at a secret Herculean Society base. Whether it was George's team that had been attacked or Chess Team. Only then did the thought occur to Duncan to have someone check him for a tracker.

And sonofabitch, he thought to himself again.

It was there.

Ward's medics removed the chip, and it was immediately destroyed. Ward theorized the thing would have only been effective once the group had left the metal confines of the sub and travelled up the long elevator shaft to the Society's base, located under a factory. The signal would have been strong enough—and close enough to the surface at that point—for their hidden enemy to launch a missile strike.

What worried Duncan the most was that their as-yet-unidentified enemy had been able to mobilize so quickly—and globally—and launch a strike at their location within minutes of the team getting close enough to the surface.

And halfway around the damn world from the Desolation Islands!

Unless their enemy knew *all* the Herculean Society locations, which King had been doubtful about.

Either way, they had all been examined for tracking chips, and the sub would soon arrive at Diego Garcia in the Indian Ocean. The joint US and UK military force there would be all the protection the team would need to recover and organize their response. Once they determined who was at fault.

Until then, Duncan had only himself to blame.

He grunted in disgust, not thinking that he would wake anyone. But the bunks in the sleeping quarters of the submarine were close together.

"Thomas," Asya said from her bunk next to his. "Are you alright?"

"Sorry. Didn't mean to wake you," he whispered, and he meant it. He had taken a liking to the young woman as soon as he'd met her, after the Norway incident, but he had never seriously considered he would develop feelings for her. Her own feelings for him were hard to ignore. The fact that he was older than her—or that he was a former President—made no difference to the Russian-raised woman. To her, he was simply 'Thomas,' and she clearly adored him. Since his release from the cell on the Desolation Islands, Asya had not let him out of her sight, even quickly selecting the bunk adjacent to his, when he had insisted to Ward that he could sleep in the same quarters as everyone else.

Asya sat up in her bed, and swiveled to face him, her broken left arm still in a sling. Her wavy black hair cascaded across part of her face. She looked at him with concern, but also a slight trace of annoyance.

"You can't keep blaming yourself for what happened," she said, and once again he was amazed at how quickly this woman had lost all trace of her accent. Asya took to all new learning with gusto, and she had mastered everything she had touched from weapons to explosives to language.

Even knowing my thoughts.

"If I had—" he started.

"No," she cut him off. One of the nearby sailors shifted in his bunk at the volume of her voice. Asya reached out and took his hand in hers. "You were a prisoner for *years*. No one expects you to be a fully functioning field operative—even before you were taken. Any one of us might have missed the incision. Especially if they kept you sedated until it had healed. There would have been nothing for you to even feel."

He sat in his bunk and looked at her, but he didn't withdraw his hand from hers. Even though she was rebuking him for his maudlin thoughts, her touch was gentle. Not for the first time, he marveled at this woman and her ability to persevere through all manner of adversity. Despite her fracture, he had yet to hear her complain about the broken limb even once.

"Once we get to DG, we can get out of this tin can, get you a good solid meal, and then figure out who the bastards were that did this. They're the ones to blame. Not you. And Jack and the others—including Erik—will need your mind to help them find those fuckers. Have you heard anything from Lewis?"

She was referring to Aleman, who was supposed to rendezvous with the team before the attack.

"He's on his way to Diego by air. He'll be waiting for us when we arrive. I'm just glad he wasn't there..." Duncan trailed off.

"We just need time to regroup. And rest." When she looked in his eye, something sparked in his chest, and she saw it, as clear as day.

She leaned forward and kissed him gently on the cheek.

The tenderness of it made him smile in a way he hadn't for a long time.

The submarine's klaxon shattered the moment.

Ward's voice came over the loudspeaker. "Battle stations, everyone. Eagle and King, I need you with me." The message was terse, and Duncan was already on his feet, leaving Asya behind. As she and the other members of Chess Team—and Pierce's group—were all passengers on the boat, their battle stations were in their bunks, out of the way of the rest of the practiced crew.

Duncan rushed toward the comm, and King joined him in the tight corridor.

Admiral Ward looked angry.

When he saw Duncan, he took a deep breath. "We've come up to the surface, just outside DG. Mr. President, President Matthew Chambers was assassinated, and we are on a war footing."

Duncan was flabbergasted. "What? What do we know so far?"

"From our own government? Very little. As you know, Sir, when a president is killed or dies unexpectedly in office, SOP is to be battle ready. All I know for sure is Mr. Chambers was shot and killed by a sniper, and the *New Hampshire* is to be recalled to Norfolk, just as soon as I drop you all here in DG. I'm not sure what level of help I'll be able to provide your team moving forward."

Duncan nodded. "Understood."

"There's something else. And I'll swear on a stack of Bibles I didn't provide you with this intel if I'm ever asked."

"I never heard it from you, Jon," Duncan assured him.

"Russian intel confirms that Putin is dead, too. And then there's this. Broadcast worldwide less than a minute *before* the gunshot." Ward tapped a seaman on the shoulder, and the young man hit a key on his keyboard. A video monitor came to life, and Duncan gasped.

"Sonofabitch," King whispered.

The image was of a man they both knew quite well.

Richard Ridley. He wore a crisp white suit, although they could only see him from the shoulders up. His bald head was gleaming in the harsh light his video crew was using, and a bead of sweat dripped down his brow. Then the man spoke.

"Oh, Matthew. We told you. You defy us at your peril. Your toy soldiers are gone now, too, along with Tom Duncan. So, Vice President Beaman? Once you're sworn in? Stay out of our way."

Then the screen went dark.

HOSTILITY

TWENTY-TWO

Xining Caojiabao Airport, Qinghai, Western China

The private hangar was all the way at the western end of the airport, where taxiing planes made their final one hundred and eighty degree turn before beginning their take-off runs. The hangar was thought by all to be a military facility, and copious warning signs in Chinese, Tibetan, and English warned everyone to stay far away from the small building.

To the structure's side was a small helipad, and the entirety of the area was surrounded with chain-link fence topped with far too many rolls of razor wire.

The message was clear. Any unauthorized attempt to access the facility would be met with the harshest of penalties.

Most of the pilots that flew commercial flights out of Xining—nearly always to somewhere better in China—ignored the structure completely. Some had never even noticed it, situated as it was to the left of a right hand turn they took before takeoff. They were simply too busy at that stage to be sightseers.

But the virtual invisibility of the structure's location had less to do with keeping looky loos away and more to do with the efficiency of starting at that end of the runway with a private plane—which was all the building held, beside a comfortable office that was barely ever used, and a large commode.

Senior Colonel Li Wan Jian knew the advantages of being able to cut the line of commercial flights and immediately take off in a private plane. And he had taken this particular flight twice before. Neither had been pleasant. As his limo travelled the poorly paved road out to the building, passing two armed guards at the gate, he recalled again, with a shiver, the woman he was coming to meet, and on whose private plane he would be flying.

Her formal title, to those in the People's Liberation Army Ground Force who were aware of her existence at all, was 'The High Honorable Lady' and, although technically a civilian, she held a power greater than that of a four-star general. A few of the highest Party members officially held more sway, but Li suspected even President Xi Jinping would cower before her. Such was the fierce intellect, steely nerve, and ruthless tactics of the woman they all referred to informally as 'Lady Crimson.'

No one knew her real name, or where she had come from. Many suspected she was not even Han Chinese. But there were rumors, of course.

As the limo pulled into the facility and parked next to the plain concrete building, Li gathered his small travel bag and his briefcase. He resented not being allowed a valet on this journey and needing to carry his own belongings, but he also reminded himself of Lady Crimson's whispered history.

What was known for certain was thin on the ground. Supposedly she was a powerhouse in the Hong Kong and Macau crime syndicates. But that taste of power had not been enough for the giant woman, and she had quickly found her way to expand her power, via local politicians. She used, manipulated, or threatened them all, until she rose her way up to Province level government, rarely holding a government position of her own for longer than a month before climbing farther up the ladder.

If there was a glass ceiling for female members of the Chinese Communist Party, she soon shattered it into deadly slivers. And why not? The woman was terrifying to behold. At nearly seven feet tall, with arms and legs like a champion weightlifter, Lady Crimson filled any room she walked into. Li guessed her weight at over three hundred pounds, but all of it was muscle. Her face was hideously ugly with several tiny scars that could be seen if you got up close. Li had only done so once, when the woman was screaming at him for a past failure. He suspected she'd had some kind of plastic surgery after a horrible accident. But the surgeons could only do so much. Still, the woman hid it well, with long flowing hair that usually covered half her face, and thickly applied makeup.

'Lipstick on a pig' was the expression he had heard on American television, and it resonated when he thought of her.

He passed another armed guard, heading into the building, and he needed to remove his sunglasses to see. The hangar door was still closed, but the lights on the aircraft wings were lit, so he knew the pilot, at least, was aboard. Li moved across the slick concrete floor at an angle, so he would be able to see in through the office's glass wall. If Lady Crimson was in the office, he would go there. If she was already aboard the plane, he would board—or someone would arrive to let him know which to do before he could determine it for himself.

As he suspected, the latter was true. Before he could get close enough to the office to look through the window, a slim Han Chinese woman approached him wearing high-heeled shoes, and a plain black business outfit. She carried a digital tablet, and she did not look up at Li as she walked toward him. Li recognized her as one of Lady Crimson's personal secretaries. He had seen six different women in the post, and he wasn't sure if they rotated frequently or if they all serviced their employer full time. He had a hard time keeping them straight, but this one, a younger woman named Rong, he recognized from his last trip.

"Rong," he said, holding out his carry-on bag.

The woman swept close to him and took his bag, with a final few taps on her tablet. "Good morning, Colonel. Lady Crimson is already aboard, and we are ready for takeoff. Please climb aboard and take your seat."

Li huffed and walked ahead of the woman, climbing the short folding flight of stairs into the doorway of the small Gulfstream plane. He suspected it belonged to Lady Crimson. It certainly wasn't a military plane. He knew from his last flights that the interior was plush, decorated with thick carpet and real wood paneling on the walls. Swiveling leather chairs filled the small interior and at the back of the cabin was a private bedroom. Li was grateful Lady Crimson had not ever invited him to see it firsthand.

As he stepped inside, he could see that she was most likely in the private quarters, because Rong had said she was aboard, but he couldn't see her anywhere. He glanced left at the pilot, but the co-pilot seat was empty—and Li honestly thought the giantess would have a hard time squeezing into the cockpit at all.

He took a seat and belted in, and Rong sat next to him, still furiously working her tablet.

A moment later, the plane began rolling forward and, as Li glanced out the window, he saw a ray of sunlight flash across the smooth concrete floor as the hangar door opened.

Then the plane was on the runway, and seconds after that it was in the air.

Must be nice, Li thought, *to have the power to inform an entire airport that it should pause all operations while your personal plane uses the runway.*

It was his third time riding on the plane, and he still marveled at the audacity. Only the highest-ranking members of the Party would be so brazen.

Not even a Beijing four-star would have gotten away with it.

The Gulfstream climbed at a steep angle into the sky, and Li looked out the window at the ugly brown hills below them, which covered most of Gansu and Ningxia provinces. They were on their way to Beijing, so it would be hours before the landscape turned greener below them.

As the plane leveled off, the door to the private quarters opened, and Li turned his chair to see her.

Lady Crimson needed to bend her head so as not to scrape the curved roof of the plane. She was in a smart cream-colored business pantsuit, and her enormous feet were crammed into a pair of low heels, which only added to her immense height. As usual, her face was slathered with thick makeup, and her long wavy hair, which today was dyed blonde, fell like a curtain over her face. She lost no time getting down to business.

"Colonel, your people destroyed the Chess Team and, as I instructed, you ensured that the tracking chip stopped transmitting?"

"Yes, Lady Crimson," Li said, feeling the need to unbuckle and stand from his seat. "As soon as the signal was sighted in South Africa—just as you suspected—we launched a missile at the location."

The large woman made a noise like a growl, as she stepped closer to him. "And the tracking signal stopped when the missile hit?"

Damn this woman! How does she always know? Li wondered.

"Within seconds, the signal was lost."

She waited on anything further, again, like she knew there would be *something*.

Li cleared his throat, nervously. "A few minutes later, there was another faint signal..."

He could see her visibly becoming enraged.

Her face reddened.

"But then the signal died again!" Li quickly corrected. "We checked for it for hours afterward, but there was no further blip. We assume that there was either a technical glitch or the man was buried under rubble in the explosion, and he was still alive for a few minutes before expiring."

"Or," Lady Crimson said, her arm flashing out like a cobra striking. Her meaty hand closed over Li's throat, and she hefted him off his feet, his head slamming into the curved ceiling of the plane. "He survived the attack, and then discovered the tracking chip—and disabled it."

Li's hands scrabbled and clawed at the woman's gigantic hand, but he couldn't pry her fingers loose. She swung his body to the side and moved forward in the cabin. Rong remained seated and only slightly leaned to the side, while still tapping at her tablet, when his body was carried past her.

As if she had known what would happen.

This close to Lady Crimson's raging face, he could smell her breath and see the yellow tint to the whites of her eyes, as if the woman was suffering from liver failure.

"I warned you what would happen if you failed me a second time, Colonel."

The plane's door cracked open automatically, and a wind unlike any he had ever experienced filled the cabin. The giantess was unaffected by the hurricane blast.

Li could no longer breathe from the crushing grasp around his neck, but the thought that he was going to be thrown out of the plane sent a surge of adrenaline through his body and boosted his strength. He struggled and fought, clawing now at her face, his hand tangling in her long hair.

As she reached her arm out the door with his body flailing along in her powerful fist, he saw that his attempts to grab her hair would do him no good.

It came away in his grasp.

The huge woman snarled at him and released his neck.

He began his long fall to the ground, clutching the woman's long hair—a wig—in his hands.

In seconds, the plane was gone overhead, and Li's voice had gone hoarse from screaming.

But he still had a long way to fall.

TWENTY-THREE

15,000 feet over the Pampas de Jumana, Peru

The plane was a mercenary flight paid for with funds Chess Team had stored away for years and years since Tom Duncan had been President of the United States. There were several such accounts around the world, and King hated to tap into them. He had his own similar accounts around the world, tied into the Herculean Society, but now he didn't know if Ridley's forces had found the base in Cape Town through the tracking chip in Duncan's neck, or if somehow Ridley had located all the Society bases and offices around the globe.

Either way, King couldn't take a chance.

So, they had used older Chess Team funds to get from Diego Garcia to Caracas, and then had hired mercenary forces to fly them from Venezuela to Peru, and now to fly them out to Nazca. Duncan, Aleman, and the surviving civilian members of Pierce's Cerberus Group had relocated to a new base of operations in Oregon, where Ridley would be unlikely to search for them.

King looked across the tight confines of the battered cargo plane at Erik Somers, fully garbed in black-market military gear and ready, like the other members of the team, for a HALO jump down to the Nazca plains. Because Asya had broken her arm in the collapse in Cape Town, she had been left behind with the others.

Secretly, King was happy about that, because he knew she needed the break, and the time would allow her to pursue her feelings for Duncan. They both tried to hide the attraction from the rest of the team, but King had noticed and was happy for them, despite the age difference. They still had plenty in common. But mostly, King was pleased to leave his sister behind because he knew if her team was attacked, she would do serious damage before going down. Between her and Fiona's powers to move inanimate objects, plus Duncan's and Aleman's military backgrounds, King felt better about leaving them on their own and without any additional military support.

As expected, Ward had needed to leave with the crew of the *New Hampshire* and report to the boat's new tasking—in the Gulf. The Admiral hadn't even had time to tell his crew they were heading to Norfolk before the newer orders had come in from the Pentagon. After President Chambers had been shot, the Pentagon went to an all-out war footing, shuffling military pieces around the world in a show of force designed to deter the Russians, the Chinese, and any other potentially hostile states in the Middle East from any further aggression.

Stuck with his crew in the Gulf, Ward was now unable to offer any additional intel or military equipment. But he knew that Chess Team had a better chance of finding—and stopping—Richard Ridley, so Ward was still allied with them. He just wasn't freed enough from scrutiny to lend any actual help.

King's more immediate concern was how well his five-person team would function again with Somers. The man had been reluctant to leave Felice Carter's comatose side at first, but after Tom Duncan had assured him the woman would receive the best of care, Somers—the newly reinstated callsign: Bishop—had asked King if he could join the field operations team. Especially since Asya would not be.

As far as King could ascertain, Queen and Rook were fine with it, and although Knight had not expressed any enthusiasm for Bishop's return, he hadn't objected in any way either. He had just been his mostly quiet self about it. For his part, Bishop appeared calmer than he had in the past. More self-assured and competent. King probably put that down to the love of a good woman these last few years, and a chance for Bishop to get his head straight after the horrors he had faced with Chess Team.

The man's explanation for his sudden resurrection had been brief. "I needed time. You all thought I was dead. Eventually you moved on. When I felt I'd had enough time to get my head straight, it didn't seem like the kind of thing I should send you an e-mail about. George was supposed to smooth things over when we met up in Cape Town." But the mention of the deceased George Pierce quieted the man. King assumed it was also what quieted any further comments from the other three members of the team as well.

Privately, King had spoken with Bishop about some of the work he had done with George's Cerberus Group, and he'd thanked him for watching out for Fiona. King's friendship with Erik had not been damaged by the time away or the prolonged absence of contact, and for that he was grateful. Longer lived than the other members of the team, King understood the need for a man to just disappear and start a new life. He had done it himself—dozens of times over the centuries of life he had lived. Although much of his time trapped in the past had faded from his memory, he still understood the process and the need.

Now, as they approached their HALO jump point, King let his concerns about how well the team would work again with the prior Bishop fade. They were all professionals, and they all knew how to do the job. King's mental energy needed to be on one man. Richard Ridley. He needed to focus on what he knew of the continually resurfacing megalomaniac, and how Chess Team would be able to stop him.

At first, they had just the thinnest of leads to follow. They had no idea where in the world the man might be now, but King knew without a doubt where the man's remains should have been.

Nazca.

King had hoped the last time he was here would be the last for the rest of his days. His knowledge of Ridley had begun over a decade earlier, when George Pierce asked King to come to Nazca to provide security for an archeological dig. Pierce had helped uncover the head of the Learnean Hydra. When Ridley's men attacked the site and abducted Pierce, King had been left for dead in the same cave in which the relic had been discovered. King escaped with the help of a local, and he'd chased the men down, rescuing his friend. Chess Team fought Ridley's forces and genetic creations for years to come after that. But after a knock-down drag-out fight in Tunisia, King had taken the ruined remains of Ridley's shattered head and buried it in the same cave in Nazca where everything had begun. With the aridity of the desert, there was no way Ridley could have reanimated his own remains. The geneticist had used different life-giving serums on himself over the years—and he could speak the mother tongue, the same language Fiona could use to manipulate the inanimate—but still...

There's no way he came back on his own, King thought for the hundredth time. *He must have had help.*

That help was their only lead. The team was heading back to that cave in Nazca to see if they could find some clue or some hint of who it was that had assisted Ridley. That was the only trail they had available to them. The missile in Cape Town was a non-starter. Aleman had found the vehicle that launched it on CCTV in Cape Town, but then the truck vanished in traffic and, even with Aleman's and Duncan's joint computer prowess, they had no further ways of tracking the thing.

So, for King and the rest of Chess Team, it was back to the beginning.

Nazca.

King looked around at the group.

They were all silent for a change. No banter. No wisecracks from Rook. Everyone determined and deadly. Ready for business.

The mercenary loadmaster, a man named Haim, stood up and gave them the signal they were approaching the drop point. The Chess Team members all quickly performed a final inspection of their equipment.

Then they were standing, and the rear load door of the plane opened. Below them, the dry brown plains and the mysterious stunning lines that cross the desert.

Haim gave the signal, and Knight moved to the edge of the ramp and jumped. Bishop followed him. Then Queen, then Rook.

King jumped last, with a solemn promise in his heart.

I'm going to end Richard Ridley, if I have to burn him down to the last molecule.

TWENTY-FOUR

Underground, Siletz, Oregon

Fiona had mixed feelings about returning to Siletz, Oregon. On the one hand, it was her childhood home with her grandmother. On the other hand, it brought up suppressed memories of the massacre Richard Ridley had perpetrated here a decade earlier. The entire population of the town, and most of the Siletz Tribe living on the contiguous parcels of reservation land immediately east of the town proper, had been slaughtered in Ridley's hunt for the last living speakers of ancient languages.

When King found her as a little girl, Fiona was thought to be the last member of her tribe. As it turned out, many other Siletz Confederation Native Americans had indeed survived the purge—either because they had escaped notice or because they lived on some of the non-contiguous parcels of their reservation land. Still, after the slaughter, those survivors had moved farther away from the reservation, aided by funds Tom Duncan quietly supplied, while President of the United States.

Now, the entirety of the town, and the lands that formerly comprised the reservation, belonged to Fiona. That was a situation she found she had quite complex feelings about. Eventually, she hoped to lure other tribal survivors *back* to the land, and to give them an income based on something besides gambling casinos. For the moment, she wasn't sure what to do with the land, and so it had just sat waiting for the day she would return to it. Duncan paid long ago for the restoration of some of the buildings, although some still showed their battle scars. He'd also paid for the creation of a 'community center' building, under which Chess Team could have a small, but fully functional base of operations—should they ever need it. Before having it constructed though, he had formally asked Fiona's permission. When she was twelve years old. She still remembered the conversation, when he talked briefly about some of the many atrocities that had befallen Native Americans over the years, and that, since she was a survivor of the attack, the decisions about what was to be done with the land should involve her.

At twelve, she thought a secret base for Chess Team on the land was a good idea. Today, she wasn't so sure her ancestors and the other survivors of the massacre would agree with that choice. But every last one of them, when given a choice and money to relocate, had chosen to abandon the reservation, feeling the place was cursed after the Ridley attack. Some of them even blamed the U.S. government for the attack and what they saw as *another* forced relocation.

She could understand that feeling of resentment, but, she noted, none of them had turned down the money when it had been offered. While many might have objected to a paramilitary strike team—which was only sometimes under the control of the government—operating off these lands, Fiona had the final say.

Today, those concerns were not utmost in her mind.

Today, she wanted vengeance against Richard Ridley for the murder of a man she had thought of as an uncle, for the killing of Augustina Gallo, whom she'd thought of as an aunt and hoped would marry George Pierce, and for the death of Cintia Dourado, who had become Fiona's best friend.

Today, Fiona was angry.

She would use her land, her abilities with the mother tongue, and anything else she could to find Ridley. Then they would finally stop that crazy bastard.

The base was underground and, since arriving at it, she and Lewis Aleman had quickly installed a number of additional security measures and perimeter alarms at the edge of town. Tom Duncan had, at Aleman's insistence, slipped back into his role as callsign: Deep Blue, orchestrating Chess Team's intel and operations. Asya was by his side at all times. Fiona's grandparents—King's mother and father—were on their way to the facility, and so was Sara Fogg, Fiona's adopted mother, and King's wife.

Everyone alive who was affiliated in any way with Chess Team was going to be kept safe. Pawn was still in Thailand following up on some unrelated thing, but she was a professional operator. Domenick Boucher, the former director of the CIA, was also being called in, for the sake of his safety.

"No one else dies," Duncan had said.

If Fiona had anything to say about it, she would ensure he was right.

Now, after spending the morning with some language studies, she walked the gray concrete hallway from the sleeping quarters to the operations room. She hated the long wait while Chess Team moved into position, and the talk in operations would get dull. To keep her mind off her anxieties, she would instead occupy her academic curiosity. But she knew the team would be close to the Nazca Lines now, so she had set her books aside.

She didn't think the team would find much, but any tiny clue as to the madman's whereabouts would feed her thirst for vengeance.

When she walked into the room, she found Aleman and Duncan already sitting. Dom Boucher was seated next to them. He must have arrived earlier in the morning. No one had bothered to tell her. But she assumed they would come find her when her grandparents showed up. Asya was not present, and Fiona guessed she was checking on the comatose Felice Carter.

Five body cam feeds—one for each member of the team as they dropped from the sky—were displayed on a wall-mounted TV divided into six segments. The sixth segment of the screen remained dark.

Fiona slipped into a chair beside Aleman. He turned to her, and said, "They should touch down in under a minute."

She just nodded. Each video square showed a tiny icon of a chess piece in the upper right corner. She kept an eye on King's square, knowing that whatever they found at Ridley's burial site, he would probably be in the lead.

"Do we have audio?" she asked no one in particular.

Duncan replied. "They'll stay on radio silence until they're down on the ground and sure the LZ is safe."

Fiona lapsed back into quiet, keeping her eye on her father's video feed. In moments, the screen jostled, letting her know he had landed on the desert floor. He quickly dropped to a crouch and swept the barren landscape with the barrel of his rifle. She couldn't tell from the feed, but she knew it was the latest Sig Sauer protype. King, after seeing nothing but the desolate plains, hauled in his parachute. Then he stood and moved over to the giant stone adjacent to the entryway to the cave, where Ridley should have still been buried. The tunnel itself had been unsealed, the giant stone rolled away and lying cracked on the ground. Fiona knew King had sealed it the last time he was at Nazca.

King examined the dusty ground for a full minute, and Fiona wondered what he was doing. Then she understood. Footprints in the Nazca dirt would stay put for centuries. He was looking for tracks, but the ground had been disturbed too much for her to discern anything.

When King raised his eyes—and, by extension, his video feed—back toward the tunnel, Fiona knew the team would be going in now.

Then King's voice startled her, coming in over hidden speakers in the room so clearly that it sounded like he was standing right next to her. "How are we looking, Blue?"

Duncan wore a wireless headset microphone, and he toggled a switch in his hand, making it live. "We have nothing on radar or Sat images. Far as we can tell from here, it's just you out there."

"Copy," King said. "Mic check?"

The other four members of the team called in, each one clear, as if they also were in the room with Fiona. When Erik sounded off, she was startled by the deep timbre of his voice. Despite knowing better, she was expecting to hear Asya's voice instead.

"Bishop. Watch the door. We're going in, Blue."

Duncan did not reply, as Bishop moved to the side of the tunnel, with Queen, Rook, and King taking up cover positions on the opening.

Knight's camera view kept changing, as he maintained a watch in all directions for distant aircraft or distant ground vehicles and their telltale plumes of dust. There was nothing but a clear blue sky and a dry whitish desert in any direction Knight looked, though.

When Fiona looked back to King's feed, he was making his way down the tight confines of the dark tunnel that led into the cave.

King wore a shoulder-mounted LED flashlight, but he was entering the tunnel with a night-vision monocular. The camera feed switched to all shades of green, but it still looked dark. Then Fiona could see it looked like he was at an opening, at the end of the tunnel. King peered around the corner with a small mirror on a collapsible rod, but the chest mounted camera could not see what he could.

It was infuriating.

But Fiona's wait was short.

"The cave is clear," King said.

Then he activated his shoulder LED, and the video feed went white for a second. He switched off night-vision mode, and suddenly Fiona could see the entire cave.

It was small. No bigger than a bedroom. Fiona had heard about the cave but she had never been inside of it.

Across the surface of the gritty floor were a few discarded lights on tripods, a video camera on another tripod, and twenty empty plastic water canteens. A shovel leaned against a wall. Beside the blade was a frayed burlap sack. A green sheet had been hammered into the opposite stone wall, as a photography backdrop.

And lying on the floor in front of the sheet, was the half-regenerated body of Richard Ridley, his lower jaw ripped away from his face, and his eyes wide open.

But he was very dead.

TWENTY-FIVE

Nazca Plains

"**Well, shit. Did** anybody see Ridley's legs anywhere? I hope I didn't step on them," Rook said.

King didn't laugh, but he heard Queen make a slight grunt that could have been a chuckle.

The corpse looked like it was only part way through regeneration when someone had killed Ridley. His upper torso and arms were dressed in a white shirt and suit jacket. He wore boxer shorts, but no suit trousers over his partially formed thighs.

This makes no sense...

Then King understood. "Someone came here and revived him..." he started.

"How?" Queen asked. "I thought he was done for."

"He was," King said, squatting down and prodding the exposed ligaments and blood vessels that extended from Ridley's raw thighs. "We removed his original Regen serum, by counteracting it with an herbal concoction we got from Alexander. It was similar to what I used to end my own immortality. Then his mouth and tongue were removed in the hand grenade blast. Without the ability to manipulate the mother tongue with his mouth, he couldn't regenerate himself that way either. He should have remained here...inert...forever."

"So, someone used a Regen serum—or something like it—to bring him back," Rook said.

"Partially," Queen added. "Or enough to make that video clip we saw with Ridley warning the new President. But why kill him right after doing that? Why even bring him back just for that?"

King looked around behind Ridley's limp torso. In the dirt behind the body, King found a small mark. Clearly drawn by Ridley with a finger in the grit—and done behind his back. King motioned for Queen to come over and look.

"The Herculean Society symbol. The symbol of Alexander. You don't think—" Queen started.

"That this was Alexander?" King interrupted. "Doubtful. I don't think the man I knew would leave his other-dimensional home, and the love of his life, to come back here and resurrect Ridley for *any* reason. Plus, Alexander tended to stay away from human politics over the centuries. No reason to think he would get involved in them now."

King stood up and went over to examine the video camera. Its memory card had been removed. The battery was long since dead. He flipped the device upside down, looking for a manufacturer's label, and found it—covered in Chinese characters.

"I think someone from the Consortium did this."

"Stands to reason," came Deep Blue's voice in the ears.

"That shadow group your sister, Julie, was involved with?" Rook asked. "Why them?"

"Because," King said, slipping the video camera into his backpack, "President Chambers wasn't the only one attacked."

"Yeah," Rook said. "I *remember* digging out of the rubble. That was only a few days ago."

"The Russian president—the original Rasputin. My grandfather," King reminded him.

"You think this is about you?" Queen asked.

"No," King dismissed the idea. "But I think Chambers and Rasputin were likely aligned with the Consortium. The same group responsible for a lot of our headaches these last few years."

"So why the Herculean Society symbol then?" Queen asked.

"Someone used a Regen serum on Ridley. Enough for him to start regenerating. Maybe he even helped the process along with the mother tongue, once his face reformed. Then, whoever it was, encouraged him to record the message. He was probably eager to help at first, when he thought he had a newfound ally that would help rid him of us and regain his life. But then, something would have tipped him off…that his apparent savior's plans didn't involve healing him completely."

"Like what?" Rook asked. He was examining the burlap sack for any further clues, but he discarded it.

"Maybe they were pressing him for information on his genetic projects. Or on the Society. Maybe something else. I think the symbol he drew was for us. Or for someone else…"

"Then before he can fully reform," Rook said, "this partner of his, what? Injects him with another serum to nullify the Regen sauce? Then rips off his jaw?" His disgust was visible on his face, and his lack of typical sarcasm backed it up.

"And ripped out his tongue," Queen confirmed, peering into the ravaged corpse.

"Look for tripwires but check everything in this cave," King said. "Nothing in its original position. If there are any clues—anything that might point us toward whoever did this, I want it."

King started following his own directions, and the other two followed his lead. In ten minutes, they were sure there was nothing else in the cave they hadn't seen. Ridley's suit and shirt had no labels. The tripods were all generic items that could be purchased online. The sheet once had a tag, but it had been removed. The only thing with any writing on it was the video camera King had already taken.

"Let's get out of here," King said.

When they had rejoined Bishop and Knight outside the cave, Queen filled them in. King pulled a grenade from his belt, called "Frag out," and tossed it down the length of the tunnel. The resulting explosion was muted, but the blast still erupted out of the tunnel opening.

"Now what?" Rook asked.

"King, a single vehicle is approaching your position from the highway to the north." Deep Blue's voice did not sound concerned.

"That will be our ride out of here," King said. He turned to the others. "Let's walk out to meet him."

"Someone we know?" Bishop asked, as they started walking across the hardpan plain.

"An old friend," King said. "A local. Atalhuapa. Saved my life once."

In the distance, they could see a dust plume, as an open-topped Jeep made its way to their position.

When it got close enough, King waved. The man driving was brown and leathery, with deep creases in his face. When he pulled up close to them, he shut the Jeep off and leapt out of the vehicle with a surprising grace.

"Mr. Jack, sir!" he said. "So good to see you again."

He shook King's hand. Then he looked closely at what King and the others were wearing and asked, "Is there trouble again?"

"Not this time. We just need the ride to Ica and the airport, like we discussed on the phone."

The man smiled wide. "Of course. Anytime for you, sir."

The group got into the vehicle, with Bishop, the largest, up front. It was still a tight fit for six people, but the Jeep had an extended rear section with a double roll bar. King sat right behind Atalhuapa, so he could speak to the man.

"How is your lovely wife, Azucena?"

The old man laughed. "She speaks of you all the time, sir. You are much beloved in our home."

The group lapsed into silence for the often-harrowing, three hour drive to the airport. Along the way, the team packed their weaponry and anything identifying them as soldiers, besides their boots, into the packs, which they would leave with the old Peruvian man. King assured them he would keep their things out of harm. They dressed in civilian clothes, but the video camera stayed with King in a small satchel.

Atalhuapa dropped them at the airport and hugged King, then drove off, waving an arm until he was far down the road.

"What was that all about?" Rook asked.

"He saved my life out there on the plains, years ago," King told him. "I made a lot of money on my journey through time. So, I went back and visited him and his wife, and bought them a new house."

"Extravagant," Queen said, but she was smiling at the kind gesture.

"Not as expensive in his district as you might think. Call it a pricey taxi ride for today."

As was typical at smaller airports in South America, several people were milling around the entrance to the building. Some looked like they were on the hustle, trying to find newly arrived passengers looking for a taxi ride to somewhere. Others looked like they just had nothing better to do all day than hang around the entrance to an airport. This airport was strange in that it was little more than a small landing strip with some low buildings around it. There was no parking lot. Just a few cars parked outside the main building.

King eyed everyone he saw, checking for any hints of malice or danger.

Two men set off his mental radar immediately. They saw King and his team, and immediately began checking their cell phone screens. As if they were checking photos of him and the others.

"Crap," he said. "Rook. Two o'clock. Everyone be prepared to take evasive action."

Before anyone could move, both men withdrew Glock pistols and got off the hood of the old Ford sedan they had been sitting on.

"Move," King shouted.

Then a fusillade of bullets was headed their way.

TWENTY-SIX

Knight rolled to the ground behind a parked Ford sedan, as soon as King shouted.

Bullets from the two assailants riddled the glass front doors to the airport's lobby, and the concrete walls on either side. Two civilians went down in mists of pink. *They're terrible shots, and they're scared,* Knight realized. He recalled having spotted the shooters on the hood of a parked pickup truck across the street, and he wondered if they had ever fired weapons before. *Maybe they're just local thugs.*

Either way, they were a danger, and Knight suspected they would call for reinforcements. Worse, if the local army showed up—whether they were on the payroll for these thugs or not—they were likely to shoot everyone and ask questions later.

Knight could see Queen and Rook crouched down behind another parked car. He thought he'd seen King dive through the closing glass doors to the airport, just before they had disintegrated into a shower of cubed safety glass crumbles.

Knight looked around. No sign of Bishop.

Bishop.

Shin Dae-jung, callsign: Knight, was not thrilled at the revelation that his friend was alive. He should have been. He knew that. Instead, he felt betrayed by the ruse and furious that, even though Erik Somers had felt he needed time away, he had let his friends think he was dead.

That he let me *think he was dead.*

Knight kept most of his emotions to himself, but he could tell when his fellow teammates had finally processed their grief after Bishop's supposed death in Africa, years earlier. Rook, oddly, had seemed to take the longest to get over Bishop's death. But by two years after the event, it seemed to Knight that even Rook was done grieving. The others moved on with their lives and the new missions and the ever-present dangers.

Knight still wasn't done grieving.

All the members of Chess Team had formed bonds. They were all family. But Knight had developed a special bond with the huge man formerly, and now once again, known as 'Bishop.' They had come to a point in the field where they could predict each other's movements and thoughts.

The fact that Knight had no idea where Bishop was now, or what he would do next, as the two assailants continued firing bullets at the airport building, only served to highlight the absence of the bond that had been there and was now broken.

Knight seethed inside about it, but he knew now was not the time. They had no weapons since they had been about to board a commercial flight. Not even a pocket-knife. He was going to have to find something else to use as a makeshift weapon.

Knight lunged, rolling on the concrete sidewalk, and came to a crouch next to Queen, behind the car she and Rook were using for cover.

Bullets ripped up and sparked off the sidewalk where Knight had roll-ed, just a second too late.

"Sup?" Knight asked Queen, but she didn't respond to the humor. He rolled low and peered under the car's chassis, trying to figure out where the shooters were—and where Bishop had gotten to.

"So, this is great," Rook said. "What do we do? Wait until they run out of bullets and rush them?"

But before Knight could suggest a plan, King emerged from the shatt-ered glass doors of the lobby with a gun in his hand.

From a security guard, probably, Knight thought.

King fired three rounds, then dodged back for cover.

Knight used the opportunity to peek around the trunk of the car.

One of the shooters had taken cover behind their truck. The other was lying in the road bleeding from a shoulder wound. The man's greasy long hair covered his face, as he screamed in pain. His pistol was in the dirt of the road—halfway between the shooter and Knight's position. Knight weighed the possibility of rolling out there, scooping up the weapon, and taking cover on the far side of the road before the other gunman popped back up.

He never had the chance.

Knight heard a roaring voice, and he looked to his right. Bishop stood up from where he had been taking cover. There was a metal trash can surrounded by a thin concrete housing, just twenty feet away, but Knight hadn't seen the big man behind the small structure. But now, Bishop grab-bed the base of the concrete housing and ripped it up off the ground, the veins on his huge arms bulging from the strain.

Just as Bishop raised the chunk of concrete above his head, the shooter reappeared. Bishop threw the masonry across the street, as the man fired his gun at the building. The target caught a glimpse of motion, turned to look just as the concrete chunk bounced off the truck's roof and then impacted his face. The makeshift missile obliterated him.

Knight looked over at Bishop, who was now casually walking toward the discarded weapon in the street. Knight was still angry about the big man's deception, but suddenly, he was very grateful to have him back.

Knight stood up and joined Bishop in the street, leaning down to scoop up the discarded automatic, just as King emerged from the lobby.

"We're going to need to find a different way out of the country," King said.

Bishop reached down to the bleeding assailant and grabbed the man's phone. He tossed it to King, and then Rook and Queen joined them in the street.

"We should take their truck," Knight suggested, and he slipped into the driver's seat. There was a bullet hole in the side of it, from one of King's shots, and the roof's metal was all scraped up from the trash can housing Bishop had thrown, but with the other patches of rust and general decay on the vehicle, no one would notice.

Bishop climbed into the truck bed. Queen ran to the far side of the truck, retrieved the dead shooter's weapon, and hopped in back next to Rook and Bishop. King slipped into the cab next to Knight.

The keys were still in the truck, so as soon as King was mostly in the vehicle, Knight floored it and they sped down the road the way they had come with Atalhuapa.

"Police or army will be here soon," Knight said, casually. "What's the plan?"

King was looking through the shooter's cellphone. "Head southeast. We could get lost in Lima for a while but, with the locals looking for us and who knows how many other shooters, it might be easier to drive to the Bolivian border and try to get across and into La Paz. Look."

King flashed the phone in Knight's direction. On it was a close-up picture of King from a year or two ago. King flicked the screen with his finger, and the picture changed to one of Queen. Then he flicked it again, and Rook's grinning face appeared.

"They have us on playing cards," Knight said.

"No picture of Erik, but they have Asya. So, their deck is a little out of date. These guys didn't seem well trained. They're 'local knowledge.' But somebody sent them our pictures and told them to be on the lookout." King flicked through the phone a bit more, and then breathed a sigh of relief. "They didn't have time to send a text. But it won't take long before people hear we survived."

"So, who hired these guys?" Knight asked.

"The pictures came from 'Primate Industries,' and there's a bounty on each of our heads—a million dollars."

Shit, Knight thought.

That's going to make movement tough.

"If word gets out to every local security guard and soldier..." Knight left the thought unfinished. He knew King understood how hard it was going to be for them to get out of South America now.

"Just head for the border," King said. "They'll expect us to head to Lima and get lost in the city or try to get another flight out. They won't expect us to go deeper into the continent.

Then King used the phone to call Deep Blue.

Knight listened as King said simply, "We were made on departure. Tell Sis that she's on a playing card. We'll be taking the long way home."

TWENTY-SEVEN

Chess Team HQ, Siletz, Oregon

Asya walked the corridors of the subterranean Chess Team base for the third time that morning. She was going stir crazy. It had been a week since they had received word that the team was ambushed at an airport in Peru, and that their faces were on cards.

Using a deck of playing cards to remind soldiers of the faces of the enemy's most wanted valuable targets supposedly went back to the US Civil War and World War II. But the practice became more widely known after the 2003 United States Invasion of Iraq. The faces and identifying details for the fifty-two most wanted targets were printed on playing cards made by the Defense Intelligence Agency and distributed to US and allied troops. Saddam Hussein was on the Ace of Spades card. The thinking was that, as soldiers had down time, they would use the cards and become that much more familiar with the faces of high value targets.

Of course, since then, with the advent and proliferation of pocket-sized digital devices from PDAs to smartphones, most operators now had these so-called 'playing card' images digitally.

What it meant for the field team, who should have been back six days ago, was that they now had to split up and pursue different techniques for returning to the United States. Aleman had sent a plane to collect Erik—Asya still had trouble thinking of him as 'Bishop' now, after she had worn that title for so many years—from New Orleans, just this morning. The others had not been heard from yet.

For Asya, what it meant was that she was confined to the building. King had mentioned that she, too, was on a card. Presumably, whoever was looking for Chess Team—and they now knew it *wasn't* Richard Ridley—had no idea that Erik Somers was alive and back with the team. That gave Erik an advantage, and it allowed him to return to the US faster than the others. But it also presented Asya with a serious disadvantage. Although she was largely happy to stay at the base in Siletz with Duncan, the notion that she couldn't go outside of the building for fear of being spotted chafed her soul.

So, she paced the hallways.

Normally, she didn't care too much one way or the other about being indoors or outside. She took situations as they came. But the sun was shining outside, which was rarely the case in this part of Oregon. And the notion that she needed to stay indoors made her psychologically want to go out that much more. Waiting on news of her brother, or the rest of the team, was always hard when she wasn't with them. But feeling locked up in the underground hallways beneath the surface's Community Center was so much worse.

When she tired of pacing, she ran.

The hallways were laid out in a huge square, so she could do loops, as she had done every day since learning she'd be a prisoner in the facility because of her face. Despite her broken arm, which was still in an annoying half cast, held on with an Ace bandage, and which still rode in a sling around her torso, she was able to exercise. Mostly running, and she would stop periodically to do one-armed pushups. It was something, at least.

She sprinted down the first leg of the corridor, the stripes on the sides of her jogging track suit swishing as her legs pumped. It would be another four weeks before her arm was fully healed, although if she was careful with it, Aleman had said she'd be able to completely lose the cast in two. She planned to lose it in one and a half. If there was a goal, Asya would hit it. Or she would hit it early. Or she would completely destroy it.

That was just who she was.

She turned the right corner at the end of the corridor, without missing a stride. All the doors to either side of the corridors were shut. A general safety precaution. But she knew where everyone was. Her parents were sleeping in their guest room. Sara Fogg was in Felice Carter's room, taking a shift at keeping an eye on the comatose woman. Sara was Asya's sister-in-law now, but the woman still seemed distant to Asya. She wasn't sure whether it was because the scientist didn't like her or because the woman was just so preoccupied at most times with her work. Fiona was studying in her room. The younger woman seemed determined to follow in George Pierce's footsteps with archeology—perhaps more so in the last few days since his demise.

Asya reached the end of the loop's second leg, and she turned the corner. She knew that, even at full speed, as she was sprinting now, it would be another minute or so before she started sweating. Halfway down the hall were the double doors that led into the operations room. Duncan, Aleman, and Boucher would be in there, waiting for word from the team.

As she was. But Asya passed the doors at full speed, and turned the last corner, racing down the fourth leg of the loop.

In addition to burning off her irritation with exercise, she knew she had a decision to make.

The Bishop problem.

The choice wasn't so much about Erik's return from the dead. She wasn't even sure whether he would stay with the team now. Asya expected a lot of that had to do with whether Felice Carter came out of her coma or died. As Asya understood it, there was a remote possibility that, if Carter died, nothing else would matter anyway. The woman's consciousness was somehow quantum connected with every other living person on Earth. King had tried to explain it to Asya once. But she couldn't live her life in fear of some weird possibility of dying in the blink of an eye because something happened to a woman she didn't even know. Asya figured that Erik was likely to either vanish to some far-off place to grieve if Carter died, or he might want to suddenly rejoin Chess Team on a permanent basis if she passed away.

On the other hand, if the Carter woman came out of her coma, Erik might just go with her back to the type of work the two were doing with Pierce's group—or they might go off to do something else entirely. Asya had no idea.

Lines of sweat dripped from her forehead as she finished her third loop at close to her full speed. The bland corridors, with their faint scent of industrial cleaner, held nothing to sway her internal debate.

There was no reason that Erik returning to Chess Team or not needed to affect her own decision about whether or not to stay on the team. She could always pick a different callsign. Or the team could have two Bishops. The Chess analogy wasn't as important as what the team accomplished.

She slowed her pace to a leisurely jog, finding a good rhythm, and wiping the arm of her jogging suit across her forehead.

Her choice was not about Erik Somers or whether he would continue on with the team. Her decision to stay on the team was entirely about another man.

Thomas Duncan.

The man had been a prisoner for years, and she assumed he would resume his role as Deep Blue full time. But, after so long a period of imprisonment, when the current crisis was over, he might want to resign. *Thomas*, as she always thought of him, was not a young man anymore. In his late fifties, he was still far younger than most American ex-presidents, but age would be catching up with the man soon.

She hadn't had time to ask him what his longer-term plans were—or even if he had any. But Asya knew two things for sure. If Thomas wanted to be with her, she would be with him. If he wanted to retire and be a pig farmer in Bolivia, she would follow him there, and she would be happy. The difficult part would be if he didn't want to be with her. She knew how she felt about the man. And she knew he was twenty years her senior, but that didn't matter to her. If Duncan was not interested in a long-term relationship with her, the problem for Asya would then be whether to stay on the team, interacting with him but always at arm's length, or whether she would leave the group and attempt to find a new life of some sort for herself.

Asya slowed her jog to a walk for the final lap to cool down. She wasn't tired, but she was sweating. Any more laps and she would need to mop the hallway floors when she was done.

She had other interests besides being a paramilitary soldier, but her family and her life were intricately wrapped up with Chess Team, its history, and its mission to keep the world safe from rogue factions and power-mad maniacs like Ridley. And Asya was good at it. Although she felt sure she could be good at anything into which she threw her efforts and talent. But could she see herself as a college professor or as a small bookstore owner? She wasn't sure she could find fulfilment with that sort of a life.

She would need to make a decision at some point. But first she would wait to see how things progressed with Thomas. Maybe everything would fall into place on its own. Or maybe they wouldn't survive this latest threat.

Or maybe that Beloruchka*'s strange brainwaves will kill us all!*

Asya stopped in front of the operations room's double doors and went inside. As expected, she found Duncan and Aleman seated in chairs in front of computer screens, furiously tapping at keyboards, while Dom Boucher was refilling an enormous mug of coffee at a side table. Fiona must have come in during Asya's last lap. She was tapping away at a keyboard of her own.

"Any news?" she asked.

Dom nodded. "Rook. He just called in."

Asya turned to look at Duncan, and he had already turned in his chair to smile at her. She noticed the smile was more than just his relief at hearing from one of the field operatives. "He's in Boston. Called the voicemail and left a coded message."

"What did he mean about the cabin?" Dom asked.

"Hang on," Duncan said, and he played the message again, so Asya could hear it.

A second later they heard Rook's voice on the room's hidden speakers, but he was putting on a thick Boston accent.

> *Hey, Uncle Tommy! I just gaht in at frickin' Logan. The flight was the balls, even though the trip went to Chelsea. Dat horsehead bastid left to go find love, so I figured I'd head out to the cabin Way Westa Woostah. See ya soon.*

"Okay," Asya said. "I know my grasp of English idiomatic expressions isn't on par with native speakers yet, but I'm not even sure that *was* English."

Duncan laughed.

"You're not the only one," Boucher said.

Duncan invited Asya to sit near him.

"The translation is that he arrived safely at Boston's airport. Despite the mission going badly, he was pretty sure he wasn't being surveilled. Something being 'the balls' is good. Knight decided to go to Thailand to meet up with Pawn, apparently. And finally, Rook is going to get himself to extreme Western Massachusetts—probably by Greyhound bus, and we'll need to pick him up at a 'Cabin,' probably near the town of Lee. 'Cabin' is a prearranged term for the nearest landing strip, and there won't be one in Lee itself."

Aleman chimed in, as he looked at Google Maps, "There's a municipal airport to the north of Lee, in nearby Pittsfield. We'll pick him up there."

"Cripes, Tom, your people have better spycraft than the CIA," Boucher said as he plopped into a chair and sipped from his freshly filled mug.

"It's how they're still alive, Dom," Duncan said. "In fact, it's—"

Tom Duncan never got the chance to finish, because the lights in the room changed to flashing red, and a loud insistent beeping noise filled the room's speakers.

Asya understood that what she was hearing were the base's proximity alarms. Someone, up top, was trespassing.

TWENTY-EIGHT

"**You have to** let *me* go," Asya insisted.

"It could be nothing," Duncan said. "A salesman. A tourist. A kid on a dare. Whoever it is, they're not on any of our cameras yet, but we know that someone is looking for you because—"

"—of the playing card," Asya interrupted him. "I know! But I have the best—and most recent—training." She added the part about 'most recent' when she saw Duncan's eyebrows go up. He had been a Ranger. And Aleman was a Delta sniper before his injury.

"I'll go," Fiona volunteered. She didn't expect them to agree to it, but she knew it would interrupt Asya's outburst.

To her surprise, Duncan agreed. "You be careful. I know your... abilities...have grown, but you're to use them only as a last resort. Lew will go with you." He looked at Asya's bright red face and quickly added, "And if things go sideways, Asya will come out with heavy ordnance."

The comment diffused the Russian woman's tirade.

Fiona, for her part, decided to move fast before anyone could change their minds. She was on her way out of Operations' doors before Aleman was even out of his chair. Fiona knew where the weapons lockers were, and how to use everything in them. She raced down the hallway leaving Duncan and Asya to bicker amongst themselves. She knew Boucher would know to stay silent.

That just leaves...

"What are you doing, young lady?" Sara Fogg asked, just as Fiona was whipping open the doors to a weapons locker mounted in the hallway.

Mom.

But before she could reply, Aleman had caught up to her and reached into the locker, removing two Sig Sauer P226 pistols. He handed one to Fiona. "Intruder alarm, but it's probably just a looky loo or more likely a loose wire or something. We're going to be extra careful though, just in case." Aleman turned to Fogg, and at 6'2", he towered over her. He gave the woman his best shit-eating grin and held up his weapon for her to see. "Hence the guns. But you know Fi has had the best of trainers over the years. Always safety first."

Then he was loping down the hallway with his long stride, and Fiona raced after him before her adopted mother could offer any more objections.

"Thanks for that," Fiona said, when they got close to the door that led up a concealed staircase to a maintenance shed in the back of the community center.

Aleman smiled at her. "She's going to read me the riot act later, but now wasn't the time."

He handed Fiona an earpiece, which she slipped into her ear. The tiny white plug fit snugly, and instantly she could hear Duncan's ongoing monologue.

"—was moving on the west side of the compound. Looks like just one infiltrator. Either he knows exactly where the cameras are, or he's just racing from cover to cover behind the older buildings."

Aleman chimed in through the mic built into his earpiece, and Fiona could hear him both because he was next to her, and in her earpiece.

"Seems odd to attack during broad daylight."

As he said it, he and Fiona exited the stairwell into blinding sunshine.

It was a warm day, and it hadn't been this sunny in a while. Fiona didn't have any sunglasses, so she squinted against the glare.

"Split up and pincer him?" she asked Aleman.

He just nodded and started moving north. She understood she was meant to go south, and she took just a second to be proud that the man trusted her to be competent in the field.

Soon she would get a chance to see just how competent. She had been practicing in secret. The intruder wasn't the only one who knew where all the cameras were. Fiona had helped to place them.

Deep Blue was still speaking. "Target is behind the old Necotat House. I'll advise if I've got any movement. Fi? Wanna give me a mic check?"

She growled a quiet "Yes, Dad."

Duncan laughed. "I'll be sure to let King know I'm your new father."

Fiona crept around the corner of an old firehouse building. She often resented the place when she was younger, since it had been no help when her people were slaughtered and many of the buildings had been razed. As an adult, she recognized that the firefighters had been a volunteer force, as was the case in most rural areas around the United States. She also understood that there was little a volunteer fire squad could do against golems of animated rock.

That gave her an idea.

Instead of rounding the abandoned brick firehouse, she slipped inside of it, climbed the still intact stairs to the upper floor, and then used a metal ladder that was bolted to the wall to climb the building's old clock tower. From the outside of it, she would have an excellent view of the battlefield with her opponent. If it was just a trespasser, Aleman would be able to handle the person with no trouble. If it was an attacker, she would be more use from above.

As she moved up the last rusted rungs of the metal ladder, Deep Blue was in her ear again. "Fi, I've lost visual on you. I had you rounding the old fire station..."

"I'm inside," she said. "Getting to the roof to get some overwatch."

Deep Blue's next comment, "Excellent," and Aleman's comment of "That's a great idea," both overlapped, but Fiona got the idea.

She slipped out onto a small catwalk that rounded the clock tower. It was windy at this height, but not so bad that she would lose her balance. She could see the Necotat House—a small farmhouse style building with the second floor entirely gone, from fire. Its blackened stumps of timber and planks looked like stalagmites to Fiona.

To the north she could see the next house, which was little more than a pile of rubble. She waited for Aleman to emerge from behind it. He would be moving across soft grass, so if the intruder didn't move from cover, Aleman would be able to get up close.

"In position," Fiona said.

"Nothing new here," Deep Blue said. "He's off my visuals, but still behind Necotat."

They had named each remaining structure as a part of their security protocols. Fiona had chosen the Clatsop word 'Necotat' in honor of the tribes that once lived in the village. They had no records of who once lived in the house.

Fiona watched as Aleman slipped out from behind cover, and cautiously approached the northern side of Necotat.

"I'm going to flush him," Aleman said softly.

Fiona kept her eyes on the south side of the Necotat house.

If their quarry fled from Aleman's advance, that was where they would show up.

She could probably hit the person from the clock tower with her Sig if she needed to. But if the intruder posed a bigger threat, she could definitely hit them a different way.

Fiona concentrated and stared at the field of grass on the south side of the Necotat. She muttered softly in an ancient tongue, and the words sounded as if she were murmuring or even humming to herself. She started to lose herself in the rhythm. As she did so, several small sharp rocks pierced the grass below, moving upward like erupting incisors. The largest of them was no more than a few inches tall, but each spine of stone was flint thin, and would either trip a running human or possibly even puncture a shoe and foot—if the intruder didn't see the obstacles and avoid them.

Fiona strained her hearing, but she couldn't discern Aleman creeping toward the intruder—or any other sound over the birdsong in the distant trees. One way or another, something would happen soon.

Fiona's murmur became a recursive chant, and she was poised to alter it as soon as she saw motion.

Then she did.

A man ran around the southern wall, staying close to the Necotat's stained white vinyl siding. Roughly six feet tall, and thin, he was wearing an untucked button-down shirt and jeans. His hair was shoulder length and concealed his face. But there were two important features to the man that Fiona discerned immediately.

The first was that he was avoiding all the stone spikes as he ran.

The second was that he held a gun.

Instinct took over, and Fiona's low hummed murmur of the mother tongue, the ancient protolanguage she could use to animate the inanimate, burst forward from her lungs into a roaring Tibetan-esque shout.

Below her, giant slabs of granite shot upward out of the ground, encasing the intruder in a stone box. The walls were four inches thick. The tallest granite slab cracked, the top portion falling over, atop the box to form a lid. The intruder might be able to shove the top aside, but it would take time. Plenty of it.

"Tango's pinned on the south side," Fiona said. "I'm leaving my perch."

Without waiting for a reply from Deep Blue, she went back inside the access hatch, and descended the tower's steps. Just as she was exiting the old firehouse, she saw Aleman by the stone phone box she had created. He seemed relaxed, although he still held his weapon in his hand.

When he saw her, he waved her over.

She jogged across—and at the same time hummed a low deep chant that made the remaining stone spikes retreat into the overgrown grass.

"Who is it?" Fiona asked.

Aleman smiled and just gestured toward the slabs. "Ask for yourself."

Fiona leaned close to the stone and called out. "Who are you?"

The responding voice was familiar. "Good work, kiddo. You wanna let your old man out of the box?"

"Dad!"

TWENTY-NINE

Bank of China Tower, Hong Kong

General Bao Chen hated Hong Kong. At sixty, he was old enough to remember when it had been a cherished possession of the British and a bastion of all things capitalist. Now, over twenty years after the handover of the leased land back to China in 1997, his countrymen viewed the city with a mixture of lust and loathing.

On the one hand, the city and its colonial economic past was all the communist nation stood against. On the other hand, by even two years after the handover, capitalism and materialism had infected the people of China from Beijing to the deserts bordering Tajikistan. Now, everyone from the celebrities to the hoi polloi, saw Hong Kong living as the pinnacle lifestyle, or as the symbol for what others had and they did not. Expensive dinner party with Chinese actors and Chairmen of the military? Have it in Hong Kong. Planning a protest about wages or the treatment of Uyghurs? The streets of Hong Kong were the place.

As an old school communist who had lived through Mao's Cultural Revolution as a child, Chen despised the place and wished the damned British had insisted on keeping it.

Rather than a limousine—which he was entitled to as a Vice-Chairman of the Central Military Commission—Chen preferred public transit, and he had taken a cab in from the lavish airport to the Bank of China building. Located on Garden Road on Hong Kong Island, the tower was easily identifiable with its giant triangular patterns and its glass walls. At over a thousand feet in height, the tower was the tallest building in the city in 1990, but now was only the fourth tallest. The CMC owned the top eight floors. Like everything else in the city, to Chen's mind, it was ostentatious. He paid his driver, strode past the doorman, and strutted up to the elevator. No one attempted to slow him. He was in full dress uniform. The placard of ribbons on his chest, and the gold stars on his epaulets were enough to dissuade anyone from standing in his way—even if they didn't recognize him as a CMC chairman.

Rather than selecting the button for the plush lobby of the building's CMC section, he chose 70—the floor where the computer laboratories began. He had no need for coffee or pleasantries. He just wanted to see Lady Crimson's vaunted test.

The elevator whooshed upwards, making his stomach lurch. He could feel the car rapidly accelerating, heaving his body into the sky. Everything about the city put him in a bad mood, but Lady Crimson, a former criminal who had clawed her way into power in the People's Republic—*somehow*—always annoyed him further. The woman was savage and ruthless, but she was also impatient. The other members of the party all had plans. Long range plans. None of them had achieved their positions of power by a lack of vision. But Crimson's ideas were edgier and accelerated the timeframes for global domination in all fields. The other members of the party were impressed, so the woman had inched higher into power.

They haven't made the hideous bitch a member of the Central Committee yet, but that will be next.

The elevator ground to a smooth stop, and the doors slid open. The room's chilly temperature shocked him. With over forty computer stations and walls lined with giant LED television screens, Chen expected some warmth from the packed electronics. Instead, the air was kept at a chilly fifty degrees—twenty degrees colder than the outside air. The room was bustling with people, all quietly performing a variety of tasks at different workstations. The air had a hint of lemongrass and the volatile organic compounds of new electronics.

Chen strode out of the elevator, and across the room, the employees taking no notice of him, which was unusual. His attire commanded respect.

"General, I'm glad you're here," came a low rumbling voice from behind him. A voice far too deep and gruff to be feminine, but Chen recognized Lady Crimson's throaty tone.

He turned and saw her moving quickly between workstations, leaning down and over the shoulder of several workers, sometimes tapping a key or two on a keyboard. Then moving on. The woman was immense. Like an American linebacker. She was muscular and looked uncomfortable in her charcoal business pantsuit. Her face was coated with caked makeup and, like the last time Chen had seen her, she had long wavy red hair, although he had heard a report recently that she was now a blonde.

"You seem busy," Chen said, letting his irritation at the complete lack of reception show in his face.

"We're in the middle of testing the process," Crimson said, patting another computer jockey on the shoulder as she rushed past him, and then past the General. "I hope you don't mind. We just need a couple more minutes here, and I should have some very pleasing results for you, sir."

Chen liked the sound of that, and his hackles folded. "When we last spoke, you thought you wouldn't be ready for tests for another month." He walked after the woman as she bustled through the room, adjusting settings on panels of touch screens, before moving to the next seated terminal operator, and glancing over that shoulder.

"We were very lucky, General. We had several breakthroughs all at once. It's very exciting."

Indeed, even though he greatly disliked Lady Crimson, her enthusiasm was contagious, and he found himself becoming excited at the prospect of success with this new experimental weaponry.

The hulking woman reversed direction and started back toward him. She stopped at a complicated array of computer communications equipment beside an old-fashioned phone handset.

"I feel like I don't have enough hands. Would you hold this for ten seconds?"

The woman pointed to a red spring-loaded lever, and then pivoted away to the next screen she needed to adjust.

Chen sighed and held his wide thumb against the lever, watching the woman move from screen to screen. "The results from this are going to be revolutionary, General."

"Yes, you've said," Chen released the red lever in now regrowing irritation. "But I must tell you, High Honorable Lady, there are those in the Central Committee who still have their doubts about this approach."

Crimson stopped her frantic motion and turned to face the General slowly. "Yes, sir, and I know that you are one of them. But I assure you, in a few minutes the results will erase your doubts."

Chen was not about to be placated. "You really believe it will be in the best interest of the People's Republic to murder several million people, just to divert suspicion when we utilize this weapon on other nations? You realize how insane that sounds? The Great Chairman Mao was responsible for the deaths of nearly fifty million of our own people—but not intentionally!"

"General," Lady Crimson said, straightening up to her full height, "I really do understand your concern but, as we've discussed, a weapon of this magnitude is going to send shockwaves through the world. Everyone is eventually going to figure out who's behind it. But, for a short period of time, the element of surprise will be on our side."

Chen slammed his hand down on the console. "You act like we have already decided to use this experimental weapon of yours. You have convinced some, including the President, but the Central Committee has not approved moving forward with this project. There are still many questions to be answered and many decisions to be made. Before anyone decides to execute several million Han Chinese, we must be absolutely certain of victory."

Lady Crimson smiled, not viciously, as she was known to do, but gently, like she was about to impart some wisdom. "You see, General Chen, this has always been your greatest problem. A lack of certainty in your own ability to succeed. I suffer from no such self-delusions. We *will* be victorious. We will activate the weapon. We will kill six million Chinese men, women, and children. Well, I say *kill*... But you know what I mean. The rest of the world will be too busy looking at America and Russia and wondering which of them tested the weapon on us, for anyone to consider that the source was here. The Committee *will* get on board with it. They really won't have a choice. This is going to happen. Well, I say *going to...* It's actually already happening."

Chen was astonished.

"What?"

Now Crimson's gentle smile transformed into her usual predatory leer. "This wasn't a test, General. The satellite is live, and the weapon has been fired."

Chen was flabbergasted now. His mouth dried up and he had a hard time asking questions, "What– How are–" Finally he settled simply on, "When?"

Lady Crimson's lip snarled even higher into a deadly sneer. "You activated the weapon minutes ago when you touched that red switch. The people of Kunming should be feeling the weapon's effects right now. All six million of them."

Kunming, Yunnan Province, China

Over seven hundred miles away, in the provincial city of Kunming, a woman named Ying Yue suddenly felt nauseated. She'd had a normal breakfast and, as she walked along the shore of Dian Lake, she was feeling fine—until she wasn't.

The lake, at only a quarter of the size of Lake Champlain—the United States' sixth largest freshwater lake after the Great Lakes—was still immense when seen from its shore. It resembled an ocean fringed with low mountains and hills in the hazy distance, and it was large enough that the strong wind whipping off the mountains struck up little waves across its murky green surface. But the sun was shining, and people were all going about their business in the bustling city. Until Ying Yue looked up from her cramping stomach, and saw people stopping in their tracks, grabbing on to benches for balance, and wobbling on their feet, as if they were all suddenly dizzy.

She doubled over in pain, her head throbbing and pounding, and her limbs increasingly heavy. She collapsed to her knees just as the bones in her forearms extended, jutting spikes backward from her elbow joints. The newly elongated ulna bones tore through her skin and grew to fine points.

She screamed in pain but couldn't hear herself, over the agonized howls of all the other people in the small park. She had time to glance upward at the nearest man, to see his forehead bulging under his skin, and the seams of his suit jacket ripping as his musculature swelled, before the next wave of pain struck her.

Her feet grew as she watched, and the toenails—now pointed claws—savaged their way out of her running shoes, separating the rubber from the leather uppers, as if they were made of nothing more than tissue paper.

Ying Yue's mind revolted at the sudden and unexplained hypertrophy of bone, muscle, and ligament. In moments, her brain stopped processing the pain entirely.

Just like every other human in the metropolitan area of the city.

Their cognitive capacities reduced to bare creatures, their bodies altered and distorted, their backs hunched, and limbs elongated. If there was anyone left in the city who knew what a gorilla was, they might have remarked on the similarity. But they'd have been wrong. Gorillas were peaceful. Herbivores. And highly intelligent.

The newly transformed populace recovered from the event that had devolved them. They struggled to clawed hands and feet, tentatively moving around in an environment that should have been familiar to them but was now unrecognizable.

Unseen by human eyes, unnoticed by world governments, a small satellite swept over the Earth's surface, in Low Earth Orbit, 1200 miles above the calamity, on its way to its next target.

THIRTY

The White House, Washington, D.C., USA

"You can go right in," Cathy Bennington, the President's personal secretary said, from her desk outside the Oval Office door.

Dom Boucher and Danielle Rudin walked into the office. It wasn't the first time for either of them. Boucher was the former Director of the CIA, and Rudin was the current Director. Before Boucher's retirement, they had worked together. The room was empty except for the new President, who was leaning back on one of the two sofas that sat astride the carpet's Great Seal of the United States. The central portion was a circular cutout, and it showed a bald eagle clutching an olive branch in one set of talons and thirteen arrows in the other. The familiar banner with *E Pluribus Unum*–'out of many, one'–was fluttering from the great bird's mouth. Boucher knew that, in times of war, the circular piece of carpet was removed and replaced with an exact replica, except that in the wartime circle of carpet, the bird's head faced the side holding the arrows.

He was pleased to note that the bird was still facing the olive branch.

But for how much longer?

The new President, Jonathan Robert Beaman, was looking across the eagle, past the facing sofa, at a large video screen that had been installed on the Oval Office wall since the last time Boucher had set foot in the room. On screen was a very familiar face.

Richard Ridley.

"Mr. President," Boucher said, as if announcing himself.

Beaman simply turned his head and waved a hand at Boucher and Rudin to join him seated.

"Did we get the count yet, Dani?" he asked.

Rudin sat and bowed her head solemnly. "Six million, eight hundred thousand, and forty-two."

"Sweet Mother Mary," Beaman swore under his breath.

Boucher had never met Beaman before—Dom retired before the previous President, Matthew Chambers, had chosen Beaman to serve as Vice President. But from everything Boucher knew about him, Beaman was a good man. And every piece of intelligence Rudin, Boucher, or Tom Duncan and his team could find, indicated that Jonathan Beaman had no connections whatsoever to the Consortium. He could still be working with them, but Boucher doubted it.

"Domenick, Danielle tells me you are the man with all the answers. So, what can you tell me about this homicidal maniac on my TV screen who just somehow turned an entire Chinese city into a bunch of walking barbarians?"

"The first thing I can tell you about him, Mr. President, is that the man is actually dead," Boucher said.

"What?" Rudin sat forward in her chair, and Beaman was also at attention now.

Boucher continued. "This video, and the last ones, when former President Chambers and the Russian premiere were assassinated, were filmed before any of those events took place. I have it on good authority that this man's corpse was found in the Peruvian desert. So, someone from this 'Consortium' is trying to deflect attention by pointing the finger at a dead man."

"I think you'd better start at the beginning, Mr. Boucher," Beaman said.

"It's quite a tale, sir."

Hours later, Boucher finished summarizing the last several years of Chess Team's adventures and their attempts to stop the megalomaniac Ridley. He recounted the story behind the team's founding, Tom Duncan's imprisonment—with interjections from Rudin, who had placed Duncan in a custom prison site in the Arctic—and his subsequent abduction and years as a prisoner at the hands of unknown enemies. Boucher told the President of Chess Team finally finding Duncan on the Desolation Islands, and about the attacks on the team in South Africa, and about their losses.

Beaman, understandably, had many questions. At the end, he looked exasperated. "So, you're telling me this Ridley character is gone for good this time, and that someone else is behind the murders of world leaders and turning the brains of six million people to pudding? We don't even know how this was done yet?"

"The Agency's best are hypothesizing that it was a space based weapon," Rudin put forth.

"That tracks with what Mr. Duncan believes, sir. But again, it's just conjecture. We haven't seen the weapon system."

Beaman stood up and began pacing the room. Rudin and Boucher also stood.

"No idea at all who else was in this damned Consortium? The Chinese are pointing the finger at us and at Russia, and they're screaming pretty loudly about it. And now that I find out Matthew was involved with these people, I don't really have a leg to stand on when I deny we had any part of it. I mean, did we, Danielle?"

"Not to my knowledge, sir," Rudin seemed flustered. Even as the Director of the CIA, knowing what the last President had been involved in was way above her head. Boucher expected Beaman might have more information on that than she did.

"Nothing definitive, here, sir, but Mr. Duncan and I have a strong contender."

"I cannot believe that I am taking advice from one of the only people ever convicted of treason against this country," Beaman said, referring to Duncan, "but lay it on me, Dom. We are one step away from a global World War III. No ideas are too crazy."

Rudin looked at Boucher expectantly.

"China."

"I take it back," President Beaman said, sinking into his chair behind the broad Resolute Desk. "Some ideas *are* too crazy. Explain."

Boucher did.

He explained the entire LCROSS fiasco during Duncan's time, and the plausible deniability theory of using a weapon of mass destruction on your own people first, to throw off suspicion when you start using it on others.

Beaman sat silently for a moment considering the ramifications.

Then he stood rapidly.

"Danielle, am I correct in understanding that Tom Duncan is still *persona non grata* with the United States of America?"

"Yes, sir," Rudin replied.

Beaman turned to Boucher. "And am I also correct in understanding that this Chess Team is currently a free organization, no longer under the control of the US Military?"

Boucher nodded.

"Well, let's start here, Domenick. Duncan is pardoned of all crimes effective immediately. I don't need your operatives to come back under control of Admiral Ward, but I do want them reporting directly to Duncan, and I want him reporting to me. This organization will have my full but private support. I can't publicly endorse this paramilitary squad, but it sounds like, when things end up going bananas, Chess Team is always in the center of it. I'd rather have them at my disposal than at my back."

"Yes, sir," Boucher said, smiling.

He knew what was coming next.

"I want you on board until this crisis is over as well. I can't give you Director of National Intelligence because Congress would make it take forever..."

"I completely understand, sir. Title is unimportant. I serve at the pleasure."

"Thank you, Dom. Work with Dani. Work with Duncan. Track down your leads and keep me updated. If this is China or some rogue faction operating out of China, I need to know about it yesterday. If this was someone in our own government, I need to know about it sooner than that."

THIRTY-ONE

Siletz, Oregon

A few days after his arrival at Siletz, and his daughter's successful ambush of him, Jack Sigler walked into the operations room to a crowd of smiling faces.

"What's going on?" he asked.

Duncan and Aleman were at their traditional places at the computer terminals, but the room was stuffed with most of his team and his extended family. Sara was there, and his parents. Fiona was in the room. Asya, Rook, and Queen, too. Knight and Pawn were overseas. Erik was not present, but King felt that was natural, since the man had hardly left the comatose Felice Carter's side since he had returned. Before the obvious additional absence of George Pierce had a chance to put a scowl on King's face, Duncan answered.

"I just got off the phone with Dom. Chess Team is now an independent mercenary force, fully funded by the United States government. Oh, and I now have a full Presidential pardon." The man smiled broadly.

It was good news indeed. But it didn't get them any closer to the perpetrators of the Kunming Attack or the assault on the Herculean Society base that had killed Pierce, Gallo, and Dourado.

King got right to business. "Do they have any more intel on the attack?"

Duncan seemed to understand right away that King was asking about Kunming. The intel on the Cape Town attack was already stale, and no one seemed to know anything. "We have a lot more scientific information on what happened. Cognitive degradation. Accelerated skeletal and musculature redefinition. Actual changes to the victims on a genetic level. I'd hazard a guess that Manifold Genetics research was involved, but as we know, Richard Ridley himself is already dead. What we still don't know is the who or the how."

King pulled up a chair next to Queen at a nearby conference table. Rook smiled at him and slid him a bottle of water.

"I might actually have some ideas on the how," Lewis Aleman interjected. "I remembered reading a white paper by an Air Force colonel on weaponizing genetically engineered bioweapons. And I was thinking about it. There's a clear zone of delineation between the attack zone in Kunming and the surrounding area. If people were inside the zone, they were 'devolved' by the attack, for lack of a better term. If they were outside the zone, they were completely unaffected. Information coming out of the PRC is scarce, as you might imagine. But we do have confirmation that there was no halfway measure—either people were devolved, or they were just feet away outside the zone of effect, and they were not."

"Means the attack wasn't airborne," King said.

"Is that what it means?" Rook asked. "Couldn't have been a directional attack from outside this zone?"

"Wind patterns," Duncan said. "If the attack was aerosol, the wind would have carried it past a firm line or demarcation."

"But there is a solid line," Asya said, pulling up a map onto a large wall-mounted LED screen for everyone in the room to see.

Peter and Lynn Sigler had been sitting quietly off to the side of the room, but now Peter stood up, as if asking permission to be a part of the conversation.

When Duncan looked at him, he spoke. "You know, the Soviets were experimenting with satellite technology that would allow a clear border attack like that, using nanoparticles attached directly to light wavelengths. My understanding was it never really went anywhere, but if the attack was space based..."

"That was my presupposition, as well," Duncan nodded. "Especially since my captors were so intent on learning about the LCROSS mission. And if you're correct, Peter, the genetic material could have been delivered via nanoparticles, and the beams of light would only have blanketed the target area. That might explain the non-dispersal of whatever the infectious material was."

Queen leaned forward at the conference table. "That's the *how* of it then, or something similar. What we need is the *who*. Where are we with the camera label?"

"Nowhere," Aleman said. "It was made and probably sold in Hong Kong, but it gave us no more information than that."

Duncan sighed and leaned back in his chair. "It's not completely nowhere. It points a stronger finger at the Chinese—or someone operating out of China, with or without their knowledge. But Peter's information suggests Russia's involvement, too."

"Unlikely," Lynn Sigler chimed in. "Russian security is lousy. Far more so in the last twenty years. It's like a revolving door of mobsters and terrorists over there. The experimental satellite attack idea could easily have been pilfered—or sold. To any bad actors."

"That brings us back to the Chinese," King said. "Any word from Knight and Pawn?"

Aleman tapped on his screen, bringing up a map of Hong Kong, which he then transferred to the room's larger screen. King could see the familiar shape of Hong Kong Island, and he saw red dots on eight locations across the island and the nearby Kowloon peninsula. "Knight is with Pawn, and they've been tracking down the locations that sell the camera that was used. All the businesses are legit. So far only three of them had the cameras in stock, and no one recalls selling any in the last year. Not a popular model, they were told. That might work in our favor."

"And Primate?" King asked.

"Nothing. They don't exist as far as we can tell. Peter and Lynn have put out feelers in Russia but, so far, no one knows anything about an organization called Primate Industries."

"In this room, we have the gathered intelligence might of Chess Team, the Herculean Society, the now-defunct Cerberus Group, the US military and intelligence communities, and the Russian military intelligence communities," King said.

"And the scientific community," Sara Fogg said. "I've asked around in my circles, too. Nothing, I'm afraid."

"Right," King nodded. "So how is it that no one anywhere has heard a peep from this Primate Industries?"

"The answer," Tom Duncan said, "Is that they are exceptionally good...or exceptionally small."

Just then, King's cellphone vibrated, and he glanced at the screen. Then he stood up. "Bingo. Doesn't matter how good or how small. Our network is too broad. One of my Society contacts in Macau just got back to me. He's heard whispers about Primate in the criminal underworld over there. Just faint hints. Nothing too solid. But that's another connection to China. Looks like that's where we're heading."

THIRTY-TWO

Chungking Mansions, Kowloon, Hong Kong, China

Anna Beck was not a fan of China. She had spent too much time in the country—and much of it running for her life. She could speak the languages and knew her way around, but it never felt welcoming to her.

Pretending to be a shoestring backpacker chafed even more. But the days of Chess Team having endless resources were largely over. Even with their new-found forgiveness from the US government, she and Knight hadn't been able to blast into the country in their own private military aircraft with guns blazing. But that was mostly down to the nature of this work. Not espionage. Not battle. But shitty legwork, slipping in and out of seedy electronics shops in the shabbier parts of the city, looking for leads on a generic video camera.

She had met up with Knight in Thailand, and they had flown over separately as tourists, staying in the largest and most notorious backpacker slum in the city. Chungking Mansions was a building that was meant to be residential, but it had turned into low budget 'guest house' accommodations for travelers, shops, cheap-eats restaurants, and a gathering place for ethnic communities. It was also a great place for low-level street crime, and to score illicit drugs.

Anna Beck, callsign: Pawn, was after the criminal element, but not for what they could offer the world-weary traveler. Knight had received word two days ago that Chess Team had a lead on Primate Industries having connections to the Macau underworld. The city of Macau was just an hour's boat ride away, so it stood to reason if organized crime in Macau had heard of Primate, she might be able to get a whiff of them in Hong Kong, too. Besides, operating in Macau itself would be too difficult. There were fewer tourists, and the criminal underworld was more closed. It would have to be Hong Kong. But what went down in one city usually went down in the other as well. The trick would be in gaining information without putting herself and Knight in danger.

Her room was just large enough for a toilet, a sink, and two smaller than normal twin-size beds. The communal shower was down the hall. The buildings were a warren of skeezy travelers, and the scabbiest locals and thugs. The idea of actually using the communal showers filled her with thoughts of any number of potential scenarios where someone might attempt to rob or rape her. 'Attempt' would be the key word. She could hold her own, but she didn't want to blow their cover. She would wait until they could get a room at a proper hotel for the shower. Until then, her unwashed state helped her blend in with the other occupants. Her room was on the inner core of the building, and there was an air shaft outside her window, into which people had been throwing trash for decades. Her room was on the seventh floor, but she could only see windows down to floors six and five. The lower windows would have been covered with trash.

Everything about the place oozed age and disrepair. She was surprised no one had bulldozed it yet.

She checked her phone for any final messages from Knight—he should have been in place by now—and then she left her room with her one small bookbag-sized backpack. It contained all her belongings in China. She traveled light.

Chess Team had several ID card drops in countries around the world. Lockers where she could go, swap out her existing passport and other ID cards, grab a stack of cash, and even pick up a gun. With the cash, she could buy new clothes on the go, discarding the old outfits, especially when she needed to throw off pursuit. So, it wasn't necessary to carry much more than what she had on her. And if any of the multiple pickpockets in the building tried their trade on her, they would walk away with broken fingers at best.

She kept her money and ID in a secure belt around her waist, inside her clothes. A thin sweatshirt was wrapped around the black Glock 17 in her backpack. Along with a Lonely Planet guidebook, a notebook, pens, and other assorted crap to disguise her as a typical backpacker. The gun was the only reason for her to cling hard to the faded and battered red backpack as she boarded the elevator with three gaunt and probably drug-riddled Malaysian men for the ride down to the shopping arcade. The heat in the city meant she couldn't wear a thicker outer garment under which she could conceal the gun, so it had to ride in the backpack.

The Malaysians were not interested in anything except their next score, so the elevator ride was uneventful. She stepped out into the noise and chaos of the mall. Loud music blared from several different store fronts, beckoning customers in, but usually repelling Westerners. The hallways were packed with people coming and going, store vendors loudly hawking their wares, and the occasional pickpocket slipping past them all.

Pawn knew the terrain though, and she knew the shop she was heading toward. It was a place that sold bootleg Blu-Ray copies of brand-new films that were still on cinema screens in the US and the UK. But the shop also sold every illicit drug you might think to ask for and twenty you'd never heard of. Pawn knew you could also find jobs, where the pay was under the counter, and sometimes did *not* involve the tourist getting abducted and sold into human trafficking rings. It was just the sort of place where she could buy some illegal crap, while dropping hints that she was looking for work with Primate Industries.

She made her way through the crowd and walked right past Knight, who was wearing a nondescript Adidas track suit, and looking at scarves on a spinner rack as tall as he was. She was tempted to goose him as she passed, but she wanted to maintain her cover, just in case anyone was watching them. No one was supposed to be, but it paid to be cautious—especially since his face was in the Primate deck of digital cards. Hers was not, she had been pleased to discover. And in a city like Hong Kong, crowded as it was with thousands of individuals from every Asian country on top of China, Knight could pretty easily get lost in the crowd. He was Korean-American, but his looks could pass for Chinese, and he had frequently been mistaken for Singaporean. Knight would have examined every way in and out of the shop already. He would know who worked in the store, and he would be ready to react if anything went wrong when Pawn was inside.

She continued past him and into the door of the store, moving straight for the New Releases wall, looking impressed and excited, as many tourists do. She had exactly zero concerns for her safety. Knight suffered a terrible eye injury, years ago, in Africa. Since then, he had been fitted with many cutting-edge cybernetic eyes, until they found one that worked exceptionally well and caused him no pain. One of its many features was an X-ray mode. He could stand outside the shop and literally keep his eye on her and what was happening with her, *through* the wall.

It didn't take long for Pawn to attract the attention she wanted.

"You need help, lady?"

Pawn turned to the slim Chinese man. He was wearing jeans and a T-shirt that was a size too small for him, and he was sizing her up, trying to decide how much he could sell to her.

"Actually, I heard this was the place to come to get a little work. Just something to keep me on the road for a while, you know? My friend said she got a part time gig with the Primate Company."

The man's demeanor changed immediately. His guard was up but he also thought this might be a big score for him. "Primate Industries, you mean?"

"That's the one," Pawn said, smiling as if the man had just saved her life.

"We should go talk in back," the man said.

THIRTY-THREE

Undisclosed Location, China

Lady Crimson walked through the nondescript hallway of the underground base, pretending she didn't know where she was being led by her military escort. But she knew precisely what was waiting for her.

The People's Republic of China, a communist nation since 1949, had a government like many other twenty-first century, power-player nations. It was comprised of numerous organizations, committees, and commissions, both civilian and military. Power appeared to be dispersed across all these governing bodies and offices, along with the courts and political groups with affiliations in each of the above. But when it came right down to it, a small handful of individuals held the true power and, in China, many of them held multiple titles and leadership roles on multitudes of departments and bureaucratic bodies. For instance, the President was also the Paramount Leader, the Head of State, the Commander in Chief of the armed forces, and the Leader of the Communist Party. Along with the Conference Chairman, the Congress Chairman, and the Head of Government, the President and the three other men controlled most of the nation's systems.

As such, just like with most governments, it was rare to have an event that brought them all together under one roof, with their seconds, and the heads of military and civilian bodies.

But that was what this would be. A formal rebuking in front of the entirety of China's government, all gathered in one enormous room.

She was certain that she was meant to be terrified, but she was having too much of a good time. Lady Crimson liked all the pomp and ceremony, but she especially loved anything that pulled the elusive men—and they were always *men*—who truly held the power, out of their normal hidey holes and elaborate offices. Her military escort had showed up to collect her just a week after she had tricked General Chen into launching the de-evolution attack on Kunming. He had been furious. Understandably so.

But she had patiently explained her plan to the ruling powers on more than one occasion and, while she knew Chen and several others had reservations, she also knew that those few shadowy men higher than Chen in the hierarchy—the National Leaders—were all in favor of the plan.

Still, she had made Chen look like a fool, and she had moved ahead with the plan, forcing China into going down the path that entailed, without authorization and approval.

Now would come the rebuke. The men in the room at the end of the hallway would all feel smug right now. Until she stepped through the doors. Then, like always, they would cower from true power.

Hers.

Her escorts stopped outside the double wooden doors, and executed smart marching turns, taking up positions outside the door. Without any words or instructions to her, she was expected to understand that she should walk through the doors and into her dressing down.

In fear.

Instead, she strode through the doors like the physical powerhouse she was.

Inside, the room was a circular auditorium. Large enough to house several hundred people. And all the chairs were filled. The chairs circled around a table with four men seated at it, which faced a single podium, behind which the accused could stand and explain themselves.

This wasn't a rebuke.

It was a tribunal.

A court that had already determined her guilt and her punishment.

She walked slowly down the center aisle, spotting the heads of Committee, Politburo, Secretariat, and various chiefs of commissions like National Security and Central Military.

She knew she had some friends in the room. Not in the top slots of power. But that would change. They just needed to know that she could succeed where others had failed.

General Chen was one of the four men seated at the table in the center of the huge room. Lady Crimson noted that the Conference Chairman was not present. She understood. Chen had whined so hard that in addition to giving him this circus in which to punish her, he had also been given a high-ranking position in the Chinese Communist Party—a higher position even than he had held as the chief of the entire military. It was just the sort of reward for which a good, life-long communist like Chen strove.

Chen leaned forward to the microphone on the table in front of him and said, "Lady Crimson, would you please take your place at the podium, so we might begin."

His voice echoed around the chamber slightly. She was close enough already that she would have heard him speak without the PA system. That was for show. Just like all of this.

It also did not escape her notice that he had referred to her in this company as 'Lady Crimson' rather than as 'High Honorable Lady,' which was her formal title. It wasn't an oversight. She assumed she had been demoted. Perhaps they even planned to execute her.

Rather than obeying, she stopped in place, halfway down the aisle toward the center of the arena, and she looked around the room. Junior members of the party were at the outer circumference, but no actual security guards or soldiers had been admitted into this most elite of spaces.

That was a mistake, she thought.

She waited in place, looking around the room, until Chen leaned forward toward his mic again, and then she took slow strides forward, making him look foolish, should he again request that she start walking—since she already was. She watched him struggle to stop himself from speaking, and she smiled directly at him. He saw her and understood how she had manipulated him. His face turned beet red, and he diverted his eyes from her gaze.

Rather than subserviently waiting on formality, she approached her podium, tapped the microphone, and heard a reverberating thud through the auditorium's hidden speakers. She leaned down and spoke into the black grill on the end of the mic. "Paramount Leader, Head of Government, Congress Chairman, and our newly promoted Conference Chairman General Chen, please allow me to say just one thing, before we begin."

She waited, and the President, also the 'Paramount Leader' she addressed, nodded. He was a very short man with a wide face that suggested maybe somewhere in his lineage were more ethnic groups than just the Han Chinese, but that had been scrubbed from any official records long before he became a well-known face in politics.

Lady Crimson could see that General Chen had been about to deny her the chance to speak, but even he had to take his cues from the President. His face was crestfallen at the simple nod.

She leaned in, to the mic again, and simply said, "China thanks you for your services, but they are no longer required."

There was a moment of shocked silence, followed by exactly the indignant uproar she expected. But by the time the uproar began, she had shoved the wooden podium out of the way and was leaping up into the air.

She cleared the table in front of the four men, reaching out with both hands. Her leap took her between the President and his cousin, who was seated next to him and acted as Head of Government. Her huge hands landed on each man's throat, and with a quick twist, she ripped away skin and trachea from both, in an arc of arterial blood spray.

Her powerful legs absorbed the momentum of her landing, and she twisted her torso, lunging to the side as she came out of her squat. The impact broke the next man's neck. The Congress Chairman, a very skinny man, stood no chance.

Her lunge into him knocked General Chen sideways out of his chair, and onto the floor.

Before he could scramble away, she was on him, clawing and tearing at his clothes, like a wild beast.

Most of the rest of the assembled government employees raced for the auditorium's locked doors, where they were crushed to death in stampedes. The doors never opened. The soldiers guarding them were on Lady Crimson's payroll and they were loyal to her and her vision of the future.

Those who did not run, stayed in their seats, and witnessed the carnage, waiting for their turns at the hands of the woman's murderous rage, while the seventy-two-year-old Chinese Communist Party gasped its last breaths.

THIRTY-FOUR

Chungking Mansions, Kowloon, Hong Kong, China

Shin Dae-jung watched through the wall with his artificial eye's 'x-ray vision' mode. Of course, it wasn't really *x-ray*. The eye could function as a passive backscatter receiver. It utilized things that were all around us, like background radiation, cosmic rays, and radio waves. The eye rendered an approximate image based on the diffusion rate. So, human bone showed up because it blocks more radiation than flesh or clothing.

The scene before him was like black mist, with certain shapes—the denser ones—standing out in more contrast against the murky background. But it was enough for Knight to keep track of Pawn as she walked with the salesman toward the counter and then around it.

Knight moved down a small alley at the side of the store, glancing at the wall with his cybernetic eye, acting like a lost tourist searching for a bathroom. He knew from previous recon that the hallway led to a very narrow service corridor that was usually locked. The corridor ran behind most of the shops in the arcade, so they could load wares into their stores out of sight from customers. Today, the door to the corridor was unlocked. Knight had jammed its lock mechanism.

He waited outside the door, lurking in the shadows. If the man stepped into the corridor with Pawn, he would want to pursue them—but only when he wouldn't be seen. If they stayed in the back room, and things looked fine, Knight would just wait it out. Pawn was the leader on this mission. He would take his cues from her. He'd known Anna Beck for years now, and he knew her to be extremely competent in the field. More than him when it came to stakeouts and periodic espionage activities. He was a soldier. He could do the James Bond stuff, but he didn't love it. It was usually around too many people, and one of the things being a sniper afforded a person was space and quiet. He was used to being out in a distant field, concealed by trees, or hanging out in the window of an abandoned building. Most of his activity with Chess Team over the years was either frantic action, or relaxed waiting from an overwatch position.

Knight leaned against the wall, watching the back room, as the employee led Pawn into the room. They stood in the center, facing each other for a moment, apparently talking. Then the discussion looked like it was becoming heated, because Pawn's arms went out from her sides for emphasis.

Two shapes moved from the corner of the room—two more men, and Knight could see them moving toward Pawn from behind.

Shit, he thought.

Although he couldn't see the fabric with his eye, he saw one man come up behind Pawn, and the other slide what had to be a sack over her head. Every fiber of Knight's being wanted to move, but he had to first wait to see which direction they would go. He was closer to the back door, but the men could take her out the front of the shop if they were brazen.

Pawn struggled, but then the larger of the two assailants that had snuck up on her head-butted her, and then slung her body over his shoulder, making way for the back door from the shop to the corridor.

Here we go, Knight thought.

He moved closer to the door and grabbed the handle, but he was surprised to see Pawn moving just a bit. She had been faking being knocked out. As he quietly slid into the narrow loading corridor, he could see her head moving slightly from side to side, behind the back of the man carrying her over his shoulder. Knight knew she was listening and trying to get a read on the space around her before she made her move.

Now fully in the corridor, Knight could use his regular vision to see the two armed men down the corridor. The larger of them was carrying Pawn. These were muscled toughs—or at least the larger of the two was. Knight figured the second man wasn't much bigger than he was. Both of them had zero operational awareness, though. The men just turned and started down the long hallway toward a loading dock at the far end.

With no need to be subtle, Knight started jogging after the two men, a pistol already in his hand. He didn't have a suppressor. No point, really. If shooting had to start anywhere in China, things were going to go horribly wrong. In the tight confines of the corridor, the weapon would be obscenely loud, so he planned not to even use it, if possible. It was in his hand more for persuasion.

As it turned out, no posturing would be necessary.

Pawn suddenly lunged up off the larger man's shoulder, grabbing his head with both hands and twisting hard. As the man's dead body began to slump downward, she thrust herself up and off him, windmilling her legs out sideways, and clocking the second man in the face with her heel. Then as the second body began to follow the first toward the floor, she starfished her body outward, her legs and arms reaching the walls on either side of her, and she stopped abruptly, poised in midair, listening hard for any other attackers or movement. She heard Knight running toward her, because she whipped her still covered head up and toward him. Then she dropped to a crouch on the floor and tugged the black cloth off her head.

"Knight," she said, relieved there were no more assailants.

Knight smiled at her. *God, she is beautiful,* he thought.

"I was coming more for moral support, really," he said.

Her smile said she knew perfectly well that he wasn't certain she'd had the situation under control. But rather than being offended by his lack of faith in her abilities—which had grown tremendously since he'd first met her—she appeared to appreciate him worrying about her.

As he reached her and the fallen men, the smaller of the two, who had taken her heel to his face, began to stir on the cheap linoleum floor.

"Interrogation time," Knight said, squatting down and slapping the man's cheek a few times, until his eyes snapped open.

Panic instantly filled the Chinese man's eyes, as he saw Knight and Pawn hunching over him. He glanced around and saw his dead companion, and then his panic ratcheted up to full-on terror.

"We're not going to hurt you," Knight said in passable Cantonese. "Where were you taking her?" Knight pointed his thumb toward Pawn, but the man on the ground didn't look at her. He was still glancing around, as if attackers might materialize from anywhere, despite the fact that the tight corridor only had doors at either end, or to the shops it serviced along the way on one side of the long passage.

The man was even looking at the blank wall as if a threat might erupt from there.

It was then that Knight peered hard at the man's eyes, and he saw the dilated pupils.

"He's off his head on something," Knight offered.

"Great," Pawn said. "We can't stay here too long. Someone is bound to come looking for them."

At that moment, the loading bay door opened at the distant end of the corridor. But rather than a worker pushing a long slim cart with cardboard boxes on it, like Knight was hoping for, four larger men with guns already drawn came running into the hallway.

"Looks like they already are," he said.

THIRTY-FIVE

Before Knight could decide how to handle the armed gunmen at the far end of the hall, his cybernetic eye detected movement behind him. He had gotten in the habit of allowing the eye to look backward, through his own head, to keep alerted to anyone approaching him from behind, as a default mode. After all, he could see perfectly well with his biological eye, and the depth perception issues were ones he'd mastered during the long adjustment time when he and Aleman were trying to find a replacement eye that worked well enough.

So, if he wasn't actively using the new eye, it slipped into a defensive posture, cycling through its various modes slowly, watching his back.

It made sneaking up on Knight very difficult. And as a sniper, who had once been *stepped on*, while he was in the field and camouflaged, he considered the additional perimeter awareness to be a great boon. It was certainly serving him well today.

He was about to suggest that he and Pawn retreat through the back door to the same shop Pawn had been 'abducted' from, but as men came in from behind him, Knight's eye could detect not just the raising of their weapons, but the movement of trigger fingers.

"Down," he shouted, and Pawn dropped to the floor with him.

A fusillade of bullets roared past him from behind, slamming into the four armed men that had first entered the narrow hallway in the distance. Knight rolled back to face this new threat, and grabbed the large, dead man and lifted him up. When his new meat shield didn't take any hits, he realized two things.

The first was that the newest arrivals had used silenced weapons. The second was that, once they had killed the armed men at the corridor's far end, they'd held their fire.

Knight poked his head up over the dead man's shoulder. He recognized the three newcomers, who were quickly approaching his position.

His cybernetic eye was great for detecting threats in a variety of spectrums, but it couldn't always help him identify a friend from a foe in ultraviolet or X-ray mode.

"Aww," Rook said. "You look like a little whack-a-mole poking his widdle head up."

Knight ignored him and stood. "King."

Chess Team's leader slipped his sound suppressed weapon inside a thin button-down shirt he was wearing loosely over an Elvis T-shirt. Next to him, Queen and Rook were likewise packing their weapons away. "Didn't think you'd mind the help," King said.

Rook shrugged. "Plus, I was hoping to pick up a knock-off Rolex while we were here."

"Where's Bishop?" Pawn asked, as she searched the drugged-out man still lying on the floor, glancing around as if a swarm of insects might attack him at any second. She took the man's phone and then stood up.

"He's in the mall," Queen said, handing Pawn and Knight earpieces, so they could all communicate.

"Nice timing," Knight said. "How did you find us?"

"Deep Blue has been keeping an eye on things from the sky."

Knight was dumbfounded. He and Pawn had been off grid, working solo, and without any support from Deep Blue or the others at HQ. "That is so creepy," he said as he slipped the earpiece in.

Deep Blue—Tom Duncan—replied immediately in his ear. "We didn't put trackers on you or anything, Knight. Ale and I just figured out which places you would be likely to hit in the Kowloon part of Hong Kong, and we gently nudged a satellite in your direction. Didn't take long to figure out where you were."

Knight chuckled. "Still spooky."

Pawn interrupted the online reunion. "I'm glad for the backup, and the help. Maybe you can tell us where number 1 Garden Road is, over on the island." She held up the mobile phone she had taken from the drugged man on the floor. In his Contacts, she had found a listing for Primate Industries.

"Never mind, Blue. I know the address," Knight said.

But Deep Blue had already looked it up and found it. "It's the Bank of China building. Triangular frames all over the glass walls."

Pawn nodded, having seen it.

King started back the way they had come in, but the back door from one of the shops snapped open. In a fraction of a second, all weapons were up and out, but as the mountainous form of Bishop slid into the hallway, he simply turned and closed the door. After all, he had been listening, and knew the threat was over.

"What about him?" Pawn asked, pointing toward the lone survivor of the shootout, the man who was still tripping hard.

"Local EMTs are already on the way for him," Deep Blue's voice slid into all their ears. "You're going to need to relocate while we come up with a plan for the Bank building. Getting into it isn't going to be easy."

"We've cracked some tough nuts," King said. "An aerial drop might work. Or we could probably just break in at night."

"This one might be tougher than you think, King," Deep Blue sounded tired. Knight realized it was close to midnight on the US West Coast. "Primate isn't listed as having leased any of the floors or even a suite in any of them, but a trail of holding companies *is* showing that the Chinese Central Military Commission bought the top eight floors a few years back. Four of those used to be owned by the Bank. But the local courier services have been delivering packages addressed to Primate Industries to the lobby on the sixty-fourth floor. If we had any doubts about whether the Chinese government—or at least the PLA—was in bed with Primate, we can now lay those to rest."

"Drop a deuce on the Pontiff's pointy hat!" Rook said. "Looks like Chess Team is going to war with China."

THIRTY-SIX

Cheung Kong Center, Central, Hong Kong

It took a few days for the team to get in place, acquire the equipment they would need, and to lay low, keeping an ear to the ground for any police or military movement after the assault at Chungking Mansions.

Oddly, there had been no news about the fight in the tight corridor. Someone had kept it away from the press. In fact, Deep Blue and Lewis Aleman had been continually surprised at how little news of any kind was coming out of China. Everything seemed calm on the surface, with the local news broadcasters relying on puff pieces and human-interest stories. Newscasters' tranquil smiles pointed to absolute serenity in the Middle Kingdom.

But there were signs that something was deeply wrong.

Behind the scenes, all foreign journalists had slowly been deported or jailed. There was an absolute news blackout for Western news sources regarding China. Intelligence services were concerned that no one had seen or heard anything first-hand from anyone in the Chinese

Communist Party in days. No bloviating statesmen. No jingoistic military blather. The last anyone internationally had heard was China moaning on the international stage about the Kunming attack, and pointing fingers at every country in Europe, the US, and Russia, before all went quiet.

World leaders were deeply concerned about what China's reprisals might look like. Then China started withdrawing their diplomats from Western nations. These withdrawals were made to seem like simple reassignments and promotions, with new replacement officers to follow. But replacements did not come. The Chinese embassy on International Place in Washington, D.C. was shuttered. As was the embassy in London and the China Visa Applications Centre, which was in a separate facility. Yet, oddly, Chinese commerce continued apace, as if nothing was wrong.

International intelligence agents from organizations such as the CIA, MI-6, and the Mossad, who had been embedded in China were suddenly silent.

Taiwan was naturally panicked.

Russia offered no information—if they even knew what was really going on.

Deep Blue was busy trying to discern what was happening in China, while prepping the team for their incursion to the Bank building, and also working with Aleman to narrow down the list of possible satellites that could be armed with the de-evolution weapon.

He sounded exhausted.

"Keep in mind that you are the only foreign agents in-country that anyone in the West is in contact with. The President is down my neck for more intel, but that needs to wait until after tonight's mission."

King leaned back on a plush sofa and sighed. "I'm still not sure this is the best plan. Yes, it gets us into the Military Commission's offices in the Bank building, but even if we're stealthy and get in and out without being noticed, it'll take them all of five minutes to figure out how we did it."

The team had been holed up in a penthouse apartment belonging to Raymond Park, the chairman of a multinational conglomerate—who was also one of Deep Blue's personal friends. Park's conglomerate owned the entire Cheung Kong Center skyscraper—which was adjacent to the Bank of China tower. Park himself was in London on vacation, but he had allowed the team access to the building using the ground level parking garage entrance, and a service elevator. No one had seen the team slip into the building. No one would see them leave, when they departed from the roof—via a rope fired across the one-hundred-and-fifty-foot distance between the giant buildings. No one would see the team use motorized winches to travel that distance, almost a thousand feet off the ground, gliding into the top floor of the Bank of China building at night, when the employees had all gone home, and the exterior of the structure was dark, hours after it had been lit up with neon light displays.

But the next day, after the team had departed, a trail of evidence would reveal the team's actions. There would be a broken window on the seventy second floor of the bank tower, facing the nearest corner of the CKC building's roof. There would be a hole in a concrete support pillar inside the room, just beyond the broken window, from their rocket-propelled grappling hook. A beat cop on the Hong Kong Police Force would be able to figure out that someone had crossed from the roof of the CKC building with a rope. The team had debated their entry for days, but there was no way past the security on the ground floors without causing a massive international incident. The only way in was from the top. And conveniently, there had been no activity in the Military Commission's top floors of the building. Day or night, no one entered the floors. Park's penthouse had a fully programmable Celestron telescope, and Knight had been using it to keep an eye on the adjacent building.

Deep Blue felt (and King agreed) that parachuting onto the Bank building from above was probably out of the question. With all the air traffic in Hong Kong—one of the world's busiest destinations—that approach probably wouldn't have worked anyway. With no way to know what the Chinese government was doing these days, anything that had the appearance of a paramilitary strike team dropping into one of the busiest and most politically unstable cities in the country was out of the question.

"I've thought about that some, King," Deep Blue said, over King's earpiece communicator. "We'll have Pawn retract the rope on her end, before her rendezvous with you at the Park."

King shifted on the plush penthouse sofa, nodding. "Leaving us to remove the anchor at our end and take it with us."

"Exactly," Deep Blue said. "There will still be the matter of the broken glass, but with luck most of it will be inside on the carpet when you transfer over. When you're ready to depart, I'll check the street below. If you're still undetected, you can sweep the glass outward, and maybe anyone investigating will think the window blew out instead of in."

"That's a big 'if' and you know it," King said, smiling.

"Yes. But so far, we've seen no indication of any other forces, besides the basic bank security guards on the ground floor. Raymond hasn't seen anything either, although he hasn't really been looking for that per se."

"Any chance we get Mr. Park in trouble with this?" King asked.

He stood and walked through the stunning living room to a wall of windows that faced northeast and the amazing view of Hong Kong's Victoria Harbor.

"Shouldn't be," Deep Blue answered. "Raymond is doing good work in London. If local police or the Military Commission or whoever comes looking for how anyone got into the Bank from CKC, they don't have anything to lead them to the penthouse. The roof is accessible to anyone in the building. And Raymond will deny having had anyone in the penthouse. If it blows up, he's planning to act offended and demand stronger security at CKC. After all, if you can get into the Bank building from his building, then anyone could get into his building from the Bank, using the same tactic. He'll make such a stink that no one would ever suspect him of anything."

"This is all a lot of work to go through if we don't turn anything up. That place has been deserted," King said, leaning in close to the window, to glance to his right, where the Bank building loomed, taller than King's location—not counting the building's antenna arrays.

"It's worth a look," Deep Blue said. "We have literally nothing else to go on. Also: you should get a shave."

King blinked in surprise, then stepped back away from the window, realizing that Deep Blue was watching him from a satellite somewhere far out of the range of human sight.

"If you ever decided to use your powers for evil..." King started.

"I know," Deep Blue said, mirth in his voice. "I'd be invincible."

THIRTY-SEVEN

In the next room, a large opulent foyer, the other members of Chess Team were gathering their equipment for the incursion into the Bank of China building, checking sidearms, the rope, and its rocket-propelled launcher.

Queen walked over to Rook, where he was cinching a backpack, and tapped him on the shoulder. "I need to talk to you for a minute. Privately."

Wisely, Rook made no smartass comment, and simply stood up and followed her into the guest bedroom, where they had been staying. As soon as the door was closed, though, his concern became apparent. "What's going on, Zel?"

Queen looked the man she loved in the eyes, steeled herself, took a deep breath, and said "I need you to stay calm and quiet, and listen to what I have to say."

A thick crease appeared on Stan Tremblay's forehead. Queen knew it was something that happened on his face only when he was deeply worried.

"Relax," she told him. "It's not bad news. But it's important."

The crease diminished, but only slightly.

She sat him down on the end of the bed and took his hand in hers. "At first, I wasn't sure what to do, and I really wasn't ready to say anything just yet. But I can't go on this mission."

Rook was about to speak, and she gently placed a finger on his lips. "Let me finish. This is hard enough."

Rook closed his mouth and Queen took another breath. "I'm pregnant, and I want to have this baby. Your baby."

An array of emotions shot across Rook's face, before he simply leaned in, kissed her, and then hugged her. When they parted from the embrace, they both had tears in their eyes.

"Listen," she said. "I don't want any shit about continuing with the team. I know I'm going to have to step down soon, but I know that, for a little while, at least, I can still keep on doing what we do. Within reason. But wearing a tight climbing harness across my abdomen for a traverse, isn't one of them. I'm worried what the tight pressure might do to the baby. I'm worried enough about what that might do to your recently healed ribs. So, I'm going to join Pawn on support for this one. When things get hairy enough, or when I start feeling like I can't do what we do, I'll be sensible about it and stop. This decision today, should be all the evidence you need that I'll be sensible about it."

Rook's face had turned impassive, and he still said nothing. Then she realized she'd asked him to stay quiet so she could get that all out.

"Question?" she asked.

"First," he said, "I love you. Second, I never would have doubted your ability to make sensible decisions for cutting back on this life. And we were already talking about pulling back some..."

"I know," she said. "I wasn't ready yet, but sometimes life has a way of telling you when it's time."

Rook's concern crease returned. "Are you okay with that?"

"It took me a while. I've known since just before the Desolation mission. But yes. I'm good with it now. Let's get through this mess with Primate. Then we can think about what to do."

Rook squeezed her hand. "Look, I know about your past, so, yeah, your concerns are valid. But I know you, Zelda Baker." He leaned forward and kissed her forehead which today was uncharacteristically bare, the scar from her former torture still visible, but faded. "I know you. I know you'll be an amazing mother."

She started to cry again and said, "Stop it."

Rook just nodded to himself, and she could almost hear him say to himself in his head 'But you will.' She knew he believed it, and she believed it, too. He made her feel more confident in herself than she had before, and she had come a long way from the broken woman she had once been.

"Just one more question," Rook said.

Queen just raised her eyebrow.

"When can we tell them?" he asked, a huge grin spreading across his eager face.

"Can we do it with at least a trace of tact and grace, though?" she asked.

THIRTY-EIGHT

"Best stock up on cigars, motherfuckers! We're having a baby!" Rook shouted as he entered the foyer.

Queen laughed as she came into the room behind him. King was the first to sweep her up in a hug and offer congratulations, and Knight was right behind him. Bishop was shaking Rook's hand and Pawn was smiling wider than Queen had ever seen. There was back clapping and then offers of congratulations from everyone in the room, and from everyone back in Siletz over comms. Rook was cracking jokes, and everyone was laughing.

It was the best Queen had felt in a long time.

These people were not just her teammates. They were family. She allowed herself these few minutes of contentment and happiness before it was time to compart-mentalize it all and be back on task, ready to help with the mission. She might not be able to join them, but she could help Pawn with support operations. And if the shit hit the fan, she would still wade into battle. She was only about eight weeks in, and she had experienced no morning sickness yet. She hoped she might still be okay for another few weeks.

She took King aside after a few more minutes to explain that she wouldn't be joining the mission. King understood her reasoning completely.

"You'll go with Anna?" he asked.

"Yeah," she said. "But I'll be ready if you need me."

King just nodded. He knew she would be.

At the tail end of the twentieth century and the start of the twenty-first, it became apparent to military strategists that new thinking was needed for mobility in urban terrain. As the new millennium continued, R&D think-tanks and YouTubers with too much time and money on their hands alike were hard at work perfecting a grappling hook gun. The ideal was the fictional hand-held weapon Batman used, but in true military fashion, conventional forces focused on designing a weapon that relied more heavily on force.

Although pneumatic rifles existed, capable of firing a grappling hook up to three hundred feet, the version Chess Team was using was rocket-propelled. Resembling a 50mm cannon more than a grappling hook gun, the weapon was attached to a tripod, and the legs had to first be bolted into the roof of the CKC building.

Queen assisted Knight in drilling the final bolts through the tripod's feet.

The barrel was over five feet long and would easily fire its projectile across the 150 foot distance to the Bank of China building. But unlike pneumatic rifles used by police forces worldwide for urban rapid entry systems, this projectile would smash through the inch thick glass wall of the bank building, continue into the room, and drill itself into the concrete support pillar, before deploying a series of spring-loaded anchors that would widen the projectile's circumference. In theory, it would act like a series of cam lobes to fix the device in place.

Trailed behind the projectile would be an 11mm rope that the team would use motorized ascenders on. Queen knew that the team could have traversed the rope under their own steam, but the top floor of the

Bank building was about twenty feet higher than the roof of the CKC tower. So, they would need to cross and ascend at the same time.

"Ready," Knight said, and Queen just nodded to him. Her leg of the tripod was done.

King looked around at everyone on the roof. "Are we all set?"

Every team member nodded.

Without prompting, Deep Blue spoke in their ears. "You're all clear on the ground. Everything looks quiet."

Queen glanced around. The surrounding skyscrapers were no longer lit-up with neon lights that danced and flitted on the metal and glass of the structures, making night-time Hong Kong look like a surreal playground. The show, called the Symphony of Lights, was performed every evening at 8pm. But it was close to midnight, and now everything was dark and gloomy. On the ground, most of the traffic would have thinned out—if not vanished entirely. It was a Tuesday, after all. Not everyone was out partying until all hours during the work week.

"Stand clear," Knight said, moving to the rear of the grapple launcher and laying his hand on the grip, but his finger nowhere near the trigger yet. He looked to King for confirmation.

"Do it," King said, and Knight waited just a second, then pulled the trigger. The resulting sound was loud—but not much louder than a car backfiring. As Queen watched the shot through a small pair of binoculars, the glass wall shattered inward, the smash across the chasm barely audible. As far as she could tell, none of the glass had fallen down the thousand feet to the ground.

She couldn't see the projectile embed itself into the concrete pillar, but Deep Blue apparently could from his vantage point with a satellite in space. "It was a perfect shot," he said in her ear.

Rook worked controls on the cannon that would ratchet the rope taut. In a worst-case scenario, if the rope didn't hold inside the Bank building, it would still be securely anchored on the roof of the CKC. The swing and fall against the side of the tower could kill the team, but at least they wouldn't plummet to their deaths from an anchor failure.

"We're good here," Rook said.

He moved over and placed a kiss on Queen's cheek, then attached his lunchbox sized ascender to the line. He tested his weight on the line, then dangled from it, and used the ascender to move toward but not yet over the edge of the CKC building.

Without a word, Knight followed, then Bishop, and finally King clipped on to the taut rope.

"Final check?" King asked.

"You're clear," came Deep Blue's reply.

"Go," King said.

The four Chess Team members slid along the rope with a barely audible mechanical buzz from their four ascenders, as the wind buffeted Queen and Pawn, still standing on the rooftop.

In a few minutes, the team was across the distance. "All clear," came Rook's voice in Queen's ear. Once she saw the other three pass the threshold of the Bank of China building's missing window wall, she turned away, checking the roof access door behind her again.

"We're in," King said. "Slack."

Pawn operated a switch on the grapple rifle, and the taut line loosened slightly.

"You have slack," Queen said.

"Detaching rope," came King's reply. "Detached. Haul it in."

"Hauling," Queen replied. At that point, she knew King would actually release the rope, allowing it to spill out into the chasm over Garden Road.

"Haul away," came King's final practiced reply.

At that command, Pawn activated a switch on the weapon that began spooling in the rope. By the time the slack rope had fallen across the distance between the two buildings to hit the side of the CKC tower, more than half of the length that had been let out for the crossing was retracted. In another minute, Queen saw the end of the rope zip up over the edge of the building and toward the tripod's legs before Pawn shut off the motor that pulled the rope back.

Queen knew, as she and Pawn began to disassemble the weapon that on King's end they would be removing the projectile from the concrete pillar—if that was possible. Sometimes the anchors jammed themselves in at a weird angle and couldn't be retracted.

Then the team would slowly explore the floor they had entered. Pawn and all the other members of the team, along with Queen, had practiced assembly and disassembly of the grappling weapon. Soon the pieces were all stowed in black nylon zippered cases so the two could remove any evidence of the weapon—besides the holes in the roof where the anchoring bolts had been.

"Anchor removed," came King's voice. "We're proceeding."

Deep Blue was silent in their ears.

Queen nodded to Pawn and they grabbed the cases, heading for the roof access door. They had another part to play if things went to plan.

If they didn't, she and Pawn were the team's only chance of rescue.

THIRTY-NINE

Bank of China Tower, Hong Kong

Gusts of wind buffeted King as he released the rope and watched it fall into the chasm between the skyscrapers. Although it was dark, he could still see it, but he doubted anyone at street level would have been able to spot anything. There wasn't anyone down on the streets anyway. It was too late, and Central, the district of Hong Kong where they were, was the city's business and banking area. Government, office, and other historical buildings filled the area, but besides hotels, there were few residences. Even most of the light displays from hours ago were intended to be seen from afar.

"Anchor removed," King said. "We're proceeding."

They had privacy.

It's a good thing, too, King thought. He looked at the concrete support pillar inside the window that had shattered. Two feet below where the rope's anchor had embedded itself in the support, a dinner platter sized chunk of the concrete had dislodged itself onto the floor from the impact.

"No way we're undetected now," King told Deep Blue. "Part of the column fell apart."

As King reported to Deep Blue and the others at Siletz, Rook worked quickly to pack away the dislodged anchor, while Bishop and Knight had taken up positions a few feet away on either side of them, keeping a lookout.

"Regrettable," Deep Blue said, "but we knew that was a strong likelihood. Still no movement on the lower levels, and the city below looks like it's asleep. I'm about to lose visual coverage, but I'll still be on audio. Happy hunting."

"Got it," Rook said. "Not that it's going to matter much, I guess."

"They'll know we were here, but no need to show them how we did it," King said, "besides, anything we can do to deflect attention from our host will be a good thing."

The team was in a small foyer near a stairwell. Because the top several floors of the tower tapered into a triangular shape, the actual office layouts in the building were odd. Elevator banks, stairwells, and restrooms filled the center of the triangular floorplan, but five large offices lined two of the triangle's walls, with a large boardroom at the point. The walls and the floor were either bare concrete—like the pillar they had damaged—or a rich walnut wood paneling. The team searched the seventy second floor's perimeter, ensuring that they were alone before they started looking through offices.

When they neared the elevators on the building's far side from where they had entered, Knight leaned his head against a wall by the elevator's call buttons. He pointed a small hand-held LED flashlight that shone just a tiny beam at a plaque by the buttons. He peered at the raised brass plate. It read:

PRIMATE

INDUSTRIES

But what was *behind* the plate had captured Knight's interest.

"What is it?" King asked in a low voice.

"A familiar shape," Knight said. He pulled out a KA-BAR knife, slid it under the Primate plaque, and pried. The screws holding the plaque popped out on one side, and he bent it back to reveal an older, slightly faded brass plate that had been sealed flush against the wall.

"But we know Ridley is toast, right?" Rook asked. "We saw his dry, dusty, peener-lookin' noggin."

"What is it?" Deep Blue's disembodied voice asked.

"Manifold Genetics logo on the wall under a Primate Industries sign," King said, disgust in his voice. "I thought we knew about all of their Asian facilities, but it looks like we missed at least one of them." He started back along the hallway, popping into each office as he went, looking through folders and paperwork.

"Nothing in leasing records indicates Manifold's presence, but some of Ridley's properties were buried in so many shell companies, that it could take even me a few weeks to unravel," Deep Blue replied.

Much of the paperwork King could see was in Chinese, but he could read enough to know that he was looking at basic operating reports with no actual content information to explain what Primate was doing here. The team took turns with two people checking rooms, and two standing guard.

After they cleared the first five offices along one wall, they headed toward the next five, with Rook passing by the open doors to the board room and declaring, "No need to check in there, it's empty." King followed him toward the next office when from behind him he heard Bishop softly say, "Wait."

King backtracked. The huge man had paused near the open door to the board room and his eyes were closed. King thought he was listening for something, so he didn't speak. Rook and Knight took up guard positions around the other two, also not speaking. Knight dropped to a crouch on the carpeted floor.

After a minute, King whispered, "Erik?"

But without answering him, Bishop strode into the board room, and shone his small light all around it. The room was filled with a large oval wooden table with six expensive leather chairs around it. The wooden walls were unadorned except for one small cut-out shelf in the middle of one wall. The rest of the room was empty.

Bishop walked directly toward the shelf.

Centered on the foot-wide wooden shelf was a decorative display.

The base was a lacquered wooden stand, on top of which was a vertical growth of crystals, almost the orange color of a Himalayan salt lamp, but resembling a clump of finger-sized shafts of quartz.

When Bishop pointed his LED at it, the light refracted, split, and shimmered around the room in a wavering display of colors.

"These are from Mount Meru," Bishop said. He reached out a finger and gently touched the tip of the crystal display. Then he closed his eyes again.

"You're sure?" King asked.

"I wore one around my neck for years. They give off a slight humming vibration. Not strong. Not like an annoying refrigerator compressor going bad. It's almost musical. Subconscious. I could feel it from the hallway." Bishop opened his eyes and turned to look at King. "I'm sure."

Years ago, the team had engaged in a protracted battle at Mount Meru in Vietnam, while hunting for the source of a deadly virus. A crazed cryptozoologist named Anthony Weston had tried to kill them, and Queen had been tortured by a sadistic Vietnamese army general before the whole mess was over. But King had shot Weston, the mountain was destroyed, and the crystals had been buried deep underground. Bishop had used a small crystal for a time to negate the effects of genetic tinkering Richard Ridley had done to him, which caused him to lose all control in a berserker rage and rapidly heal all injuries. But Bishop had long been cured of being a 'Regen,' and he no longer needed the Meru crystal to keep his composure.

"What the hell is going on, King?" Bishop asked. Not much scared the huge man, but the prospect of losing control of himself again was probably high on that list.

Before Jack Sigler could answer, the elevator in the hallway chimed.

FORTY

Santiago de León de Caracas, Venezuela

Maria Rivas held her sign high and shouted, "No more blood for oil!" As did a dozen of her fellow protesters. The group, People for the Planet, had set up the protest weeks in advance, and now that they were here, Maria could see why the location was so perfect.

The group stood on the wide concrete plaza at the foot of the Parque Cristal building. Constructed in 1977, the building was a cube shape made of glass and steel, with a giant square cut out of the middle of it. Not only built with funds from the Venezuelan oil boom, the business building had come to be seen as a symbol of capitalism, and also as a marker for gentrification in the Altamira neighborhood in which it sat.

But as Maria glanced around and saw the fruit stands across the street, shabby wooden crates hastily assembled under torn and dirty tent like awnings, she noted the dichotomy of wealth between the poor farmers selling their wares and the slick businessmen leaving the Cristal for their lunch.

"No more blood for oil!" the group chanted again.

She could see one of the fat-cat businessmen, an older man with a thin white beard, heading toward the protesters, as if he meant to force his way through their line. This wasn't the group's first protest. They would stand their ground. Block his passage, and she would start accosting him and try to hand him leaflets. He would probably walk away in feigned disgust, but Maria believed she might one day reach one of these monsters and make him see the truth.

But as the man came closer across the concrete plaza, his steps faltered, and he fell to his knees next to the trunk of a decorative palm tree that jutted up from the ground.

Maria was going to bark out a laugh.

Instead, a jet of projectile vomit burst from her mouth, splashing the concrete all around the man, as he too began to heave.

Maria attempted to look around at her fellow protesters, but they were all on the ground already. And then so was she.

Her fingernails involuntarily grasped at the concrete, and as she watched, her wrists began to grow hair before her eyes. Her nails elongated.

The older businessman looked at her with pleading eyes as his arms distended and buckled.

Rather than feeling spite for the man, Maria felt a wave of empathy. He was going through the same thing she was. The same torture afflicting them all. Her body lurched hard again, and the force of it shattered her ribs. A large splinter of the broken bone pierced her stomach. On the next heave, the bone fragment was wrenched from her body, and out her mouth to clatter on the ground next to the businessman's swelling forehead.

In her last moments of consciousness, Maria felt only kinship with the man. The playing field was level. None of their political or cultural beliefs mattered now. They were both suffering from the same thing, human beings brought low by the unexpected.

Lijia Dam, Qinghai, China

A cool breeze blew across the balcony, as Lady Crimson took in the night air. It was well past midnight, but it was lunchtime in Caracas. She liked to make her statements when people could see them. If that meant staying up late once in a while, she was all for it.

The station was above the dam complex, looking out over the vast beauty of the dammed Yellow River, in a canyon streaked with green vegetation and red sandstone. Of course, none of that was visible now. All she could see was a vast black void over the manmade lake. She could smell the water, but she could not see it. She could hear the roar of water powering through the penstocks and the fishway, keeping the mighty Yellow River flowing beyond the facility.

She breathed in deeply, yearning for when her new palace would be finished. It was being constructed for her all along the nearby Likan Highway, crawling up the mountainous expanse of the Kanbula National Forest Park, close to 10,000 feet above sea level. But the palace would not be ready for a week yet. She could have her pick of accommodations, but she chose to be near the dam—and the control station from which the satellites could be manipulated.

Before he cleared his throat to get her attention, Lady Crimson heard her underling approach her from behind.

"Majesty?"

She turned to face her general, Huang Shuchang.

He was dressed in his best uniform, as befitted the occasion—the second firing of her mighty weapon, followed by the press conference. In his late forties, Huang was physically imposing, serene, and exceptionally competent, making him perfect for her needs.

Both in the new Army, and in the bedroom.

"What is it, Huang?" she asked, before turning back toward the dark void and breathing in the night air. "Please do not spoil the evening by telling me there is a problem with the Venezuela implementation."

"Not at all, Your Majesty," Huang said, stepping up beside her at the balcony rail. One of the other things she appreciated about the man was his complete lack of fear. He respected her and was formal at all times, but he never exhibited the slightest hint of dread. "All indications are that the entire Zone of Effect has experienced the de-evolution. If anything, this particular instance was more successful than the Kunming application."

"Interesting," she said. "How so?"

"I hypothesize that the proximity to the Earth's equator in Caracas may have played a part. My secondary hypothesis is the relocation of the launch facility from Hong Kong to here, much closer to your...power source, might have somehow affected the process, but that would of course require testing. If you would have a firm answer, I can task some men to–"

"It won't be necessary, Huang, but I like the initiative," she said.

Lady Crimson had decided, after dealing with the Party's impromptu meeting, that it was time to finally relocate all operations from their former Hong Kong facility to the new base that she had been overseeing in Qinghai Province for the last two years. The area suited her needs, and she liked it far better than Hong Kong with its glitz and gleam.

"Was there anything else?"

"Yes, Majesty," Huang said. "It concerns the Hong Kong facility. There has been a break-in."

Lady Crimson turned slowly to face her general. "A break-in? How?"

"I do not yet have that answer, Majesty. Our men reported a silent alarm was tripped on the seventy second floor. They are investigating it now."

Lady Crimson frowned. "The burglars are on Seventy Two? They were not intercepted in the lobby of the building?"

Huang's demeanor did not change even slightly. "The very same question I asked. I should have more information momentarily. Shall I ask them to keep the intruder or intruders alive for questioning?"

Lady Crimson smiled and turned back toward the night.

"Oh, yes. Let's have some entertainment," she said.

Without a word, Huang left her on the balcony to contemplate the night, until it was time for the conference.

She stood motionless, peering into the darkness. A moment later, she spoke aloud again, even though he was beyond earshot.

"Unless," she said to herself softly, "it's who I suspect. In which case, your men haven't got a chance."

FORTY-ONE

Bank of China Tower, Hong Kong

As soon as Rook saw the first raised Heckler & Koch MP5 rifle barrel come out of the hallway of elevators, he knew two things: the shooting was going to start soon, and he wanted one of those rifles rather than his suppressed 9mm Sig Sauer handgun.

He also realized he wanted the men in the elevator hallway pinned between two groups of combatants, so rather than waiting for orders, he lunged toward the first man exiting the narrow hall, tackling him to the far side of the larger corridor.

The other men inside the hallway started shouting and shooting in Rook's direction. But rather than tussling with the man he'd tackled to the floor, Rook scrambled behind cover, allowing the assailants to shoot their own man in the first spray of bullets.

"Oh-ho, shit! No one told you guys friendly fire was turned on?" he yelled, rolling out from behind the wall at the back of the elevator bank. He fired two shots, taking down the first of three men emerging from the narrow elevator corridor.

Then Rook quickly dove back behind cover, as a storm of bullets hit all around where he had just been. He glanced down at the dead man's MP5, but there was still no chance to retrieve it.

No matter, he thought. *Three, two, one.*

He counted in his head as long as he figured it would take the men to clear the elevator hallway, stepping fully into the main corridor. Distracted as they were, Rook thought...

They won't even think of checking—

Two suppressed shots fired, and Rook heard the last two men thump to the floor.

—behind them.

He stood up and crept back toward the hallway junction. Knight was watching the elevator bank, and King was stooping to collect an MP5. Bishop stood by, looking concerned.

"These guys are not security guards," Bishop said, looking down at the dead men dressed in black fatigues and body armor. "There will be more."

"Another car is coming up," Knight said, looking up at the digital display above the elevator doors. "Stairs?"

"Let's go with my side," Rook suggested. He stooped to collect the MP5 he'd been coveting and snagged three spare magazines on the dead man's tactical vest, while the others ran past him and around the corner he'd been using for cover, heading for one of two stairwells.

By the time Rook joined them, Knight was saying "Clear," in his ear and slipping into the door to the stairs. Rook took up a defensive position, watching the elevator hall. When he heard the faint *ding* of the elevator car arriving, he slid into the stairwell behind King, and gently shut the door.

King whispered an update to Deep Blue as the team made their way down the stairs to the seventy first floor. Knight glanced through the stairwell door window, and then slid in, with Bishop and King following. When Rook got to the door, there had still been no sound from above him. He hoped the pile of dead bodies above would stall the second team with indecision about what to do. At least long enough for them to find firing positions.

When Rook entered the seventy first floor, he immediately noticed its layout was identical to the floor above, but rather than the two diagonal walls being lined with offices, this floor was lined with what looked like medical offices or science labs. White walls and strange equipment filled each room, along with simple desks and computers. Rook thought they were unlikely to find any paperwork on this floor.

"Knight, the elevators. I'll take the far stairwell," King directed. He and Knight started off along the corridor. "Bishop, the labs. Rook, our six."

More and more often, Rook found himself silently coming up with the exact plan that King would order them to follow. He wasn't sure if that was because exposure to the man over the years had taught him things about leadership or whether they all shared some sort of gestalt mind now. The other possibility was that he knew King well enough to predict how the man would think.

Either way, Rook agreed with the decision—and even if he hadn't, he would have followed the orders. He trusted King. He trusted every member of the team. Even Bishop, who had weirdly allowed them all to think he was dead for years. Because Rook had temporarily pulled a similar stunt in Russia once, when he needed to get his head on straight, he had been willing to throw the big man more than the lion's share of goodwill on the issue.

But although there were tons of things for him to dwell on at the moment—Bishop's return, Queen's pregnancy, or the deaths of their friends, Rook was able to shut all that out and focus on the issue at hand. For all his reputation on the team as the wisecracking joker, Stan Tremblay was a finely tuned machine of death when he needed to be.

And that was the man that crouched at the side of the stairwell door with a SOG Seal Pup knife. The blade was just under five inches long with a glass reinforced nylon grip. If just one of their pursuing soldiers came through the door, Rook would attack him from behind, slip the knife into the base of the man's skull, and gently deposit his rag-doll-like corpse on the carpet. If more than one man came down the stairs, he would use the MP5. But neither happened.

"One tango down," King whispered from the far side of the building. "Where are we, Bishop?"

It seemed their adversaries had sent just one man down King's stairwell, and he would have dropped the guy—either with a knife like Rook had planned, or with his suppressed handgun. Rook hadn't heard a sound.

"One more lab," came Bishop's soft reply.

"Regroup on Rook," King said.

A moment later, the others joined Rook and they again slipped into the stairwell, moving to the next floor down. Again, Rook found himself agreeing with the strategy. When the one man they had sent down King's stairwell never reported back, they would send someone else down to find him. Chess Team had a small lead in time, but it would grow shorter and shorter. Eventually men would come down—or up—from both stairwells, and the elevators, all at once. But for now, Rook's stairwell was quiet.

As they reached the seventieth floor, Rook noticed the different architecture. No offices. No labs. Just all open space with over forty computer stations and walls lined with giant LED television screens. The air was frigid—several degrees colder than upstairs. Rook smelled lemongrass on the air. Racks of servers, electronics, and cabling filled all the available space, except for a narrow walkway around the central elevator banks and stairwells.

Before King could order them to multiple positions around the floor, Rook heard two elevators ding—and footsteps racing down the stairwell behind him. That moment Rook had been concerned with, where there would be men coming from all sides? It was here.

FORTY-TWO

The White House, Washington, D.C., USA

"Danielle!"

He was shouting. She had only known him a short time, but Danielle Rudin was well aware of President Beaman's wrath when things were going wrong. And lately, they were *always* going wrong. Plus, when he wasn't mad at her, he called her 'Dani.' It was a nickname she hated coming from other people, but he made it sound regal when he was in a good mood. When he was in a bad mood, it was 'Danielle.' Again, she had known him only a short time, but it was long enough for her to learn that he was a decent man with a good heart. If he was pissed off about something, it usually meant incompetent or evil people had made life harder for everyone.

Cathy Bennington, the President's personal secretary, just nodded at the door, and Danielle went in.

Beaman was pacing behind the Resolute Desk, his jacket off and draped over the executive leather chair.

He was clenching his fists.

Oh no, she thought.

"What's happened?"

He looked up at her with a pleading look, as if he truly hoped she could fix the problem. "I just got off the phone with Southern Command. Caracas was just hit with the Kunming Weapon."

"Oh god, Mr. President," she was stunned.

They knew there was an orbital weapon.

The United State Space Force's Space Delta 2, the unit in control of satellites via the Satellite Control Network, was working around the clock trying to find out which of the thousands of satellites around the planet had launched the first attack on Kunming.

So far, they had come up blank. In addition to the multiple nations that had successfully launched satellites, there were hundreds owned and operated by private corporations. Hell, Elon Musk's SpaceX had over fifteen hundred of them alone. China had several hundred. Some were even multinational devices. Even Bangladesh had a satellite in orbit. Tracking them all and scrutinizing each for any hint of the invisible weapon that had somehow devolved an entire city's populace in China was like looking for a needle in a stack of needles—with more needles raining down on them.

Now, another city had been hit.

"I'll get a call in to Schriever Space Force Base," Rudin said.

"No need. They'll call here in a minute," The President said. "Damn it, Danielle. Short of destroying all the damn space junk in orbit, what can we do? Have you heard anything more from Duncan's people?"

"Yes, sir. They've gone dark for the moment because they're on an op. It's our only lead in China. Hopefully we'll hear something within the hour."

Beaman sighed. "China is my other big problem. After all the hand wringing and accusations, they've gone totally dark. I still don't understand how Duncan's people are the only operatives we're hearing from."

"Sir, it's looking very much like all of our people in country were compromised."

Beaman was aghast. "That had to be hundreds of people that— No. No, don't tell me how many. I don't want to know. I just want to hear that you've got more people trying to get in, at least."

"Of course," Danielle said. "As do other nations. This had to be a huge cyber operation. They would have needed to know who all the foreign assets were. They needed to shut down any and all journalists."

"Are we getting the journalists back?" the President asked.

"We're trying, sir. State is making a lot of noise, but literally no one in China is answering. Phone calls are going unanswered. E-mails. Texts. Civilians are in contact with the outside world, but we can't find any ranking Party members or military contacts. The whole country is just silent. The Chinese businessmen we can reach are panicked, because they can't even find out anything on the ground. The amount of coordination, and the complete lack of leaks? It's unheard of. We're certain most of the Chinese population have no clue that anything is going on. Yet. It won't be long before the absence of political figures is noticed on the news. But our best people cannot come up with any kind of a plausible reason for why the whole country would go silent. It isn't their style. They should still be dominating every news channel, shouting about the decadent West, and now blaming us for Venezuela, too."

"Unless China is behind it..." Beaman said, now clearly having come around to Domenick Boucher's and Tom Duncan's hypothesis.

"Unless it's them, yes," Danielle said. "But they've made no demands. And there's so little to tie China to Venezuela. I mean, if they wanted to throw off all suspicion that this weapon was Chinese, then attacking Kunming first fits. But what about Caracas? The Chinese have made billions off Venezuelan oil and other trading. It's almost akin to a second attack on themselves."

"So maybe Dom was wrong, and this is someone *targeting* China," Beaman sighed. "I don't need to remind you that the PRC has three hundred and fifty nuclear warheads, and they've stopped talking to literally everyone. If this is an almighty pout, it could end in complete annihilation."

"We've had some of the best Sinologists on the planet consult with all our China desk analysts," Rudin said, still standing, because Beaman was still pacing. "They all agree that the silence is completely uncharacteristic. And no one at Defense can come up with a potential tactical strategy for the quiet."

Behind her, Cathy Bennington slipped into the room. "Mr. President, you're going to want to turn on CNN now. They have a big announcement from China coming in a minute."

Beaman and Rudin shared a meaningful look, and then Beaman moved to the center of the Oval Office, while Bennington walked over to the wall and turned on the flat screen TV.

CNN's anchor was in the foreground with a smaller inset showing a room decked out in flowing red tapestries. There was a small stage, a large chair on a raised dais and a small wooden podium to the right of the stage.

"—and we're being told that the momentous announcement will begin in just a moment. China has been relatively silent for days. Speculation about the government's announcement is running high, and we're told that... Oh, just a moment, it looks like we're starting."

The screen changed as the inset filled the entire screen, and a large woman in flowing yellow robes, with her face veiled, walked across the stage, ascended the dais, and sat down in the chair without speaking.

"What the hell is this, Danielle?" the President asked.

With no answer, she didn't speak.

On the screen, a military general in full dress uniform approached the podium. He took a deep breath, and then leaned slightly forward toward the microphone.

"The People's Republic of China...is no more."

FORTY-THREE

Bank of China Tower, Hong Kong

"Let's deal with one group, instead of three," King said, motioning back to the stairwell door, and unhooking and dropping his lunch box sized ascender to the floor. There was no point in not leaving evidence behind. Each man wore one of the devices attached to a harness, and they all followed suit, dropping their devices. Now they just had backpacks and harnesses, their handguns, and the pilfered MP5s, but that was all they needed.

King nodded toward the door, and said, "Go."

He watched Rook simply nod, then open the door. He rolled across the concrete landing and fired a spray of bullets upward at the men descending the stairs. They were not expecting any resistance in the stairwell itself, so the first three men were caught off guard, two of them falling down the steps and the third crawling back. A fourth man farther up the staircase ducked backward and around an inner concrete wall.

Knight dove through the door, and leapt upward onto the stairs, firing his pistol up the staircase. He caught the crawling man and then landed on one of the fallen men's bodies. His cushion grunted when Knight landed on him, and Knight swiftly pointed his suppressed weapon downward and fired off another round.

While Bishop watched the corridor, King slipped into the stairwell leapfrogging past Knight and using his same maneuver, his handgun and hand reaching around the concrete wall.

He fired three rounds blindly, and landed on the previously crawling man that Knight had just shot.

King's cushion made no noise when he landed on it, but he did hear his target groan from around the wall. Before he could clamber to his feet though, Knight had passed him and put a final round into the fourth man, who had initially fled up the stairs.

King next heard a burst from Bishop's MP5 rifle before he slipped into the stairwell next to Rook.

"The stairs are ours, for a hot minute anyway," King said. "I don't think we're grabbing anything useful from a room full of server racks. I think it's exfil time."

Deep Blue's voice came over their earpieces with agreement.

"Up or down?" King asked.

"I don't have any—" Deep Blue started to say, when Bishop interrupted him.

"Up," he said. "They think we're heading down floor by floor, and they're throwing team after team down at us. They won't expect us to head up."

Without a word, Knight started up the steps, and King followed him. The other two would be right on his tail, but one of them would guard the door until they were all clear of it. No words or orders were needed. And Bishop was right. If they could get back up to Seventy One and slip onto the floor and get the door closed fast enough, their foes might just bypass that floor and head straight down to the bodies near the seventieth floor's landing and assume that was where all the action was.

No one was coming up the stairs yet. Seventy floors were too many to take by foot, so the guards were probably sending men to Seventy Two first, by elevator, and then they were descending the stairs and coming down in the elevator cars, checking each floor.

If the team could slip into a lab on Seventy One—a floor where the conflict was already theoretically over, and if they could get the door closed, they might have a minute or two of peace and quiet. King figured it could even be an hour before the men thought to check every room again on the upper floors.

As he reached the door, Knight was propping it open with his foot, and King slipped through and past him. Now, King was on point, and he quickly raced toward the apex end of the hallway, where it intersected with the elevator bank's shorter hall. As he suspected, it was empty. He glanced around the other corner, looking down the third corridor, and shining his LED light. The lone man he'd shot at the far stairwell was there, still dead where King had left him.

King revised his estimate of the enemy's forces as he made his way back toward the others. They had never sent another team down the western stairwell, where he had just been. All their forces had come down the elevators and the eastern stairwell, where Chess Team had just killed another four men.

They're undermanned, King thought. *But that won't last long.*

"This way," he said, and turned and ran back toward the dead man at the western stairwell. The others followed, with Bishop stopping at the corner, to keep an eye on anyone attempting to approach from the elevator banks.

"Queen, Pawn, we're getting ready for exfil," King said.

Before he could request a sitrep from them, Queen replied.

"We're in position," she said, sounding so clear it was as if she was in the room with them.

The original exfil plan required the team to make it to the roof, but now that they were lower than their enemy forces, King wasn't so sure that was going to happen. They would have to sneak past Seventy Two, which seemed to be the new enemy base of operations from which they were sending down their men in small groups. Then they would have a lot of stairs after that, potentially with shooters coming up after them.

Then came Bishop's voice.

"Contact."

Shit, King thought.

"Hold them there," King said. Then he turned to Rook.

Having read his mind, Rook simply asked, "Kaboomi?" He pulled a fragmentation grenade from his vest.

"We'll have to do it from the stairwell," King said.

He glanced back toward Bishop just as the man dropped to a crouch and fired a burst from his stolen MP5.

Knight was already moving into the stairwell, stepping over the dead body at his feet.

King slipped into the stairwell next, and Bishop was there a moment later. Then Rook slid into the door and threw the grenade out the doorway, toward the wall of glass windows, just as the door was shutting.

Even twenty feet away from the detonation and protected by a concrete wall, the explosion was loud. The second it was over, Bishop was out the door, and again heading toward the corner with the elevator's hallway, providing cover for the team's escape. But even before Knight could make it through the door, King heard the rushing of feet from above.

"Bishop, pull back. Everyone go now!" King shouted.

Their lead was just seconds, and every second would count.

At their end of the hallway, the wall of glass windows, despite being an inch thick, had been decimated by the fragmentation grenade's blast. Wind was rushing through the opening. The hallway was now just an open, gaping wound that led to a nine hundred foot drop. With no seconds wasted, Knight sprinted for the right side of the hallway, and leapt out that side of the open wall. Rook was next, bearing left along the wall and exiting the missing window at the leftmost edge of it.

That left the center space free for Bishop and King. As Bishop came running, King matched his speed and they both jumped out of the skyscraper, just as bullets started pinging off the walls around them.

FORTY-FOUR

On average, a human being falls two hundred feet per second on a skydive or a BASE jump. King knew, just as well as the others did, that falling from just slightly above nine hundred feet wouldn't give them long, but they also needed to put some distance between themselves and their pursuers.

It wouldn't do to jump out of a giant skyscraper, only to get drilled in the back by your enemy.

King counted, *One one-thousand, two one-thousand...*

Then pulled his ripcord. He sailed away across Cotton Tree Drive and over the neighboring Hong Kong Park. He noted three other parachutes, although they were all hard to see with black nylon against the night. It would make them hard targets to spot, let alone to hit.

The sprawling park covered almost a million square feet, but from the height they were jumping, they could glide right over it and land on Kennedy Drive to the south of the trees. In addition to trees and a playground, as well as several historical buildings, the park was home to everything from a greenhouse to an aviary and a sports center. If one of the team didn't have the altitude to clear the park, then the backup plan was to aim for the wide, circular concrete amphitheater in the center of the huge expanse of trees, known oddly as 'Olympic Square.' Failing that, landing on the chain-link fence roofing of the aviary would be preferable to getting tangled in a park tree.

Thankfully, no bullets came for them as they swept over the trees below. King needn't have worried about their landings. Each man made it to Kennedy Road, which was about thirty feet higher than the ground of the park, and just over a chain-link fence with barbed wire that surrounded the park. Yet none of them had the slightest problem clearing the fence.

King and the others had performed hundreds of jumps over the years, and the newer BASE jumping chutes were easier to steer. Plus, it wasn't a very windy night. All things in their favor.

They landed in the road, right in front of an empty guard booth at the front of a curved building King knew to be the Ministry of Foreign Affairs, an organization analogous to the US Department of State. Two black Mercedes GLE SUVs were parked in front of the building, and the four men detached their chutes, gathered them quickly, and stuffed them into the back of the first vehicle.

King and Rook climbed into the first vehicle, King in the passenger seat, and Rook in back. Queen was behind the wheel. The second they were in, she drove off. Bishop and Knight would get into the second vehicle, driven by Pawn.

They were all still tense, and on high alert, keeping an eye out for any pursuit, but none came. Queen followed Kennedy Road for a bit but then looped back out of the Central district, crossing through the Wan Chai Gap, and eventually brought them to the marina on the far side of the island, at Aberdeen—also known as the Southern District.

Pawn's car was right behind them the entire way.

Still, there was no sign of pursuit.

In Aberdeen, they boarded a pre-arranged luxury yacht that would take them across the harbor to the Hong Kong Disneyland Resort, on Lantau Island. They had checked into three rooms—with Queen and Rook posing as the couple they were—two days ago, before transferring to Raymond Park's swank penthouse.

The next day they would check out of their rooms, as if their respective vacations were over, and take separate commercial flights out of the nearby Chep Lap Kok airport.

A strong wind buffeted the harbor at Aberdeen, and King was once again reminded how different the weather was on opposite sides of the mountainous island. He had been here many times, and usually he enjoyed it. The city had a strange mix of civilization and nature. Despite being one of the most densely populated cities in the world, and one of the most significant trading centers on the planet, the city and its surrounds also managed to contain thousands of miles of parks, rugged mountains, and spectacular coastlines, with dozens of secret green spaces embedded in the concrete and glass jungle. An aerial view of the city showed just how much greenery there was—even in the densely packed urbanized areas.

In King's mind, the place just always looked like it had been constructed with care and consideration for what it would look like when they were done building.

Not something he could say seemed apparent from most other metropolises he'd visited.

But now, at the Marina Club, this late at night, there was nothing to see. The team boarded a forty two foot Catalina sailboat, greeted their captain, a small woman named Lin, who had worked for the local office of the Herculean Society for thirty years, and headed below decks to change their clothing.

Although the vessel had a sail, they would travel the roughly six-mile distance using the 54HP engine, and taking things at a leisurely 5mph, so as not to get noticed in the middle of the night. It would get them to the resort's pier in about an hour, where they would then slip into the hotel, and pretend to be extremely inebriated, returning from a night partying in Kowloon.

The craft had three staterooms, and a curved couch that could be used as a bed. But King was wired, so he went above deck, content to just sit next to Lin, feeling the wind in his hair. The night air would calm him down. Rook and Queen headed for the stateroom in the bow, and Pawn and Knight quickly disappeared into one of the aft staterooms. King figured Bishop would take the other or crash on the sofa. Instead, he followed King topside, and sat down next to him.

They sat in silence for twenty minutes, just listening to the lapping of water against the hull and the thrum of the engine. King could detect that Bishop wanted to talk with him. The man looked tense, but it was almost as if, after all the time apart, he didn't know how to broach the subject.

King figured he would take the lead.

"Something on your mind, Erik?" he asked. He didn't have to shout to be heard over the engine, but he did have to speak loudly.

"I'm concerned about what the hell we're getting into," the big man said. "Felice is in a coma. You know what could happen if she dies."

King knew perfectly well.

Felice Carter's consciousness was somehow quantum linked with every person on the planet. There was a real possibility that if she died, so would the entire human race.

"I remember from when I first met her in Ethiopia," King said. "What else? The Meru crystals?"

"Yeah," Bishop said. "And someone partially resurrecting Richard Ridley? Trying to take us down at the base in Cape Town. Trying to kill you all in the Southern Ocean when you grabbed Blue. All of it."

The big man reached into his pocket and withdrew a steel capped glass tube, slightly larger than a test tube in diameter. He looked at it, and then handed it over to King.

"Then there's this, which I found in one of the labs back there..."

The Catalina had a stern light, but it wasn't bright enough for King to see what he was holding. He pulled out his LED flashlight and beamed it at the tube. The light glittered off the silvery end caps, which were designed to keep the glass tube from shattering after a mild impact. King knew they were probably padded inside the metal.

The glare of the light on the glass made it hard to see what was inside, so he shifted the angle of the tube in his hand, until he could peer into the liquid within.

"What the fuck is this?" King asked.

Swimming in the liquid was a two inch long creature, which undulated like a snake or an eel, but the scales and fins on its body, the tiny legs fore and aft on its underside, the whisker like feelers coming off its face, and the crest around its head made it look very much like a different type of animal—from ancient legend.

"I don't know. But let's hope what it *isn't*, is a goddamned baby," Bishop said.

FORTY-FIVE

Chess Team HQ, Siletz, Oregon

"For the love of god, Tom, I don't know how you did this job for as long as you did," President Beaman said. He looked like he hadn't slept in days. His image on the digital screens in the operations room of Chess Team's Siletz headquarters made the man's face appear in critical detail.

Tom Duncan could see the pores of the man's face. "The People's Republic of China was overthrown, and there's now an Empress in charge of the entire nation. How the hell did we not see that coming?"

"Because this was planned for a very long time, sir," Duncan said. "For them to have controlled all the media as they did, and eliminated any opposition... Well, it would have required meticulous planning, and absolute loyalty from her followers. Does anyone at Langley know who this woman is yet?"

"Nothing," the President sighed. He leaned back in his chair and ran his palm across his face. "Absolutely nothing. As you know, she was veiled when the announcement went out, and the general—we've found out his name was... Hang on a sec."

The President leaned forward and shuffled some papers on his desk. "Huang Shuchang. Pretty sure 'Huang' is the surname. Right now, Dani doesn't have anything else on the man, although he was a high ranking general in the Communist Party. And we still haven't heard from a single Party member, so we have to assume most of them are dead somehow."

The announcement had been broadcast worldwide, and Duncan's team had watched in real time as Huang had acted as the mouthpiece for the entirely silent and motionless Empress, who sat on the dais the entire time.

Huang explained the people's dissatisfaction with the Chinese Communist Party—especially in the light of the recent attack on Kunming. He announced that the Empress had removed all the standing members of the Party, and President Xi Jinping.

Huang continually referred to the Empress as 'Her Majesty,' and he announced that the Chinese people would be cared for and would prosper under her excellent leadership as the nation moved deeper into the twenty-first century.

Huang had then explained that the media blackout had been necessary for a smooth transition, and that the Kingdom of China would soon be sending new diplomatic envoys and accepting media requests.

He said there would be another announcement in days, and then the feed had cut.

"What about your people, Tom? Have they come across anything? As far as we can tell, they are the only operatives on site. We're desperate for some information over here."

"Yes, sir," Duncan said, leaning back in his task chair, most of the way across the nation from the President. "We've come across more evidence that Primate Industries has been involved in genetic engineering of the sort Richard Ridley had been working on. The suite of offices in the Bank of China building could very easily have been a command center for the weapon that hit Kunming and Caracas. But we have no hard proof of that. It could also have been used for pretty much anything else. While there was nothing else going on in Hong Kong that could shed any light on this, I was about to pull the team from China when the Imperial announcement happened. I had people checking for signals coming out of that skyscraper. The signal came from western China, sir. Somewhere in Qinghai province. But the broadcast was simultaneously backed up at the Bank of China complex that my people had literally just left."

"You want to send your people to Qinghai," the President said.

"There's no hard link yet that this new Empress is in any way involved in the attacks on Venezuela and Kunming, sir. It's the thinnest of threads, but it's all we have, and my team is already on the ground."

In fact, he had already sent them on to Qinghai, but it would be a good idea to get Beaman on board—even though he would deny their existence later, if things didn't go as planned.

"Jesus, Tom, if they're caught, it could start World War III. I need 100% full deniability. We never had this conversation. If you even think the operation is going south, my people need to hear about it so we can start spinning things and I can swear up and down on a stack of Bibles that I never heard about your team."

"Of course, sir," Duncan said nodding, "that's the way it works. That's how it worked when the team was working for me, when I sat in the Oval. Hell, they didn't even know who I was back then. I was just a digital voice and face on a screen to them. Dom will already have gone over a number of contingency protocols with Danielle. If things go wrong, my people will vanish into thin air, and you'll never hear from us again. If members are captured, they know that no rescue will be coming."

"That's harsh," Beaman said, "and you know I wish it didn't have to be that way."

"Understood, sir. Every member of the team understands that, but it's the nature of the job. When I was whisked away from Danielle's black site in Canada, I understood perfectly well I might never be back in this country. It's the price we pay, Mr. President."

"That cost is too high, all too often. Let me know if you hear anything, Tom." The President's feed closed, and Tom Duncan sat back in his chair and thought, not for the first time, that there had to be a better way. A better world. A better life. Some way to stop genocidal madmen and unknown terrorists from launching space based weapons that evolutionarily devolved humanity.

Hope was a slippery eel of a concept that all too readily attempted to slide through his grasp. Apparently, Beaman felt the same. Duncan had obviously had his bouts with depression through the years of his incarceration and abducted relocations. He knew Chess Team would never stop looking for him but, for a long time, he really did not think they would find him.

And now that he was free at last, the maniacs of the world wanted to end it yet again. His people were in danger, the entire planet was under threat from a mysterious weapon that was likely—but not yet confirmed to be—a space based ray that belonged to the Chinese.

He just didn't know why. Or even how. The power source needed to genetically change an entire city could hardly be contained on an unobtrusive satellite. He had a guess that the weapon was powered by something on the ground that was first fired into space, and then bounced off a satellite toward its target at a different location on the ground. That was basically how simple satellite communications worked.

And the genetic tinkering with the lab samples Bishop had found in Hong Kong concerned him even more, after the team's run-in with the megalanias in the Southern Ocean. Then there was the question of what their secret opponent had wanted from Richard Ridley.

And the backdrop to all of it was poor Felice Carter, who could snuff out all life on Earth at a moment's notice. Everything was falling apart, and it was all happening at once—

Asya walked into the command center and smiled at him. All his stress melted away. If they could get through all these insane problems, if they could stop the lunatics, prevent World War III, help stabilize the new political landscape, and save the world just one more time...if they just had a moment to *breathe*, they could do all of that, and then for Tom Duncan...

He smiled back at her, and she lit up the room with her radiance and happiness.

...then there just might be a future of peace and quiet for them all.

That's what he thought—for just ten seconds. Then another intruder alert went off. The room filled with a piercing klaxon, and the lights kicked over to flashing emergency red.

FORTY-SIX

Aboard a Train, Zhengzhou, China

Getting from Hong Kong to the source of the Empress's broadcast in Qinghai province was no easy feat when you were trying to lie low. Knight had suggested they take the train, after Deep Blue had asked the team to head to Qinghai. When they had checked into it, Rook had found to his utter horror that it was a nearly thirteen-hour ride. He had insisted that they at least pay for first-class sleeper compartments, but as it turned out, the class of train on that route didn't even have sleeper cars. And the Business Class section actually looked a bit more comfortable than First and was pricier, so they went with that. The seats reclined and there was a full six feet of space between rows, with only three chairs to a row. They had a modicum of privacy since the car was mostly empty besides them, but it wasn't operationally safe for them to discuss much in public.

Rook took the chance to get some shut-eye. But after a few hours, as they blasted north over the Chinese countryside at almost two hundred miles per hour, he woke up and found himself unable to go back to sleep.

Queen slept in the chair next to him. Knight and Pawn were sleeping in their chairs at the back of the car. Bishop sat alone in a chair halfway down the car, reading on an e-reader, and King had opted to take a solo seat in the next car, in First Class, just to maintain the impression that this group of five Westerners (and one Korean-looking man) all traveling on the train at the same time, did not know one another.

Rook wasn't sure it would make a difference. If anyone was keeping an eye out for them, his towering frame and white skin stood out like a lighthouse in the dark. No harm in trying though.

He used to love riding on trains when he was younger, in New Hampshire. But now the feeling of movement without being able to see the country whiz past in the dark, made him feel a little ill. He wondered if he was experiencing some kind of strange sympathetic morning sickness, but then he recalled that Queen had not really been sick yet—if she was going to be at all. In the few down moments the team had experienced since coming to China, he had been searching the Internet for blogs on being a father. He wasn't too worried. He had siblings. Some of his sisters had kids now, and he was a great 'Uncle Stan' to them. He'd seen his own parents in action, and he'd even helped change a number of diapers—whether his sisters' or those of his nieces and nephews.

But with a baby of his own on the way, he felt a pressure to not screw it all up. Queen's painful past made him want to be an even better husband and father.

If she would marry him, that was.

He understood that she would retire from the team with him and raise a child with him. He had no illusions about their relationship. She would be with him until the end, and he with her. What he didn't know was whether she would want to be legally married or if she would prefer to do the modern twenty-first century relationship that his mother would have called 'Living in Sin.' Rook told himself he didn't really care one way or the other, as long as he had Queen's love. But deep down, he knew he wanted that traditional marriage—especially now that they were going to have a child. He just didn't know how to broach the subject with her. Or whether he should.

He glanced at the woman he loved, asleep on the chair next to him, the scar on her forehead revealed, now that she was snoozing. She was stunning. She was smart. Hyper capable. Funny, too. The more private time they spent together the funnier he had learned she was. But rather than falling into the category of team joker as he had done or competing with him for the role, she kept her sense of humor for the quiet moments. He loved that about her.

He let his gaze linger for a moment, but then turned to the darkness outside the train's window. It was punctuated by moments of light as they passed near a road or a building but then he was plunged back into darkness. His mind started to wander, first to the events in the Desolation Islands when they had retrieved Deep Blue. A trap had been waiting for them with the giant lizards, and Deep Blue was the bait. Then he thought of the attack in Africa. Much too quickly after they had arrived at the Herculean Society's base. He thought of how little they had found on the Nazca plains, and how men were waiting for them at the airport. He tried to leave out all the geopolitics, and just see the team's actual interactions on the ground over the last few days. Too many men coming to the rescue for Pawn's abductors in that corridor. Waves of poorly trained, but much too heavily armed men in the Bank of China building.

Regular security guards don't have MP5s, he thought.

The more he ran the events through his mind, focusing only on the team and not the larger global problems—the assassinations of world leaders, the attacks on Kunming and Caracas, and the overthrow of the Chinese government—he started to see a very simple pattern emerging. Everywhere they went, someone was expecting them. Not just any team but specifically Chess Team. Their faces had been on digital 'playing cards' in Peru, but it was more than that. Whoever they were facing knew them. Each of them. The opponent not only knew the Chess Team, but where they were heading at each stage of the game.

Of course, he thought, *they were tracking Duncan when we came into Africa. They couldn't track us when we were underwater in the submarine. But when we surfaced, they moved on us.* But after that horrific incident, and the loss of life, the team had found Duncan's tracker. For good measure, the rest of them had checked themselves over. No additional trackers.

So how did they know? Rook asked himself. It was a mental exercise, like doing Sudoku. To keep him sharp. He wasn't expecting to come up with an actual answer. But he went through the motions.

The video of Ridley led us to Nazca, where they knew we would go.

The ambush at the airport was simple then. If you knew the team and understood how they traveled, then you could have guessed the team would have been in Ica. San Juan airport was too close to Nazca, and they would have travelled by land some distance first before trying to fly out. Cusco was too mountainous a region and too hard to get to. No, it was either Ica or Arequipa in Peru. Rook guessed their opponent would have covered both airports, just to be safe.

After the airport ambush, the team had split up and become ghosts, travelling from different ports back to the US. Too hard to follow them all. Even Rook had had no idea where he was heading in South America before trying to get himself to Boston.

Too hard to track us then.

But then Knight and Pawn went looking for information on the Chinese video camera. *Pretty much the only frickin' thing left behind in Nazca other than Ridley's shriveled corpse.*

Then he understood. If someone knew the team, guessing where the team would look was easy. If they knew the camera was the team's only lead, they knew where it would lead them. Local thugs to abduct Pawn, with another team of better men standing by in Kowloon somewhere. *If that failed, then armed men at the Bank of China building?*

Then what? It took him just a minute to backtrack. *What led us here?*

The Empress's takeover broadcast. *Which had been backed up to the computers at the Bank of China building.*

He asked himself, of all the places in China a computer broadcast could have been backed up—or anywhere else in the world for that matter—why Hong Kong? Why would a new world leader, based in the middle of China—in almost the exact geographical center of the country—send a signal to the exact same building the team had just vacated hours earlier?

We're being played so frickin' hard, Rook thought.

He figured their opponent wanted them to go to Qinghai. They would no doubt run into a trap there.

Then he realized two things.

The first was that even someone who knew the team well couldn't have anticipated every move they would make so well. Not without inside information.

We're not being played, he thought. *We're being hacked.*

The second thing he realized was that if their security was truly compromised, then their enemies would be able to deduce exactly where they were.

Right now.

Rook leapt up. "Bishop," he shouted. "Get them up and off. Evac now!"

Queen startled awake when he shouted and was on her feet already. When Rook looked to him, Knight was already moving for the First-Class cabin to get King. Pawn was groggy but on her feet.

"Lose the comms!" Rook took his earpiece out and stamped on it. The others did the same. "We have to get off this frickin' train. Now, now, now!"

Pawn opened the door. Wind blasted into the compartment, and she held on to a safety handle.

"We're moving at over a hundred miles an hour," Bishop shouted over the noise.

Queen had moved to a door near the front of the compartment and yanked the emergency brake. A piercing alarm went off and a bright white LED light flashed upward at the ceiling. The train began to decelerate immediately.

Rook moved next to Queen and opened the door next to her. The countryside outside was still dark, with distant lights visible.

They could see the ground rushing past, way too fast.

"As soon as it looks survivable, we have to get off," Rook said.

"What happened?" Queen wanted to know.

"Someone has been tracking our every move. They probably know we're on the train. We have to—"

Before he could finish his sentence, a missile slammed into the middle of the train.

FORTY-SEVEN

Chess Team HQ, Siletz, Oregon

Deep Blue knew exactly how this would play out.

Not well.

He and Lewis Aleman had strategized and run scenarios on an attack on the support team multiple times and in multiple ways. He knew they could fend off a small attack team. But he also knew without Chess Team, the support crew could be easily taken by one simple tactic: over-whelming force.

On his monitors, Tom Duncan could see at least a hundred soldiers in black, moving on the headquarters from multiple angles. All armed with rifles. All wearing night vision headsets. No identifying insignia. The enemy was here to capture or kill the support team, and it was unlikely that these were US forces.

"Fiona," Deep Blue said into his microphone. It echoed in every room and every chamber of the base. "Activate the Panic Room Protocol. You know what to do."

"On it," came Fiona's reply, and he was pleased to not have an argument from the young woman. She was potentially their strongest team member, with her mother tongue-based earth-moving powers. But she knew there were more creative ways to use those powers. Right now, her job was to stay safe.

The panic room was nearly indestructible. Once inside, Fiona would hit a large, convenient, red button on the wall, just inside the door. The room was filled with nonperishable food, water, medical supplies, radios, and so forth. This being Chess Team's headquarters, it was also filled with computers on a separate networked connection, weapons, and communication equipment. Passports in fake names, money, and a secret exit that no one would ever find.

The walls in the room were thicker than a bank vault's, and Deep Blue knew that short of using a thermobaric bomb, no one would be getting to Fiona once she was locked in. Her safety was not just paramount for peace of mind, but also as a tactical backup plan. To make things better, the room was completely hidden in panic mode, with a fake wall in front of the door. Unless their opponents *knew* that Fiona was present in the base, they might not even think to look for her.

The rest of the present team, Lewis Aleman, Asya Machtcenko, Deep Blue himself, and security officers were what was left to fight off the threat. A few soldiers to fight off a hundred.

Still, despite the lopsided numbers, Deep Blue was grateful that some of their compatriots had left. King's parents had used their spycraft to vanish from the grid. Dom Boucher was currently in Washington, D.C., assisting Danielle Rudin and the President with intelligence.

That left Sara Fogg, King's wife, who had insisted on returning to her work in the jungles of Brazil as an epidemiologist. Deep Blue did the best he could to keep tabs on her, but he had no idea where exactly she was at the moment, and no way of knowing whether their enemies were hunting her as well.

There were, of course, extended family members, but it was Deep Blue's experience that the enemy rarely went after distant aunties and second cousins twice removed. If they were after non-combatants, the enemy was looking for leverage, which meant immediate family. This attack on the Siletz HQ was almost certainly designed to accomplish that. If Fiona and Sara Fogg were to be captured, that would make King less of a concern in the field. If Felice Carter were captured, Bishop would almost certainly lose his mind.

The other possibility nagged at Duncan, though. He had finally found some personal happiness after years of imprisonment. If this black ops team was here to simply cripple intelligence and communications, by executing the support team, rather than capturing them for leverage, then he was about to die. And so was Asya. And so was his best friend.

It was a narrow possibility. Deep Blue figured it was five percent or less likely. But it existed.

And he wasn't ready to die.

Of course, they all could have hidden in the panic room, but then the enemy would have hunted for them, and possibly found it. They would never have believed that the HQ was empty, so someone had to remain behind as sacrificial goats.

It was just that, after years of imprisonment and his newfound freedom, Duncan wasn't happy it had to be him. But using skills he had learned two lifetimes ago in the Army Rangers, he compartmentalized those feelings, altered them with a mental hammer and anvil, and transformed that anxiety, despair, and unhappiness into cold rage, cool calculation, and unyielding determination.

Aleman and Asya would have heard his orders to Fiona, wherever they were in the facility. There was no need to give a final order. They would already be on their respective ways to battle positions and would already be armed. Instead, Duncan flipped a glass cover off a red button on the desk and hit it.

The room plunged into darkness.

He stood up quietly and began moving toward a concealed door on the wall. Halfway across the room, hidden emergency lights flicked on for a single second, in filtered red LED. He was expecting it. The light was enough for him to see where he was going, to ensure he was on target for the weapons locker he was heading for, but the startling burst would have been unexpected for an intruder.

Duncan knew the irregular schedule of the lights—as did the others. They all had smart wristwatches with the schedule if they forgot. Knowing when lights would come on and go off would be a tactical advantage for the home team.

In addition to the control over lights, the base's panic mode Duncan had activated killed outside communications—not just for those in the base, but for those in the entire Siletz neighborhood. Amplifiers had been installed on the town's telephone poles to act as jammers for intruding forces.

Doors had locked shut with blast-proof metal shields. Additional hidden air vents had been activated while extant vents were snapped closed. In two minutes, after Duncan and the others had secured their hearing with special helmets, blaring noise, music, and static would alternately and unexpectedly roar through hidden speakers in the base and the community center above it. Anything to throw off the enemy. Necessary data would have been backed up off site, and on-site computers would be disabled—the hard drives melted with acid.

This wasn't Duncan's first *in situ* siege, and he had learned from the last two times in New Hampshire.

The first time he had successfully managed to repel the invading force led by an Irish mercenary named Martin Damien—although at the cost of the lives of some of his people. The second time had been against the US Army, and he had been reluctant to use lethal force against his own people.

For this assault force, whoever they were, the gloves were off. Right before Duncan closed himself in the weapons locker—which held a ladder that descended to a subterranean network of tunnels—he tossed a fragmentation grenade into the command center. It was connected to a motion activated timer on the fuse, which would obliterate the room as soon as someone attempted to breach the space. He closed the reinforced door to his weapons locker, little more than a closet with a hatch in the floor for the ladder, and then counted to ten, when he knew the device would arm itself.

Then he waited.

FORTY-EIGHT

Gabu Village, Huangnan Tibetan Autonomous Prefecture, Qinghai, China

Knight couldn't wait until dark. He knew they weren't safe in the village, and he would feel better once he and Pawn had embarked on their mountain hike, across the two miles of terrain between them and the dam where they suspected the transmission to the skyscraper in Hong Kong had originated.

After the middle of the already decelerating train near Zhengzhou had detonated, the Chess Team members—all up front on the train—had leapt off to relative safety. Despite moving fifty miles an hour, the lack of obstructions in the desert, and a mostly soft landing had left them with little more than Knight's bruised ribs, and a sprained ankle for Rook.

King had made the decision that they should all partner up and then ghost away into the night, choosing different ways to reach their destination. Queen and Rook would continue to play tourists enamored with rural China. King and Bishop were rock climbing buddies looking for the next mountain thrill. That left Knight and Pawn as budget travelers heading toward Tibet for cultural enlightenment. But despite those mild covers, they would each endeavor to stay off the major lanes of transit on their way to Qinghai Province. Luckily, where the train had exploded in Henan Province, there were plenty of small villages and smaller roads where the subteams could lose themselves over the next few days. But they all understood there was a ticking clock. Take too long and another city would revert to a Neanderthal lifestyle. If they'd been hacked, using comms was a bad idea. They had discarded all electronics and personal belongings, just to be sure.

There was no way to stay in touch with each other, and no way to contact Deep Blue for any support. They would simply plan to rendezvous near the dam. And that was still at least an eight-hour hike in the dark, for Knight and Pawn, despite how close it looked on a map. The distance crossed ridges and hills that would more than quadruple the distance in vertical loss and gain. It had taken them a week to reach the small village. It was definitely the scenic route, but if they got too close to the dam on any vehicle and the area was controlled by their enemies, they would have been detected immediately.

Even this tiny village was suspect, in Knight's mind. But it was far better than Kabula Town, which was the last actual town before the dam, and only about a ten minute drive from the structure.

Instead, they were off in the foothills of the mountains that made up the Kabula National Forest Park, and they would seek the cover of trees and sharp mountain ridges, just as soon as darkness fell. Until then, they were stuck playing tourists, wondering what might have become of their compatriots.

The village was little more than a half mile wide collection of dwellings with nearby factories and terraced rice fields. Everyone either farmed or worked in the long concrete buildings, manufacturing who knew what, most likely for people in Europe and North America. But life continued as usual for a people so far from the demographic centers that they were used to keeping on, despite political upheavals stretching back millennia.

There were two small restaurants in the village—not much more than buildings with open fronts, and two or three tables on the dirt road in front of them. Knight and Pawn had picked the one that was less busy. Although foodborne illness was a possibility, fewer people to gawk at outsiders was better.

The place they had picked was run by a little old woman named Li Fang, and she had been thrilled that both a man who appeared Korean and a clear Westerner were fluent in Mandarin Chinese, and she had quickly sat them down at her table and offered to fix them a meal. No orders were taken. Knight understood she would just get them something, and they would eat it. That was how it was at smaller places in rural China sometimes.

After Li had busied herself in the kitchen and left Knight and Pawn alone, they began to talk. But rather than using Mandarin, or English, or even Korean, which Pawn had been learning, they chose Finnish. It was a random language they had chosen so they could speak to each other privately in this part of the world. Finnish was a tough language for a casual speaker to pick up and, with a population of just under six million in Finland, and a diaspora of fewer than one million worldwide, the chances of running into a Finnish speaker in most parts of the globe was slim. Making the language tactically smart for them to use in potentially hostile situations. Plus, they both liked learning tough languages.

"Gonna be a fun hike, if I'm shitting out crawling noodles," Pawn said, her accent maybe not perfect enough to fool a native Finn, but, Knight thought, still really good.

He smiled at her. They both had tough stomachs from eating in all manner of places around the world, but she was right. Intestinal problems could slow them down. They would cross just two winding mountain roads on their journey and skirt a large mine, before descending hills toward the dam and the Yellow River. Google Earth wasn't great in the region, but it was enough on the crappy Chinese burner phone they had picked up in Lanzhou for them to see the difficulty of the journey ahead.

Even though they would depart tonight, they had paid in advance for a room in a different part of town for three nights, so it would be a few days before anyone thought to look for them—if anyone ever did.

As Knight was about to twist in his chair to look toward the kitchen for the old woman, he caught something with his artificial eye. A fast-moving vehicle, two streets over. From the shape of it, it looked like a military vehicle. Some kind of tricked-out Humvee with an armored gun turret mounted on top.

"We need to move," Knight said, springing to his feet, and running into the back room—the structure's kitchen.

Pawn was right behind him, and Knight wasn't surprised to find the kitchen was empty, the back door open, and the old lady nowhere in sight.

"She called the army," Knight said.

They sprinted out the back door, quickly winding through the warren of small dwellings and weaving their way west toward a thin line of trees that separated one part of the village from the next.

They couldn't hear the vehicle anymore, but Knight's eye tracked it as it skidded to a stop in front of the restaurant where they had been seated. The line of trees led them into the next neighboring village of Gabucun, and they were not surprised to discover there were no more people on the streets. Everyone in the villages knew that the army was looking for someone, and they would all be hunkered down in their homes, or oblivious to what was going on while out in the fields or at their factory jobs.

Knight and Pawn needed to make it five hundred feet through winding lanes before they would hit the next wooded strip of land when the wilderness of the mountain park began.

They split up, each taking different lanes. Knight used his eye to scan north along the main road into town. Two more Humvees roared toward them. He and Pawn weren't going to reach the park.

FORTY-NINE

Yellow River, Qinghai Province, China

Queen felt bad, but she ate the last of the food they had anyway. She and Rook, rather than heading straight toward the region on the Yellow River where the dam was located, had taken the main highway well past it, and then doubled back. They had stocked up on supplies, visited the Qinghai Guide National Geopark Museum as tourists, and then quietly slipped away. They had approached the dam on foot, from upriver, skirting the artificial reservoir, and creeping ever closer to the structure over the rippled hills by night.

But without a plan, and with far too much activity in the area by day, they had been reluctant to move any closer to the actual structure. After days of waiting, their food had run out.

"Well, this has sealed the deal on one thing, at least," Rook said softly.

They were lying on the hard, rocky ground, concealed from view by scraggly desert bushes. They would stay on the ground until nightfall. The terrain around them was either barren rock or dusty, dry soil with sparse clumps of short grass. Outside of the few bushes and caves they had found, there was no cover during daylight, and anything standing over three foot tall would be spotted from over a mile away, clear across the artificial lake.

"What's that?" Queen asked, but he could tell from her tone she knew he was just about to make a wisecrack. He pressed on anyway, too irritated with the situation to do anything more. He hated waiting for things. "We're *never* moving to Arizona. This desert shit sucks. Reminds me of that mess in Mongolia."

Queen turned her head to look back at him, where he was spooning her on the rough ground, as they hid under the bush. "Your problem is you always need to take on every Mongolian Death Worm you run into."

"So does your mom," Rook countered, without even thinking.

Queen chuckled softly.

Jokes about each other's mothers had become a regular running feature of their relationship—despite the fact that Queen's mother had died when she was a child. She'd told Rook that she was much more horrified at the thought of one day meeting Rook's still-living mother in New Hampshire and keeping a straight face. Worse, she was terrified she might slip up and make a 'your mom' joke in front of the elderly woman. "I always figured you'd want to be somewhere near your family and the White Mountains anyway."

Rook thought about it seriously for a moment. "I've always liked the Presidential Range, but I don't need to be too close to the farm, or they'll want me to come over and help do shit all the time. But it doesn't need to be New Hampshire. You never really said where you want to be. We could go anywhere in the world."

Queen turned away from him again, but she snuggled backward tighter against him. "I've seen enough of the world. I just want to be where you are."

Rook was crafting his next joke in his head when he heard a persistent buzzing hum.

"Contact," he whispered.

Then they both fell silent, straining to hear the hum. He was certain it was mechanical and not some strange Chinese insect. The bush they had chosen concealed them from the air and from anyone travelling the area by boat. There were no nearby roads, so behind them was just slopes of rock and scree. The bush was one of the largest bits of cover, but it was also pretty sparse. They could see clearly through it. If a boat came along, they would be able to see it on the water without even moving their heads. And presumably, if anyone were to look directly at the bush from below on the water, as long as Rook and Queen stayed still, no one should have been able to spot them.

So now it was a waiting game, and the hum grew steadily louder, but far higher pitched than the engine of a boat. "What the hell is that?" Rook whispered.

"Not a boat," came Queen's whispered reply, and it was so soft Rook could barely hear it.

The buzzing hum began to doppler back and forth, and Rook imagined it in his head. It was something small, and fast, and it was down near the water, its racing sound echoing across the lake and bouncing off the rock on each side of the basin.

Rook leaned his mouth right up to Queen's ear, and very slowly and very softly whispered the word, "Drone."

A second later, they could see the source of the noise.

Rook was right. Three quadcopter drones, each maybe a yard across, sped just over the water's surface. The craft flew so close to the top of the lake that they left a wake as they flew by. All three were dark gray, and their buzzing propellors helped them race past and out of view as fast as a sports car.

The buzz just grew louder, and then the craft passed.

Rook knew that the military now used drones for all manner of purposes, from espionage to attacks on personnel. He hoped these were civilian craft, but they seemed too large and the fact that there were three of them indicated it was a team of operators flying them—or a computer. His lips still near Queen's ear, he whispered, "Don't move."

But that plan went to hell almost immediately. The drones rose into the night sky and circled back. They flew directly over their heads and sped past them in the opposite direction from which they had come. Then they turned again, and came to an abrupt halt, about fifty feet west. Rook could just barely see the hovering fleet through a gap in the branches. A small door opened at the belly of the quadcopter in the center of the three, and something black, and the size of a human fist dropped out and fell toward the ground.

"Oh shit, get ready to run," Rook said, no longer with any pretense of whispering.

The fragmentation grenade detonated with a tremendous roar, echoing back and forth across the lake, and spewing dirt, dust, and grit into the air in every direction.

"Go," Rook said.

They both scrambled up, and started running across the rocky slope, toward the distant dam, and away from the quadcopters. Queen was faster, as Rook was still dealing with the ache of a sprained ankle, but it was a relatively mild sprain, and the hike across the forbidding terrain around the Yellow River's artificial basin had helped loosen the injury over the previous two days. As Rook glanced back, two of the copters moved slowly in their direction, and they also opened bomb bay doors in their bellies. The lead quadcopter raced ahead, well past their position as Rook and Queen ran. Rook bent down and scooped up a fist sized rock as he went. Without needing to discuss it, Queen stuck to their escape plan, veering toward the water as she ran.

The water was their only chance of an unseen escape. They were each excellent swimmers and could hold their breath for long periods of time. As long as they weren't facing boats, they could easily submerge and come up for air around a bend of rocky promontory, keeping hidden from aerial or land-based pursuit.

The lead copter swung around, dropping to a menacing ten feet off the ground, and hovering in place.

The two copters behind them each dropped grenades. The twin detonations boomed loudly in the rocky canyon, but the blasts were much too far back to injure them.

We're being herded, Rook thought.

The lead copter moved toward Rook another two feet and then stopped. As if it was daring him to take action. He kept running toward it with Queen, but still veering slightly toward the water. The quadcopter changed trajectory, only now detecting his plan.

They must have cameras on them, Rook thought.

Ahead of him, Queen suddenly jagged to the left, away from the trajectory of the oncoming lead copter, and she headed straight toward the water.

Rook stayed on his path, heading right toward the drone. The two back up copters swept out to the water, and around over the lake, heading back toward Queen as she still raced to the water's edge.

The message was clear. These things were way faster, and Rook and Queen would not be permitted to reach the water.

Rook continued toward the lead drone and hurled his rock. At the last second, the craft tried to dodge the throw, but it was too late. The hard smooth stone mashed into one of the drone's propellors, and the craft wobbled for just a second before plummeting downward and cracking loudly into the slope of rock. To his left, Queen slowed to a halt and started running back up the slope toward him.

Rook scanned around for another sizable rock, but all that was near him were pebbles and tufts of grass. Of the remaining two quadcopters, one of them ascended to a fifty foot height again. The second raced over to where the first had fallen, and slowly descended to almost the height at which Rook had pelted the first.

In range of my throw, he thought.

Why?

Then he heard a voice speaking English, but with a thick Chinese accent.

"Mr. Rook. Please halt all hostilities. Ms. Queen. Please stand near Mr. Rook."

Rook stared at the nearby copter and could see a small speaker on its underside. He also noticed that the bomb bay door was still open.

"Uh, how about no?" Rook said.

"Unacceptable, Mr. Rook," the drone replied. "You'll notice the other unit far above, out of your striking distance. We have no shortage of grenades. As we speak, additional fleets are heading your way. There is nowhere for you to go. You cannot escape. You can surrender peacefully, or we can detonate the hillside until nothing remains but rubble and very small specks of the both of you."

Rook glanced at Queen, and he could see in her eyes that she thought the best strategy was to go along for now. He looked back to the drone.

"Who am I speaking to?"

"This is Colonel Bao, of Her Majesty's Imperial Army. Why?" The voice sounded too young to Rook for the man to be a Colonel. Across the water, Rook spotted another five quadcopter drones approaching them.

Just wanted to know who I'm gonna kill later, he thought.

FIFTY

Chess Team HQ, Siletz, Oregon

Tom Duncan ran through the subterranean passage below the headquarters. He expected a spectacular explosion in the command center, but one never came. Instead, he heard automatic rifle fire in another part of the complex, and he didn't want the others to face a hundred troops on their own.

The storage locker he'd been in led down a ladder into a network of winding tunnels. The passage was constructed that way on purpose, so it would be easy to defend, with plenty of places to seek cover along the way to any destination. Now as he ran, checking corners as he went, Duncan could hear the muffled sound of Mötley Crüe's "Kickstart My Heart" blasting through the hidden speakers in the complex above him.

He knew the lights throughout the building would be flickering on and off at random intervals, too, which would play havoc with the enemy's night vision equipment.

Armed with a Swiss-made Brügger & Thomet APC9 submachine gun with a collapsible stock, Duncan cleared each twist and turn, expecting resistance, but not meeting any. He'd heard some firing from above in the main complex, but then all weapons had fallen silent. Now it would be cat and mouse.

Where the hell are they? he wondered.

All the rooms in the complex above him had blast doors. He should be hearing explosions or some kind of fracas above, as the soldiers attempted to breach the rooms. But all was eerie and quiet. After the initial bout of shooting, he heard nothing but silence.

This isn't right.

He'd seen a hundred men approaching the base on the monitors upstairs.

They couldn't all have given up—

A single shot rang out from his right, down a twisting corridor he knew led to the southwest corner of the complex...and an emergency escape tunnel that ran half a mile away into the woods.

Duncan turned, taking the corners slowly. As he checked the next, he caught a glimpse of someone crouched and facing away from him. His head darted out and back in a fraction of a second, but the image was imprinted on his brain. Asya's hair.

Rather than popping around the corner to join her and risking friendly fire—or using his voice and risking enemy fire—he placed his hand around the corner and tapped a spare magazine against the wall three times.

He waited for a beat and heard the same tapping noise repeated. Then he turned the corner. Asya was still crouched by the next corner, waiting with her back to him. She raised her left hand and gestured for him to join her.

He slid up behind her but remained standing. Bending over her and about to whisper to her, she answered his unasked question.

"One man. He's down," she said. Her voice wasn't a whisper, but it was low enough that it wouldn't carry far.

"One man," Deep Blue mumbled to himself.

It made no sense.

How are they even down in the tunnels? he wondered.

Asya, likewise armed with an APC9, slid down to the floor, and darted out around the corner, spraying the tunnel ahead with a controlled burst before she was back behind cover again. *Unless...*

The pounding jackhammer beat of glam metal from the building above them cut off abruptly and they were plunged into complete silence.

Tom Duncan had tried to come up with contingency plans for everything—everything except the possibility that they would be hacked, and the enemy would know all about their contingency plans.

Damnit.

Then a voice came out of the darkness ahead. The English was flawless, but Duncan could hear in the timbre that it was a smaller man. "Mister Duncan..."

"What is this?" Asya asked Duncan.

He sighed. "This is where they negotiate our surrender. We're pinned on all sides."

Asya flashed him a look of defiance. He knew she would fight to the end, but he also knew there would be no way out of this one. Close to a hundred men? They would be covering all the exits. If he was right about the hack—and he had to be, or they never would have found the tunnel network or the music system—the enemy would have covered all their bases.

"Mister Duncan. Miss Asya. Your security officers are dead. We have Mister Aleman already. My men are on all sides of you. Your plan to defend yourselves in a tunnel was great—as long as you're not surrounded by men with grenades. You only have two options. Surrender or die. And since I was sent here to capture you, I'd rather you *not* die."

"Proof of life for Aleman," Duncan demanded.

A second later, Aleman's pained voice called back. "I caught a round in the leg. Sorry."

Duncan let the silence spin out. He and Asya were too far from the nearest ladder back up to the surface, and with so many men, they would never get far. They might take out a few soldiers, but never all of them. And as he had suspected, the men were here to collect the Siletz support crew as leverage against Chess Team.

Time to be a prisoner again, Duncan thought. At least he had a lot of experience with the process.

"Hold your fire," he said. "We're coming out."

Stepping around Asya, Duncan led them deeper into the tunnel, and around another corner. Waiting there were five armed men, the leader of whom had only a holstered pistol. Up close, Duncan could see that each of them were Chinese, but not all of them were ethnic Han. He thought one of the men looked Uyghur. He was the man keeping his rifle trained on Lewis Aleman.

As soon as they approached the men, the leader nodded, and his lieutenant spoke rapid Mandarin into a small, old-fashioned, two-way radio on his chest.

More soldiers came up the tunnel from behind Duncan, as he and Asya were cuffed with zip ties.

The leader, a man with subdued black captain's bars on his uniform, spoke again. "Thank you for seeing the light, Mister Duncan. Would have been nice if you could have done that before killing my men. But my Empress only asked that I bring her two captives..."

The man drew his pistol in a flash and brought it up toward Duncan.

"No!" Aleman shouted. Despite his injuries, he shoved past the Uyghur and lunged from his uninjured leg.

Lewis Aleman leapt up between Duncan and the attacking captain, just as the man's suppressed sidearm barked in the tunnel.

The echo of the shot continued in the tight confines of the space, long after Lewis Aleman's dead body collapsed to the floor in a heap.

"Lew!" Duncan shouted, dropping to his knees next to his best friend.

But there was no time to mourn or even react, as the captain ordered the men to drag him away, and a black sack was slid down over his head.

FIFTY-ONE

Cha Rigongba Village, Hualong Hui Autonomous County, Qinghai

King and Bishop took a very different route from the others. They followed the main highway from Lanzhou toward Xining, the latter being one of the last outposts of civilization with a functioning airport on the way deeper into Tibet or the deserts of Xinjiang. But shortly before the city of Xining, the men boarded a smaller bus and followed a winding mountainous highway that ran roughly south, before it would eventually dead end at a Tibetan temple that overlooked the Yellow River—right where it let out on the other side of the dam.

But they never made it to the Xiaqiong temple. Instead, as their bus rolled into the town, right near a Buddhist Academy, a crowd of police officers in navy blue trench coats halted the bus at a roadblock. They were right before the last turn off point before continuing onward south toward the towns and villages surrounding the dam. King had seen that point on a map but, as it was still a two hour drive from the village down to the dam's environs, he figured there would be no point in setting up any surveillance this far north.

"They might not be here for us," Bishop whispered.

King wasn't so sure. Then men surrounded the front end of the bus. They were all armed with AK-47 style rifles, which was fairly standard for officers of the law in rural China, but these men were leveling their weapons at the bus. And they seemed worried.

It was still another mile through the village before they would run out of road and they'd be able to lose themselves in the rugged countryside, far above the waters of the river.

King assessed the situation, and came to a conclusion that he never liked, but usually worked: run away.

He and Bishop were seated two rows from the back of the bus. When he turned to check the back door of the vehicle, he knew the jig was up. Twenty more armed men stood arrayed across the road behind them, all nervously pointing their weapons.

"They're here for us," King confirmed. "But it's a two hour trip down to the dam from here. Let's just see what happens. Too many civilians around."

He looked at the faces of the largely elderly men and women on the bus. Only now did he notice there were no children. He still didn't want to see these people suffer. There was no look of recognition in the faces of the passengers. They didn't know why the bus was being stopped, but they could all guess that it was the two foreign men who wore the clothing of mountaineers or die-hard hikers.

Then King heard one of the police officers speak to the bus driver in sharp Mandarin. "Send the foreign devils out."

King just waited a second, not willing yet to reveal that he understood Mandarin fluently. The driver turned to him, and they made eye contact. Without a word, the older man pointed to the door of the vehicle.

King just nodded, and stood up, indicating that Bishop should follow him.

The drive down the mountain took two hours, and King was surprised that the men had not bound them. In fact, one of the officers had held the rear passenger door of their battered SUV open, and politely indicated they should get in. There were plenty of opportunities for escape along the way. But King weighed the benefits of enjoying a quick ride to their destination versus being hunted across the landscape and hiking for hours to reach the same place. He decided he'd rather conserve his strength.

Bishop sat silently. His head was back, and his eyelids appeared closed. But King knew he was still observing everything, noting every opportunity, and readying himself for the battle to come.

Neither man spoke. And the police officers seemed pleased that their prisoners were cooperating. At last, their route came down out of the mountains and swept around to the west, following the bends of the river toward Kabula Town and the dam structure beyond it.

Kabula Town looked to be little more than a wide spot in the road, but as they continued along the river toward the dam, King began to see signs of what he had both hoped for and dreaded: Gigantic antenna arrays. Parabolic dishes that dwarfed anything he had seen before. The road toward the dam ran pretty straight, and he had time to appreciate the giant metal towers, piercing the sky like knives and growing taller with every thousand feet they drove. There was an immense complex where the dam sat, with concrete structures and buildings with pagoda like roofs stretching far up the hillside, past where he could see from the edge of the vehicle's ceiling.

There was no known technology he could think of that would combine a hydroelectric dam with massive towers and communications antennas. This entire facility was not what it seemed. He'd found the source of the weapon that had genetically altered and devolved human beings. But for the life of him, he couldn't figure out what the technology was or how it could be powered. There was no way a simple dam on the Yellow River could supply the energy to blast a powerful genetic weapon into space—and control the corresponding satellites that maneuvered it to pinpoint accuracy around the globe.

Unless this is just a control station, and all the energy comes from the satellite, he thought. *But then why is this control station so immense?*

King had seen major space related bases around the world. He's seen the Very Large Array and Arecibo Observatory. They were tiny compared to this facility in the middle of nowhere. King even doubted the dam could keep lights on in a facility this size. He bent forward slightly, pretending to cough, so he could glance up the hillside. The step-like buildings just kept going up the mountains.

He didn't understand any of what he was seeing, but he knew, without a shadow of a doubt, that this facility was behind the attacks on Kunming and Caracas. He understood why the Chinese would attack Kunming first. But he didn't understand why the Venezuelans were a threat to whatever the longer-term Chinese plan might be. But one thing was clear. If this facility was knocked out, the strange new weapon probably would be as well.

Unless...

Unless this was just a command-and-control facility...and there were others.

Either way, King thought. *This one has to go. We can deal with the problem of other stations later.*

He and Bishop just had to stay alive long enough to do some damage. Sooner or later, the other members of his team would show up to do their share as well.

The vehicles stopped in front of an array of tinted glass walls, windows, and doors.

He and Bishop were motioned toward the doors by some of the young men, who now seemed relaxed. Not at all afraid that King and Bishop might try something. They probably felt secure that there were enough men in the area to track them down no matter what they tried.

King had seen numerous opportunities for escape if that had been on his agenda. Even now, the men around him had their rifles casually slung on shoulders, as if they expected no resistance.

He knew the time to make a break for it would be before he reached whatever holding cell he was headed for, though. Still, he wanted to see more, and understand more, before that time came.

A man with a crisply pressed uniform and colonel's insignia on it approached and led them inside the door with a gesture. "My name is Colonel Bao," he said in flawless English. "You might not have heard during your travels, Mister Sigler, but the former People's Republic of China is now ruled by Her Imperial Majesty, Lady Crimson the First."

Things were worse than King had suspected. They were waiting for him and Bishop. Not just because they were foreigners. That meant the rest of the team was also in danger—or possibly already killed or captured. Worse still, he now had zero knowledge about China's current political landscape. Was there resistance to this new Empress? Was there civil war throughout the country? Too many questions. Rather than playing coy and pretending to be the hiker he was dressed as, King owned up to it.

"No," he lied. "I hadn't heard. An Empress?"

"Oh yes, Mister Sigler," Bao said, smiling, as he swept open another door leading from the glass foyer into a large ballroom decked out in red velvet tapestries and an intricate gold-embroidered, wall-to-wall carpeting. At the center of the large space was a raised dais, and an ornate throne. On the throne sat a huge woman, in flowing red and black robes, with a crown seated on her very red, straight hair. Even under thick pancake makeup, King could see that the face was not right. When she smiled broadly at his entrance, and he could see her teeth, he understood why.

And he recognized her.

Bao continued, "Her Imperial Majesty is *very* much looking forward to meeting you. *Again.*"

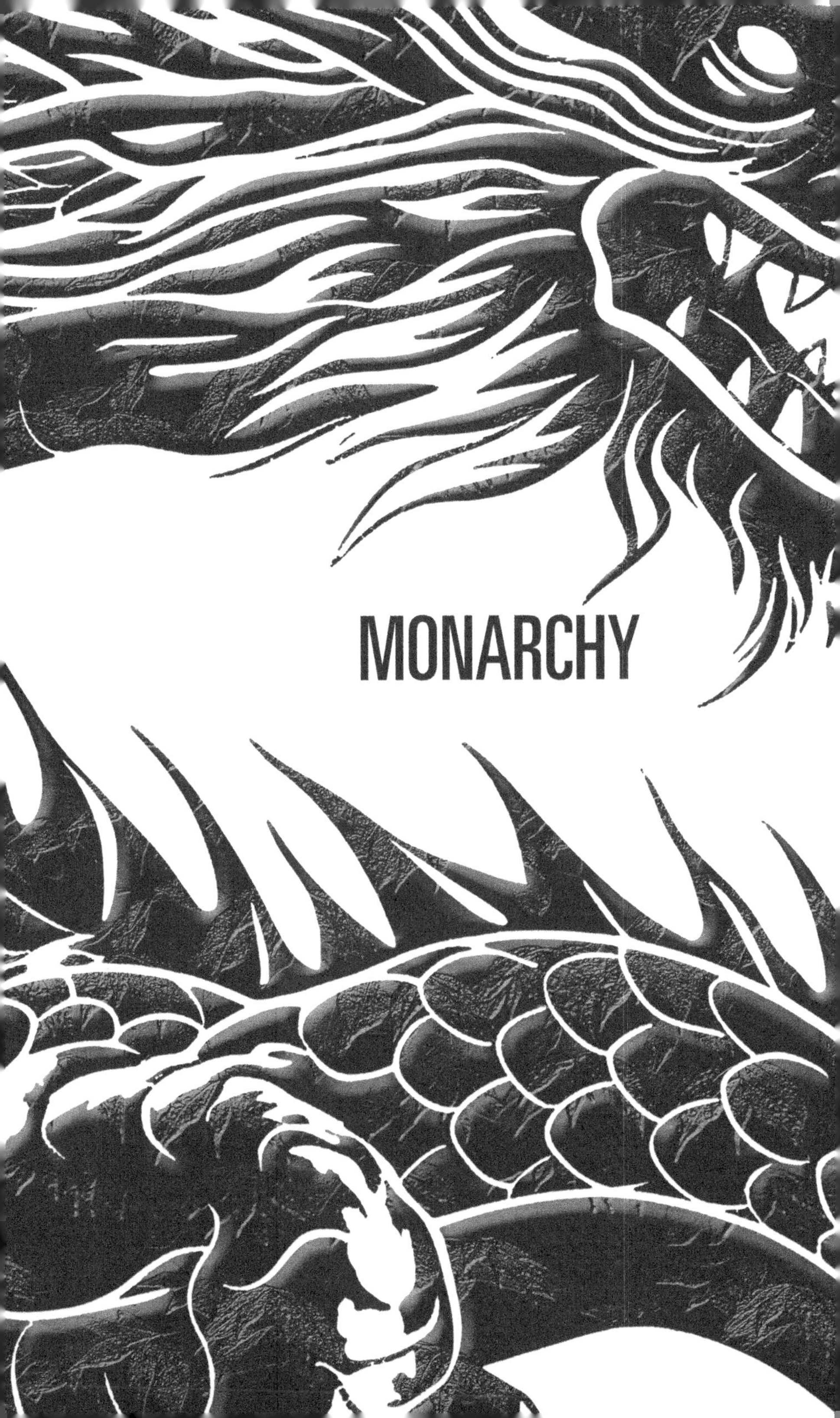
MONARCHY

FIFTY-TWO

Bishop looked at the woman rising from the throne and wondered if he would ever be freed from his past, or if it would cyclically continue to return to haunt him.

Although technically this woman was more from Rook's past, she brought up everything for Bishop again. On one of their earliest missions, Bishop's DNA had been genetically altered by the rogue geneticist, Richard Ridley. Bishop had been turned into a super-strong, nearly mindless zombie version of himself. A 'Regen,' as they had been called. There were positives, of course. He'd become nearly impervious to injury.

But the rage that coursed through his being took a terrible toll on his psyche.

The team tried many cures, after Ridley's seeming defeat. Gene tinkering. A medically induced coma. Pharmaceuticals. Bishop even tried alternative approaches from yoga to meditation and aromatherapy. Nothing much helped.

Chess Team then encountered a cryptozoologist who stumbled into the last female remnants of devolved Neanderthal survivors living in the jungles of Vietnam, called the Nguoi Rung. They mated with the local human population, creating a tribe of over two thousand, and they excelled in the jungle, moving rapidly through trees overhead, and possessing the strength of silverback gorillas.

At the end of the Vietnam mission, Rook insisted that the remaining creatures and their offspring be left in peace. A year later, though, the tribe was slaughtered by Ridley's forces in a separate incident.

During that first mission in Vietnam, Bishop had come across crystals with a curious curative property. He started wearing one around his neck. The crystal kept his rage in check until it was lost but, shortly after that, Ridley removed his Regen fury during a battle—but that same cure robbed him of his nearly superhuman strength and regenerative abilities. Still, Bishop had viewed the change as a positive development for him personally.

He fondly remembered the crystal, and its soothing effect on him, though.

The same crystals Bishop had found in Hong Kong.

Now he understood why.

The woman descending the steps in front of the dais and approaching them, the woman who was now apparently the imperial leader of China, was the matriarch of that tribe of devolved creatures. A woman that Rook had watched die in Vietnam.

"Red," King said, his mouth hanging open in surprise.

"Empress Crimson," Bao corrected, although his tone betrayed no hint of actual irritation with the verbal faux pas. The man continued to stand behind King and Bishop, so relaxed he appeared either drugged or bored.

The woman loomed over them, and Bishop was six foot four. She looked to weigh over three hundred pounds of coiled muscle. Her face was covered in tiny scars like it had repeatedly undergone plastic surgery, but she was walking erect, like a human. The Nguoi Rung that Bishop remembered had more closely resembled animals, moving on all fours. The amount of orthopedic restructuring it would have taken to make her appear more human would have been extensive and costly. And painful.

But now she casually approached them, a long cape flowing behind her, a broad smile on her face. There had been no attempt to restructure her teeth, Bishop saw. They were still terrifying fangs. But they were a perfectly polished, gleaming white color.

"Jack Sigler and Erik Somers. How nice to see you again. And how nice to finally complete the set. Tremblay, Baker, and Shin are waiting for you to join them in their cells."

Bishop noted something. There was a slight sneer when Crimson said Queen's last name. He wondered if she still had a thing for Rook.

That could work for us...or against us, he thought.

To Bishop's left, King reined in his astonishment, and he was back on task, trying to get whatever information he could from her in whatever time they had. "How? Rook saw you die."

Bishop was surprised when she turned her attention to him instead of answering King. She looked him over, as if she was assessing him. It took him a second, and then he realized she was smelling him.

"*You* know the power of the Meru crystals. You know what they can do. Their energy is still mingled with your scent, even after all this time," Crimson walked around him, and he turned, his eyes following her.

Bishop was trying to run the calculus in his head of whether he and King could take her and Bao. The Colonel was still relaxed, his hand nowhere near his holstered firearm. But Crimson was massive, and no doubt extremely strong. Both Bishop and King could fight, and both were quick, but it didn't seem like the time—and if she could smell the crystals on him, years after the fact, maybe she would be able to detect his aggressive intent before striking.

King stood still and his face was impassive, as she swept behind him and around to stand in front of them again. Bishop couldn't detect any hint that King was ready to spring into action.

"The crystals healed my body. But surviving in the jungle on my own was another story. And I knew too much about the outside world by that point." The Empress's face soured, as she recalled her past.

"You sought out civilization," King guessed.

"Yes," she said, her face still showing the horrors she most likely faced. "The criminal underworld in Hanoi was easy to enter, and climbing the ranks was child's play. Transitioning from criminal power to *true power* in a world government was much trickier. But patience and knowledge got me there."

"That's impressive," King said.

Bishop knew it was part of a plan to keep her talking. The longer she went on, the more time they had to plan an escape or look for an opportunity. Anything that kept them alive, out of a cell, and not being tortured.

It was Bishop's turn to prolong that fate. "So, you took your revenge on Ridley, and framed him for everything."

She laughed. A huge barking, grating sound that filled the throne room with a thunderous echo. The sound was so sudden and so loud that it made Bishop jolt in surprise.

"Oh no, dear boy. I had no idea at first that Ridley's forces were the ones behind the attack that nearly killed me. Or the murder of my sisters. I can't tell you how long I tried to bring my siblings back with the crystals, once I realized that *they* were what had saved me. But it was no use. No, I didn't know I needed to 'take my revenge' on Ridley at that point. I just knew that you and your Chess Team brought all that hell to my world."

She sneered at him, and then turned her gaze on King.

"Your team and your missions. Your world, clashing with mine, Jack. Do you know how I climbed the ranks of the criminal underworld? With computers. I started out with no knowledge. The more I gained, the more I craved. Once I understood the world at large, and what computers could do, I opened the eyes of the crime lords to what could be accomplished with more information—on everyone and everything. And once I took over and moved my organization out of Vietnam and into China? I found out what I could accomplish with an *enormous* work force and cutting-edge computing power."

She walked around them again, but this time she continued toward the door to the throne room.

"Come, Bao," she said. "Let's show them what I've built. It's no fun to brag without visuals. Besides. I'm in the mood to devolve another major metropolis."

FIFTY-THREE

King understood that the situation was now dire. Keeping Red talking would stave off whatever hell she had planned—but only for so long. He couldn't guess what she had done and how many bodies she had left behind along the road, as she clawed her way from forgotten creature to ruler of an entire empire. But he knew she would have few confidants, and that she craved recognition for her mighty efforts. He would use that on the outside, while frantically searching for a tiny opening on the inside.

As she led them into the corridor and down a stairway toward double doors, King took in his surroundings. The palace—if that was what it was—was a nearly labyrinthine structure that stretched up the hillside. The building's interior was all twists and turns, with doors and unremarkable, unlabeled corridors. Everything was still new and had the look and smell of recently poured concrete and freshly laid carpet.

"Empress," he said, thinking that while she was unlikely to fall for direct flattery, following etiquette might keep him and Bishop alive longer, "You've clearly risen to great heights from your start in Vietnam. You've taken over one of the most powerful nations on Earth. You could have just stopped there. I don't understand. Why attack other nations?"

Crimson turned and smiled at him, as Bao opened the double doors for them. The look wasn't a good one. Almost a leer, King wasn't sure whether she was pleased or thinking of eating his spleen. "That's a great question, Jack, but it tells me you've bought into a specific belief."

She turned and strode into the room. King shared a quick glance with Bishop and held his fist across his left chest. A Chess Team sign language gesture that meant 'Be ready for anything.'

Bishop's nod was nearly imperceptible as he followed Crimson into the room. King was right behind him, and then stopped in his tracks.

The room was more realistically a cavern. It stretched a mile under the mountain and was just as broad. The floor was terraced and sloped downward, so that King could see the entire technological wonderland spread out before him. Rings around the outer edges held hundreds or maybe even thousands of workstations, each with a Chinese man or woman manning the desktop computers on them. Cables and wires were cleverly hidden and, when King looked down to the grated metal floor, he could see the bundles of wiring that ran through a molded concrete trench just under his feet.

Beyond the desks were lower tiers of laboratory stations. King recognized many of the cyclers and sequencers used in genetic research. Below that was a ring of crates—both wooden and metal. Deeper down the conical space were giant machines with overhead wires behind chain-link fences he couldn't even guess at. Above the cavern was a complicated gridwork of iron support trusses, air conditioning vents, and lights, casting a uniform industrial glow over everything.

When he lowered his eyes from the cavern's ceiling, Crimson was standing next to him, watching him. "In the United States, a large number of people believe that China is the greatest threat America has ever faced. They believe that the technological acumen and massive population of this country poses the single biggest risk to worldwide security and peace. There's just one problem with that narrative."

She looked at King and stepped closer to him. He could smell the lightly applied and, no doubt very expensive, perfume she wore, but her breath reeked of something raw and meaty. Still, he held her gaze without flinching.

"The problem...is it's a false narrative."

"False how?" King asked, now genuinely interested.

"Completely." She turned her back on him and began descending the steps through the amphitheater of technology. "China imports the necessary resources for its energy. All the inputs needed to grow our own food are brought in from other countries. And the two million-man army? Dwindling."

She stopped abruptly and whirled around to look King in the face again. "In the last five years, the birth rate in this country has dropped by seventy percent. That's not the fastest drop in China's history, Jack. It's the fastest drop in birth rate that humanity has ever experienced! Think about that. Let it really sink in. The population of China—and the world—is aging without sufficient replacement births across generations. The time to fix that problem was twenty or thirty years ago."

"So," King said, really digesting what she was saying. "You're saying we're all going to die out? All of humanity?"

"Not all and not immediately, no," she resumed her descent. "But there are going to be too few people to keep the globalized economy truly global. It's going to all fall apart. The US will pull back from performing as the Planetary Policeman and focus on keeping themselves alive. The rest of the world will fend for itself, and things will devolve into warlordism."

"So, you're starting things early?" King asked, really not following her logic.

"I made all my gains by accumulating and manipulating information, Jack. Computers and what they could achieve were my way up the criminal ladder. Well, that and brute force." Again, she flashed a grin at him, and he felt like a gazelle being eyed up by a starving lion. "I studied demographics, economics, geopolitics, and the history of empires. I became fascinated with strategic forecasting. If you know the general direction the future is likely to go, can you make a change here, drop an invention there, and intentionally affect the outcome of the future? Yes. You can.

"So, I tracked down all the information about your Chess Team. I found Ridley and slowly resurrected him. I explained to him my philosophy and my plans. I offered him a deal. He could make my recordings and give me the secrets of his genetics research, and I would let him live and be an equal partner. He was eager to take me up on that."

"But you killed him," Bishop said. "Cold."

Crimson took no insult from the comment. "He was untrustworthy, of course. As soon as I had what I needed from him, he needed to be removed from this world again."

"And you left that camera for us to find," King guessed.

"Of course," Crimson said. "I took Ridley's research, and I took all the secrets from your organization, Jack. When my operatives learned that Tom Duncan was being whisked off to a black site years ago, I made arrangements to get him. I took what information I could from him, too. But yes, the camera and the other tidbits were to lead you right here in the end—if any of the traps along the way didn't kill you. But you, despite your interesting life, Jack...*you* were not what I wanted. I needed all the secrets you held. Chess Team had a lot. But your Herculean Society, that you and that buffoon Alexander cared for all those years? Treasure trove of information. I'm especially interested in the immortality recipe. I'm sure it's in there somewhere."

King blanched. He knew she'd gotten past Deep Blue's extensive firewalls and security. She'd been one step ahead of them the entire time, but to think that she had access to the centuries of secrets the Herculean Society cared for and hid from humanity? She could do untold damage. He realized she'd somehow discovered the Society's base in Cape Town, but he assumed that was just her following the tracker in Duncan and getting forces in place quickly. Now, he suspected she had been staking out not just that base, but all the Herculean sites around the globe.

Crimson led them past chain-link fences around the giant buzzing machines near the inner rings of the massive arena, and toward a circular central hub into which hundreds of cables were plugged in an arc rising up from the floor and diving down again into the center. King couldn't see what was at the very center of the space now because he was too close to the arched technology.

Crimson stopped abruptly again and turned to face King and Bishop. Bao hung back, one tier up the ringed cavern. "I gathered information so I could predict the future, and the future is grim, Jack. I took over a country, yes, but as soon as the world really starts falling apart, I would be constantly fending off invaders. Empires usually fall because they grow too big and decay, or because someone else conquers them. The United States was too smart at the end of World War II to attempt global imperialism. It would have been too costly and too much work. And they didn't really have the manpower to lord it over the whole planet. Instead, they offered global protection with their superior navy for worldwide industry and trade. The rising tide would raise all underdeveloped nations. All those nations had to do in return to be a part of the coming prosperity was to join the cause against communism in the Cold War. The US got worldwide allies, kept the Russians in check, and got on with prosperity. The rest of the world caught up quickly. Just one problem with that model..."

"The Cold War ended," King said.

"Precisely," Crimson looked like she was pleased with her pupil for learning so quickly. "No more advantage for the US in safeguarding everyone, especially when they need so little from the rest of the planet. Oh, they still need some of the things they can only get from Central and South America, sure. But no point in keeping global trade routes open and safe from piracy and plunder anymore. The Americans saw the future and saw that everyone would benefit from some peace. So, they enforced it. Now, they see the future again and realize they no longer need to enforce world security. Simple as that."

"And the rest of the world can fall, if necessary," King said, realizing the broader picture.

"As you say," Crimson agreed. "The future is now a Zero-Sum Game, Jack. Resources and manpower. That's what it all comes down to. The Cold War worked first because the US had nukes and no one else did. Then it worked because of Mutually Assured Destruction. So, I now have a weapon that can turn a populace into *de*-evolved creatures—not too genetically dissimilar from my deceased siblings. A loyal work force. And a deterrent all in one. Easy to control; unlikely to rebel. And these new devolved hybrids won't be consumers, Jack. That time is past. They'll just need to be fed. I keep other countries afraid and subservient. The Chinese have long believed China to be the center of the world, and the peoples of the rest of the planet to be uncivilized barbarians. Now that will be literally true."

"And the Consortium?" King asked.

"Oh, they were useful for a time. Chambers. Putin. Others. But once my weapon was fully functional? They, too, were surplus to requirements. It's really just business, in the end."

King pointed at the mound of wires and thick cables all arcing into the center of the enormous stadium. "And what's that, then?"

Crimson's teeth glittered like diamonds when she smiled, and King understood this time there was actual menace in that leer. "That...is the power source that drives my weapon. And I have you to thank for it, Jack. Go ahead. Have a closer look." She strode around the circular arc to the right, leading King and Bishop in her wake.

There was a break in the wall of cables, and she beckoned them toward it to look past the mass of machinery.

King stepped forward and saw a platform at the center, the size of a bed. On it was a strapped down man, whose body was shriveled and frail, his skin a sickly gray color. Every one of the arcing wires and cables was plugged into his body. There were ring-like ports that covered most of his legs and arms, and nearly all his torso and groin. The ports and the cables stopped just before the man's wrinkled neck and head.

Even though King was looking down on the head from behind, he could still recognize the man, who had once been known throughout the ancient world as the legendary Hercules.

FIFTY-FOUR

In the early days of the Chess Team's exploits, Rook and Queen encountered a man who would play an important part in their future—but more so in King's personal exploits. A six-foot-five man of rippling muscles, tanned skin, and dark features, Alexander Diotrephes was a fierce defender of a hidden site in Gibraltar. A man of deception and threats, he eventually provided Chess Team with a serum that would help end their initial conflict with Richard Ridley.

Over time, the team repeatedly came into conflict with the man who it turned out was the Hercules of legend. At times adversary, and at times ally, Alexander eventually became King's personal friend. The last King saw of him, the man had been reunited with his long lost wife, and the couple retreated to another dimension of reality.

Now, the shell of a human creature wired up to dozens of thick cables, looked one step from death—on the wrong side of it.

"Alexander!" King shouted. "What have you done to him?" He made to move for the man but was restrained from behind. Two armed soldiers had silently joined Bao. No one was restraining Bishop, but the soldiers were keeping an eye on him.

Bishop looked at King, waiting for a signal. If they were going to fight, this might be the time. But Bishop didn't think their odds were good. They were at the bottom of the massive conical space, and the huge banks of machinery surrounding them left them with no clue how many reinforcements might already be on the way. He couldn't even see up the slope of the terraced cavern. The humming, buzzing equipment looked like an electrical substation. Transformers, arresters, and a network of overhead girders and wires, were all held back behind chain-link fences from the walkways.

Then Bishop realized it *was* an electrical substation. Carrying power from Alexander's body to—well, to who knew where. Bishop supposed it went to power the weapon, antennas, and parabolic dishes outside the building complex. But he didn't understand how so much energy could come from Alexander. The man had come from another dimension, but could their physiology be so different?

There was no time to think about it.

King made a signal with his face—a slight squint—that he wanted to make a break for it. But Bishop just closed his eyes, the message being that he knew the time wasn't right.

Although they had been through many missions together, and knew and trusted each other, Bishop could see a small amount of hurt in King's face. He felt betrayed by Bishop's disagreement. But it had been years since they had worked together on the regular. Bishop's doing.

I suppose I deserve that, he thought.

The entire exchange took a fraction of a second, but then Bishop saw King refocus and resign himself to wait.

Crimson was laughing, first at the sight of a withered Alexander. Then she turned and sneered at King. "I tried to get the secrets of his immortality out of him, but he wouldn't talk. You know, Jack, it's funny. I wouldn't have even known about him if it wasn't for Chess Team's files and the Herculean Society records. We tried to drag him back through a dimensional rift, and mistakenly got his wife."

Acca, Bishop thought. He'd never met the woman, but he understood that Alexander and King had once engaged in a very complicated plan to save her life.

"She didn't last long," Crimson said, dismissive of the woman. "But as we expected, Alexander came looking for her. 'Hercules...'" She huffed a laugh. "He didn't put up that much of a fight."

King's face was impassive now, but Bishop knew he was probably seething and formulating another plan of attack. And Bishop was reconsidering himself. Maybe this *would* be their only chance...and he certainly wanted to choke the life out of Crimson, too.

"There was so much dimensional rift energy in his body from having gone back and forth. I knew we could power the de-evolution ray with this boy. I really need to come up with a better name for that. It's a mouthful." She chuckled as if everyone would think that was hilarious.

Bishop understood how deadly this she-beast was, but he also started to see that she had been in a position of power for so long, that she was no longer used to any dissent...on anything, even her feeble sense of humor. So wrapped up in imperial narcissism, she had started to believe herself infallible.

That chuckle was what did it. The last straw for King. Bishop saw the man nod hard—a silent communication to him that they *were* going to make a break for it, and that it was an order.

Then King lunged for Crimson. He'd been standing only a few feet from her, but the creature moved with lightning speed, turning her body sideways, grasping King by the neck with one meaty hand, and by his upper thigh with the other, all in one smooth motion.

Before Bishop could rush the armed soldiers and Bao, he was shocked into stillness by how quickly Crimson had grabbed King, hoisted him above her head, and flung his body at a nearby eight foot tall, chain-link fence.

King crashed into the fence with a loud exhalation, and he then immediately plunged to the floor, all the fight taken out of him by the vicious blow.

Bishop hadn't even had a chance to move.

Bao directed the soldiers to get King to his feet in Mandarin, and Bishop was pleased to see King was alive, just bruised and shocked.

Crimson turned back toward Alexander's shriveled supine form, completely unfazed by the attack from King. "As you can see, poor Alexander is running out of juice now. Oh, he can probably power this next attack, but then I think he'll be finished."

She turned back to King and the hungry leer reappeared on her face. "But not to worry. As I understand it, from your own files, Jack, you, Knight, and Bishop have all traversed the dimensional barriers as well. I don't expect any of you have the same energy as ol' Hercules did, but it's going to be an awful lot of fun finding out. I *was* going to let you both stick around to see the weapon fired at Moscow. But if you're not going to behave, I'll just have to savor Alexander's screams by myself."

Then she pointed to Bao.

"Take them to the cells."

The soldiers dragged King away, and Bishop noticed Bao's hand on his holstered sidearm.

He'd have to go willingly.

"Don't worry, Jack," Crimson called after them. "We rounded up all your friends from Siletz, too. You'll have plenty of company!"

FIFTY-FIVE

1600 Pennsylvania Avenue, Washington, D.C.

"Once again, Yuri. You have my deepest sympathies."

President Beaman hung up the phone and just sighed in his chair behind his desk.

"How are the Russians holding up, Mr. President?" Danielle Rudin asked him from where she stood on the other side of the desk. She had heard his side of the conversation, but it seemed polite to say something.

Beaman stood slowly, and then pulled his jacket from the back of his leather chair and whipped it behind his back in one smooth, practiced move, twisting the fabric onto him. "How is the Russian President handling the entire population of the greater Moscow area being reduced to little more than human apes?" He sighed again, realizing his ire wasn't really directed at Rudin. "Not well. Yuri is damn glad he was in the Urals. He's grateful for whatever assistance we can offer."

"But the Russians are now on our side?" she asked.

"Yes."

Rudin followed the man as he strode across the Oval Office. She knew he would be heading toward the Situation Room again. As this was a call of condolences of a sort, Beaman had insisted on making it from his desk. In his place, his Chief of Staff, Nancy Hubbard, would be speaking with the generals in the Pentagon, and the Chief of Space Operations at United States Space Force.

"How will they handle it?" Rudin asked, more out of curiosity and so the walk back to the Situation Room wouldn't be in abject silence as the President brooded.

"Containment for now, walling off the Zone of Effect, just like with Caracas." Beaman shook his head like he was trying to clear a pesky thought from his consciousness. "What the hell do you do with twelve million feral, animal-like humans?"

After passing security, the President strode into a conference room (one of three attached to the 5000 square foot operations center known as the "Situation Room") with Marines at the door announcing his presence. Everyone stood as he entered, even as he was waving them all to remain seated. Before Rudin had crossed the threshold after him, and before the doors were closed, he was asking Domenick Boucher for intel.

"Where are we on the weapon, Dom?"

Boucher looked exhausted, and his suit looked rumpled. Others in the room, from the National Security Adviser to the Director of Homeland

Security and the Duty Officer, all looked more tightly pressed than Boucher. But they all had offices on the premises, where they could freshen up. Boucher was staying in a Foggy Bottom hotel room, which he hadn't even seen yet. He'd slept a few hours here and there on a sofa in Danielle's office. But when he spoke to the President, there was no lack of energy in his voice.

"We have it, Mr. President. It's some form of pulsed light beam that was fired from the Lijia Dam complex in China. It was sent to a satellite, which bounced the beam off another and down toward Moscow. Space Force already has a few satellites redirected toward them."

"Can we blow them out of the damn sky?" Beaman asked.

"Yes," Nancy Hubbard immediately spoke up and with emphasis. She was former Army and served as Beaman's Chief of Staff. She normally advised him on all military matters, and Rudin had observed that she tended to drive him toward action—sometimes recklessly.

Boucher cut in before Hubbard could defend her stance. "I'm advising against that action, for now, Mr. President."

Beaman slumped into his chair, and Rudin took her seat by Boucher.

"Why?" was all the President said.

"There are a few things going on," Boucher began.

"Tell me about it," the President said, his stare oozing sarcasm.

"Sir, we've lost contact with the Chess Team. They were en route to the Lijia facility. Now I've lost Deep Blue."

Beaman sat forward in his chair. "What do you mean you've lost... Blue?"

Not everyone in the room knew of Tom Duncan's role in organizing things with Chess Team, so he paused for a second to stop himself from saying the man's name aloud.

"The entire facility is unresponsive. A Sat pass over the area shows a protracted battle. We've sent Marines stationed nearby to check on the support personnel. But the silence is...well, Deep Blue isn't in the habit of going completely radio silent. We have to assume they've been killed or taken."

"Damn it," Beaman fumed. "They were our point men in this."

Boucher continued, "If we move in on the satellites too soon, the Chinese—and until we hear otherwise, I am assuming it is this new Empress behind these attacks—will be alerted that we know how they're doing this. Maybe they have other satellites beyond the two we know of. If we show our hand too soon, the Empress could resort to a backup plan we know nothing of yet."

"We barely know anything about this main attack plan, Dom," the President complained. "What do you suggest we do?"

"Space Force will have our satellites in position in about two hours. But they're also moving a few other civilian satellites around. We don't know if their intel knows which of ours are military and weapons capable. By moving a few more, it looks more natural. If the Chinese satellites don't react—and that's a big if—then we just remain in place. We're watching the complex in Qinghai. If they launch another shot, we'll be in position to destroy their relay satellites before they can forward the beam."

"Aren't we talking about a laser style weapon here? How much time will we have to react?" Nancy Hubbard asked.

"Space Force tells us there's about a one-minute delay on board their satellites between receiving the shot and reflecting it, Ma'am," one of the Colonels in the room replied.

"Our people are ready for another shot," Boucher said. "We don't quite understand yet how they're attaching the 'de-evolutionary' aspect to the beam of light. We don't know if it's a biological contaminant attached to the beam somehow, or if the light triggers something else on the ground. But we'll know the second they launch another strike, and we'll be able to destroy their satellite in seconds."

Then Beaman turned from Boucher and began rattling off a series of questions aimed at the National Security Advisor and the military representatives in the room.

As far as Rudin could see, hers and Boucher's part in this was finished—or at least it seemed that Beaman felt that way.

As the President consulted his people on air strike and land invasion options, as well as talking about the possible science involved in causing rapid mutations in human DNA, resulting in the horrific creatures they had all seen footage of, Boucher picked up a phone with a blinking light.

"Boucher," he said. After a minute he hung up and looked over at Rudin. Then he smiled.

"Mr. President," he called, and the conversation in the room stopped. "We might have just had a stroke of really good luck."

FIFTY-SIX

King was dumped into a small room, its metal door slamming shut behind him. There was a vent in the door that allowed airflow, but he couldn't see anything past the louvres. The space was new and clean, but devoid of anything else.

No window. No other doors. No cot or toilet. It wasn't even necessarily a cell—yet. Just a room without a designated purpose. But it would hold him just as effectively. The walls were cinderblocks with a thin coat of gray paint, and a plain smooth concrete floor.

Bishop had been led somewhere else.

But the thought that kept going through King's head was Crimson's parting shot. She claimed she'd captured the support crew from Siletz. His sister. Tom Duncan. Lewis Aleman. And...

"Fiona..." he whispered her name, and cursed the situation they had wound up in. His daughter, although now a young woman, was the light of his life. He was disappointed that she'd been captured, concerned for her well-being, furious at Crimson for abducting her, and simultaneously filled with hope that Fiona might actually be here. Her ability with the Mother Tongue might be a Get Out of Jail Free card for the entire team. She could alter inanimate objects. Like the concrete floor of his makeshift cell.

The jumble of emotions was confusing, and he needed to think, plan, strategize, and come up with alternate options. He needed quiet, and although a cell wasn't the best place to have some, in this case it would do.

King sat in the center of the room, on the floor, and closed his eyes, which had provided him little information about the space. He tried to clear his mind, and focused instead on the smells and sounds around him.

He could still smell the dryness in the room, but the concrete floor was perfectly smooth in many places—and cracked in a few. He could feel a line under his hand. The room, and probably the entire facility had been built quickly. New hairline cracks in freshly laid concrete were normal.

He could hear no industrial humming or buzzing noises. No background HVAC. His hand felt no—

Wait.

He placed his other hand flat on the floor and felt it again. A slight tremor.

King swept his hand along the floor in front of him in a slow arc. The thump was stronger from the wall to his right. He slid across the floor, closer to the wall, and the tremor was stronger. And irregular. Not mechanical.

He raised his hand up and touched the cinderblock wall, and the feeling grew in strength. Something was impacting a specific block in his wall, low down near the floor.

King got on his hands and knees and peered closely at the wall. The block didn't appear to move, but as he inspected it, he could see a bit of grit shift in the crack on the left of the block.

He sat back on his heels and watched the block. For a minute. Then another.

A tiny puff of dust came out of the crack and hit his floor. He swiped his hand through the dust and held it up to inspect it.

He was still wearing his heavy-duty hiking boots, so slid forward toward the wall, and rammed his heel toward the vibrating stone. He hit the stone three times quickly, then three times slowly. Then three more times quickly.

Then he touched the wall again.

He felt a thump. Then another. Another quickly after that. Then a final thump.

Then the block stopped vibrating.

Morse code. For the letter 'Q.'

It was Queen.

King quickly responded with a thump, followed quickly by another. Then a brief pause before his final thump. The letter 'K.'

The response was a furious flurry of thumps.

He understood that the communication phase was over. She was trying to break the wall. He joined in and repeatedly slammed the heel of his boot against the stone. He felt it shift, then pulled his foot back to see the block slide forward into his cell by a few inches.

King moved to the side, and stood up, now kicking his heel against the edge of the stone as Zelda Baker slammed it from the other side. Instead of sawing back and forth, now they were working the block in the same direction.

In another minute it was free, and King slid it across the floor.

Then he dropped down toward the floor and looked through the hole they had made.

Queen's face was waiting, sans the bandana she normally wore around her head to hide the old scar on her forehead.

"Funny meeting you here," King said.

Queen swiped a lock of blonde hair away from her face and said "Room service is a little slow here. WiFi is crap. Nothing on TV. Bullshit accommodations. One star."

King filled her in on what he knew. From the last day. Then he asked her for her sitrep.

"They separated us. I don't know where Rook is. They pinned us out by the lake with drones dropping grenades. A Chinese Tango named Bao."

"Colonel Bao. We've met."

"I haven't seen this Crimson yet. You're sure it's Red? The Old Mother from Vietnam?"

"Yeah," King nodded, although he was lying on the floor now, looking at her sideways. "And she said she got the Siletz team, too. No visual confirmation on that yet."

"Fuck," Queen whispered under her breath. "What are we gonna do?"

King thought for a minute. He hadn't gotten the quiet thinking time he'd needed to plan. But some other things had come along—a partner and a tool. "No cameras in your space?" he asked.

"Not that I can see."

"We need to scuttle the whole operation here. If we can save Alexander, great, but I doubt it. He looked a little too far gone. We need to get the others; we need to get the Siletz crew. Blow everything the fuck up. This place can't stand."

Queen laid down on her side of the wall now, looking at King through the hole. "Still waiting on the 'How,' boss."

"They'll be back for us eventually. And now I've got a blunt object weapon. Let's get you a block of your own."

They worked until they had a second cinderblock section freed, this time kicked into Queen's cell.

After she slid it away from the wall on her side, she laid down next to the hole again and asked, "How much work do you think it would take to get this whole wall down?"

FIFTY-SEVEN

The door to Knight's cell snapped unlocked and whipped open with no warning.

Colonel Bao was unsurprised to see no one standing in the middle of the cell. Not Knight. Not Queen or King. His men had opened King's cell first and seen the hole in the wall to Queen's cell. They had backed out immediately and opened Queen's room next, only to find that the prisoners had also burst through to the next cell. Knight's.

Bao stood against the corridor wall, the farthest he could from the door, and also to the side. He could see that the group had not yet slammed their bodies against the far wall and into Bishop's adjacent cell.

His men stood arrayed around the door in a loose arc, their Type 56 rifles, aimed at the opening. He gave them credit for the fact that not one of them looked dumbfounded at the absence of the prisoners. Not one of them relinquished their focus and aim on the doorway. Each man had been chosen exactly for his steely nerve. No weapon wavered.

Bao understood what he was seeing and called out to his prisoners.

"Mr. Sigler. Ms. Baker. Mr. Shin. We know you are in there. We've seen the holes in your cells. Please tell me that the extent of your plan is not to hide at the side of the door with a breezeblock each and hope to brain us. There are five rifles trained on you. Thirty 7.62 millimeter rounds per man. Plus, I have my sidearm. I like my odds against your concrete projectiles."

Bao waited, then shifted behind his men, along the corridor wall, hoping a glance in the other direction would yield a slice of fabric or skin that would give him an indication of where his prisoners were hiding. But there was nothing.

He radioed for more men. Then waited in silence.

His soldiers kept their aim leveled at the open doorway.

A second five-man team came running down the corridor and slid to a neat halt by Bao.

"Back to King's cell. If it's empty, come through the holes they made to this cell. We'll pin them."

The soldier in the lead nodded, and the group of five ran back down the corridor and yanked open the door to King's cell. Four men cautiously entered it. The fifth maintained his stance at the doorway, ready in case the prisoners got past the other four men.

In less than sixty seconds, the men were at Knight's cell, and called in Mandarin, "Clear. Cells are empty."

Empty? Bao thought. *Where the hell did they go?*

He pushed his men aside, and they lowered their rifles, as he walked into Knight's cell. There was a bunch of wall debris and dust in the room, scattered along the floor. But no sign of the cell's occupant.

Bao walked through the shattered wall, into Queen's former cell. Same thing. Piles of debris on the floor. Most of the concrete blocks were still intact but had just been knocked out of the wall.

Bao cursed the shoddy craftsmanship and inexpensive materials that had been used.

"Son of a monkey's diseased testicle," he swore.

He passed through the final wall into King's ruptured cell.

Likewise empty. The only real difference was that there were fewer blocks on the floor in King's cell. But that made sense. He had burst through into Queen's unit. There were more blocks on the floor in her cell.

Bao walked back through to the middle cell, noting that there were indeed more breeze blocks on the floor and more dirt and grit. He continued back into the third cell and saw fewer blocks.

"Check Bishop's cell," he ordered.

Three men ran from the room and came back in less than a minute. "Prisoner is accounted for."

Huh, Bao thought. *Three of them gone, but they left the fourth man.*

Rook was being held elsewhere in the facility, and the new arrivals from Oregon—the Chess Team's support crew—were still being driven in from Kabula Town. They were due to arrive any minute.

Something was tickling the back of Bao's mind as he tried to puzzle out to where his prisoners had escaped. And a new thought was creeping up his spine—what his Empress would do to him when she found out they had escaped. Probably the same thing she had done to General Huang when the team escaped the train. Bao shivered.

He stepped back into Queen's cell, where most of the blocks were piled on the floor. He stood with his back to the wall that faced the door and looked down at the pattern of the blocks on the floor and the piles of dirt and dust.

There was something.

He knew he should be sending out search teams. He should be setting off alarms. But another part of his mind cautioned him to wait.

Just wait. Pause. Reflect.

He needed to solve this problem first. There was something off...

He went again into King's cell.

Fewer blocks.

King, probably with Queen's assistance, burst into her cell.

Bao moved through the broken walls again, all the way back to Knight's cell. The holes in the walls were not small. Large enough for an adult man to walk, without bending. They were giant doors in the walls.

Bao looked down. Chaotic and messy debris in Knight's cell across the floor. Queen's cell was far neater and contained more blocks.

Bao returned to her cell and took up his position again, facing the door. He looked down. Neater piles of blocks. No other differences.

He looked left into Knight's cell through the hole, and then slowly swept his eyes to the right, past the door, and through the huge hole into King's cell.

The answer was right there in the front of his mind. Almost on his tongue.

He slammed his hand against the intact wall at his back. "Damn it!"

As the cloud of dust dislodged by his strike puffed forward, past his body and into the cell, the answer dawned on him.

"Not enough blocks!" he shouted.

Bao whirled and kicked the wall as hard as he could—and it shattered outward, into the grassy area behind the cells at the back of the building.

As the concrete blocks rained down in a crumpling heap, Bao realized what they had done. They had broken the outer wall as well, and then, rather than retrieving the dirty blocks from the dusty soil outside, they had used the blocks on the floors of their cells to temporarily restore the wall, probably packing the creases with dirt and dust, so no light would shine through to the cell from outside.

"Should we pursue, sir?" one of the men asked.

That nagging thought lingered in Bao's mind.

"Not...just yet," he said.

He knew there was no way they would leave Bishop behind.

There is no way, he thought. Then he realized the thought that was nagging in his brain.

They are still here.

Then he motioned the soldier over to him and whispered in the man's ear.

The soldier quickly rounded up three other men and departed into the hallway through the open door in Knight's former cell.

"You two," Bao shouted, for show. "Search down to the river. That must be the way they went." The two men leapt through the hole in the outer wall and ran from sight, toward the dam.

Bao motioned to the other three, that they should quietly retreat to the hallway. The men retreated, without question.

Bao followed them back to the hallway. He indicated the men should remain silent. He moved quietly down to Bishop's cell, bringing the men with him, and taking up position outside Bishop's door.

They wouldn't leave the man behind, he thought again. *They would climb to the roof.*

If the walls were shit, the roof probably was, too. The other men he'd sent to the roof would flank the escapees, while Bao and his men would catch them in the act, as they tried to free the big man.

FIFTY-EIGHT

Anna Beck felt like she had lived many lives. She'd compartmentalized sections of her years, as if each brief period of her life was an entire lifespan.

Her time in the Army was one such life. Then her years working for the 'Gen Y' security team at Richard Ridley's Manifold Genetics. That came to an end when she saw what kind of hideous work Ridley was up to. She assisted Chess Team in taking him down in New Hampshire, but then she had slipped away in the confusion.

Her next brief life was when MI-6 dragged her into helping them hunt down former Manifold facilities around the globe. She had seen a future in that life and thought the intelligence field would be for her.

Fate had other plans.

Before that life had really gotten started, she ran into Knight again, in Shenhuang, China. And while she had been hoping to move into intelligence, battlefield action was upon her again.

That incident led to her working for Deep Blue at the same New Hampshire facility where she'd helped to take down Ridley years earlier. After another protracted battle, this time with the remnants of Gen Y when they came back to New Hampshire looking to reclaim their base, Tom Duncan had promoted her to his bodyguard and Endgame's Chief of Intelligence.

She'd ultimately gotten the intel work she'd wanted, but that role hadn't really suited her, and she was soon back out in the field with Chess Team, acting as Knight's spotter, and functioning as a permanent member of the group. Her most recent life.

The designation of 'Pawn' had originally been reserved for temporary members of the team. But Beck had now made it her own and saw no slight in the moniker. She understood now that a pawn could be the most important piece on the board.

In this case, it was literally true.

All the others had been captured. But Pawn had evaded discovery. She'd also taken out two lone soldiers on the periphery of the base, and successfully hidden their remains. That no alarms were sounded suggested to her that if the forces at the installation were even aware that the two men had vanished, they were not in any way concerned.

In any case, now she was armed.

She'd found in her long experience with secret bases, by the very nature of them being secret, their owners were usually paranoid and had lots of security in place. That meant there were only two ways to get around those bases undetected—over them or under them.

This place, terraced as it was, in stages, ran several thousand feet in elevation. The complex climbed the hillside from the dam on the river, and its step-like structure presented problems with going over *or* under. There was no way for her to discern, from the exterior of the sprawling complex, what each level did or what she'd find there. Worse, the roofs of the different levels were all tiles and pagoda like turrets. It looked more like a palace or a monastery than a control and operations center for the dam complex. But it *was* connected. You could travel from the top of the mountain, down through the levels, all the way to the river, the communications arrays, and the dam without ever stepping outdoors.

But terraced as it was, Pawn thought it unlikely there was a single basement that ran all the way up the mountain. And, with the periodic pagoda towers, there were too many places where she would have been spotted if she ran along the rooftops.

So, she had done the only thing she could think of—pull some tiles off a section of the roof behind a tower, and then slip into it, replacing as many tiles as she could behind her. It still left a gaping hole in the roof, but as long as no one was looking at that one spot—and as long as it didn't rain—she guessed it could be days or even weeks before anyone noticed.

Then came the tedious part.

She had crawled in the interstitial spaces between rooftops and drop ceilings, along AC vents and ducts, for what felt like miles. Before she'd entered the complex, she'd seen a large section—far wider than the others, about halfway up the mountain. It had looked like a main lobby, an auditorium, or a control center. If it turned out to be an auditorium, she would curse her luck. But if it was a main lobby, she'd likely find an infographic or directory, a map or something similar that would get her where she needed to go in the gigantic complex.

She'd been on the move for what felt like hours when she reached the edge of the larger section of the staged building. She didn't know what she'd found, but she knew she was on the right track. There were larger and larger bundled networks of telecommunication wires all leading out of a wall ahead of her, and maintenance doors every few feet leading through the wall. She had seen similar set ups in actual auditoriums for lighting crews, but there were far too many electrical cables running through the wall ahead of her.

This is definitely the place, she thought.

She crept to one of the metal doors and slowly eased it open, her stolen QSZ-92 pistol, raised and ready.

Pawn peeked inside, but she was shocked to see that her view went on seemingly forever. When she realized she was looking down on a gigantic human-constructed building that turned into a natural cavern, extending deep into the mountainside, she took a chance and opened the door wider to get a better look.

A single metal girder led from her door to a network of them. Above the girders were handholds, making the metal I-beam a catwalk of sorts. The entire connected metal landscape above the yawning chasm of a room was an intentional maintenance and construction system for workers to access the vents, lights, and wiring that went into the arena like space below her. She saw rings of desks and computers, all manned with workers ensconced in furious typing and clicking. There were science labs, all manner of machinery behind chain-link fences, and a central hub that looked like a nest of wires and cables sinking into the floor.

There were thousands of people in the gigantic cavern, but no one was looking up at the rafters.

Pawn spent a while checking all around the upper haven of metal makeshift catwalks, ensuring there were no guards present. Then she slipped out onto the walkway and closed the door behind her. As she moved deeper into the space, she could see a glassed-in control room, forty feet below her and off to her left.

What she didn't see were armed soldiers, which was a relief. As she moved across the girder toward the center, she paid more attention to the rings of equipment at the center, which resembled a power station.

She didn't know what they were powering with so much tech, but she could take a guess. When she'd entered the building and started her long journey toward this space, she'd had two goals in mind: find Knight and the others, and burn this whole place down somehow. She wasn't sure how to get that done at first, but everything in the cavernous space was connected to a central point. If that went boom, the whole complex might be useless.

She was making for the center to do something about that when she glanced back at the lower control room and saw several people being dragged into the room.

King and Queen were brought in first, Bishop was followed by an officer. Knight was in back. Rook wasn't there. She hoped that didn't mean the worst. The other four had all been brought in by armed men, and were stood in front of a large woman, whose back was to the glass.

She was looking at them, and they were looking at her...but not Knight. He took in the view outside the window. And like he always did, he looked up.

Right at Pawn.

FIFTY-NINE

It was the craziest of flukes. The most unlikely stroke of luck. The last person that Shin Dae-jung ever would have expected to see was Pawn. That he hadn't seen her since his capture had led him to believe she was either killed or being held elsewhere. He didn't think she was free, and he didn't think she'd be roaming the rafters behind an immense sheet of glass.

His temporary escape with Queen and King, had led to their immediate recapture as they tried to also free Bishop. It had been a calculated gamble, but King thought it was worth a try. They restored the cinderblocks in Queen's outer cell wall, and then scrambled up onto the roof. Knight had seen the pursuing soldiers race out of the building and head down toward the distant dam.

King led them to the adjacent cell after a few minutes, creeping across the loose clay tiles of the roof. Then Queen had started removing them, so they could descend into Bishop's cell from above.

But they were met by Colonel Bao, with his pistol raised at them, and several soldiers with rifles aimed at Bishop's head. Knight was about to start running, but another group of soldiers, each no older than twenty, were coming across the roof from lower down the structure. A second and third group approached their position on the roof from opposite sides of the building on the ground. Knight and the others were pinned, so they quickly surrendered, and would wait for the next opportunity to escape.

Knight didn't think it would be so soon.

Bao and his men, to their credit, had not roughed up the escapees, but calmly collected them, and led them through inner corridors in the building until they had stepped into this observation room. On the side wall was a series of computer terminals, all manned by young Chinese women. Bao's men pushed and shoved the team members into the room, and then swept to the side to take up stations along the wall, by the door.

In the middle of the rectangular room was a giant glass wall that looked out onto an immense cavernous space, the distant floor of which was ringed with machinery and thousands of workers and computer technicians.

And waiting in this observation room was the new Empress of China.

She was dressed in a simple pantsuit now, all white. And her hair color—a wig—had changed. Now her hair was long, blonde, and straight. But the outfit and the wig did little to disguise the beast of a woman who was actually a Neanderthal.

"Bao tells me you all went for a stroll. I'm glad you came back. You would have missed the fireworks. Washington, D.C. is coming into range." The oversized woman said with a sneer.

Things were moving too fast. Knight's brain was already reeling from the sight of Pawn up in the rafters. His habit upon entering a new space was to inspect every direction—especially upwards. He'd only been expecting to see the ceiling of the massive space beyond the glass—not the woman he loved.

"Where's Rook?" Queen demanded.

Crimson acted like she hadn't even heard the woman. "What do you think, Jack? Should we contact the White House and let them know we plan to devolve the Capitol, and then fire the weapon before they have a chance to evac, or just let it rip?"

King took a cautious step forward. "I'm not sure why you even need to use the weapon, Empress. You've already got what you want—the world's full attention. I know you said you need resources in the world to come, but surely the US will recognize you hold all the cards now. They'll deal with you. You just have to talk to them."

Knight knew he was stalling. But he also knew that King probably didn't know *what* he was stalling for. They had no plan, and no way to stop things...as far as King knew.

Knight turned his body, like he was just shuffling around, shifting his weight so he could see Pawn again. She had moved closer to the center of the huge space. But he could still see her clearly, and she was watching his every move. She mimed pulling the pin out of a grenade with her teeth and throwing it downward into the huge cavern.

King had described the space to Knight, and he knew Alexander was down there in the center of it all. But by King's account the man was nearly dead, a fragment of his former self.

Knight raised his arm and scratched the top of his head. A soldier behind him by the door stepped forward, but said nothing as Knight scratched, as if he had a mild case of dandruff.

It was an affirmative signal to Pawn, and she moved deeper into the complex, above the huge ring of machines on the floor.

"There's no point in speaking to Americans, Jack. Not until they've seen sufficient force to know they are beaten." Crimson said.

"You and the others proved as much when you tried to escape. Once you saw the forces arrayed against you, all three of you backed down," Bao added.

Crimson just smiled.

"There's no escape, Jack. I have your support team. I have Duncan. Again. I have all five members of the Chess Team."

In his best Peter Falk impression, Knight took a step closer to Crimson, "Oh, there's...just one thing...that you forgot."

Crimson turned to face him, examining him with a look suggesting she'd never really considered the diminutive man before.

"And what is that?" she asked, her voice dripping with sarcasm.

In the distance, over her shoulder, Knight saw Pawn hold out both her arms, to either side, and drop a grenade from each into the middle of the complex.

Glancing quickly back to Crimson's leer, he said, "There aren't five members of Chess Team. There are six."

SIXTY

United States Space Force Chief Master Sergeant Kyle Mohr answered the landline telephone at his station in Cheyenne Mountain. He was in a relatively small room with banks of computer terminals showing the positions of dozens of space satellites. Two other enlisted men were in the room at their own desks and, behind him, a Colonel stood from his terminal and walked over to Mohr.

The voice on the phone was another non-commissioned officer, Technical Sergeant Ray Willis. "We have confirmation that Tango 'X-Ray' is active, and Pentagon has given the firing order."

Mohr replied, "Affirmative on firing. Hold."

He set the phone down on the desk with his left hand and moved the mouse of his computer with his right to an open window on his desk's second monitor. There was no need to target the Chinese terrorist satellite. Mohr had been tracking it for hours. His own Anti-Satellite Weapon (ASAT) satellites had long since moved into position and were constantly keeping the enemy weapon locked in. Everyone in command knew they'd have just sixty seconds from the time the weapon at the Lijia Dam in China began powering up, before it fired its de-evolution ray into space, to bounce off the target satellite, which had been named 'X-Ray.'

They still weren't sure what the energy source was, but they knew *how* it was transmitted. There was a measurable pulsed light beam. After it hit X-Ray, it would be redirected to another satellite. USSF was tracking the second satellite that had been used in the Moscow attack, but since it was still over Asia, the thinking was that there might be several more that could be used as relays.

There were more than 10,000 satellites—colloquially referred to as 'birds'—in orbit around Earth. Most were for communications and remote sensing. Some were in Low Earth Orbit, where the Hubble Space Telescope and the International Space Station were also located. Those accounted for probably 5,800 of the man-made objects circling the planet. Others were in Medium Earth Orbit—mostly used for navigation systems. Sixty birds were in a 'Highly Elliptical Orbit' used primarily for communications. Several hundred others were in geosynchronous orbits over specific locations on the planet. Over 3,200 birds were junked and abandoned.

The private company SpaceX owned almost 1,700 of the birds around the planet. One hundred and twenty-nine satellites were the property of the Chinese Ministry of National Defense. The China Academy of Technology and half a dozen other supposed science organizations based in China were responsible for another hundred and fifty. The US Space Force assumed all of those were potential hostiles. They had been tracking every single one since long before the sixth branch of the US military had been formed in 2019.

Most concerning were eighteen satellites that no one had claimed. Their owners were simply unknown. Space Force, and the US Air Force before them, had no clue how those birds had even been placed, but the widely held presumption was that they had been assembled in space and set loose up there rather than having been launched from the surface.

Had they been launched from Earth, multiple countries would have seen the launches and known their origins.

One of those eighteen, Space Force was pretty sure, belonged to Kazakhstan. The others were all mysteries. And X-Ray, the bird that Mohr was now about to destroy, had been one of the unknowns. He was pleased to see it obliterated. One less threat in the sky.

The Chief hovered his mouse over the red button clearly labelled 'Launch' on his screen and clicked his mouse's button.

Over 12,000 miles above the surface of the planet, a laser fired from one of Mohr's ASAT birds named simply '37.' Space Force controlled over a hundred birds, and they were officially designated with complicated numbers and letters, but generally just referred to by their simple number.

The laser would strike X-Ray and incinerate it in seconds.

"*Semper Supra*," he said under his breath. Latin for 'Always Above,' the United States Space Force motto.

On his screen, Chief Mohr watched the satellite wink out of existence, and the words 'Target Lost' appear on the screen in the satellite's former place. Software would track X-Ray's former orbit, with those words in the place of the red dot that used to be the bird, for weeks still. But the enemy satellite had been destroyed.

Unfortunately, by unleashing on X-Ray, they had just revealed to the world that 37 was armed with a laser and capable of destroying other satellites. There would be diplomatic hell to pay, and the element of surprise had been removed from 37, but all of that was not Mohr's problem, and a problem for another day.

"Thank you, Chief," the Colonel standing behind him said. He leaned down and collected the landline phone off Mohr's desk and said, "Sergeant Willis, please inform the Pentagon that X-Ray has been intercepted before the beam reached it."

Then he hung up the phone and started walking back to his desk on the other side of the room.

"Colonel," Mohr called.

The man turned on his heel and strode back to Mohr's desk.

"I'm seeing five other Unknown Tangos repositioning, all at once." Mohr ran a quick orbit calculation program on each and arrived at the same conclusion others would be reaching in a different part of the building and at other sites. In under a minute, the phone would ring again, he was sure of it.

"Trajectory?" the colonel asked.

Mohr turned in his seat to look at his commanding officer. "The precise spot where X-Ray was a minute ago."

The colonel sighed. "What's the nearest bird's ETA?"

Mohr turned back to his screen and typed and clicked furiously for a minute. He knew how to get this information, but collecting it wasn't normally his job. He was the guy who blew shit up. Usually someone else discovered when it needed to be blown up and passed that information on to the White House and the Pentagon, and they sent a message back. Willis would then pass the message to Mohr to pull the trigger.

But despite that chain of operation, Mohr still knew *how* to do the work.

He had the answers in under a minute.

"We have about two hours before the first will be in position to take X-Ray's place," he reported.

"Shit. Let's get on the horn and get permission to blast those bastards out of orbit too, Chief," the colonel said.

But by that point, all the other USSF personnel watching the sky had come to the same conclusions and raced through the command structure as well.

The desktop phone rang, and Chief Mohr answered it again.

SIXTY-ONE

Stan Tremblay hurt all over. He was reclined on a cot in his cell, his head by the wall, and his eyes closed. But his lids were cracked, just a bit. Oddly, a soldier had stayed stationed in his cell with him, after Red had given him his latest beating. The man stood on the inside of the solid steel door, his gaze never wavering from Rook's battered form on the bed. He was armed with a Type 56 rifle—a variant of the famous AK-47—and the barrel was always pointing in Rook's direction. Otherwise, the man's face was impassive. But he didn't scratch itches. He didn't let his gaze wander. The man did not seem bored. He clearly took his job seriously. He also looked afraid.

Red had last visited Rook's cell just a few hours ago. That time she just knocked him around a few times. It was bad, but it wasn't like the first time. That had been brutal. She'd bitten him. The puncture wounds in his left shoulder were deep, and they still wept blood through the bandage Red's medical team had applied to him. His right arm was broken for sure, and in a sling. His ribs hurt, and he wondered if some were broken again. They had only just finished healing. His legs were sore, and he was bruised all over. His left eye was swelling shut on him, and he had a killer headache.

But after each of the beatings, the medics had come and administered acetaminophen injections that kicked in faster than the medication did in pill form. He guessed there was also a narcotic in the injections because he slept after each one.

But when he woke, he was still in the cell and the guard was still there. He was almost certain that it was the same young man. But Rook was too injured to know for sure.

There had been no questions. No words. Red had just burst into his cell the first time and started slamming him around. Picking him up and hurling him into walls. Punching him and kicking him once he was down on the ground. Rook didn't understand how Red was alive. He didn't know how she'd gotten here or what she wanted. He just knew she was pissed at him. He was separated from Queen and the others. He was a prisoner.

And injured as he was, rattled as he was, he understood something else perfectly well: the beatings would continue. They would only stop if he could beat Red and, in his current state, there was just no way. The only other way they would stop was if he could escape.

Maybe he could do that.

Maybe.

From his position on the bed, pretending to sleep, Rook examined the guard. The young man was maybe twenty-five. His skin clear, his body slim. If Rook wasn't injured, he'd be able to take the kid and maybe two or three more all at the same time. But right now? He let his head loll to the side slightly, his mouth fall open a bit, and he test shifted his left arm. The puncture wound in his shoulder stung, but the rest of that arm felt okay.

The trick would be whether he could get up from the bed at all, and whether his legs would support him if he did.

And more importantly, whether his captor would ever take his damn eyes off the prisoner.

The guard had a rifle but no sidearm. He didn't have a visible knife on him, and Rook let his surreptitious gaze lower to the man's boots. Small feet. No knife clips visible anywhere.

So just the rifle, Rook thought. *That works.*

He was worried about Queen, and about whether Red had likewise battered her. If so, the baby could have been harmed or even killed.

No, Rook thought. *Focus up, sucker.*

He had to keep his mind off what might be happening. The 'what might have beens' could kill him. He needed all his focus on the job ahead. Looking for the slightest crack in the guard's concentration and pouncing on it.

When the opening came, just a minute later, he almost wasn't ready for it.

He heard a muffled thump, and then a second later a gigantic rumbling clap of thunder sounded, shaking the walls of the room.

The guard turned his head.

Maybe the kid had never heard such a huge booming cacophony. But Rook had. Many times. He knew exactly what an explosion sounded like. He'd caused dozens of them himself.

The second the guard turned his head, Rook lunged.

By the time the man's head turned back toward him, Rook's left arm was up and horizontal to the ground, just six inches from the guard's neck. With his broken arm, he deflected the barrel of the rifle away.

Hurt like a bitch, but the guard didn't have time to fire.

Rook's arm bar struck the guard's neck, slamming the young man against the concrete wall to the side of the door. There was a sickening crunch as Rook's forearm crushed first the man's larynx and then the spinal cord behind it.

The guard's head flopped to the side.

Rook yanked his arm away, catching the body with his hand and gently lowering it to the floor.

He pulled the rifle away from the corpse and checked that its magazine was fully loaded. The guard didn't have any spare magazines, but as Rook searched the pockets of his uniform, he did find a small locking pocketknife. Rook scraped the side of his thumb across the blade's edge. Sharper than a Ginsu, which actually wasn't saying much, but if he needed to poke a hole in someone, it would get the job done.

Still, with the explosion, he guessed the rest of Chess Team had just made their move. The time for quiet had probably passed.

He knocked on the metal door. Three loud wraps of his knuckles.

Then he stepped off to the side with the rifle raised to his shoulder, listening as the door was unlocked.

The man was shouting in Mandarin and panicked as he whipped open the cell door and ran in, his own rifle still slung behind his back.

Rook just placed the barrel of his stolen rifle against the man's temple. He didn't need to say anything. The guard just stopped and held up his hands.

Rook was thinking of how to deal with the situation, when another explosion sounded—louder this time, with the door to the cell wide open. He was just going to knock the man out. But at the sound, the guard tried to use Rook's own trick against him, swinging his shouldered rifle upward in one slick maneuver.

Rook pulled the trigger, firing a single shot through the Chinese guard's head.

The time for quiet *was* over. He stooped and retrieved the second guard's magazine, stuffing it into his right arm's sling.

"Now it's time for the thunder," he said, turning and running out of the room, the barrel of the rifle leading.

SIXTY-TWO

The explosion shattered the massive wall of glass in the observation room, sending shards and slivers flying inward.

Right after his comment about Pawn, Knight had dropped to the floor, and King, Queen, and Bishop followed him.

Crimson turned around and caught the flying shards of glass, and the smoke and force of the blast, head on. She stumbled backward but didn't fall. The center of the huge chamber was far enough away that she wasn't receiving the brunt of the blast. A secondary explosion, from the electrical station ring around the central hub of the cavernous room below, was stronger, but she'd braced herself by then.

Before the guards in the room could recover from flying glass, the Chess Team members were up and on them. The women who had been at computer stations all took refuge under the desks. Bao had fallen into a corner of the room, and Crimson was still facing the now vacant window, her back to the battle.

King launched a kick at the man nearest him, dropping him to the ground. Bishop ran across the room like a linebacker, hitting three different guards in his first strike.

But Queen had been eyeing a huge M95 knife/bayonet on the hip of one of the guards since she had been captured. Now she made her move.

She lunged from the floor and launched her fingertips into the man's throat with her left hand, while smoothly drawing the knife with her right. She then swept it across the man's neck. The strike would have slit the man's throat, but he recoiled downward after the first strike. Instead, the blade slashed the man right across his eyes, and he howled in pain, his body flying backward as a spray of blood spritzed Queen's face.

She didn't notice. She had already turned and was making for Crimson, the seven-inch blade extended in front of her. To the right, King was collecting a rifle from a fallen soldier on the floor. On Queen's left, Bishop was picking up a soldier and throwing him.

Crimson turned around and faced Queen.

Her face was hideous. Dozens of glass shards were sticking out of the woman's skin, and all over her chest. That she was still standing was amazing.

If I have anything to say about it, Queen thought, *that won't last long.*

Crimson sneered at Queen, then glanced to the side of the room. "Bao!" she yelled.

Queen wasn't going to pass on the opportunity that Crimson's distraction provided. She lunged with the blade, but Crimson was expecting the strike, batting the knife strike away with one arm. The edge of the blade still sliced her massive forearm, and a spray of blood arced away from the big woman.

The force of Crimson's blow nearly knocked the knife from Queen's hand and, rather than staying still, she went in the direction of the blow, diving down to the floor, rolling, and coming up in a spinning kick in case the huge woman followed her.

But to Queen's surprise, the kick met no resistance. Crimson hadn't given chase. Instead, she had climbed up into the window frame, and was clutching the edge of it. "Bao!" she yelled again. "Release Qiángdà de! Do it!"

Queen nearly lost her balance, but she landed on her feet. King moved up beside her with the barrel of his rifle pointed at Crimson.

"There's nowhere to go, Red," he said.

Crimson just sneered again and then dropped backward out of the shattered window.

King ran to the window after her, but Queen turned to find Bishop approaching with a rifle for Queen. All the other soldiers in the room were down, and the women had fled, but Bao was still crouched in the corner.

Queen approached him cautiously and kicked out at his hunched back. The man turned, with a face full of anger, as he stabbed his finger down at a phone.

A shot rang out, and his head exploded, a fine pink mist decorating the wall just as his finger made contact with the screen.

"Shit," King ran past Queen with a thin wisp of smoke still trailing from the barrel of his appropriated rifle. He crouched down and looked at the phone in Bao's dead hand.

Bishop stepped closer and asked, "What is it?"

"Qiángdà de," King read. "Means 'the Mighty One' in Mandarin."

"What the hell is that?" Queen asked. "The Mighty One?"

"Not sure," King replied. "Crimson escaped. We need to find the others and then take this place apart. Queen, go with Bish and look for Rook. I need to check on Alexander."

"You think he's still alive after that blast?" Bishop asked, picking glass out of his black fleece jacket.

"I have to check," King said. "I owe him. A few times."

"Understood," Bishop said. "Rendezvous down by the dam?"

"After we blow that dam," Queen said. "So, on the shore."

"Yeah," King said. "But not before we find Deep Blue and the others."

"Wait a minute..." Queen said. "Where the hell is Knight? I didn't see him after the fight started."

King and Bishop glanced around the room. "I didn't see him either," King said.

Bishop just grunted.

"Well. Okay. We need to find Rook *and* Knight, and Blue and the others. And preferably before we find out what this Mighty One might be."

In the distance, they heard another explosion, this one more muffled. A second later, like a call and response, they felt the ground rumble and vibrate, and they heard an ear-piercing shriek.

"I think that could be the Mighty One," Bishop suggested. He opened the door to the room, which was already ajar, and pointed the barrel of his rifle out.

King put his hand on Queen's shoulder, and she whipped her head toward him. Then she instantly felt bad about it. They were friends, but her adrenaline was pumping hard, and she was deep in 'fight mode,' ready to kill anything that needed killing.

"I'm sure he'll be alright, Queen. We'll find him," King said. And she could see the concern in his eyes. She knew King and Rook were also friends, like brothers. Rook had known Bishop longer than the others, but he and King had just connected. It was like that sometimes in battle.

But the fear Zelda Baker saw in King's eyes rattled her.

He was usually the confident one.

The one in control. And he always seemed to have more faith than the rest of them that things would work out in the end. More importantly, he'd always been able to make her believe that things would work out. If he believed it, she could.

There was doubt in his face. But there was no time.

"Go," she said, as the rumbling in the floor became more pronounced.

King turned and made for the shattered window. She knew Crimson had gone that way, so as he climbed into the frame, she assumed there was a catwalk or a staircase or something, even though she hadn't seen it herself.

"Jack," she called at the last second.

He looked back.

"If you see that bitch..."

"I'll end this," King said.

SIXTY-THREE

After the initial grenade blasts, and just a fraction of a second before the larger explosion, Knight had rushed out the door. At first, he thought the others would have followed him. Then, as he ran down an empty outer corridor looking for a stairwell, he justified abandoning the others by reasoning that between King and Queen, they could take the soldiers in the room. And if any of them had a chance against Crimson, one-on-one, it would be Bishop, who was nearly her size.

The second explosion slammed the door shut after him and muffled any further sound in the room behind him, so Knight kept running. Forty feet down the hallway, he found what he was looking for, a plain door with the Chinese symbols for stairs.

He ripped the door open and raced up the metal steps. After two landings, he was at the top, and kept his momentum going, hoping that the element of surprise might help if there were soldiers on the other side of the door at the top.

Instead, he came out in a small concrete room not much bigger than an elevator car. But there was a metal ladder bolted to the wall and a hatch at the top. And up was where he wanted to go.

The hatch was unlocked and unmarked, but it opened into a cylindrical, ridged metal tube with the ladder continuing upward on the other side of the hatch. But the tube was open at the top, ten feet farther up. And the ladder continued about a yard past the top, ending abruptly.

He slowed as he reached the top of the tube, entering the girders where he had seen Pawn. It was unlikely any soldiers would have beaten him to the girders—even if they knew that was where the attack had come from. Plus, the smoke would give him some cover.

Then he felt and heard another distant explosion that echoed in the tube's confines.

Next, he felt an even louder and deeper rumble that rattled the ladder against its bolts. There was a horrible shrieking, inhuman noise.

He didn't know what it was, but he didn't want to be stuck in the tube. He climbed to the top of the ladder where it let out on the side of a metal girder. A thick metal pipe ran parallel to it, about chest height.

A handhold, he thought.

He climbed onto the girder and started making his way toward the center of the massive cavern. Below him, the outer ring of desktops was strewn with bodies, and the laboratories had been utterly destroyed. Smoke swirled around the cavern's upper reaches and poured out near the ground. The good news was, he was alone.

He glanced back toward the control room. The glass was shattered, and there was no sign of anyone.

The smoke was getting thicker, so he took a chance, and called out, "Pawn!"

"Knight!" came the reply. She was off to his left. He was on the wrong girder.

He called out. "Head down. Observation deck!"

"Affirmative!"

He ran back along the girder to the tube and descended the same way he'd come. He was checking for weapons or makeshift objects he could use on the way down the staircase this time. The complex was crawling with Chinese soldiers—he just hadn't encountered any yet. He knew that luck couldn't hold out. The best he could do for a weapon was a fire extinguisher in a metal case.

Extinguisher in hand, he ran back down the corridor toward the observation room.

When he reached it, he found the soldiers inside were all dead—and weaponless. That answered his questions about the others.

"Dae-jung!"

Knight's eyes snapped up to the now missing glass wall, and he saw Pawn stepping around and into the frame from the outside on the left.

He ran over and helped her into the room. She had a rifle slung over her back, a pistol tucked into her waistband, and a Chinese belt with six more grenades on it.

Once she was on the floor, she wasted no time unslinging the rifle. There was no time for hugs and reunions. That would come later. Right now, she handed him the long gun, and pulled out the pistol. Then she handed him a grenade.

He took the weapons, checked the rifle, and chambered a round. "Plan?" he asked her.

"Find you. Find the others." she said. "Blow shit up."

He smiled. "I like it. King, Queen, and Bishop are on the move. We're missing Rook and the support team."

"Shit," she said. "They have everyone?"

"Not for long. Did you see Alexander?"

"Hercules?" she was shocked.

"He was in the center of the floor down there," Knight said.

"Oh my god," Pawn threw her hand over her mouth, and her eyes went wide. "That's where I dropped the first two grenades."

SIXTY-FOUR

As King made his way down through the wreckage of the conical cavern, he saw far more body parts than living people. The few who were up and mobile were already making for the exits and paying him no attention.

The wreckage was a tangled mess with whole sections of the chain-link fencing that had surrounded the electrical equipment flung upward and out, toward the labs and workstations. Fires were still burning, and smoke choked the whole area. He'd pulled his moisture-wicking T-shirt off and wrapped it around his face. He had to backtrack a few times when obstacles were piled too high for him to continue forward.

Eventually, he found a way to the center, though.

The plinth Alexander had been on had been moved several feet. All the cables and wires were in disarray, but the man's nearly skeletal body was still attached to the plinth, with some of the wires still jutting from their ports. Others had come loose, and others still had been ripped away, ports and all.

The man's gaunt face was unmoving, and his eyes closed. It was hard to believe the pitiful thing before King was once a six-foot-five powerhouse of a man. His curly black hair was all gone. His skin scorched. His muscles were all atrophied.

King gently laid a hand on a space free of ports and cables on the man's chest, thinking of what few words he could say—and had time for.

But the chest was rising and falling under his hand!

Somehow, Alexander was still alive, after all he had been through, and after the devastating explosion that ruined most of the cavernous space around them.

"My god," King said. "You're still breathing. You never were one to give up."

The man's wrinkled eyelids snapped up, his deep brown eyes still looking focused and clear. His voice, once booming, was now a hoarse scratching, like sandpaper on concrete. "That really you, Jack?"

"It's me," King said, pulling the T-shirt away from his face. "Lie still, we'll figure out how to get you out of here."

"They came for Acca, Jack."

"I know," King said.

"I tried to stop them."

King nodded. "I know," he said again, his own voice almost a whisper.

He realized he had no access to any of the ancient healing serums the Herculean Society kept secret. They were miles from friendly ground and without any modern medical facilities, beyond what they might find in this complex. If they could take it and keep the complex. Plus, the fires were not dying down. They were spreading.

He needed to leave.

Soon.

King looked around the cavern.

Where can I take him? he wondered.

"Jack," Alexander said in his scraping whisper.

"Just a second. I'm trying to figure out—"

"Jack," Alexander said again, and this time some of the former thunder returned.

King turned his gaze back to his dying friend.

"It's...too late...for me. My wife...is...dead. My body is—"

"But the healing serums," King tried to say. "We could find a—"

"—too far gone. It's too far. I'm done, Jack. But I'm glad I got to see you one more time, my brother."

King leaned in close, as Alexander's voice got softer and harder to hear over the noise. It was only then that he realized he'd heard more shrieking in the distance, and there were alarms going off all around the huge arena like space.

"Jack, did I ever tell you about the time..."

But Alexander didn't finish the sentence. His eyes stayed open as he died, and his voice didn't diminish as he had spoken. It just abruptly stopped.

King couldn't find his voice, as he tried to say aloud, 'Safe travels, Brother.' So, he just *thought* them, as tears streamed down his face. He rocked back and forth, just slightly, and he still touched the body of the friend with whom he had shared so much history, and so many adventures.

In about sixty seconds, King had reined in his emotions, tightly compressing them in a ball and shoving them deep down inside of him, allowing a wave of anger to rise and take the place of the grief.

He had a new mission objective: find Crimson and kill her. That would prevent any further lunacy from her, and his now secondary mission objective—preventing the Chinese weapon from devolving any more cities—could be assured. He suspected that, with the facility's destruction, and with Alexander's death, the weapon couldn't function.

But what if there's another command center? he wondered.

As far as he knew, the weapon system was still operational. The satellites still in orbit. If Crimson escaped, she might relocate anywhere in the country—or anywhere else in the world. As the newly crowned Empress of an entire nation, King assumed she had plenty of resources in place. Even if there were no other operations centers from which she could launch her weapon's devastating effect, she could always build another one somewhere.

He had to find her.

When she departed through the shattered window of the observation room, she would have seen the full extent of the damage. She would have understood that this place was compromised, even though King and the others were a small force with which to contend.

And then there was this 'mighty one,' which sounded to King like a code for a self-destruct weapon. The entire facility could soon be coming down on his head. He didn't hear any more shrieking noises, but the fires crackling all around him could be blocking it out. And the ground was still rumbling. He could feel a thrumming through the soles of his boots.

He raced up the cavern's concentric rings, scrambling over destroyed equipment, and finally overturned desks. There were dead men and women—Chinese, and all wearing lab coats—at the outer ring. Many of them scorched and burned, or perforated with jagged pieces of metal. As he moved past the bodies, he saw that some were still moving.

Any other time, he might have stopped to assist the injured—even though they worked for his enemy. He guessed many of the lab techs were just simple people doing jobs to make a living. Many of them might have even been completely ignorant of Crimson's agenda.

But he couldn't stop. She already had a lead on him, and he didn't know where she would go.

He raced to the cavern's end, to a door. He didn't know where it would lead, but out of the cavern was a start.

As soon as he began to open it, the wood surface began to splinter under automatic weapons fire pounding it from the other side. His hand snapped back, and he edged backward from the door, following the wall's curve. Once the shooting stopped, he expected the door would blast open and soldiers would burst in.

But the door stayed silent. No one attempted to come inside.

Maybe it's a small force, he thought. *Maybe they're waiting for me to come out. Or they've been ordered to hem me in.*

King looked behind him. Farther along the curving outer wall—a good thirty feet away—was another wooden door. He backed toward it, his eyes never leaving the first door.

When he reached the next exit, he felt another rumble in the ground.

Shit, he thought. *Running out of time here.*

This time, he got down on the ground on the far side of the door, able to keep his eye on the shattered door thirty feet away, and the new door. He slowly reached up for the handle and readied his rifle.

He yanked the door wide open, falling to the floor, and pointing his rifle toward the opening.

He expected a barrage of fire, but there wasn't any.

He wished he had a grenade. Instead, he inched along the floor toward the doorway. An empty concrete corridor greeted him outside.

Now he positioned himself perpendicular to the door, but still on the floor. He belly crawled forward, edged his face close to the doorway, and darted his head out and back, just at ankle height.

The view down the corridor had lasted a fraction of a second—but long enough for King to see what was outside the distant door.

For fuck sake, he thought. *One man!*

King extended the rifle out the doorway at floor level and started shooting, without looking, spraying the hallway, until he heard the guard grunt and thump to the floor.

Then he stood up and peeked around the doorframe.

The dead man was sprawled on the concrete floor, a pool of blood forming around him from having been riddled by King's pray and spray technique.

The hallway cleared, he raced out of the door and toward the dead man, but skidded to a halt halfway there, when he spotted a red and white laminated diagram attached to a concrete pillar.

He could read the words in Mandarin on the map:

In Case of Fire, Follow This Path to the Nearest Exit.

He did just that, reversing down the hall, away from the fallen body, until he found another hallway with natural light at the end of it.

As he got closer, he could see the double glass doors that would lead outside, but before he reached them, his eyes saw something moving outside the compound.

Something...*mighty.*

SIXTY-FIVE

Bishop and Queen met some resistance as they moved through the corridors and down the stairwells of the terraced complex. But rarely were there more than four or five armed guards present in a single group.

As Queen bent down over a fallen body to retrieve magazines for her weapon, she whispered to Bishop. "I think this place might have been run on a skeleton crew. Either that or everyone is abandoning the sinking ship."

They felt another deep rumble in the ground, this one closer to an actual earthquake. Bishop stood up, slapped a magazine into his rifle and charged it. Looking around, he said, "Might be a bit of both. But whatever that rumbling is, it's getting stronger."

Queen stood and they pressed on—down deeper into the complex, and closer to the dam at the bottom of the mountain. They had first started their search for Rook and the others by heading up the mountain, above the giant cavern. But they quickly discovered unfinished masonry, piles of construction equipment, and pallets of machine parts still wrapped heavily in plastic. They'd concluded that the complex had been built from the bottom, stretching up the mountain, with each new section added after the last had been completed.

They abandoned searching up the mountain and now raced down through the complex, eliminating each small pocket of armed men they encountered.

The corridor ahead of them arced to the right with open doors on each side. Bishop ran along one wall, aiming into each new room on the opposite side of the corridor, and Queen did the same on the other wall. She heard a loud *clack* come from the door she was approaching. She placed her left hand over her right forearm, while still training the rifle toward the door with her right hand. Her left index finger and thumb formed a circle and her remaining fingers pointed at the door.

Bishop spotted the movement and understood that she'd heard something. He kept his rifle trained on the doorway.

Queen backed up a few feet, signaled Bishop to be ready, and then ran straight ahead, diving and rolling on the floor, past the doorway.

A split second later, a barrage of gunfire came out of the doorway, completely missing her.

Queen rolled to a halt in a crouched position, her rifle still trained on the doorway across the hall.

Bishop opened fire on the doorway right behind her. Inside, a body slumped to the floor.

A second soldier charged out of the door across the hall—her target. She fired a single shot at an upward angle, and the man's head exploded backward in a cloud of skull fragments and bloody mist. The soldier dropped to the floor in a crumpled heap, his torso weirdly balanced on collapsed legs, and what was left of his head hanging backward, behind the dead man's shoulders.

Queen didn't think the human neck could bend that far backward.

She heard Bishop step up behind her and whisper "Clear."

She approached the dead soldier, ignoring the body, and 'sliced the pie,' widening her angle of approach and slowly increasing her view into the room, around the doorframe.

When she was sure there were no more shooters, she approached the door and continued the sidestepping movements until she could see all the way inside the room and pronounce it clear.

"Only two men," she said, thinking.

"But working together," Bishop added.

Queen turned to look at her partner. "Like they were ordered to lay a trap."

"Thinking Crimson came this way?" Bishop asked.

"Or that this way leads to Rook and the others," she said.

They were just about to return to their search when Queen heard running footsteps. There was little cover in the corridor, besides the occasional concrete support pillar. Queen rushed up to the nearest column and took up a position there, while Bishop crossed the hallway to his original target room and slipped beyond the doorframe.

Queen was positioned for ambush. Bishop was in place to spot the oncoming person as soon as they came around the middle of the corridor's curve.

She listened to the approaching footsteps. Running, but then stopping. The hallway was silent for thirty seconds, then she heard running again. One person. The footsteps stopped again, and she guessed the soldier had come maybe thirty feet before coming to a halt.

The distance down the corridor between the doors.

Someone is checking all the rooms.

It was either another enemy, or a friendly. She doubted King could have gotten around them, but she hadn't seen Knight since the explosion.

As the footsteps again ran toward her, she decided to take a chance, and called out, "Identify!"

She knew if it was an enemy, she'd be alerting them to her presence but if it was a friendly, she didn't want to accidentally shoot them.

"Queen?" came Rook's voice from down the hallway. His running steps sped up.

She came out from around the pillar, and Bishop joined her. There was just one opposing set of doors between her and Rook. The doors were like the ones she had already encountered. Staggered, so you couldn't see from one doorway into the next. And helpfully, so you could clear each one yourself. Rook had been doing that, working his way up the curved hallway.

The last doors were closer to Queen than to Rook.

She raced up to the first doorway on her side, and cleared the space while Bishop appeared and approached the other and checked his doorway.

Meanwhile, Rook raced toward them, his boots slapping on the concrete floor. Queen could tell he was limping slightly, and she saw one of his arms was in a sling.

Before Rook could get any closer to them and before he could say anything, the shaking returned, this time as loud as a hurricane. The hallway behind Rook disintegrated, ripping toward the outward side of the curving hallway. Everything behind Rook just vanished in a rumbling fury. The walls, floor, and ceiling scoured away in the blink of an eye.

Rook, stopped stationary, his entire body clenched in shock, looked like an old comedy actor startled by a crashing chandelier just steps behind him.

Queen expected dust and debris, but the speed with which the event had occurred whipped all the dust out of the building with the rest of the structure. It was like a fast tornado strike. Or a massive train just blasting through the hallway wall, whisking away everything it touched.

Rook's eyes were huge. He slow turned and looked at the devastation just a few feet behind him. "What in the name of Mother Theresa's switchblade was that?"

The hallway just a step from where he was had been removed. Raw earth made up the ground, where the concrete floor had been. Daylight poured in from the open wound in the building. A section of hallway twenty feet long was just...gone. All traces of it removed.

Rook stepped toward the absent portion of the building and scrambled down onto the dirt.

Queen raced forward and slipped her head around the corner in the direction the hallway had been carried, and she saw it. Her mind couldn't compute what she was seeing.

Bishop was next to her, looking, and he said softly, "Damn."

Rook took a step forward, toward the trail of devastation that stretched out ahead of him, snaking its way down the mountainside, toward the reservoir beyond.

The creature was distant and moving at an incredible speed for something longer than a train and wider than three of them side by side.

Rook turned to look back at Queen and pointed in the direction of the concrete-strewn hillside. "Just when you think the weirdest shit you might see in a day is a hulking Neanderthal chick with a hard-on for torture, all slathered in make-up, a god damn fucking dragon shows up."

SIXTY-SIX

Tom Duncan knew how to spend his time while incarcerated. He'd been imprisoned enough these last few years. He worked on his body, keeping it in top shape. And he worked on his mind, exploring pathways in the mental palace he had constructed to store knowledge and contain memories.

He'd become quite good at recalling things from his past, and an expert at walling off painful memories. He could amuse himself with puzzles, passing time. He calculated possibilities, considering the future, and different outcomes based on specific actions taken, or not taken, in the present. His thought process was keenly strategic, and his talent for projecting probable and even plausible outcomes was second to none. The trick was in nudging current and future events from possible to preferable. And he spent a great deal of time considering all possible and even improbable variables that might divert the progression toward a desired result.

In short, he had a rich internal life.

Even when he had served as the President of the United States, he had carved out time each day to be alone with his thoughts, structuring and arranging ideas, predictions, and likely resulting scenarios. Duncan found it crucial to maintain such a robust mental regimen, but he also found the process to be a welcome refuge from interacting with other human beings—even those he liked.

One of the things he enjoyed most about Asya's company was that the woman intuitively understood his need to do so. They hadn't spent a ton of time together but it was as if she either needed similar time alone with her thoughts, or else she was just superbly content to sit in abject silence. Most people, Duncan had realized in his youth—especially Americans—felt a need to fill silence with talk. Even if they had nothing to say.

Asya both wanted to be with him and didn't need to fill the stretches of silence with chatter. When they spoke, she was direct and clear, and also very capable of thinking 'outside the box,' a skill he prized in people. She was very well read, and highly intelligent. Duncan enjoyed discussing all matter of subjects with her.

But when he began to think deeply about a subject, the lapse into silence remained, as if she was either respecting his process or perhaps slipping into her own deep thoughts at the same time.

Imprisoned in the same cell, they now sat side by side on the sole bed in the room. As Duncan's thoughts travelled backward to the assault on Siletz, he wondered if Asya was grieving their dead. Although they had lost many in the battle, one was still too raw for him to even allow his thoughts to graze.

The ground rumbled again and, without a word, Asya slid to the concrete floor of the cell, sitting cross legged and placing the flat of her palms on the ground, as if she was hoping to discern the cause of the tremor by touch. He wasn't sure she'd be able to feel too much through her left hand's nylon splint, which she'd been wearing after her cast had come off.

"The sound is too irregular and lasts too long to be a natural earthquake," he said, his voice soft.

Asya showed no sign of being startled by him speaking up after his hour-long silence. They had each heard the explosions and the vibrations in the earth that had followed. But neither had commented on it or discussed the action outside their cell.

"Earth moving equipment, perhaps," she replied.

They had tried to escape from the cell, testing the walls, the door, the ceiling, and the floor for weaknesses. But this room was designed to be a prison cell, which was obvious from the one aluminum toilet mounted on the far wall, and the fact that the single bed in the room was bolted to the wall. There were no windows, the door was solid steel, and lacked even a handle on the inside. Once they had jointly concluded that there would be no escaping the space, they had settled down to wait for something to happen.

Eventually, their captors would come for them—followed by escape, or death.

The steel door to the room had a wide slot in the bottom, where food could be passed into the cell on a tray. The slot was closed and couldn't be budged from the inside. Duncan had tried. The door also had a small face height, six-inch square window that could be opened—again, only from the outside—so the guards could check on their prisoners. Since they had been placed in the room, the window had not opened.

Duncan didn't know whether the guards had been instructed not to peek in at their prisoners, or whether the door was completely unguarded.

Either way, when he heard the latch on the small window snap open on the other side, he was surprised. Without a word to Asya, he readied to strike if an opportunity presented itself. He knew she would be ready, too. She shifted into a crouch with characteristic smooth grace, ready to spring up.

The steel window flipped open, but no face appeared.

Asya stood to her feet, and Duncan did, as well. He took a step toward the door. "Hello?" he asked.

Knight's face appeared in the window, while the locking mechanism for the door clunked from the other side. "Hey, boss. How about we get you out of here?"

Duncan's relief was instant. "It's getting to be a habit, you freeing me from jail cells."

"Eh," Asya said. "Jack did it last time." She moved in front of him, stepping through the door first as it opened.

Pawn was on the other side, and Asya fist bumped the woman, then took the offered Chinese semi-automatic QSZ pistol from her.

Duncan followed her out of the cell and Knight handed him a Type 56 rifle.

Asya looked at the rifle, looked down at her own pistol, and then held the QSZ out to Duncan and snatched the rifle from him, with her other hand.

He just chuckled and took the pistol.

"Sitrep?" he asked Knight.

"Crimson on the loose. Some kind of self-destruct system set off. Major machinery here damaged—hopefully what was powering the weapon. King, Queen, and Bishop escaped. Haven't seen Rook. You?"

"The Empress is here?" Duncan asked.

"The Empress...is our old friend Red, from Vietnam," Knight added.

Duncan stood dumbfounded for a moment. He'd considered a number of theories, but never her. Red had been a primal powerhouse, not a sophisticated leader. She was also supposed to be dead. "That's..."

"Surprising?" Knight said. "No shit."

Duncan snapped out of his shock.

"We've only been here a short time." Duncan didn't state that the Chinese had taken the Siletz base. That much would be obvious. "Aleman's dead. So are most of the security forces we had with us. Haven't seen any others. It was just the two of us on the plane. We overheard our captors decide to leave Felice behind."

"Damn," Pawn said.

"Where's Fiona?" Knight asked. His voice was urgent. Like the others on the team, Shin Dae-jung had practically raised the girl.

Duncan looked down at the floor, not meeting Knight's gaze. "She wasn't on the plane with us. Either she escaped, or they killed her."

SIXTY-SEVEN

Two Miles West of Ping'An, Qinghai Province

The experimental stealth plane flew just barely two hundred feet above the ground. Larger than a B21, this particular vehicle had been retrofitted for cargo and fast troop deployment. There were two Chenowth Advanced Light Strike Vehicles—which were basically fast attack dune buggies—in the cargo area, ready to be dropped into battle. There was also an M1126 Stryker armored personnel carrier. The beast looked like an eight wheeled tank with no treads, but it was lighter and faster, and particularly suited for the mountainous terrain.

The Stryker would hold nine passengers, the Chenowths an additional four each. It was a tiny strike force, but it was really just the tip of a larger spear. A larger cargo plane was en route from Mongolia and would be bringing in Abrams tanks and a full battalion of soldiers.

This first plane, still referred to as a 'Raider,' despite its different size and payload, would swoop in toward the Lijia Dam, and drop its three squads, before peeling away, and high-tailing it out of Chinese airspace.

The hope, Fiona knew, was that the squads, to which she had been attached as a 'liaison' at Dom Boucher's insistence, would be able to cause enough havoc and disruption on the ground to distract anyone from keeping an eye out for the full invasion force coming in from the north.

Boucher had also explained to her that the US hoped that, with a speedy overthrow of the new Empress, they might be able to install a democratic leader—or at least someone from the older regime who might be easier to work with. If the imperial station could be quickly destroyed, and the Empress captured or killed, the US propaganda machine could declare that she and her forces were a terrorist threat, and this invasion of sovereign Chinese soil by Americans was really a 'tiny, probably not even really necessary' assistance force to the formidable People's Liberation Army of China. It would allow whatever new government was installed to save face over the entire affair.

But Fiona's job was slightly different from the rest of the men and women in her squads. She was here for just one reason—using the mother tongue, she would wreak destruction on the Danxia Landform that surrounded the entire dam complex.

The Danxia was a gigantic, unique area of petroglyphic geomorphology, composed of red sandstone and mineral deposits. The land was characteristically streaked with stripes of green vegetation, red stone, and brown and tan dirt and soils. The whole area was pocketed with caves, odd peaks, and cliffs, as a result of geologic uplift from the Qinghai-Tibet plateau.

In other words, it would be a playground for Fiona, and she could aid the US Army Delta teams deploying with her, by rupturing landforms and structures, wrenching apart stone pillars, and mangling opposing forces with her ability to move stone and rock.

And she was in the mood to do it. After the attack on Siletz, she had slipped out of her panic room to discover Duncan and Asya were gone, but the whole support team was dead. And a man that had been like a big brother to her, Lewis Aleman, had also been shot and left behind like so much refuse.

Fiona had contacted Dom Boucher, and he had arranged for her to be flown to Washington state, to meet up with the strike team he and the

President had put together. Boucher had informed her about Chess Team being on the ground in this part of China, and Fiona was certain they would be here already.

Then it was just the long flight to Mongolia, and then the nap-of-the-earth flight along the hills and mountains down through the Chinese provinces of Inner Mongolia and Gansu. Now, they were just a few minutes away.

Sergeant Cooper came by her seat and jerked his thumb toward the rear of the plane. It was time. She quickly unbuckled from her passenger seat and headed past the attack vehicles, standing to the side of the aircraft's fuselage, while the rest of the operators did the same.

"Sure you don't want a sidearm, Fiona?" Cooper asked her.

"Won't need one," she said.

A rotating green light filled the space as the rear cargo door opened, and a drogue chute released. Then the Chenowths were pulled from the back of the plane, whizzing right past the lined-up operators. Finally, the massive Stryker slid past. Then the men ran after the vehicles, flinging themselves out the open hatch.

The plane had climbed slightly, providing just enough of a height above the mountains for a low-altitude, low-opening (LALO) jump.

Then it was Fiona's turn, and Cooper would be last to follow her out of the plane. With nothing but anger coursing through her, she launched into the air. She was furious that her home had been attacked...again. Her ancestral land desecrated a second time. Her family killed or abducted. She was cut off from Chess Team and had no idea whether they were alive or dead. Lewis Aleman, a man who had helped raise her since she was a tween, was in a coffin back in Oregon. And this upstart Chinese Empress was behind it all. Her friends killed in Cape Town. All of it.

She was here at Boucher's request, but she had also made it plain to him that if he didn't send her, she would have found a way over here on her own.

The parachute snapped open, jolting her frame and her thoughts out of the spiral of pain, helplessness, and a desire for retribution. She took in the sight of the variegated hillsides, the sprawling pagoda like complex that decorated the side of the mountain, crawling all the way down to the dam, the communications towers, the parabolic dishes, and the action already occurring on the ground.

"What the hell?" Cooper said through the headphones built into her helmet.

Fiona glanced forward at the chaos. "Looks about right," she said, shaking her head.

"Is that—?" Cooper started.

"Yep," Fiona said. "That's Dad. Going up against a three hundred foot, Chinese dragon. With an AK-47."

SIXTY-EIGHT

Imperial Palace, Kanbula, Qinghai Province

King had seen a lot of things in his very long life. Terrorists with no conscience. Child soldiers with skin, limb, and mechanical grafts. Alligator-like Komodo dragon creatures. Murderous capybaras. Unstoppable regenerating soldiers. The mythological Hydra. Neanderthals. Animated golem monsters. Zombies. Underground Bigfoot-esque animals. Black holes. Dimensional tears in the fabric of reality.

And all of that was before he'd been thrust 2,800 years into the past, made immortal, and forced to live through the years until he regained his original place in the present. He later had his immortality removed. He fought dinosaurs in Africa and murderous apes in Asia. He'd even run for his life from giant Mongolian Death Worms and, more recently in the Desolation Islands, faced off against prehistoric, giant lizard creatures.

He'd fought some large monstrosities. Each one beyond the normal range of human belief.

But nothing like this.

He was looking at an actual Chinese dragon.

The long, undulating snake-like kind, with blood-red eyes, a ridge of spikes down its back, green and blue scales, long flowing whisker-like appendages streaming from its elongated snout, and four stubby legs with five claws each—one facing backward like a hawk's talons. The creature had no wings, and King was grateful for that. It seemed restricted to travel over the ground. But it was easily three hundred feet long. The beast's weight rumbled the ground like an earthquake as it raced and coiled along the hillside. Behind its head were several long horns or spikes that faced backward, protecting the back of its neck, as well as vivid green feathers.

It was exactly the image King always had in his head of a Chinese dragon—but it was huge. It was so big that he couldn't see all of it at once, and he was awestruck as the beast raced across the hillside, propelled not by the talon-tipped legs, but rather by its side and belly scales pushing it like a snake.

And the creature was fast.

Like a speeding train, winding and careening around curves. The dragon blasted its way through a part of the building, disappearing for just a few seconds before exploding back out again a hundred feet farther up the hillside, onto King's side of the mountain. It trailed a stream of debris and decimated masonry behind it, the beast's scales carving troughs in the soil as it passed.

King's eyes expanded in wonder as the creature raced by him. The breeze left in its wake ripped across his clothes, like he was standing on an underground platform next to a subway train that wasn't stopping. Then the horrid stench of the beast hit him. It was a deeply spoiled fish scent, and it nearly made him gag. He felt his stomach contents begin to rise, but then the rushing wind in the creature's wake cleared, bringing the fresh mountain air with it.

The head of the dragon curved up ahead, swishing and twisting, until suddenly it was racing back up the hill, right toward King. He raised his rifle but quickly realized how futile it would be.

He started to dart to his left, but then he quickly shifted his weight and threw himself to the right.

The creature blasted past him on his left, moving so quickly that, by the time he stood and realized it was passing him, half of its enormous length had already gone by. Before he could congratulate himself on his successful dodge, he realized he'd forgotten about the beast's rear leg. The appendage was coming right at him, but the talons were not stretched out to grab him. The limb was simply being carried along, but it was about to collide with him.

King did the only thing he could.

He jumped.

Like a track star throwing established rules and style out the window and attempting to clear a hurdle headfirst. He dove over the on-coming limb, but the tips of his boots still caught on the scales, and he tumbled forward out of control. There was no way he would be able to dodge the tail if it snapped at him as it passed, cracking like a thunderous whip.

He hit the ground on his shoulder, and remained in a ball, rolling with the impact. A cloud of dirt erupted around him, filling his lungs, and causing him to cough uncontrollably.

He rolled to his hands and knees, and then struggled to stand.

Somewhere he had lost the Chinese rifle.

When the cloud of dust cleared, yanked away like a magician swiping a tablecloth out from under a candlestick, a burst of fresh air hit him again, clearing his breathing.

Before he could react, a string of tiny soil geysers erupted from the ground around him. Someone was firing an automatic weapon at him. He dove left again, headfirst, but this time into the shallow trench left by the dragon's passing. It wasn't much cover against the oncoming barrage of bullets, but it was something.

The dragon was gone now, perhaps to the other side of the mountain. The ground around him had stopped shaking. Was it far away, or had it stopped moving? Either way, King couldn't see the creature farther up the trench in the direction it had gone. The path ran through the nearby building, and then twisted to the left on the other side of the ruins. Crumbles of cracked gray concrete and shattered terracotta roof tiles littered the path.

What the dragon's absence did was provide King the opportunity to hear again. Chinese rifles rattled as soldiers continued to pelt his position, the rounds ripping into the soil, but not penetrating his makeshift foxhole.

Then he heard an answering round of fire coming from downhill of his position, where the massive creature had blasted through a hallway.

The incessant pocking of King's trench stopped. The gunfire from the building continued for just another second, and then all firing ended.

King darted his head above the trench's edge, getting a look at the hillside. Farther down the slope were three dead soldiers, their limbs twisted at unnatural angles from where they had fallen. Standing in a hole in the building's side were Queen and Rook, each armed with rifles and Rook with his arm in a white medical sling.

Approaching King was Bishop, already tossing him another Chinese Type 56 rifle with the wooden stock, grip, and handguard behind the barrel.

King lunged to his feet and caught the rifle by the handguard and the magazine, with both hands outstretched in front of him. He quickly pulled the charging handle to ensure the weapon was ready to fire.

He was about to make a crack about Rook not pulling his weight, as he and Queen approached King's position. But then he saw how badly injured the man was. Beside Rook's sling, his face was badly bruised, he was limping, and Queen was helping him walk. His left shoulder was bloody through the fabric of his shirt, and his left eye was completely swollen shut.

Instead, King said, "Stan, are you alright?"

"I don't care what Red said," Rook started, his voice sounding hoarse and ragged, "I don't think she's really a licensed masseuse."

Before anyone could respond to Rook's feeble joke, the wall of the building just twenty feet downhill from his position exploded outward.

SIXTY-NINE

The dragon was coming back, and Pawn managed to lunge out of the way, just as the massive beast plunged once again through the side of the building that traversed the hillside.

Knight was on the other side of the impact. He didn't know that Anna was safe until the beast had plowed through the building once again, and he saw her standing to her feet. For a second, he thought he'd seen her obliterated before his eyes. The impact of the dragon and the building happened so suddenly that he didn't even have time to think of using his cybernetic eye to see through the dragon's body and look for her on the other side.

Things were moving too quickly, and he used his eye now to track the dragon's passage on the other side of the crumbled hallway, as it raced and slithered away down the other side of the hill, colliding with, and knocking over a tall communications antenna that fell into the distant reservoir.

He switched visual sensor modes, allowing him to see the beast through the hillside once it passed a crest. But there were too many mineral deposits in the ground. It was mostly sedimentary rock layers mixed with larger chunks of igneous granite.

Knight would have to keep a watch for the dragon like everyone else—with his remaining natural eye. But he quickly scanned the surrounding hillside anyway, focusing more uphill than downhill where the dragon had fled.

"I think we're about to get some reinforcements," he told Pawn. "That or Crimson's forces are."

She knew better than to distrust his assessment. "What do you see?"

"That plane that flew over just dropped vehicles and paratroopers up near the mountain's summit."

Knight followed the dragon's newly cut passage through the building's now exposed electrical wiring and dangling fluorescent lighting. Little rubble remained from the creature's high-speed blitz through the concrete, but he had to step over a few obstacles, as Pawn followed him. He crept through the newly hollowed out tunnel, weapon raised.

"One thing I can tell you, is bullets aren't going to stop that creature," Pawn said softly to him.

Knight thought for a moment.

"We need explosives."

"I gave Asya all the grenades I had," Pawn complained.

Knight nodded. "She'll need them more than us. Unless that monster does their job for them."

As they approached the end of the tunnel—and the other side of the building's exterior—they slowed, and quieted, Knight checking the hillside for hostile targets...and the dragon.

Two hundred feet below, from behind an exposed conference room, a squad of five armed men ran to the building's corner and charged uphill toward their position.

To his left, a group of four stood near the building, and Knight recognized a mountain of a man among them—Bishop. His size, and even his posture, was instantly recognizable through the X-ray vision.

Beyond the team, up the hill another three hundred feet, Knight spotted another squad of soldiers slowly picking their way down the hill, around and through trenches left by the dragon, and the shattered fragments of what used to be the building.

Chess Team was about to be pinned between two hostile forces. And the paratroopers hadn't left the mountain's summit yet. They were at least a half a mile away.

"Does it look to you like the dragon's movements are erratic?" Pawn asked him, her voice now a whisper, having no doubt read his body language, as he tensed slightly after spotting the approaching soldiers.

"It doesn't seem to be targeting individuals. It's just in a frenzy. We have tangos coming from our left and right," he informed her.

"What about—?"

But he was already ahead of her, using his eye to look through his own head and back the way they had come.

Another wide section of the building was still standing on that side of the hill, and he could now see twenty men slowly rounding the structure, about three hundred feet away, converging on his position.

"A platoon behind us," he said, squatting down next to the fractured wall he was using as cover.

Pawn dropped down, and turned around, facing the oncoming platoon. She would cover their rear as best she could, but Knight could see that the whole team was about to be overpowered and hemmed in on all sides. And he still hadn't contacted Bishop and the others to let them know he and Pawn were right here.

He didn't think they would have time for the reinforcements to arrive…and that was *if* the paratroopers were on their side. He thought he'd recognized the plane as a kind of stealth bomber. It looked like an American plane, but he knew it could have belonged to any nation, really, and it might then have found its way to China's possession.

The only way this could be worse—

Then he felt the ground tremor.

"Fuck," he said, "On my six."

He crouch ran out from behind his cover, trying to get up the hill toward the rest of his team. Pawn followed him out of the ruined building.

"Incoming," he yelled, and he could see Bishop's head snap his way down the hill. Rook was now on the ground, and Queen had dropped to one knee next to him, but her rifle's barrel had snapped up in his direction, at the sound of Knight's yell. Beyond them, King was crouched, and had his rifle pointed up the hillside. "Coming from up and down, and through the building!"

He started running for their position, as Bishop trained his rifle downhill of Knight's position.

Knight heard rifle fire from behind him, as Pawn opened up on the tunnel freshly ripped through the side of the building. He dropped down to a squat and turned to give her support. As he was doing so, he saw the men far downhill, off to her left, start to clear the corner of the building. Leaving her to shoot at the tunnel, he fired on the distant corner of the building. The Chinese soldiers popped back around the concrete corner as his rounds found the building, sending chips of masonry flying in all directions. He could hear Bishop's rifle firing as well.

Then behind him, Knight heard King firing up the mountain, away from them.

The ground vibrated softly, growing to an ominous shaking. Knight was keeping up the pressure on the distant squad downhill, when he heard Queen yell "On your right," as she passed between him and the building, heading toward Pawn's position. Queen then dropped to her stomach and belly crawled to a three foot high, fallen slab of wall, which she used as cover. Her own rifle soon joined Pawn's, firing at the tunnel entrance, as the platoon members popped around the wall, one after the other. Pawn had dropped four, but the others kept darting back behind cover to safety.

Knight heard Rook's voice next, "It's coming!"

He turned his gaze from the pinned downhill squad to the side of the mountain, away from the team, which also led down the hill toward the distant reservoir and the communications dishes.

The dragon was racing up that hill, straight toward Bishop's position, no unplanned twists or turns. The animal barreled toward the building, and Bishop was standing in the way, with Rook on the ground right behind him. Bishop swung his rifle toward the massive beast and fired a sustained burst directly at the creature's twenty foot wide face.

The dragon, unfazed by the maelstrom of 7.62mm rounds, closed the distance at fifty miles an hour.

SEVENTY

Former Chess Team HQ, Siletz, Oregon

Felice Carter snapped awake in the dark. It took a second for her eyes to realize the room wasn't completely black. A light green hue filled the space. Just enough for her to see by. She knew from the feel of the bed that she wasn't in her Cape Town room, but the green light—from a small LED on an emergency light in the corner of the ceiling—was a dead giveaway that she was somewhere unknown. The little LEDs on the lights in the Herculean Society base in Cape Town were red. Not green.

Her body hurt in multiple places and, as she slowly tested out moving, she found that she had an IV drip bag attached to her left arm, by a port taped to the back of her hand. There was no medical heart monitor noise in the background, just absolute silence. No hum of electronics or machinery. No ventilation system. Just quiet.

She tried her voice, but her attempt at 'Hello' just came out of her dry throat as a hiss of air.

Her tongue felt enlarged and dry in her mouth.

Felice reached over with her right hand and traced the line of the IV drip upward as far as she could, and then tugged on it. The aluminum stand toppled over and landed across her legs, but she was able to extend her hand farther up the line until she felt the collapsed, empty plastic bag that had once held liquid in it.

What the hell? she thought.

She pulled the port out of her hand, the tape causing her more of a problem than the needle. Then she sat up. She was in a hospital gown, but there were no windows in the room with her. She ran her fingers over her body. No obvious broken bones, but she was sore all over. She wasn't covered in bandages, though, so she assumed they were just bruises. She pressed on a spot on her right thigh until it hurt.

Definitely a bruise.

Then she slid her feet to the floor. The tile was cold on her feet, but it felt good to stand up, even though the light in the room was dim enough that she couldn't make out any of the blurring, dark shapes in the room. She shuffled her feet and slidewalked across the room to the wall under the LED. There was no special medical equipment or medical ports for oxygen. No sharps containers mounted on the wall. This was a makeshift medical room.

But where?

She searched the wall for a light switch and found one, but nothing happened when she flicked it.

Of course, she thought. *Power is out.*

But the emergency lighting wasn't on either. Just that lone LED. She thought of the empty IV bag and realized the emergency power could have been on...and run out. She'd been unattended for some time.

Felice slid her hands along the wall, moving to her right, until she could feel the outline of a wooden door frame. She felt a small sense of triumph, but then frustration as it took her another sixty seconds fumbling in the dark to find the doorknob in the unfamiliar space.

Frustration, yes, but not panic.

She had lived all over Africa, first as a geneticist, and later working with Erik Somers and the Cerberus Group. But her ability to remain calm in stressful situations was the core of her being. Especially after discovering, during her experiences in Ethiopia, that she was somehow quantum entangled with every mind on the planet. If she lost control, she could turn off the genome responsible for human sentience in an individual—or possibly in the entire human race. Amongst the very few people who knew of her abilities, there was a very real concern for what might happen to humanity, should she die.

But Erik Somers acted as a lighting rod for her, grounding her fears and concerns in the very real warmth of his love for her. And for her part, she helped him ease the traumas he had experienced in his previous life as a member of the covert operations group called Chess Team.

Together, they had explored all manner of calming techniques like yoga and meditation, as well as different kinds of medicines—both traditional and natural. Their work with the Herculean Society, solving world problems and hunting down archeological relics, was a fascinating and fun new life for her. But, at the center of it all, was always the need to remain in control. Something she excelled at.

She opened the door, inward, and took a step out into the dark space beyond her room. Her foot made contact with something lying on the floor, but her first instinct, rather than attempting to scream with her hoarse voice, was to take a calm, steadying breath.

Then she squatted and checked on the obstacle. It was a man, in a uniform of some sort. She checked for a pulse, but he was definitely dead. Then her hand roamed over his body looking for a flashlight. Instead, she found a phone in his pocket. She turned it on and saw that it had only 13% battery life left, but that was enough for her to turn on the device's flashlight.

She was in a hallway of some type. Also windowless. The man was in a security officer's uniform, and he had three bullet holes in his chest. His uniform shirt was bloody, but his life's juices had not dripped onto the tile floor yet. Behind her, as she suspected, was a normal room, no different than a basic office, but it looked like it had been quickly converted into a makeshift hospital room.

What the hell? she wondered again. She was an expert at remaining calm, but she was not especially patient with mounting mystery.

And there was something else about her strange abilities. She could use them intentionally. She rarely did, instead opting for keeping them in check. But she could use her mind to shut down another human if she chose to. Or to peek into another soul's mind. Or see *through* their eyes.

She calmed herself with another slow steadying breath, then closed her eyes, and let the orbs roll up under her eyelids. She reached out her thoughts, something she visualized as her hands flying through an endless darkness around her, until they found a pinprick of red light. As she zoomed in on that light, it blossomed into a flowing jumble of glowing red aura that always reminded her of the designs a Spirograph toy made, with each human mind forming a geometric roulette curve. Each human being's personal hypotrochoid pattern of glowing energy appeared to her in the vast abyss of the darkness in her mind. She could zoom in on one, or she could zoom out to see billions of pinpricks that themselves formed a complicated spiral pattern.

She quickly peeked through the eyes of the first few living people she found—nearest to her geographically. In seconds, she discovered that she was in a forested area with trees far different from those in South Africa.

She let her thoughts flick outward faster, her glimpse flitting through one mind and then the next in a fraction of a second. She could rarely pick up on discrete thoughts when she did this, but sometimes she could get a theme or idea that was prominent in a person's brain. As she cast her net farther, she discerned, through stolen glimpses and prominent mental imagery, that she was somewhere in the US Pacific Northwest.

Her eyes snapped open again. *What the actual hell happened to me?* she wondered. Then her patience was gone.

Her eyelids slammed shut again, and she resisted the urge to put everyone, everywhere on Earth on pause, which would be as easy for her as thinking it. She could certainly stop the whole world in its tracks until she felt secure in her understanding of what was going on. But that was like using a hammer to turn the page of a book. Not the right tool for the job.

Instead, she let her consciousness swim farther outward into the darkness behind her eyes. The tiny dots of red aura multiplied and became blobs and misshapen humps around the world as her mind scanned for one unique, distinct light.

All the others were red. This one was blue. And it shone brighter in her mind than all the others on the planet.

Felice Carter's mind invaded Erik Somers's eyesight and, in an instant, she saw exactly what Bishop was seeing halfway around the planet.

"Oh my God."

SEVENTY-ONE

Kanbula, Qinghai Province

Asya raced along the top of the nearly white concrete dam, approaching the only guard stationed atop it. The man noticed her and began to raise his rifle toward her. He was older than some of the soldiers she had seen stationed at the complex, and his skin was tanned and leathery, as if he had served most of his days in the army outdoors, in the higher altitudes and bright sun of the Tibetan Plateau.

As she came within ten feet of him, she leapt to his left in a handspring. Rather than continuing in the direction she was heading, at a forty-five-degree angle away from the man, she juked right, her feet launching into the air directly toward him. Most of her weight in the handspring had gone on her right hand anyway, as she was still slightly favoring the left.

The man's rifle followed her through the first part of her acrobatic maneuver, but he wasn't expecting her to suddenly spring toward him. Her feet connected with his face and sent him flailing backward.

Asya deftly landed on her feet, sinking down into a crouch, prepared to spring again. But it wasn't necessary. The man's body toppled over backward, his lower spine connecting with the three foot high concrete and steel guard rail, which really served more as a guide track for the legs of the orange floodgate gantry hoist that was twenty feet to the man's left. Under normal circumstances, the wall would serve as a safety rail for a careful pedestrian. In this case, the wall cracked the man's spine, and then his torso's weight flipped his inert body over it, where he plummeted five hundred feet to the concrete platforms at the base of the dam, just before the rushing spillway waters.

Tom Duncan ran along the edge of the wall behind the lithe Russian woman, astounded at her agility and speed. He glanced over the edge of the wall to watch the guard's body tumble the perilous distance to a hard concrete demise far below. He winced. Even the loss of enemy combatant lives felt like they left a mark on his soul, and he regretted every one of them. He understood the necessity of killing enemies, but he yearned for a world where it wouldn't be called for.

The dam was a semicircular structure that curved almost 1,300 feet, and the massive one hundred and twenty foot tall, bright orange, four-legged gantry could be rolled slowly around most of the dam's top surface. The gantry looked like a squat oil platform, all steel, with staircases climbing its legs, all leading to a top platform with a two story building full of observation windows.

When there was a need to release some of the water from the 52,000 square mile catchment area on the upper side of the dam, the gantry could be moved to different locations atop the wall to raise and lower floodgates weighing several tons.

Duncan didn't know if the dam's hydroelectric power station could function to launch another space based attack on humanity, but he was certain that the structure provided power to the sprawling complex and the parabolic dishes that climbed the mountain above them. And he understood that, if the magnificent dragon didn't destroy everything, if he and Asya could damage the dam, that might be the nail in the entire complex's coffin.

There was just one problem.

The dam was built to take a lot of abuse. At just twenty six feet wide at the top, the dam broadened at the bottom to almost a hundred and fifty feet wide.

It was an immense structure filled with tons and tons of material to hold back the reservoir.

And they had just a handful of grenades between them.

At first, Duncan thought they might be able to destroy the base of one of the legs of the gantry. Although steel, that was one of the narrowest parts of the huge metal behemoth. If they could take out a foot, the entire thing might tip over the wall, just like the dead guard did, gouging a massive hole in the side of the dam as it went down.

Pressure from the immense body of water on the other side would do the rest.

But now that he stood at the orange steel base with Asya, he understood just how flawed that plan was.

"It's huge," Asya said. "The feet are three meters long at least. There's no way these grenades will even dent the steel. These were designed for anti-personnel." She held up the military web belt with five grenades that Pawn had supplied. 'Fortunes of war' she had called them after she'd liberated them from dead Chinese soldiers.

Duncan glanced over the side of the dam, then looked back to Asya. "We need a different plan."

In the distance, up on the mountain, the dragon rampaged through the building, and the soldiers running all over the mountain—both up the hillside and down toward the dam. They wouldn't have much time.

"Up the stairs. Let's look for a rope."

Asya raced to the gantry's stairwell and made it up the six flights of stairs to the huge machine's first level—and one of its lower control rooms—before Duncan even made it halfway. By the time he reached the top of the fourth flight of stairs, the younger woman was already on the way down with a white coil of nylon rope over her shoulder.

Duncan turned and raced back down the stairs to the dam's surface. He took little pleasure in the fact that she didn't manage to overtake him. He was getting too old for this sort of thing.

"Now what?" Asya asked.

Just then, a plane screamed by overhead, and Duncan was certain it was a US made B21 Raider. The plane raced up the mountain, and Duncan thought things might turn out alright after all.

Dom, I swear to God if that's you, he thought, *I'm going to buy you all the bourbon in the world.*

With no more time to consider the new arrivals, Duncan pointed down the dam's wall. "Do you think if I swung you on the rope, you could run along the wall to that opening below the leg?"

Asya looked over the wall. Ten feet below the top of the guard wall, there was a foot wide concrete lip. Without a thought for the five hundred foot height above the ground, the woman flipped the fence, and lowered herself from the metal rail by her arms, then let herself drop the remaining distance.

She landed squarely on the ledge, then dropped to her stomach and lowered her head upside down over the concrete ledge.

"It's like an open window into the structure. There're only a few feet of material between this room and the road above," she called up. "We'll do it the other way. Drop down the rope and start running for that tower."

Forty feet closer to the mountain's side of the dam was a concrete tower. It jutted out over the drop by ten feet, and Duncan could see the woman's plan.

He tossed the end of the rope down to her, and looped the other end around himself, leaving her plenty of slack. He was only just finished tying the rope to himself when she called up to him.

"Ready?"

"When you are," he replied.

"Run," she yelled.

He started running away along the top of the dam and glanced back.

Asya had tied the rope to herself, pulled the pin on one of the grenades, and tossed the belt containing the other four through the open hole in the side of the structure. There was probably an entire network of rooms in a tunnel just under the top of the dam. They wouldn't be able to do the dam any injury. But the gantry?

"Fire in the hole!" Asya yelled, flinging the last grenade into the aperture. Then she took up the slack and started running sideways along the wall of the huge concrete beast.

Duncan felt the jolt of her weight, but he was expecting it and had leaned away from the drop at an almost forty five degree angle, acting as a counter-balance.

Running in tandem, they covered the distance to the tower in just a few seconds. As the air erupted with a pressure wave and Duncan heard the deafening sound of an explosion, he reached the tower and was surprised to see Asya had reached the corner on the outer wall first and sprinted right up the side of it. She popped up and latched onto the side wall's metal guard rail, and then vaulted up and over it, landing atop the dam beside him.

She slipped the loop she'd made on the rope up and over her body and then looked back at the hole under the gantry's leg. Black smoke poured from the opening in the dam's wall. No other damage could be seen.

"Now what?" Asya asked him.

Then they heard an enormous *crack* and felt the ground under their feet shudder. Duncan slipped his end of the rope and looked up at the gantry and its brilliant orange against the bright blue sky and the puffy white clouds beyond it.

The orange moved against the white.

As they watched, the two gantry legs facing the outer side of the wall, pitched downward, sinking into the concrete tunnel that had been just under the gantry and the dam's top.

"Now we run like hell!" Duncan said and turned to sprint toward the mountain's base. Asya was right next to him.

He glanced back only once more, as the entire multi-ton steel gantry hoist flipped over the side of the dam's wall, where it would tear an ungodly hole in the concrete as it went down.

The only problem was they needed to run a hundred-meter dash before they would be off the dam and over solid ground.

SEVENTY-TWO

Bishop stared. He didn't move. Just stared.

The giant dragon had been coming at him like a steamroller and he knew he was going to die. He'd survived untold damage and pain during the years when he was genetically altered by Richard Ridley's Regen serum. Bishop had spent years trapped in an alternate dimension, forced to live like a savage. He had almost died at the bottom of a lake in Africa. There had been close calls with the Cerberus Group as well. Each time, he'd made his peace with the possibility of death.

But for some reason, with this massive beast bearing down on him, it didn't feel right. It didn't feel correct that he should die right here, with things left incomplete and undone in his life. For the first time in a long time, when faced with instant death, he really didn't want to die.

So, when the dragon abruptly stopped, its face just two feet from his body, Bishop almost thought he had somehow willed the creature to halt its frenzied attack.

But it wasn't him. He wasn't controlling the beast. For some reason, it had just stopped. Right before turning him into a smear of bloody paste.

Bishop stared. The creature's nostrils were pulsing slightly more open with its every exhale. He could smell its rancid breath. The red eyes were open, and looking his way, but they seemed...vacant somehow. As if the creature suddenly had no thoughts in its head at all. Missing its instructional software or its brain had just hemorrhaged.

Something in the creature was broken.

From behind him on the ground, Bishop heard Rook whisper in the faintest voice, "Whatever you're doing, Bish, it's working."

Bishop slowly turned his head but kept his eyes on the creature in front of him. The head was maybe fifteen feet tall, the long snout at least eight feet deep. The mouth was partially open, and Bishop could see Saliva dripping off the dragon's foot long upper teeth.

He continued to move his head back around to look at Rook, keeping his eyes on the dragon's as he did. *But it's not looking at me,* Bishop thought. *It's just looking.*

His gaze turned to Rook, Bishop said, "It's not me doing it. You should get the hell out of here. But slowly."

He turned his gaze forward again. The beast breathed in and out but showed no signs of moving.

Behind him, Bishop heard Rook staggering to his feet.

All the gunfire had ceased for the moment.

Bishop wondered if the others had killed all their targets or if, like him, everyone was staring in awe at the giant dragon.

Bishop slowly raised his hand and waved it back and forth across the dragon's view.

It slowly blinked its eyes.

Each lid—the size of a desktop—sliding silently down over the red orbs.

What the actual fuck am I seeing?

Then something flicked into his thoughts.

"Felice?" he asked. "Is that you in there?"

To his utter astonishment, the dragon raised its head two feet higher, and then lowered it to the original position, just a few inches from the dirt at Bishop's feet.

"No fucking way," Rook said from behind Bishop, and now well off to his right.

"If that's you in there, and you're in complete control of this thing, give me another nod...and then a wink."

The dragon's head raised up, and then lowered, this time all the way to the ground and rested there. Then one of its eyes closed.

Bishop turned to face Rook, and Queen had joined him from her position. Pawn was still guarding the corner of the building's newly fashioned tunnel, but no further troops were coming around the corner.

Rook's face was just a mask of shock.

For once, even he was silenced.

"No offense, Queen," Bishop started. "But Rook? I've got the coolest girlfriend." Bishop's smile was possibly the broadest shit-eating grin he'd ever made in his life.

"No argument," Queen said.

Knight was standing on the far side of her, his weapon and his eyes still trained on the far corner of the building. "So, what are you gonna do, big guy?" he called.

Bishop turned back to the dragon that Felice Carter was controlling from halfway around the planet. "What say we take this thing for a spin, baby?"

The dragon's head nodded again, but it was much less of a pronounced movement this time. *She knows now, that I know it's her,* he thought.

He walked around the side of the immense head, grabbed one of the three foot long, backward facing spikes at the back of her neck, and started to climb. Then he was standing on top of the creature's back, holding the spikes like the reins on a beast of burden.

Rook chuckled. "Someone cue *The NeverEnding Story*'s main theme for this sonuvabitch."

Bishop gave the dragon's head a pat. "Give 'em hell, baby."

The dragon's head snapped around, and with a burst of speed, they were slithering down the hill and away from the building and Chess Team.

The turn was so fast, Bishop was shocked.

He was able to hold on, but the blast of wind in his face felt like he was in a convertible travelling at speed on an interstate highway. Easily over sixty miles per hour.

Wind rushed through his ears, and he squinted his eyes to see better with the blast of air in his face. He couldn't really steer the dragon in any way, so he realized he was just along for the ride. He glanced back and saw the creature's immense length slapping side to side like a snake. The movements felt erratic, with a curve to the right here and a sudden jolt back to the left there, but as he was looking behind him, he saw the beast's tail snap out to the side, obliterating the corner of the building where Knight had been downing a squad of black clad Chinese soldiers. Two men were dead already, when the tail struck the corner of the concrete blocks. The masonry, the two remaining live soldiers, and their comrades' corpses all blasted into the air. One man arced up clean over the building, letting out a Wilhelm scream before landing on the mountain's far side.

As the renegade beast headed down the hillside, platoons of Chinese soldiers scattered in an undisciplined retreat. They were just running in all directions now. Some bolted for the perceived safety of the building, while others ran left, flailing downhill toward the distant reservoir.

The dragon raced after those on the left, sweeping through them on a curving arc, before heading back toward the building again. Bishop thought the dragon would blast straight through the structure again, and he squatted down, worried that the impact would kill him, or at least knock him from his perch.

But at the last second, the dragon curved away again, using the middle and end of its three hundred foot length to smash the fleeing soldiers into the structure and blasting apart rooms from the building, sending a rain of tiles and blocks flying over to the mountain's eastern slope.

The dragon swerved to the western slope and descended toward the enormous reservoir formed by the Yellow River and the parabolic dishes. Bishop could see the dam in the distance, where a huge orange tower atop it tumbled away, and crushed the concrete beneath it. Furious waters wrenched apart the structure's edges. It was like watching a building be demolished in slow motion.

The dragon curved away toward the reservoir, then juked a hard left again, and they were moving back the way they had come.

Then Bishop felt a piece of his calf tear away as the noise that filled the mountainside was of multiple rifles all converging on one spot: him and the dragon.

He squatted down, for cover behind the beast's enormous head. A Chinese armored personnel carrier with six wheels and a machine gun turret had driven through one of the tunnels the dragon had created through the complex. There was a highway on the other side of the structure that snaked all the way up to the summit and beyond, so the vehicle would have had an easy time getting up the hill.

The machine gunner blasted the dragon's side. Huge gouts of blood sprayed away from the creature's scaly hide.

The Chinese reinforcements had arrived.

SEVENTY-THREE

The landscape around them crackled with gunfire, and Queen briefly thought that this must have been what it was like for allied forces landing at Normandy in World War II.

Except then I'd have more guys on my side, she thought.

As soon as Bishop and the dragon departed, the Chinese forces made another push from uphill. Queen had joined King in holding off that front, while Knight and Rook were closer to the gap through the building that Pawn was defending. A new offensive was being launched, it seemed, and all three of them were hard pressed on the sides of that gap.

The smaller squad by the western corner of the building that Knight had been fighting was obliterated as the dragon swept past, taking half the building with its tail swipe.

But Queen, with her back to that spot now, was acutely aware that they were undefended from that direction. She hoped that Bishop and Dragon-Felice could provide them cover from downhill.

The soldiers above them rolled out from cover, firing small arms in their direction, and then leapt back around the edge of the building, making them hard targets. And they did it over and over, like some sideways game of life and death whack-a-mole. The Chinese had the higher ground, and they had the building as cover. She and King were forced to use boulder sized pieces of building that had been strewn around the hillside by the dragon's rampage. It was a bit of a stalemate. Until she ran out of ammunition.

"I'm out," she told King, ducking behind a pile of cinder blocks. Enemy fire strafed the top of the pile and then paused.

King didn't respond but popped up to fire again at the building's corner and, a second later, his stolen rifle stopped firing as well.

Then two things happened at once.

The first was she heard the distinctive rattling *knock* of a chain-fed machine gun over the sound of the small arms rifle fire coming from Knight's group and their opponents. That was really bad news.

She turned to look down the hill where the sound had come from and saw a six wheeled Chinese WZ-551 armored fighting vehicle. It was racing down the hill to the west, toward the reservoir. A soldier was firing the turret mounted machine gun at something beyond the crest of the hill. She assumed it was Bishop and the dragon.

Before she could react to that new threat on the field of battle, or comment to King about it, the WZ was nearly split in half horizontally and, a fraction of a second later, the big, repeated deep *thump* of an MK44 Bushmaster autocannon sounded in her ears like thunder. The WZ's armored metal sides were perforated in so many places it looked like a block of cheese had been hit by a fragmentation grenade.

She turned toward the sound and found an eight wheeled Stryker APC racing past the building, its huge turret cannon pointed down the mountain at the Chinese WZ. The Stryker kept blasting the WZ, chasing it down toward the water, even though Queen suspected it was just rolling, unattended by any living soldiers at this point.

The Stryker was unmarked, but it was definitely a US Army vehicle. She didn't care if it was owned and operated by the Mongolian military, though. All she knew for sure was that it seemed to be on her side, and that was enough.

Before she could speculate farther on the ownership of the Stryker, two light strike vehicles raced after the APC, both with machine gunners in the back, firing forward over the roll-bar roofs of their respective vehicles. One of them had a passenger who was holding her hands out in front of her like she was trying to fire a blast of energy from her fingertips, but nothing was happening.

But something *was* happening.

Large boulders of granite erupted from the hillside, some reaching up to ten feet like sudden and irate Easter Island Moai statues. Others were not as tall but shot up out of the ground like globules of spit hawked up vertically, and they reached a height of a few feet before returning to plummet back to earth.

Fiona, Queen thought.

The area of effect was larger than the girl had been capable of in the past. She was rupturing the soil all over the visible mountainside, with new rock obstacles popping up all over, as if the mountain was growing boils. Large swaths of the building beside Queen were crumbling away, pushed up from underneath by rocks that had been buried deep under layers of sedimentary rock and soil. Then the two Chenowths had passed, leaving a stunned Queen and King to look after them.

"That's your girl," Queen said.

"I *am* proud," King replied, starting to run toward Knight, Rook, and Pawn at the gap entrance.

Queen was about to follow him when she was tackled from behind and slammed to the ground, all the air leaving her lungs in one forceful, involuntary exhale.

She had felt that kind of blow before—most notably from the fists of her abusive ex-husband. She knew she wouldn't be able to breathe for a second or two until her shocked lungs remembered how, but she also knew she needed to move. She rolled over to her hands and knees, and then, rather than trying to stand from that position, she rolled forward in a somersault, stopping in a crouch just as the wind came back into her body in a massive gulping croak.

The move probably saved her life, as her attacker, Crimson, kicked out her massive leg, the army booted foot sweeping right through where Queen had been a moment before.

Queen lunged with her thighs, launching herself to her feet and taking a few running steps before whirling around to face her attacker.

But King was there already. He ran back and slammed his shoulder into Crimson's midsection. The blow would have staggered most opponents, and possibly knocked them out of the fight entirely. But Crimson was only pushed back a foot before her feet gripped the soil.

She had changed clothes, and now wore an all black Chinese military combat uniform, with no insignia. She had black boots on, and a black web belt, but she carried no armaments. She didn't need any; she *was* a weapon.

Her blonde wig had fallen off in the tackle, and Queen saw the woman's head was now completely bald. Like a strange cross between a cancer patient and a linebacker, when the woman opened her mouth and sneered at King, her sharpened teeth removed all doubt that she was more animal than human.

King stood between Crimson and Queen. He shouted behind him. "Get Rook and the others and get out of here."

"Are you crazy?" Queen yelled back.

"That's an order," King said, as he slowly moved in an arc in front of Crimson. She didn't attack, but her eyes never left King's face.

"Fuck you, Jack. I'm not letting you fight her alone," Queen said.

She darted a glance behind her and saw that Knight and Pawn were gone, and the firing from the gap in the building had ceased. They had given chase through the building. Rook was still on the ground by the opening, but he looked beaten. And his eyes were closed.

He can't be dead, she thought.

"Zelda," King said, his voice softer now. "You know why you have to go. Please."

The anguish in that 'please' almost undid her. From nowhere, the emotion swelled up inside. The emotions she had spent so many years learning to control. The fear and the anxiety.

She turned back to him as Crimson crouched slightly on the other side of King's body. She was going to attack, and she was smiling, her face like a ragged vicious curve of immense fangs.

Zelda Baker, callsign: Queen, knew exactly why she couldn't stay. If she did, Crimson would kill the life growing inside of her—if the woman hadn't already.

And King knew that.

SEVENTY-FOUR

King saw the gleam in Crimson's eye a moment before she lunged. If he'd had his trusty KA-BAR knife, he would have stood his ground and let her dive right into it. But he was now completely unarmed. So, he dove to his right, just in time, and she passed by him, close enough for him to smell her outrageous breath.

He launched to his feet in a spinning kick with his right leg coming up. His booted heel cracked hard into her jaw, breaking it, and shifting the bone three inches to the left of her face. She was already hideous to look at, but now she wouldn't be able to bite him at least.

The blow and, presumably the pain, was a shock to her. She landed in a crouch, like a furious animal. She shifted backward and sideways on all fours, shaking her head as if she could throw off the agony or maybe realign her jaw again. But the joint was firmly dislodged and rammed up against her upper skull.

King could see the bone jutting out under the skin on the right side of her face. He, too, had landed in a crouch, and he scanned the landing area for a rock or a piece of destroyed cinderblock he could use as a weapon.

But there was nothing in reach. When his eyes darted back up to his opponent, and the building beyond her, he could see that Queen had followed his order. She and Rook were nowhere in sight now. But he knew her. She would be on her way to rendezvous with Knight and Pawn, and resupplied and armed, the four of them would be back to save him. Or Bishop would come back riding that dragon. He could hear furious gunfire and screaming in the distance. The battle was hardly over.

Crimson rushed him, this time swiping with her hands, as if they still contained the claws she had at birth, but which she'd had surgically removed. She was reverting to her former fighting style, ingrained in her since her birth.

King tried to dodge again, this time to his left, but rather than clawing him, Crimson cupped her hand at the last fraction of a second, pulling him closer with her left arm, and pounding a massive, meaty fist into the side of his head with her right.

His left ear exploded with pain and a complete absence of sound and, before he knew it, he was lying on the ground, looking up at the blue sky. The power of the punch had his head ringing, but it also snapped something inside of him, releasing a fury that he'd pent up for years.

In the past, when King fought an opponent, it was with strategy and training. The blow to his head turned all of that off, and now he fought with rage. His body twisted and turned on the ground, like Crimson had done moments before and, without realizing that he'd scooped up a rock in his hand, he stood and rushed her, slamming the hand into her face repeatedly, mashing his own fingers in the process.

The violence of the act shocked Crimson, and her eyes went wide, as spurts of blood shot from her ruined, plastic surgery created nose. Without thought, King's left hand jabbed for her face, his thumb diving into her right eye socket.

Crimson screamed in agony, her entire head recoiling from the pain, and King's thumb slurped from the socket before she slammed her face forward again, her forehead connecting with his so hard that he went completely blind for just a second.

Then her hands were grappling with him, and he felt himself thrown. He opened his eyes and saw the sky and then the ground and then the sky again, before his body hit the earth hard, his right arm snapping at the humerus bone, and the gripped rock flying away from his hand.

The pain of the broken arm felt distant, and he scrambled to his feet again, once more running straight for her, and she now ran in a blind rage at him. A tiny sliver of his former training and experience slipped through his own fury in the five steps it took to be in range, and he realized he couldn't overpower Crimson blow for blow. His right arm was now hanging limp at his side. He would need to use his entire body, and every devious trick he could.

Instead of trying to punch her or headbutt her, he leapt up into the air, both of the flats of his boots connecting with her already ruined face, her own momentum making the impact worse.

Her face detonated in a wave of blood from her shattered nose. King was propelled backward, landing on his shoulders with his legs still in the air. The force of the blow sent him over, and he tucked his neck and pulled his legs in as they went over his head. He landed in a crouch, still facing her, but there was no time to counter correct.

He couldn't see her eyes anymore through the damaged face. It was all just a bloody mess. He did see that her unhinged jaw had now been ripped clean away from her face. But she still came at him like a freight train.

She followed through on her run, plowing straight into his face with her fist.

King felt his nose break—a sensation he'd experienced before. He still had no hearing from his left ear, but now the whole left side of his face felt on fire as she blasted into him with her entire weight behind the punch. His body was spun to the side where he collapsed in the dirt, and she continued on past him, tripping over a pile of rubble.

King rolled to his knees, but hadn't managed to stand yet, when he saw her coming at him again. There was just no time.

Her kick connected with his ribs, collapsing his left lung, shattering bones, and driving all the air from him. His body was flying through the air again, but before he landed, she was on him yet again. Her arms wrapped around him, preventing his lungs from pulling in the so desperately needed air. She held him upright, his feet dangling just inches off the ground. Her arms were wrapped around his chest and his broken right arm, pain coursing through him.

She squeezed hard, and the ribs on his right went with a violent crack. He hurt everywhere and wanted it to end. His left arm moved, and he realized it wasn't pinned in her death grip. Her face was right in front of his. She was watching him through the curtain of blood dripping from her brow, with her one remaining eye.

Her jaw was gone, and he could reach up for her damaged face with his left hand, but he knew the bottom of her skull, which had been protected by the jawbone, would be strong enough to stop him from getting to her brain.

But nothing is protecting your spine, he thought.

Darkness encroached on the fringes of his vision, from his own right eye. The only one through which he could see. But he felt that eye swelling shut.

King jabbed hard with all his strength, with his working left hand, shoving it deep into the open wound of Crimson's face. His fingers found her cervical bones, squeezed tight around them, and crushed.

In turn, she squeezed his midsection even tighter, and he felt something far deeper than a rib pop inside him. Instead of squeezing his hand in pain, he yanked the hand away from her ruined cranium.

He just hadn't let go of her spine first.

She dropped him and air flooded into his open mouth, a sound like an old dog's gruff bark filled the air, and he realized it was the sound of him breathing. His vision was going dim and gray, but he saw the woman formerly known as Red, now known as Crimson, the twenty-first century's Empress of China, pitch back and fall to the dirt. When the back of her head struck a chunk of masonry, and she didn't react to the blow, he knew she was dead.

His vision, what little there was of it, started sliding to the right and downward. As if he had moved his head in that direction, but he had stayed perfectly still. He felt an overwhelming wave of nausea, and the ringing in his head was louder now. He could no longer hear his ragged attempts to breathe.

Across the hillside, he could see a light attack vehicle bouncing over the earth, with Queen holding the side rail, a Type 56 rifle slung over her back. He didn't recognize the driver, who now wore no helmet, but he knew the operator in the passenger seat. He'd known and loved her more than anyone else for so many years now.

His body tipped to his left, and the vehicle was wrenched from his view as the darkness closed in.

The last thing Jack Sigler, callsign: King, heard, was his daughter screaming.

EPILOGUE

Pulaski, Virginia

The sky was clear today. Again. Fiona Sigler loved that about their new home. Well, they had been here for ten months, but she still tended to think of it as 'new.' It was a conventional nice suburban neighborhood. The house was at the very end of a circle on a cul-de-sac and had a large farmer's porch with a bright red door.

In the center of the cul-de-sac was a small grassy patch, on a circular island, a gray curb running all the way around it. In the middle of the island of grass was a natural granite boulder just two feet high. Fiona had raised it to that spot from as deep in the earth as she could reach.

But the tranquility of the entire neighborhood was a sham. Only the house with the red door was a real home. All the others were props and set dressing. After the attacks on the Siletz reservation, and before that on the Chess Team's subterranean home in New Hampshire, a decision had been made for everyone to relocate somewhere entirely new and unknown.

Pulaski, Virginia was far enough off the beaten track, but close enough to the Interstate and major airports for their needs, and the actual cul-de-sac neighborhood was far enough from the town center to not pose danger to its inhabitants, but not arouse suspicion either. They were on a small hillside, just at the edge of the state forest, so no neighbors uphill of them, and a view of the entire town below them.

The location was perfect for future team operations, and it was also the perfect place for all of them to grieve their fallen and recuperate from their injuries.

Fiona walked across the faux village toward the cul-de-sac's circle and, beyond it, her home. Her friend, Erik Somers, was walking by her side. He still needed the cane, after the loss of some of the muscle in his leg, but he didn't limp anymore. He would always be 'Bishop' in her mind, long after he'd first relinquished and later reclaimed that title from Asya.

Fiona had spent a lot of time with Bishop lately. He and Felice had married, but the woman had decided to go back to genetics research, and she did much of that work in a secret government lab in Cave Spring, an hour's commute away. She was home each evening, of course, but during the daytime, Bishop was alone, like Fiona, so they tended to gravitate toward spending time with each other.

Also, unlike the others, neither of them wanted to be indoors, if they could help it. Especially after the long winter. So, they worked on the houses in the neighborhood. They made small gardens and planted flowers in the neighborhood together. Although Bishop had not said anything to her about it, Fiona suspected the sound of the baby crying in the house grated on his nerves. Not that he was a bad godfather in any way to Rook and Queen's little boy. He just got a weird look on his face when the child needed a diaper change and the tears started. He would usually leave the room.

But for Fiona, she just wanted to be outside to soak in the spring weather. She loved the baby, and she loved being called 'Auntie Fiona.' It was one of the best things in the world. Even though the world itself was on the mend.

After the incident in China, the US government installed a democratic regime, and the Chinese publicly thanked the US for stepping in to help them with their 'terrorist group' that had falsely claimed to turn the nation into an empire. Dom Boucher told Fiona that the Chinese were secretly very relieved to be rid of Crimson, and happy to be on the mend with lucrative new trade deals firmly established with the US, a much more compliant Russia, Australia, and Japan. The Chinese would weather the coming worldwide deglobalization quite well with friends like those.

Their entire satellite network was, of course, removed from the heavens by USSF, before any ink had been applied to peace or trade agreements.

"Can you raise the stone a few feet?" Bishop asked.

"I could," Fiona said, squinting at him. "But why?"

"I think we should build something on this little roundabout," Bishop told her, as they stepped up onto the grass.

"Like what?" Fiona asked, genuinely surprised by the random suggestion.

"I'm thinking of building a wooden gazebo," he said.

Fiona glanced up at her six-foot-four tall friend. He was clean shaven these days. The first time in a long time.

She thought about that suggestion.

Fiona knew the bodies of her friends and family were not under the memorial stone, but she still felt close to her lost loved ones when they visited it. A place to sit would be nice.

"Yeah," she said. "Let's do that tomorrow."

The Chess Team still had enemies out there in the world. Sure, Tom Duncan was now completely exonerated. He and Asya would be getting married in the summer. Fiona was excited about that. Dae-jung and Anna would be flying back up from their hiking trip in Chile right before the big event. It had been a while.

She missed them.

She walked around the stone and looked once again at the writing she had painstakingly carved into the smooth slab with the enormous power inside her body and mind.

Fiona lovingly touched the top of the stone. Bishop's hand found its way to her shoulder, a comforting reminder that he was always there for her, as were the rest of them.

Then they strolled past the stone, and walked across the street, mounting the creaking wooden porch, just as Rook and Queen came out of the red door. Rook was holding the baby in his arms, the little infant boy all wrapped up with a light blue blanket to protect him from the slight chill in the air.

"Hey, Baby Jack, look," Rook said. "It's your favorite Auntie."

Fiona reached for the baby, and Rook happily handed him over. She did the same thing she always did when she got the little guy in her arms. She smiled and gently kissed his forehead.

The baby was awake and serene, his crystalline blue eyes seeming to see and know all. His mother stepped up and slid her arm around Fiona's shoulders.

Then Fiona heard a voice behind Rook and Queen, at the door.

Her father.

"Dinner's ready, kiddo. Let's go inside."

Jack Sigler had taken longer to heal than most of the others, his injuries more severe. But these days he looked just like he always did, and he was once again wearing an Elvis T-shirt.

From deeper in the house, Fiona heard her adopted mother, Sara Fogg, call out. "There's pie, too!"

Fiona nodded and smiled. Then she thought about the words written on the stone in the circle behind her, as the red door closed behind them all, separating them from the granite once more.

Beloved Family:

Lewis Aleman
Cintia Dourado
Augustina Gallo
George Pierce

We couldn't have done it without you.

Fiona missed them all. She had known George and Lew since she had been a small girl. Cintia was her best friend. Augustina was like her aunt. She would never forget them. Lew's sacrifice was especially heart-breaking, but she loved him all the more for it.

"Save some of that pie for me," Fiona called, and followed the others inside. "I mean it, Tremblay!"

From further ahead in the dining room, she could hear Rook chuckle.

Now, in this momentary lull of peace and tranquility, Fiona finally felt that all was right with the world. As long as she and her family were around, it always would be.

AFTERWORD:

The History of Chess Team's Expansion

I first discovered Jeremy's works with the hardcover novel *Pulse*, when I spotted it on a shelf, face out, in the now defunct brick & mortar book chain, Borders. I bought the book, read it, loved it, and sent the author an e-mail asking about his earlier books that I couldn't find in stores. That first contact led to me freelance editing for him, and eventually doing the job full time for the last decade. But way back in 2010, when I first started editing for Jeremy, his publisher was wanting him to put out some stand-alone titles after the first three Jack Sigler / Chess Team thrillers, and he was still keeping busy with putting books (like *Torment* and *The Sentinel*) out into the market through his own Breakneck Media imprint on the side. He was dreaming up *The Last Hunter* saga, and working on *SecondWorld*, and realizing it was going to be a very long time before he could get back to Jack Sigler and his team.

Jeremy came up with the idea of getting some of his independent thriller writer friends to help, by splitting Chess Team apart and giving each of the five core characters a chance to shine in their own adventures. His co-authors would write the first drafts, Jeremy would alter things to make them more to his taste and style or to make the characters more closely align with the personalities he had established for them in the first three novels. Jeremy got help with the labor, the co-authors got paid and got to work on a popular series that would hopefully help along their own burgeoning careers, and most importantly, the readers and die-hard Chess Team fans would have something to tide them over while they waited for the fourth full-length novel.

When I came on as Jeremy's editor, the first novella—*Callsign: King*—had already been written and edited. So, I took on editing the novellas for Queen, Rook, Bishop, and Knight. Only those first five novellas were originally planned. During the editing process, I suggested to Jeremy that he write a sixth novella, featuring the team's handler, Deep Blue. I thought Jeremy should write that one solo. But he was swamped, editing *SecondWorld*, researching *Island 731*, writing the start of *The Last Hunter*, and revising the Callsign novellas. I think when all was said and done, during the course of 2011, he released fourteen books with his name on them! So, understandably, he was crazy busy. And he met my suggestion with a suggestion of his own: "Why don't you write it?"

He was serious. I had just finished my own first novel, which he had read, liked, and very kindly offered me a great quote on. I was trying to get it released, and by this point I knew the Chess Team plots and characters really well from being neck deep in edits, while his mind was on a dozen other projects. So, I co-wrote *Callsign: Deep Blue*. Along the way, Sean Ellis came up with ideas for two additional King stories, and suddenly there were going to be eight novellas. Collectively referred to informally as 'the Chesspocalypse,' all eight stories are being repacked to be re-released as one collection called *Fracture*. The novellas did what they needed to do, though. They gave Jeremy breathing room. The co-authors got a boost to their careers. And the ravenous Chess Team fans got their fix. But they wanted more.

Still up to his neck in projects, Jeremy asked me to come on board to write the fourth full-length Jack Sigler novel, and *Ragnarok* was born. When it became a bestseller upon release, in a fit of excitement (and probably insanity), Jeremy asked me again to help write the follow up title—*Omega*. At the same time, after the success of the three King novellas, Jeremy asked Sean to co-write the prequel novel *Prime*. They would both be released in 2013, and we marketed them as the beginning and the end of the series. Yes, *Omega* was meant to be the end. There was another series Jeremy was working on that was growing to colossal kaiju size...but that's another story.

There was just one problem. Chess Team fans wanted *more*. And although fans liked *Ragnarok* and *Omega* a lot, I was a slow writer. And I was swamped with editing projects of Jeremy's, and an anthology called *Warbirds of Mars*, and my own novel *The Crypt of Dracula*, and Jeremy's *Refuge* project (which I was editing, and having to pull together with a final novella I was co-writing while my former marriage was falling apart).

So, Jeremy turned to Sean Ellis to co-write *Savage* and let Sean do the thing I wanted to do in *Ragnarok* or *Omega*—kill off a character! (Or did he?) Anyway, I was now relegated to the editor for the series, but I was keeping busy with other projects. Kent Holloway was co-authoring the Jack Sigler Continuum novellas, *Guardian*, *Patriot*, and *Centurion* (also to be re-released as one collection called *Continuum*). And *Savage* did really well.

I think there was brief talk about me co-authoring *Herculean*, the spin off Cerberus Group novel. But I ended up working on the *Endgame* guidebook and a comic book adaptation for *Island 731* instead. Sean Ellis co-wrote *Herculean* and continued the Chess Team series with *Cannibal* and *Empire*, as well as the second (and, for now, final) Cerberus Group title, *Helios*. I still kept my hand in with the long Chess Team short story "Show of Force," which was published in two different Cohesion Press SNAFU anthologies. I also worked with Jeremy on the novel *Viking Tomorrow*, which was originally envisioned to be a trilogy. Sales on that book were not as good, and in 2018, we shelved the plans for a sequel, and Jeremy asked me to co-write the next (and, this time, the last) Chess Team novel. It was originally going to be called *Checkmate*.

And the brief would not be an easy one. Write a final novel that concluded the nine Chess Team books, eleven novellas, and two short stories that had come before—oh yes, and also conclude the two Cerberus Group novels! Include all the military action, adventure, mystery, history, archeology, and monsters the series was known for, but also give each of nearly two dozen characters a chance to be in the spotlight and have a solid conclusion to their individual lives and stories. Not to mention there were dangling plot threads that needed to be tied up. The team was broken, with their leader abducted somewhere, and members of Chess Team still not having met with members of Cerberus Group—and the shock *that* would entail. It was a lot. But I figured I was up for the task.

And then...

And then everything came off the rails. Keep in mind that in 2018, when I took the job, I was still recovering from pneumonia and dealing with an obnoxious, time-chewing ex-wife. I had only just moved into my apartment at the time before the pneumonia and was still not unpacked. My new fiancée had been (wrongly) diagnosed with Multiple Sclerosis, and the usual daily emergencies were still happening. But there wasn't a rush of any kind yet, and Jeremy was still pumping out *The Others*, *Space Force*, and *Alter*, all of which I was editing and formatting for my day job. I spent a few months thinking about how *Kingdom* should be accomplished and wrote up an insanely detailed outline. It had everything! All the necessary bits. Two dozen characters had a chance to breathe and shine. Everyone had important things to do. And it all came together in one crashing conclusion. I was so proud of it. Somehow, I had found a way to get all the necessary elements into the plan. Then I showed it to Jeremy, and he hated it.

Well, 'hate' is a strong word, but he completely wanted it to be different from what I had in my outline. He even suggested just taking all the loose plot threads, all the supporting cast we didn't want to deal with, all the old lurking villains of the series, and killing them all off in one chapter and then getting on with an entirely new standalone story that just focused on the core Chess Team. If you've read *Kingdom* before checking out this Afterword (and you *should!*) you'll know that ultimately, we didn't go with his suggestion either. In the end it was a bit of a mix of what he suggested and what I had originally planned, with all new things too. But the point is, I was devastated. Up until that point, my collaborations with Jeremy had been smooth. And his critique of my outline, although presented to me politely and mildly (as is his way), still took the wind out of my sails. And it came right around the time my mother was diagnosed with throat cancer.

And then we were off to the races. I started on a new plan for *Kingdom*, even though my heart was less in it. But I still wanted to do the best job I could and make the best book we could. I loved the series and the characters, too, and I wanted us to do right by the fans. That was a major reason why we didn't just sweep away characters and plots in Chapter One—because we knew that every character or plot was someone's favorite. So, I started work, but life didn't want to leave me alone. My mother's illness progressed, and she passed away in 2019. So, I was dealing with her loss. Then settling her estate. Then I was moving my family during a little thing we like to call 'The Pandemic.' My partner Michelle needed hip surgery. We needed an emergency bathroom remodel—for the only bathroom in the house. An emergency partial roof restoration. I ruptured a disc in my spine that had me practically bedridden for six months before my own surgery. My daughter needed surgery on her arm (because my charming Ex let her use a snow-and-ice-covered trampoline in winter). Everybody got COVID (multiple times) anyway, despite all our precautions, vaccinations, and masking. And on and on and *on*. I won't bore you with the whole list, but let's just say I became a shit magnet for a few years, and most of those issues were medical for one member of the family or the other. Along the way, probably to no one's surprise, I was hitting the actual clinical definition of 'exhaustion' and had developed a sneaky case of depression. Sneaky in that I was depressed and didn't even realize it yet.

But a funny thing happened in 2023. The onslaught let up. I'd made it only three fourths of the way through the book by that stage. I started pounding the keys. The depression cracked and went away. I managed to stay out of the emergency room for a hot minute. To everyone's surprise, I finally finished my first draft of the book. Jeremy then took over and asked me to make a few tiny alterations, and he spent a few weeks trimming, nipping, editing, altering, and tucking, until the book was what it needed to be. He changed some dialogue and added some jokes. And we inserted a chapter in the middle. I had spent four years (mostly *not* working on the book) and Jeremy got his part done in a month. So, the delays were entirely on me, and blame should go squarely on *my* shoulders for that. At least the delays from 2019 until 2023. Those were me. (The gap from *Empire* in 2016 until 2019 was just that Jeremy was busy writing other novels, and the delay from 2023 to 2024 was just scheduling and getting the story narrated by the excellent Jeffrey Kafer.) Still, I apologize to all of you Chess Team fans. I'm sure you can see that some of the delays were out of my control, though. In the end, I poured my heart and soul into the project, and so did Jeremy when it came to his part. He might have only worked on it for a month, but it was every day, all day for him, and he put the same level of care and concern into the details that he does on all his projects. We were both happy with the results, and they are *better* than what my original outline would have entailed.

An important point here, too. Never once did Jeremy give me shit for the delays. Four *years*, but he understood, and gave me the space I needed to get things together. And I am so grateful to him for that. I'm not sure I could have handled everything else, and him being angry with me. Instead, he was his genuine, kind, caring self. I love him all the more for it. It's not like we were idle during that time, either. He wrote and I edited and formatted another nineteen novels during those years. So, everything above was what was happening on the weekends and evenings—after our day jobs of him writing and me doing production work.

Finally, here we are. *Kingdom* is in your hands, and hopefully you enjoyed it, and you could discern the love and affection on every page. We tried to give you a finale you'd appreciate! All that's left to say (at the end of this very long Afterword) is thank you. Thanks to Mike Pastore and Dee Haddrill for their continual support over the years. Thanks to Sally Ross for her efforts to speed up my progress! Thanks to Technical Sergeant Kyle Mohr, USSF, for his excellent military advice. Thanks to Julie Carter, Elizabeth Cooper, Dustin Dreyling, Cynthia Gregory, Dee Haddrill, Becki Laurent, Kyle Mohr, Jessica Otterstål, Jeff Sexton, and Courtney Westendorf for speedy and excellent proofreading. Thank you to each one of you readers and listeners for patiently enduring the very long break between *Empire* and *Kingdom*. And thanks to Jeremy for inviting me on the Chess Team journey in the first place!

—Kane Gilmour
December, 2023

ABOUT THE AUTHORS

Jeremy Robinson is the *New York Times* and #1 Audible bestselling author of over seventy novels and novellas, including *Infinite, The Others,* and *The Dark,* as well as the Jack Sigler thriller series, and *Project Nemesis,* the highest selling, original kaiju novel of all time (which is in development for TV with Chad Stahelski, director of John Wick). Robinson is known for mixing elements of science, history, and mythology, which has earned him the #1 spot in Science Fiction and Action-Adventure, and secured him as the top creature feature author. Many of his novels have been adapted into comic books, optioned for film and TV, and translated into fourteen languages. He lives in New Hampshire with his wife and three children.

Visit him at www.bewareofmonsters.com.

Kane Gilmour is the international bestselling author of *The Crypt of Dracula* and *Resurrect.* His short stories have appeared in *Kaiju Rising: Age of Monsters, SNAFU II: Survival of the Fittest, MECH: Age of Steel,* and *Dark Discoveries* magazine. He also writes comic books. He lives with his significant other, his kids, two dogs, a cat, and nine chickens on a farm in Vermont. Find him on the web at www.kanegilmour.com.

Made in the USA
Las Vegas, NV
16 December 2024